Mother's Child

a novel by michael conant

For more information, to inquire about rights to this or other works, or to purchase copies for special educational, business or sales promotional uses, please write to:

Incorgnito Publishing Press

A division of Market Management Group, LLC

300 E. Bellevue Drive, Suite 208 Pasadena, CA 91101

First EDITION

Printed in the United States of America

ISBN: 978-1-944589-66-0

10 9 8 7 6 5 4 3 2 1

For my mother

Blanche Edith Conant

CONTENTS

CHAPTER ONE

THE LITTLE GIRL

It was just past lunchtime during a cold October day in New England. The brisk air carried the sweet smell of autumn as it swirled the early fallen leaves. I sat on the edge of a curb, dazed.

I was vaguely aware of my surroundings and the fresh scent. I didn't take much note of the late afternoon traffic inching by or the crowd of people who had gathered along the sidewalks. Nor did I give thought to why I was sitting there. A large hand gently cupped my shoulder. A man kindly asked, "Are you alright ma'am?"

I glanced up at him and then back down. I stared unblinkingly at the gold and orange leaves plastered along the wet gutter. Flashing red, blue, and white lights danced across their surface. I didn't want to make eye contact with anyone just yet. He bent down and I could feel his eyes searching my face.

His dark blue uniform looked familiar. He stood, and I slowly tilted my head up. My gaze cleared. For a moment I stared into his concerned brown eyes.

"Yes," I managed to say. "Yes, I think so." I followed unconvincingly.

"Are you hurt?" He came around and stood in front of me. He pointed to the elongated red stain of blood, now nearly dried on the front of my white blouse.

I looked to where he pointed but said nothing.

He crouched in front of me and took my hand into his large grip.

He turned my palm upward, revealing dried blood that had settled into the thin creases of my life line. His previous question registered in my sluggish brain.

"It isn't my blood," I said quietly.

"Were you in one of the vehicles ma'am?" I didn't answer.

"Ma'am?" He repeated forcefully, squeezing my hand just a little, enough to jostle me from my stupor.

"No," I finally said. "No, I saw the accident and ran toward it. The little girl. There was a little girl in the back seat of the white car. Or brown car–I–I can't remember which one exactly."

I picked through cobwebs in my mind while I tried to recall details.

The horror of what I had seen came into focus.

"She was slumped in the back seat–blood was running from her head." I remembered. I felt hot tears welling, gathering for release.

"The car was on fire...the people in the front seat, they were...I couldn't help them." I took a deep breath, hoping the autumn sweetness would overpower the brief inhale of burning flesh that had seared my nostrils.

And then they came. The tears. Slowly at first, like when you forget to turn the faucet off that extra bit. They dripped; first one, then another. They gathered and rolled. The blue-uniformed guy took a seat on the curb next to me and wrapped his warm arm around my shoulder to comfort me.

"I undid the little girl's seat belt and dragged her out of the car," my body was shaking. "It was white. I remember. It was the white car." I looked at him.

He nodded encouragement to keep going. I tried to find some place in my head where I could logically categorize the flashing images of what had happened and relay them. The tears were now a steady stream.

"I tore a piece of my blouse away. See...here." I lifted the fabric where there was a large tear. My breath came shorter. "I don't know how I could do that. It's a good blouse—strong and new and I...I just don't know how I did that."

"It's all right ma'am," he said, calming. "You look pretty strong to me." He gave an awkward smirk. It didn't lighten the moment.

"She was bleeding, you know, from her head," I said. "Did I say that already? The car door. I caught my blouse on a piece of metal on the car door. That's how I tore it. I dragged her out into the side of the street and sat with her, pressing my piece of blouse to her head. I just held her. I don't know for how long."

My breathing returned to normal; tears slowed to a trickle.

Another man approached us. He was also dressed in a dark blue uniform. A leather belt with several leather pouches attached cinched his distorted waist line. A holstered gun rested on his right hip. I looked more closely now at the first "blue" man; he stood when the police officer approached. He lacked the same equipment as the officer; as I studied him, I discovered the yellow EMS symbol on his left breast pocket.

The officer spoke to the medical technician while giving me a cursory nod. "Is she injured?"

"No. This is the woman who pulled the little girl from the burning car. Her name is..." He looked down at me. "Oh crap. Sorry, I forgot to ask your name."

"June. My name is June Gallagher."

"Well, Ms. Gallagher," the officer said while he scribbled in a notepad, "From what the witnesses have told my Sargent, what you did was extremely brave. You saved that little girl's life. You're basically a hero." The officer bent toward me and extended his hand. I hesitantly raised my hand to meet his and offered a weak clasp for his strong grip.

"The little girl?" I asked. "She's all right? She's going to be okay?"

The EMS guy said, "My team loaded her into the ambulance a

while ago; she is likely in the emergency room about now. But I can tell you, other than a very nasty cut that will need a bunch of stitches, she looked like she should be fine. It's the fire that would have killed her...that killed her parents..." he stopped.

Suddenly, the air around me turned sooty with despair. I began to tremble and gasp. Sobs and tears rushed in a torrent. I remembered seeing the front seat of that burning white car, the distorted, bloodied bodies moments before being consumed by flames while I dragged that little girl to safety. The little girl's parents.

The EMS man sat back down on the curb next to me. "June, there was nothing you could have done for those two people." He gripped my hand again. "What could be done, you did. You saved their child. If they were here now, I know they would thank you for that."

Although the police officer was adept at dealing with life and death, the emotions of a woman who had just been thrust into the ugly side of his job were obviously not his specialty. He nodded his head then briskly turned away and joined his colleagues who directed traffic, tow trucks and street crews in the crash clean-up.

I covered my face with my filthy hands. I turned and buried my head in the chest of my broad-shouldered EMS "friend" who wrapped his arm around me. After a few minutes I was uncomfortable when I realized what I had just done. I abruptly sat up, then wiped the tears from my face with my sleeve.

"I'm sorry," I gulped. "I am so terribly sorry. I should go. I need to get home. Wait, it's Thursday. I need to get back to work. I need to go home and call work. I don't know–I just need to go."

"Is there someone I can call for you?" he asked. "Are you okay to drive?"

"Yes," I said, then shook my head impatiently. "I mean yes, I am fine to drive." I took a deep breath. Placing one hand on his shoulder, I lifted myself to my feet. I wobbled a bit but steadied as he raised himself from the curb to stand.

"Are you sure I can't call someone or get one of the officers to give you a ride?" he said.

"I'm sure," I answered. "But thank you. And thank you for being so...understanding and comforting. I don't want to keep you from your job."

"Actually, my ride left a few minutes ago," he said and grinned. "But not to worry, one of the cops will get me back to the station." He held out his hand; I took hold with a firm grip.

"You're a hero," he said. "Remember that part when you tell the story, June. I know I will. Take care."

While he walked away, I turned and gathered my bearings. I saw my Jeep Cherokee parked behind me where I'd left it in the parking lot of Dunkin' Donuts. I started to walk to it and noticed another officer in front of the donut shop doors. He spoke to a group of reporters and camera crews. He looked at me and nodded his head in my direction.

I caught his signal and knew it would lead to a rush of reporters heading my way. I didn't want to talk to strangers–or anybody for that matter–and relive the horrific experience again that I was just beginning to process. I certainly didn't want to do that for thousands more unknowns on camera.

I hastened my pace and reached my car far ahead of the pursuing press. I was so intent on avoiding the onslaught, that it barely registered that I was rushing out of the parking lot, into traffic, in a vehicle not so dissimilar from the death trap I had just watched go up in flames.

Something should have slowed me, caused hesitation to get into a car again, at least for a while. But it didn't happen. Any fear or lingering apprehension was replaced by the strong desire to put this behind me. And so I drove...home.

The drive was quiet and uneventful–a welcome change to the morning's events. It was around 2 pm when I pulled into my driveway. I parked the car and sat there.

That was the first time I had ever traveled the familiar route at a speed of about five miles an hour. Every turn was made with both hands on the wheel. At every intersection, even at green lights, I slowed to a near stop. I paid no attention to irritated honks and hand gestures. I didn't care.

Now that I was home, I didn't want to act quickly. I didn't even want to leave my car and run inside. I sat there for a while deliberately contemplating nothing. I closed my eyes and leaned my head back against the headrest. It was almost peaceful. Eventually, sounds from the street and a bird's chirping brought daylight back to my closed eyes, gently prodding my body to move. I opened the door, stepped out, and slowly walked up the pathway toward my house.

After fumbling with the front door key, I opened the door and headed straight for the kitchen to heat up a cup of coffee. I had neither the patience nor the strength to make a new pot; the leftover brew from that morning would be comfort enough. I grabbed my favorite mug from the cupboard and poured dark, cold coffee into it and placed it into the microwave, then set it for one minute.

From the kitchen, I had a clear view into the living room and to the corner of the couch, my corner, where my quilted comforter and down pillow were in a pile, calling to me to come join them. Suddenly, I longed to curl up and feel and be safe.

I sighed. As much as I wanted to fold myself into my corner of comfort, I had one chore to do. It was now 2:30 pm and I was supposed to be back from lunch and back to work. No one there knew where I was. Eventually, they would get concerned because my 3 pm appointment was due to arrive.

I picked up my cell phone and called work.

I didn't want to go into details with anyone about what had happened. I didn't have energy for any conversations that would lead to a flood of questions and more explanations and more drain on my soul.

When the receptionist answered, I told her that I must have eaten something bad at lunch and was too sick to come back–could Marty, my very apt co-worker, please take my 3 pm appointment? No prolonged conversation, no detailed explanation. Within the same minute it took to warm my coffee, the conversation had begun and ended.

I took the coffee out of the microwave and headed toward the living room. Now that my chore was completed, I was free to join my friends in my corner of the couch...and breathe.

I sat in my spot warming my hands on the coffee mug while the comforter blanketed my legs and torso. With each sip of the left-over black brew, I felt more awake and at ease, despite the fact that coffee cannot sit all day and resemble anything near tasting good. I didn't care. It soothed me and that is what I needed more than anything. That and the loving embrace of my husband.

***

I met Tim Gallagher during my junior year of college in 1996. He was a senior. We both took required accounting classes. Tim was on his way to becoming a career CPA; I was content to be a general accountant with a minor in art history.

We were sort of the Mutt and Jeff couple among our friends. Tim is six-foot tall with a long, angular face. His jet-black hair was always neatly cropped, never too long or too short, and his dress was always immaculate and conservative—polo shirts and Dockers with creases. He played a lot of racquet ball, but his thin, somewhat awkward body never could hold up to more strenuous athletics. Even in college, he looked like an accountant.

I am five foot six—in heels. My long brown curls lay on my shoulders in whichever way my morning shower dictated. I was often late for class; combing those curls would have meant being even more tardy. My round face, made to look smaller by the wild curls that framed it, is described as being pixie-like. My style of dressing, though equally immaculate as Tim's, had an artist's flair of unkemptness to it. Nothing I wore was from the local mall; I shopped at secondhand stores and avant-garde hideaways. I looked more like the artist that I had originally wanted to be. And while Tim was nearly always controlled and thoughtful about what he said, how he communicated with people, and how he reacted to situations, I had a bit of the artist's temperament.

As I grew older, my hair straightened to more of a manageable wave.

My temperament kept its twists.

A two-accountant couple is not often thought of as the most exciting pairing. Most people can't grasp the concept of debits equaling credits as it applies to double-entry accounting and couldn't care less. But for Tim and me, those things and many more advanced taxation rules formed the backdrop for our meeting and then the need to spend many hours together studying, which of course led to romance—accounting style.

Tim was very attentive; he was a throw-back gentleman who opened and held doors, brought flowers, remembered important dates, and thankfully, chewed with his mouth closed. The latter proving to hold more importance the closer we got and the longer we were together— trust me on that. We were a perfect match.

We dated all during my junior and his senior year of college and we moved in together after a year. We rented a small apartment about 30 minutes off-campus, which meant a not-too-awful commute for Tim to pursue his Master's and CPA requirements, while I found an entry-level job as a bookkeeper with a small, local accounting firm. The firm did mostly non-profit work; so, although we were paid for our efforts, there was a sense that we worked for a more noble compensation.

In May of my final semester, we married. It was a simple affair, held on campus where most of our friends were. Neither of us was very religious but we settled on having the ceremony in the campus chapel.

Tim's parents, whom I had only met on one occasion and to whom Tim was not overly close, came to the wedding and lavished us with gifts—then left on a whirlwind tour of India. They were odd that way.

My own parents had died several years earlier; my mom of heart failure when I was 15 and my dad in a car crash the following year. I spent my high school years living with my aunt. She passed away from cancer the year before Tim and I married. Because I was an only child, there was no family of mine at the wedding. But I had many college friends and it was a warm, special celebration to me.

During that first year at the firm, I became pregnant with our daughter, Elsie. We had looked forward to starting a family, so my pregnancy was a welcome surprise. A month after I came back from maternity leave I was fired. Apparently, the temporary person who was hired to fill in was told that their position was permanent and that I was not coming back. Imagine their surprise when I did. So much for nobility.

Tim's parents are of German descent; he was very close to his grandmother, Elsie–thus the name choice. I wasn't a big fan of that moniker, but I do value family history and traditions. When Tim suggested it, I understood why and the name took on special meaning. It became more meaningful when she passed away from lung cancer 18 months after Elsie's birth. She had been an ardent smoker who was fervent in her denial that smoking was bad for her.

Up until her death, Grandma Elsie insisted that Elsie's first word was Gamma. I am quite certain it was Mumma, but given Grandma's deteriorating condition and her adoration for little Elsie, I felt petty and ungrateful even thinking about trying to correct her. It was also better to support *her* claim than Tim's ridiculous idea that Elsie's first word was Dadda.

Elsie was such an easy baby. She cried when she was hungry or had a dirty diaper but was never colicky. She slept pretty much on schedule; her waking and eating times were predictable. I was the envy of all the new mothers I knew or met, as well as those with more experience and the two or three kids to prove it. Tim often joked, "We're accountants, what did you expect?"

It wasn't until Elsie turned 11 that she began to develop health issues beyond the occasional cold.

Elsie would get horrific migraine headaches that often kept her out of school–a place Elsie loved to be and where she excelled.

At first, we thought it might be related to getting close in age to the onset of her first period and all of the hormone changes that went with it. But that didn't happen and the migraines continued with varying frequency and intensity for many years. I felt for her–as any mother would–but especially because I too had suffered from migraines my entire adult life and know how debilitating they are.

When our concerns magnified, we took Elsie to her general practitioner who suggested what we had already ruled out–that this was related to her coming period and she would outgrow it. *Really there wasn't much that could be done*, he basically insisted–*here are some pills.*

When I reminded the doctor that I also had been having migraines my entire adult life and no pills had stopped them or relieved them, he just shrugged. He finally suggested that Elsie have an MRI in case there was something more to her migraines. She did. Thankfully, there wasn't.

I didn't like over-medicating my child, so I reluctantly and sparingly doled out migraine pills the doctor gave us whenever Elsie suffered through one of her "aches" as we began calling them.

I tried various over-the-counter remedies too, hoping some combination or change in approach would help, but rarely did they work, and never for very long. We took a mostly wait-it-out approach and kept Elsie still and her environment as quiet and dark as possible until the episode passed.

These "aches" could last anywhere from an hour to three or four hours; there was no telling which type was coming. I helped Elsie get better at predicting when an ache was approaching because of my own experiences and by helping her develop the ability to be attuned to her own body signals.

Sometimes, Elsie could sense a migraine coming during periods of heightened activity, such as being on the playground running and kicking a ball. During those times, she had some success in lessening the ache by immediately halting her activity and sitting in a quiet corner with her head on her knees.

This wasn't an exact science by any means; it also had the unfavorable result of other kids teasing her for stopping in the middle of a game of kickball and running to hide in a corner. Not the therapy we hoped for.

Tim was like mush during his daughter's episodes. His practical accountant side needed a logical reason that would lead to a therapy resulting in a cure–or at least a manageable outcome. When that didn't happen, all he was left with was a hurting little girl and a feeling of impotence.

Elsie was the apple of his eye–his firstborn and a reminder of the grandmother he adored. Seeing her in pain tore at him. He took some comfort in knowing there wasn't some mysterious brain malfunction happening and that, unlike other really sick children, her life was not threatened.

But when something happens to you and those you love, the force of it is felt no matter what is or isn't happening to someone else.

Whenever Elsie had an episode and retreated to her room for comfort, it became a common occurrence that Tim became quiet and almost still, never turning on the television as he normally would. He sat still, read a newspaper, and sipped a drink until Elsie came bouncing back down the stairs and into the living room.

Tim never had this reaction to my migraines. I had learned to just tell anyone that I had a headache and was lying down. In some ways I had grown accustomed to them; over the years, they lessened in length and frequency, if not intensity. I could lie down and be up again usually within an hour.

So, to Tim, mine were minor incidents; although he was always comforting and understanding, he never ceased functioning the way he did with our daughter.

Our son, Ernie, was born in 2002–three years after Elsie.

CHAPTER TWO

Einstein's Unknown Theory

It's strange how the mind works even when it feels like it's shut down.

Or you want it to, at least.

With everything that had happened that morning, through all I had seen and done, somewhere in my head, logic still ran the show.

The sequence of events from driving home to making coffee and calling work, had an order and a reason. I knew I had to drive carefully after what had happened—preservation. I knew I had to be home—rejuvenation. I knew I had to call work—responsibility. And I knew I couldn't interrupt Tim at work to console me—selflessness, or married life.

My brain worked just as if nothing had happened; or at least a part of it did.

I knew that Tim and his partners were pitching a client who would keep the firm employees in bonuses for years to come, and also end our mortgage payments years earlier than anticipated. Interrupting that meeting was not even a remote possibility.

I had to be content with my comforter and my pillow and my stale black coffee for at least another two or three hours. While I contemplated all of that, the phone rang in the kitchen. I jumped like a startled cat, splashing my coffee.

Why do we even have a stupid land line in the age of cell phones and who is calling me? I thought. *Oh...wait...maybe it's Tim.* I didn't remember where I had put my cell phone or if I had left it in the car. Maybe Tim was calling on the kitchen line.

My favorite large coffee mug had a small handle, so it was somewhat unbalanced, especially when full of liquid. Even though my mug was now half empty, I still had to squeeze two fingers through the loop to keep it steady. It was uncomfortable but gave me a strong grip and control of the mug.

I stood quickly and bent toward the coffee table to put my mug down, but my fingers were stuck in the handle. The mug tipped sideways and spilled coffee across the top of the glass table. Coffee went everywhere. Liquid apparently increases ten-fold when it spills on a glass table. I believe that is one of Einstein's theories.

The phone was still ringing. Coffee flowed over my magazines, several unpaid bills, and the unfinished crossword section of the paper—a treasured guilty pleasure—and my blood pressure was rising.

I needed to get to the phone and to Tim. *What if it's an emergency with one of the kids?* With one hand I threw my beloved comforter at the spill to contain the damage and keep coffee from reaching our large antique rug underneath the table. I tried to shake my mug loose from my fingers; which it did with enough force to careen off the glass table, fly across the room, and break into several pieces when it landed on the other antique Indian rug—a wedding gift from Tim's parents—with just enough coffee to leave a stain.

And then phone stopped.

I wanted to cry. I wanted to throw something. But I had just done that with not-so-great results, so I just stood there and cursed.

I stared at my coffee-soaked comforter, the shattered pieces of my favorite mug, and my stained antique rug. Tim and I aren't people who can afford an antique rug, never mind two of them.

Well, truth be told, the word "antique" may be a stretch. Tim's parents got them from a questionable character at a roadside market during their trip to India. Tim liked Indian rugs and when he asked his parents to have one shipped back, they figured, *why not get two and give one as a wedding gift?* Antique or not, they were prized possessions and very beautiful. And now, I had permanently stained one of them. Maybe the rug cleaner guy–there must be one of those specialists somewhere–can get the stain out.

I finally moved to investigate the stain and collect the pieces of my former mug. After I cleaned up that mess, I returned to the coffee table and made a final sweep with the dry end of my comforter, leaving streaks of coffee where the not-so-porous comforter failed to sop it up.

Broken mug pieces in one hand and sopping comforter in the other, I headed toward the laundry room which was just off the garage. At the same time that I opened the door to the laundry, the door from the garage swung open. There, in the doorway, was my Tim.

I dropped the comforter and mug pieces in a heap on the floor and ran to him, throwing my arms around his waist while burying my head in his chest. He placed his briefcase on the dryer and matched my strong hold while he gently kissed the top of my head. This was warmer and safer than the coffee and comforter. I cried.

There was something about Tim and the way he held me and loved me, that could at once make me feel like a strong, desired woman or a protected child. This time it was the latter and I needed it.

"Babe, what happened?" Tim said over the top of my head. "I called your work and someone said you were sick and left early. So I came right home after the meeting."

Babe. Tim had such a nice way of saying it, not in a derogatory way. He said it with love, with affection and caring. I loved the few times he said it but never let on how much. Not directly. I would give little hints of a smirk or a sexy kiss or maybe ask with false indignation, "Did you just call me *babe*?" Just to hear him say it again.

On this occasion, I just squeezed him a little tighter and let myself be a protected, loved little girl a minute longer before answering.

"You are not going to believe the day I had," I finally said. I broke our hold, looked deeply into his concerned eyes, then pulled him to me by his necktie and locked my lips on his.

Tim was startled and speechless, but his willing mouth assured me that it was not in a bad way. I took him by the hand and marched him over the comforter to the couch where I pushed him down and dropped in next to him. Well, sort of on his lap.

"June...*kiss*...I am in...*kiss*...my...*kiss, kiss*...good suit." He leaned forward enough to take his suit jacket off and gently tossed it onto the coffee table while I continued my kissing onslaught.

"Wait," he laughed a little, pushing me back a bit. "So you're not sick?"

"No," I said, a little perturbed at the mood killer. "I just told work that so I didn't have to explain why I wasn't going back in." Apparently, what his male ears heard was that I played hooky, scared him, and was wrinkling his best suit for no good reason.

Tim sat back and looked at me incredulously. "I rushed home because I thought you were really sick, because you never just leave work. And all that happened was that you wanted a day off? Geezus June, I left clients hanging and had a really important meeting today that didn't go as planned and was already really stressed. I don't have time for silliness."

He sat up, moved off the couch, and picked up his suit jacket.

"What the...why is the coffee table wet? Oh for Christ's sake, now my suit coat is *soaked*." He brought the sleeve to his nose. "And, wait...is that coffee I smell?"

"Yep," I replied matter-of-factly.

"How the *hell* did a coffee spill get left on the table?"

In a matter of seconds, all the nice kissy, kissy love you honey, you're my hero, hold me in your big strong arms feeling had drained from me. In its place, an ugly, vengeful monster grew with each of his harsh words. By the end of his tirade my monster had reached full adulthood.

"I'll tell you how," I said with restrained rage. I stood and clenched my fists in my pillow and held it in front of me like a shield. "Today, on my way back to work during my lunch break–which by the way had to be cut short because I picked up your precious dry cleaning–there was a horrible accident across the street from the Dunkin' Donuts. Two cars collided in the intersection and one burst into flames. I was in the Dunkin' Donuts getting a coffee to take back to work and saw the whole thing."

"Sweetheart, why did..."

"Shut up, I'm telling a story." Tim sat back down on the couch. "And please don't interrupt again–you know I hate when you do that when I'm telling a story." I took a deep breath.

"I was on my way out of Dunkin' Donuts when the crash happened. One of the cars was hit so hard the engine blew up or something. Anyway, it was on fire. A few people ran over to the car with me and we could see there were people in the front. I looked into the back seat and saw a little girl slumped over. The flames were already engulfing the front seat and heading toward the back. So I forced open the back door, crawled inside–and while I was choking on fumes and my skin was nearly blistering from the heat–managed to get the little girl's seatbelt undone, rip off a part of my blouse to use as a bandage on her profusely bleeding head, and pull her out of the burning car while her parents died–burned to death–in the front seat."

Tim stared at me with his mouth open.

"I got her away from the crash and sat with her holding my torn piece of my blouse–thanks for noticing by the way–pressed against her head while waiting for help." This was all coming out clearly and without emotion other than anger toward Tim that built in volume. "The police came. The ambulance guy was understanding and so nice, and they both told me I was a hero."

"Babe..." *(Not this time honey!)*

"I AM NOT FINISHED!" The build to the finale was coming.

"The press people wanted to interview me," I continued, "but I just wanted to get home and not relive that horrible experience. That little girl's parents in the front seat burned to death! So...I drove home with your dry cleaning–which is still in the car if you're interested– and heated up a stale cup of coffee. Then I called work and told them I was sick from something I ate. I was in a way but not from the measly donut I had for lunch.

"I really wanted to call you, Tim, but I knew you were in a meeting to end all meetings, so I just sat with my coffee. Then the phone in the kitchen rang." I was really building it now. My body was tense, my face red, my volume raised. It wouldn't be long now.

"I thought, *Oh it might be Tim*," I went on. "So, I tried to hurry to the phone, but my fingers got stuck in my favorite coffee mug and it fell sideways and the coffee spilled all over the table and I tried to mop it up with my comforter but it isn't good for sopping up spills and there's that Einstein theory and then the phone rang again and I tried to shake the mug out of my hand and it flew out of my hand, bounced off of the table, flew across the room and broke into pieces on the Indian rug your parents gave us. And that's how the FUCKING COFFEE GOT ON THE TABLE!"

The monster had blown her mind. Silence.

"Oh," I continued calmly. "And I am not certain the coffee stain will come out of the 'antique' rug." I pivoted on my heels and headed upstairs toward our bed, still clutching my pillow which was now shaped like a bow tie.

I don't know how long I was lying on the bed before Tim came up to join me; but it was at least 30 minutes. I imagined he was working on his apology speech or preparing a make-up dinner.

God knows, I was in no mood to cook. When he entered the room, he had his Basset Hound hurt puppy look on his face. Really? This was what he came up with in over 30 minutes of thought? I turned away from him with a "pfuh." Tim sat on the edge of the bed.

"I'm sorry babe. (*Uggh –do you know how you are ruining that for me?*)

I know that I am an ass sometimes. But I'm *your* ass."

He was going for humor now? *Boy is your timing off*, I thought. What I said over my cold left shoulder was, "You really need some new material, Tim. Every sitcom ever made has used that line by now."

He paused. "I really am sorry, June. Seriously. I was so caught up in my day; I didn't think to even let you explain yours. I just jumped to the idea that you were playing hooky, which you never do...so, that was another stupid thought on my part. Truth is, I *wasn't* thinking. I was just reacting."

Tim's hand lightly touched my shoulder blade and back. On top of that nice caress, he *was* sincere in his apology. I relaxed a bit, but I wasn't ready to entirely give up my well-earned pissed-off-ness. I needed more from him.

"I can't believe what you went through," he said, "...what you did! You saved a person's life. You were being a hero while I was...well I wasn't being a hero. It must have been terrible what you saw and just the whole thing. I should have been there for you and not in some stupid meeting."

I turned toward my husband. His puppy dog face had been replaced with real concern and contrition, so I let go of my hurt. I never stay mad for long. I'm not certain if that's a strength or a weakness.

"It's okay Tim," I said and rolled to face him. I put my hand on his leg. "I just wish you would listen better." He smirked. "What happened today was...*unreal*. And the people in the front seat of the car. God that was horrible to see. I don't know how I can ever get that image out of my head."

Tim leaned over me now, lightly stroking my cheek and using his thumb to wipe away a solitary tear that rolled from the corner of my eye. "I can't imagine what that little girl is going through now...losing her parents that way..."

And boom! An alarm went off in my head probably triggered by the mention of the little girl.

"Shit! The kids! Tim, what time is it?" I said and sat up on the edge of the bed nearly knocking Tim to the floor.

He looked at his watch. "3:45."

"I have to go get the kids from soccer. At 4:00. It's my turn for car-pool.

I forgot all about it."

"Yeah well, you kind of had other things to deal with." Tim put his hands on my shoulders and gently guided me back down to the bed. "Sit. I'll go get them. You stay here and rest...maybe have a cup of coffee?"

I glared at him but he knew that I knew his sick humor was funny and maybe just what I needed. He was right. I smiled and laughed. "You really are an ass."

Tim jogged out the door and quickly downstairs. "Don't you want to know what field they're playing at?" I shouted to him. I heard him run back upstairs and then he poked his head around the corner of the door.

"Good idea."

"Today is Thursday so...they are playing at Emerson Junior." Tim headed back down the stairs in a flash.

"The one on Rosa Parks Street!" I yelled after him, knowing he didn't hear me and anticipating my cell would ring in about 10 minutes when he realized he didn't know where Emerson Junior was.

I trudged downstairs and into the kitchen. I still hadn't taken any time to reflect on the crash and how it affected me. My day progressed just as nothing extraordinary had happened. I wondered if it might all hit me at once–in the middle of the night while I was wooing sleep.

"I guess this means I am making dinner after all," I muttered. I stared at the stove and then turned to the refrigerator, hoping inspiration would jump out at me and into the oven.

Then my cell rang. I could hear it but didn't know where it was–I thought I'd left it in the car. I could hear the Minions Banana Song ringtone which I had lowered for sanity's sake, but it was muffled. I followed the sound into the living room and found it lodged between the couch cushions just in time to answer. It was Tim.

"Hi honey, what do you want from Thai Palace?"

"Thai Palace? I thought you were calling because you were lost?"

"Huh? Oh, no. There's this thing called Google Maps." I could hear his smugness. "I just thought with all that happened today, cooking was the last thing on your mind, so I thought how about I pick up Thai on my way home?"

"That sounds like a great idea." Well, inspiration had jumped out at someone.

"So, what do you want?"

"I don't have the menu in front of me, Tim. Just pick something good. But not those noodles I hate or that appetizer you always get that no one likes except you."

"Umm, okay. The kids and I will figure it out. Bye. Love you."

With dinner now under control I could...get the paper towels and Windex and finish cleaning the coffee table. Then I could relax a bit. As I finished that thought, I saw that my phone indicated I had five new messages. *What the...?* Five messages in such a short period of time was a lot.

Work. That was my immediate thought. But when I checked the call list, they were all from one number...my son Ernie's school. My body immediately stiffened, and my heart began to pump wildly. This could not be a good thing.

I grabbed my purse off the kitchen table and rushed toward the front door with my cell phone pressed to my ear, calling Tim. I wanted to get to him before he detoured for Thai food. The message was from Mary Patterson, the school principal; she said that Ernie had suffered a seizure and had been rushed by ambulance to a hospital.

It didn't dawn on me that Elsie would tell Tim when he picked her up.

Before I reached the front door, Tim answered the phone. He spoke before I did, "Elsie isn't at practice and neither is Ernie. Bev, a car pool kid's mother, says Ernie collapsed and was taken to Brinker Hospital. Elsie is still at school waiting for us."

"I know, Tim. The principal called and left a message on my cell. Wait, Elsie is still at school?" I sat on the steps leading upstairs and cradled my purse in my lap.

"Yeah, she was too upset to go to practice and thought you would come get her."

"Okay. Okay. You go drop off the carpool kids and pick up Elsie at school. I'll go to the hospital and see how Ernie is. It's probably just another of his episodes and the school didn't know what to do so they didn't send him to University Hospital..."

"I don't have the carpool kids," Tim said. "When Ginny found out what had happened, she agreed to take over the carpool. I'll get Elsie, you go to the hospital. Yeah, it's probably just another of his episodes. But teachers at the school have seen them before, so I don't know why they just didn't keep him there 'til we got there."

"Well, maybe they couldn't reach me and you know they don't want to be responsible. Okay, I gotta go. Meet me at the hospital. No wait... you'll have Elsie, I don't want to worry her or bring her to the hospital. You go home with Elsie and I'll call you from the hospital if it's anything unusual. Okay?"

"Yeah, okay but call me either way."

We both hung up and I stood and grabbed my purse. Brinker Hospital was about a 30-minute drive from home, traffic pending. I was in a hurry to get there but remembered what can happen when people in cars rush or are distracted—or whatever caused the fatal accident.

This was not the first time Ernie had seized at school. Usually, they were short, subtle episodes more like fainting. He would recover quickly and go back to his normal self after his teacher or the school nurse made him take a time out just in case. I always got a phone call update, but Ernie had never been rushed to the hospital before. Not from school.

CHAPTER THREE

BEING ERNIE

Ernie's early years were the opposite of Elsie's. His issues were well beyond migraines. Ernie suffered from myriad ailments, all surrounded by mystery.

At the age of two, Ernie suddenly couldn't take food orally and needed to be tube fed. He spat up or vomited baby food for no apparent reason. We tried every sort of combination and type of food available, even some provided by his physician. Nothing worked.

His vomiting was not normal food being expelled. He had this awful granular mess; it was kind of like a dry heave without stomach contents. There was no connection to what he ate, how he felt otherwise, or any other identifiable reason.

After several visits, Ernie's doctor determined that a gastric tube needed to be surgically implanted in Ernie's stomach. This was not an easy decision for Tim and me to go along with. First and foremost, having the G-Tube inserted meant assuming the risks of surgery at such a young age. And then it meant that Ernie needed to be fed a special formula through the tube for a long time—possibly permanently.

But Ernie was not growing at a normal rate and not eating. He'd even stopped recognizing people and things around him. Something had to be done, fast.

Although the doctor didn't officially diagnose Ernie, he believed that our son's stomach had not developed completely enough to digest food and that his intestines may also be malfunctioning.

So that is when the tube feeding began. We were all hopeful that Ernie would grow out of the problem and–to our surprise and delight–he did. By three years old he was eating baby food and holding it down. The feeding tube was removed. He still had episodes of being sick, but for the most part he kept food down and began gaining weight.

When he was an infant, Ernie had difficulty with his strength. Crawling just a few feet exhausted him. He'd curl up in a ball and abruptly fall asleep. Elsie loved to play with baby Ernie, so this was frustrating to a three-year-old who thought maybe she had hurt her little brother from playing too hard.

One of her favorite games was to throw his binky a few feet and watch him crawl after it. Ernie was her pet that she controlled during those early years; making him cry and crawl for his binky was her cherished entertainment. Ernie always smiled and laughed whenever he retrieved his comfort-giver and acted as though nothing had happened and all was right again in his little world.

When he got a bit older and his sister played an annoying game with him, he pinched her. Being the older sister and considering how frail Ernie could be, Elsie could never retaliate in kind. She just put on a frowny face and called him "dirty Ern."

Of course, Tim and I did not encourage this activity. But I must admit that it was sort of funny and cute in an odd, bonding sort of way.

One time when Ernie was two, he collapsed into sleep without crawling an inch. That was frightening. We thought he might stop breathing. We rushed him to the emergency room. By the time we arrived, Ernie was wide awake, crying and carrying on like any two-year-old whose parents had forgotten to bring his binky–which we had.

Well, we were already there and already had concerns, so we asked the doctor to examine him. He found nothing wrong and wrote us off as overly-concerned parents before sending us on our way.

By the third time in six weeks that we had rushed Ernie to the same hospital for the same reason, they began to suspect that maybe something out of the ordinary was happening to our child beyond having panicky parents.

More exotic tests were ordered. Some were blood tests which meant we had to wait weeks to get results. When they came, Ernie's doctor called us to come into his office. He explained that they had found nothing.

The doctor reasoned that because Ernie was slow in developing an ability to eat and keep food down and had to be tube fed, that this–or perhaps some other temporary developmental unknown–had affected his energy levels and muscle development. Ernie was simply tired more often and needed to catch up with normal physical developmental charts.

The doctor gave us a prescription for special vitamins to boost energy. He also believed that Ernie would outgrow this phase; he encouraged us to be patient but keep an eye on him–not to the extent of fearing that he will stop breathing.

The doctor gave us a pep talk that there is nothing wrong with our son–he is perfectly healthy. He thought we should try a little harder to get him to eat and don't let him decide *when* to eat; sometimes as a parent you have to be a little tough, he said.

So, we were back to "bad parenting."

I was not a happy camper when we left the doctor's office. We were no further along in understanding why Ernie had health problems– because we both knew he most certainly did. Tim and I were also not pleased by the suggestion that Ernie's issues were *our* fault–that we were "less- than" good parents.

Truthfully, the doctor's insinuation stabbed me and left a scar of guilt that gnawed at me for years. What added to my guilt feelings was Ernie's improvement after we began the vitamin regimen and a rigorous approach to meal times.

Ernie began crawling everywhere like a mad wind-up toy; going from room to room trying to get into everything within his limited reach. We began to think that maybe the problem had been a lack of vitamins and that he really did just need to catch up to the other kids.

Well, that was short-lived. Over the next three years, until Ernie turned five, there were many instances of vomiting and fatigue; then occasional seizures happened.

So, there were more doctor visits and more tests. Ernie was seen by a gastroenterologist who ran metabolic profiles which came back saying his blood levels were abnormally acidotic. No diagnosis as to why.

There were more suggestions that we were failures as parents—even the suggestion that Ernie had gotten into something he should not have—maybe we had poisoned him by neglect. Another scar.

Along with vomiting and fatigue, Ernie had speech delays and learning problems. When he entered kindergarten, he was a year behind other children his age and had a very limited vocabulary.

Ernie could barely put sentences together beyond a few words. He often communicated with one word at a time. He pointed and said "Dahda" or "Momma" to get what he wanted. If Tim asked what game he would like to play, Ernie simply answered "play ball" or "do color" for coloring book.

That is when we began to notice other developmental deficiencies.

At first, we thought that Ernie had inherited his father's lack of artistic skills. Ernie's coloring book pictures and other art work were, well, terrible. Every mother tells little white lies about their child's efforts—I mean we love whatever they do because they are our children, right?

So, when Ernie finished coloring a picture, I said, "Wow, that's nice honey. Can I keep it?" I always said it with a big smile and Ernie always smiled hugely back. But when Tim and I sat together in the evenings when the kids were in bed, we'd look at Ernie's drawings.

Tim, with his dry way of putting things, asked, "So...why did he just draw lines in different colors over the snowman?" Or some similar comment. I feigned resentment and proudly defended Ernie and his unique artistic expression. Then I would look at the picture, then at Tim, shrug my shoulders, and laugh. Not a mean laugh. More of a God-I- love-my-kid-but-I-hope-he-becomes-a-lawyer type of laugh.

By age eight, when all of Ernie's coloring efforts and animal drawings were done with mostly the same undiscernible lines as had been done when he was three, we began to realize that our son had motor skill problems or some kind of cognitive thinking issues or both.

Of course, this meant more trips to doctors of varying specialties: for brain scans, motor flexor tests, and eventually even speech therapy.

A neurologist did find some indications of possible abnormalities in Ernie's basal ganglia part of his brain which could explain some of his learning and coordination difficulties. Once again, there was no exact causal effect diagnosis or related treatment. There would need to be more tests and possibly travel to an out-of-state specialist.

We opted to put that off for now.

We didn't want to hold Ernie back more than one year and were determined to move him on to second grade. So, we engaged a speech therapist and a physical therapist to help him catch up. This was tough for Ernie who still had energy problems and was often too tired for speech therapy and physical therapy in the same day–or even within a day of each other.

And, well, his therapies were a drain on Tim and me too–and expensive. Between all the hospital and doctor visits that required our attention, along with needing to keep Ernie close by–just in case–it was becoming exceedingly difficult for us to hold down full-time jobs. Tim's career was on an upward path; although he offered to slow it down and be content with giving up on a potential partnership to help out with Ernie's care, we both knew that was not a good idea.

We needed Tim's health insurance coverage and his growing salary and potential promotions in order to meet our growing financial obligations. Our little family needed him to stay on track. So, I began to cut down on my client list at work. The small firm I ended up with was a family business–one that truly did understand and put family first whenever possible. And they were loyal.

My boss, Benjamin, who knew much of what was happening at home with Ernie, kept me on as a part-time bookkeeper and allowed me to take work home so that I could work at night or weekends on my own schedule.

Because we were paid by clients on bookable hours, this gave me a chance to be in the office for important client meetings while building billable hours at home. Benjamin even offered to keep me on full medical benefits which I graciously declined, explaining that Tim's coverage was a bit more comprehensive.

After a year of physical and speech therapy, Ernie made tremendous progress. If Tim asked him, "What do you want to do buddy?" he would answer, "I want to play ball," or "I don't like to color, we play on swing."

Not an advanced grade level ability, but a huge advance for him at eight-years-old. Though he would still tire easily, Ernie's motor skills improved too, and he could hit the ball off the T-Ball and run to first base—albeit slowly. He even started staying in kickball games at school for longer periods of time. He gained weight and grew, even if he was still on the low end of the growth charts.

With all this progress came the hope that Ernie was outgrowing his early childhood health issues and was going to enjoy a normal childhood just like all the other kids. But just as Ernie was making this hopeful transition, his seizures began.

The first time Ernie had a seizure, he was in the back yard playing on the swings with Elsie. Despite all the health issues Ernie suffered, he never lacked courage or was afraid to try anything, even when he knew he might fail. He liked to pretend he was a daredevil and would stand on his bike seat—with training wheels, a helmet, knee pads and elbow pads, at my insistence—and glide down the sidewalk. Of course, Tim thought this was cool, but it gave me heebie jeebies!

Ernie also loved it when his sister pushed him on the swings, pleading with her to push him higher and higher. One time I was doing dishes at the sink and looked out the window. I saw Ernie fly through the air higher and higher, the two of them hysterical with laughter. I couldn't help it. I ran to the back door, flung it open and shouted at Elsie. "Elsie, don't push your brother so high! He's going to fall off and break his neck!"

I think I am a combination of the overprotective parent and being sensitive to how weak Ernie can be, *and* naturally fearful. If Tim was home and I was too busy to run to the door, I made him go scream at Elsie. He would grumble and walk slowly to the door and make a half-hearted reprimand to Elsie and then go back to what he was doing. Their shenanigans didn't faze him.

Tim's lackadaisical attitude bothered me. One time I was fed up. "Tim! Can you please take this seriously? What if Ernie gets a weak spell and loses his grip while flying up in the air like that? He could fall and really hurt himself."

"June, he is hardly flying. The swing set isn't that big, and Ernie will stop if he starts to feel bad. Don't you want your kid to have a normal life and do normal kid things like...flying through the air on the swings?"

"Yes, Tim, I want him to do everything other kids can do. I just don't want him to break his neck doing it."

"Ughh. My brother pushed me higher than that when I was only five and I never broke my neck."

"Yeah, and shall I list all the other things that *never* happened to you like G-Tubes and passing out from crawling and vomiting for years...?"

About a minute later, I heard Tim screaming out the door, "Elsie, stop pushing your brother that high or you won't use the swings for a month. And I mean it!"

One particular Saturday, we were too late with our warnings. Tim was mowing the front lawn and I was sitting on the couch with my laptop, working on a trial balance for a client as part of my take-home work. I had already admonished Elsie when she and Ernie headed out the back door–I told them to stay off the swings and go ride bikes or something.

She said,"Yeah, okay Mom" noncommittally and they were off. Twenty minutes later, Elsie came rushing back through the door and stood next to me, panting and shaking. She was white as a ghost.

"Elsie, what? What's wrong? Where's Ernie?" I knew something had happened—that could be the only reason she was so pale and now crying.

"Mommy Mommy, Ernie fell off the swing." Elsie sobbed.

That was all I needed to hear. I was off the couch, spilling my laptop and several clients' file folders to the floor, and out the back door faster than I had ever moved in my life. I ran unflinchingly through the row of rose bushes that blocked my shortest route to the swing set, barely noticing the thorns that tore into my bare legs.

I found Ernie unconscious on the ground. He had landed on the large grassy area just beyond the swings which Tim had not yet mowed. It was a softer cushion than the worn area of mostly dirt that lay beneath the swing.

Ernie was on his side, motionless. I hesitated to touch or move him fearing he may actually have broken his neck or his back.

I knelt next to him, shaking. Elsie stood behind me sobbing uncontrollably.

Through her tears she kept apologizing, "I'm sorry Mommy, I'm sorry Mommy, I didn't mean to hurt Ernie." I felt for her and I knew this was an accident. But in my head, I heard my voice telling her, *Elsie, don't play on the swings.* Why didn't she listen to me? Why don't kids listen?

I needed help and I needed my attention on Ernie and I needed calm around me.

"Elsie, go get your father." She froze. "Now!" I shouted at her. She still didn't move. "Elsie! Now!" My second shout brought her out of her trauma and sent her running to the front yard.

I put my hand on Ernie's neck to get a pulse. This was surreal. I was looking for a pulse, for signs of life on my son who just moments earlier was laughing and playing and safe in his own back yard This can't happen, doesn't happen–children don't die in their back yard like this. Then I felt it. Faint but definite. My son was okay. He was alive.

Tim came storming around the corner and bounded toward me, barely stopping in time to avoid falling over both of us.

"June what happened? Did he faint? Did he fall of the swings?" Tim knelt beside me and started to turn Ernie over on his back.

"No, no Tim! You shouldn't move him. I...he...yes, he fell off the swing but I don't know if anything is broken."

Tim dug his cell phone out of the front pocket of his shorts and dialed 911. It took a second for them to answer.

"911, what is your emergency?" I could hear the dispatcher's voice over Tim's phone.

"My son fell off the swing and he's not moving." Tim was clear but his voice was raspy and breathy.

"Is he breathing?" Tim looked at me and I nodded. "Yes. Send someone here quickly, please."

"Sir, an ambulance is being dispatched to your location. Is your son conscious?"

"No. No, he's not moving or anything."

"How old is your son?"

"How old? He's eight. Is someone on their way?"

"Sir, yes, an ambulance is on the way. Please try and stay calm and remain on the phone with me. I need more information. My system shows you are at a home on..."

As he answered more questions, Tim paced away out of earshot for a minute or two, then turned back toward me to say he was going out front to meet the ambulance.

"She says to get a blanket and cover Ernie but don't move him!" He jogged out to the front of the house. Elsie stood a good distance away, still crying and reeling from what had happened.

"Elsie honey, come here." Elsie tentatively approached me. We were both crying now. I held her arms just below her shoulders and looked into her scrunched face. I raised a hand and brushed away part of her long hair which was clinging to her damp forehead. "Elsie, Ernie is going to be okay. It was an accident and the ambulance people are on their way. It's going to be okay."

I think I was trying to convince myself as much as trying to relieve Elsie. "Go inside and get my comforter off the couch honey so we can keep Ernie warm."

It was a beautiful summer day and covering Ernie with my thick comforter seemed odd, but it was something to do—something we were told to do by people who were going to help Ernie. In my mind, that meant we were helping somehow.

Elsie turned and ran toward the house. I hoped that taking part in doing something for Ernie helped overcome her guilt.

I heard the ambulance sirens in the distance. I looked up and toward the sound, away from Ernie. By the time I turned back toward him, he was awake and staring at me.

"Hi Mom," he whispered. He shifted and began to turn onto to his back.

"Oh my God. Ernie. No, no—no don't move honey you might be hurt."

But he ignored me and turned anyway. He didn't wince or make any move or sound that suggested he was hurt badly. I wanted to grab him and hug him, I was so overcome with pure joy. But I knew I shouldn't. I settled for leaning down and gently kissing his forehead. "Honey, the ambulance is coming so just lie still baby, everything is going to be fine."

"Why am I in grass, Mom?"

"Honey, you fell off the swing while Elsie was pushing you. But you landed on this grassy part Daddy didn't mow yet, so it's nice and soft." I was trying to be light–I didn't want to worry the little guy.

"Oh. No. Elsie not push me. She said I get in trouble for the swing. I see how high I go on my own." Ernie was completely alert and awake and speaking in his normal, disjointed way. Now I was the one who felt guilty.

Elsie ran back out with the comforter *and* a pillow, bless her heart. I took the comforter from her, grabbed her, and held her close. "It wasn't your fault Elsie. It wasn't your fault." I pressed my face into her cheek and then moved her face down to land several mom kisses on the top of her head. I gave her one more big hug. She stopped crying and shaking.

While I pulled the comforter over Ernie, he saw his sister standing with my pillow, her eyes red and swollen in her pale face.

"Hi Else," Ernie said. "I fall off swing like you said."

Elsie burst into tears and scolded Ernie. "I told you. I told you not to go on the swing, dirty Ern." She held the pillow tight and molded it into the shape of a bowtie.

Tim came barreling around the corner, an EMS team on his heels. They dragged a wheeled stretcher and gear behind them. Tim wedged himself between and looked dumbstruck at Ernie. "He...he's awake. You're awake! Hey big guy, how do you feel?"

The EMS technicians nudged Elsie and Tim out of the way and unceremoniously shoved me backward away from my son.

"We need to get in here and take vitals," one man said. "Everyone please stay back and let us take care of things."

They immediately went to work; a woman took his blood pressure and heart rate while a man flashed a penlight into Ernie's eyes, one at a time, while asking him questions.

"Hey big guy. Looks like you fell off the swing huh? Are you having any trouble breathing?"

I peered over the EMT's shoulder and Ernie looked at me for direction. "Go ahead honey, you can tell the man where you hurt." Reassured, Ernie responded.

"I breathe okay."

"I am going to just touch your arms and legs, tell me if you feel anything." The man lightly touched Ernie's forearms, his fingers, and his calves in succession. At each stop, Ernie was asked if he could feel anything and each time Ernie said, "Yes, I feel."

They removed his sneakers and asked Ernie to move his toes. The woman moved her finger up the sole of Ernie's foot while asking if he could feel that while looking for a reaction at the site of the pressure. When Ernie giggled, she smiled and said, "I guess so." We had a bit of a tension-relieving laugh.

The man turned to Tim. "We're going to immobilize him as a precaution, but at this point he doesn't appear to have any spinal injury or broken bones. His speech does seem a bit slurred, so we will make note of that. There could be a possible concussion." He and his partner expertly moved the trauma board under Ernie.

I didn't feel like explaining Ernie's speech. Tim looked like he was at a loss for a response, so we just let that go. It was true that he could still have a concussion so I figured; let them note that just in case.

Tim knelt down next to Ernie while they were strapping him onto the board and took hold of his little hand. "You're lookin' pretty good there, bud. I hope this isn't some scam to get out of school."

"No school now Dad. Summertime."

"Oh, yeah right. Good point. See? You're already doing better than me."

Ernie smiled. Tim smiled. Elsie stopped crying. My pillow began to return to a normal shape. I smiled. In a matter of minutes, our world had gone from being turned upside down to righting itself. Although Ernie was on his way to the hospital *again* and we were still concerned, for the moment all we felt was relief.

The EMT team carefully lifted Ernie, strapped him into the wheeled stretcher, and headed toward the ambulance. Tim chased after. "Wait, what hospital are you taking him to?"

"University," the woman answered over her shoulder while they carefully stepped toward the ambulance.

Tim shouted in my direction, "I'll get my keys. Meet me out front," and then he was gone. I headed for the back door and realized Elsie was not behind me. I turned around and saw her standing alone, looking dejected. She dangled the pillow by a corner with two fingers. I knew that she likely assumed her place would be to wait at home. Although that was my initial intention, I hadn't the heart to follow through.

"Don't just stand there," I said. "Dad needs you to give him directions." Elsie pretended to hesitate and then nearly skipped to my side. "And Ernie needs you to yell at him again for going on the swings."

"Ha!" she said with a smirk. "Funny Mom." Elsie gave me her high-cheeked smile that lit up a room. Even at her young age, my little girl understood my sometimes-irreverent sense of humor. That is one of the things that makes our relationship special; we get each other. It helps too that Elsie looks like me; brown hair with slight curls, round face, and fair-skinned. She got my English/Scottish genes. Ernie is a combination of Tim and me, though he tends toward Tim's Germanic ancestry with an angular face, prominent chin, and strong nose. But he had brown hair like me and he had my brown eyes.

Tim waited for me in the driveway, head in his hands, behind the wheel of his little Mazda Miata sports car. A two-seated, impractical, left-over toy from his college days that he refused to abandon. Elsie and I just looked at each other and headed to my Jeep Cherokee on the other side.

Mine was the practical family vehicle, albeit on the expensive side of practical. It was my one splurge from the money I inherited when my father died. We climbed in, Elsie in the back, me in the passenger seat. I put the key into the ignition and started the engine–and we waited for Tim to realize he was still alone in his car and we were in my car.

Tim beeped his horn. I beeped my horn. Tim looked over his shoulder. Seeing the two of us perched in my car, he waved his hands in the air, shut off the engine, and headed for the Jeep. When he got in, he looked back and forth between Elsie and me.

"Elsie's coming too," I said nonchalantly. He looked back at Elsie and then backed out of the driveway. Over the years I think Tim had figured out that sometimes it was easier not to question or remark on some of the things the women in his family said or did; just accept it and go with the flow. This was one of those times.

The only time Tim's normal, practical way of going through life was thrown to the wind was when he was behind the wheel of a car. Somewhere in his head, roadways were his private speedway just waiting to be tested–thus the sports car.

He was even able to transport this fantasy from the Miata to the Cherokee–or for that matter, to any vehicle he drove. Tim made the 30-minute drive to University Hospital in 18 minutes. When we arrived, my foot was firmly planted on the passenger side brake. All of Elsie's fingers were drained of color from grasping the leather handle with both hands above the back-seat passenger's door.

Tim, cool and casual from sharing one of his fantasy drives with us, shut off the engine, popped out of the car and headed for the hospital emergency room entrance in one fluent, uninterrupted move.

I looked back at Elsie. She rolled her eyes. I smirked. Enough "said." We left the car and headed toward the emergency room entrance hand-in-hand.

Tim was already at the desk speaking with a reception nurse. He turned from the desk and met us halfway into the lobby. Elsie and I walked up to him while holding hands and grinning. Tim answered with a wry, charming smile.

"Ernie is in the examination room now," he said, leading the way into the waiting area. "Someone is coming out soon. I told them to call Dr. Reynolds, but he isn't on duty, so they might not be able to get hold of him."

"Is he okay? Can we see him?" I asked.

"No, he is being transported to X-ray I think; he's probably in the hallway somewhere between here and there. I don't know if we can go back there and look for him."

"Let me go ask and find out," I said. "You know how cold and scary it is back there." I headed toward the admittance desk.

On my way, I heard Tim ask Elsie if she was hungry. "Hey, it's 2:30 and you haven't had any lunch. They have some really awful sandwiches and stuff in the vending machines downstairs. Sound good?"

"Um, oh yeah, Dad," she said, "Maybe one of those really tasty tuna fish sandwiches they didn't sell last week. Yummm." Elsie rubbed her tummy exaggeratedly.

"Maybe just a Snickers bar to take the edge off?" he compromised. "Great idea, Dad," she said. "You buy, I'll fly." Elsie mimicked one of his childhood sayings he had used during family story-telling time. Tim reached into his wallet and handed Elsie two singles.

"Seriously, Dad?" Elsie took the bills and looked at him with wide eyes. "Ah, welcome to 2010. It will be like $1.25 for each Snickers and then we need something to drink."

"You mean you want your *own* candy bar?" Tim said seriously. Elsie took the bait and froze. "Hah! Gotcha. Here's a fiver. Don't run away with it." Tim dug into his wallet and handed Elsie a five-dollar bill.

Elsie groaned and winced when she took the bill from her dad. It was one of those, "Why are dads so weird?" looks which lingered as she headed toward the vending machines.

I returned from the admittance area just in time to see Tim settle into a chair and Elsie get into an elevator.

"Wait Elsie, are you going to get something to eat?"

Elsie hunted for the button inside to keep the door open, but in a panic threw her arm between the closing doors. They lurched a bit then slowly opened, and Elsie jumped out. But the doors stayed open.

Then they closed a few inches, banged against an invisible barrier, and opened again.

Elsie looked at the malfunctioning doors and then quickly around the room to see if anyone saw what had happened.

"Oh my God, Elsie—you broke the elevator! Nice move," I said.

Elsie turned red, grabbed my arm and tried to usher me back into the lobby toward her father.

"Come on Mom," she whispered urgently, "We have to get out of here before someone notices."

"Don't grab *me*," I teased, "I don't want people to know you're with me." I tried to shake her off , but she was determined. By the time we reached Tim we were giggling like a couple of kids who just did something naughty.

"What is up with you two?" Tim smiled. "Nothing," Elsie said. "*Mom* broke the elevator."

"How can you break an elevator?" Tim asked.

"Never mind," I said. "Where were you going Elsie?"

"Oh, Dad wanted a Snickers bar really bad, so I offered to go get it for him." This girl was having too much fun with her version of reality.

"Uh, more like little Miss Fibber here wanted one *and* a soda and *begged* me for money." Tim countered.

"What about me?" I whined, "I want a Snickers too. And a Diet Coke. Go Elsie, and hurry back. And use the stairs. Someone broke one of the elevators." I nudged her with my elbow.

Elsie held her hand out, palm upward. Tim uttered, "Oh brother," and handed Elsie his wallet. "Here ya go," he said. "Have a party while you're down there."

In a flash, Elsie darted for the stairwell like she had just won the lottery.

After Elsie disappeared, Tim turned his focus back to Ernie. "Did you find out about Ernie or the doctor?"

"Yes and no," I said, sitting down next to him. The waiting area had recently been refurbished and had the smell of fresh paint and new furniture. In one corner were a few nice, oversized chairs and a large accommodating couch. In the other corner were the customary form-fitting—no one's form I have ever seen, by the way—plastic chairs in multiple cheery pastels. Because nothing says cheery quite like red, yellow, and blue plastic chairs when you're in an emergency room, right? Those were lined up in rows that faced each other and made it impossible not to stare at the person across from you. We had decided on the comfy corner.

"I saw Ernie long enough to say 'Hi' and give him a kiss before they ushered him into one of the X-Ray rooms," I continued. "He was sitting on a hospital bed stretcher, with his legs over the side, like he was getting ready to jump off and run down the hall. He said he felt fine. The technician said the doctor was coming out here to talk to us and I didn't want to miss him, so I came back."

We chatted—normal conversation now. We weren't obsessed with how Ernie was or filled with any real concern. He was awake, no broken bones or serious injuries—or so we were told—just waiting for the confirming X-Rays on his neck and for the doctor to come out and give us the okay so we could bring him home.

It was only a few more minutes before the examining doctor came out to speak with us. I was in one of the big chairs and Tim had settled into the other. We both stood to greet him. He introduced himself as Dr. Mills as he approached, although his name was written on a rainbow-colored, plastic name tag pinned to his white coat. He invited us to sit, so Tim and I moved to sit on the overstuffed couch while Dr. Mills pushed one of the big chairs closer, turning it to face us.

The deep, fluffy cushions swallowed us up and dumped us into the high back. It was so deep that my feet barely touched the floor. Tim kept his feet firmly on the ground, but his 180 lbs. weight made him sink deeper. We were caught completely by surprise and sat there, looking like a couple of little kids just called to the principal's office.

Tim and I looked at each other with surprise. Tim made a childish expression that made me laugh. Fortunately, I stopped myself just in time while Dr. Mills repositioned his chair. My slight smirk remained though.

"So, it's Tim and June right? The Gallaghers." Dr. Mills said.

Before he could start his speech, Elsie returned from the vending machines with her arms full of junk food. She looked as though she had just done a grab and run from a local convenience store. When she approached us at the couch, she saw double trouble. There we were, her mom and dad slouched into an oversized couch, looking like a grown- up was scolding them.

I saw my little girl—arms full of what I knew were the worst food choices—about to be introduced to Ernie's very serious doctor.

I lost it and laughed out loud. This sent Elsie snorting with laughter because she tried desperately to hold it in. Tim maintained composure and kept his focus on Dr. Mills.

Elsie dumped her plunder on the couch in plain view of Dr. Mills; he stared at Elsie and me as though he was just thrust into a Marx Brothers movie and he was cast as Margaret Dumont.

I tried to break his chill with the only logical thing I could think of, "Would you like a Snickers bar, doctor?"

He pretended not to hear or see me and directed his attention toward Tim who had managed to drag himself to the front edge of the couch where he could adopt an adult posture. Elsie sat on the couch arm and bit into a Snickers bar.

"It appears Ernie is fine—there are no obvious problems such as broken bones or sprains," He told Tim. But I could hear, even from the depths of that sofa.

"X-Rays didn't show anything," he continued. "I think the fall may have knocked his breath out for a bit but no rib injuries or the like."

Pop, fizzzzzzzzz. Elsie opened a can of soda which had been tossed just enough from walking and being dumped on the couch. Soda sprayed Elsie's face and all over the front of her white t-shirt. She gasped "Oh crap!" then looked wide-eyed at me, then at Dr. Mills, then back at me.

There were a couple of minutes of silence–probably seconds but it seemed longer–before I grabbed Elsie by the arm to haul myself out of the couch. I had tears in my eyes from biting my lip to keep the laughter in that begged for release; I led her toward the ladies room while I listened to Tim and the doctor.

Still being the stoic grownup, Tim addressed Dr. Mills.

"Sorry about that Dr. Mills. So, Ernie is fine and we can take him home now? Any follow up we need to do?"

I glanced behind and saw that Dr. Mills looked as if he was still uncertain about what bad movie he might be in. He said, "Yes, Mr. Gallagher. We are releasing Ernie and he should be out shortly. No follow-up but keep an eye on him and make certain he doesn't have any other symptoms. He doesn't have any signs of concussion but it's always good to be watchful at home for any headaches, drowsiness, etc."

"Okay, great doctor," Tim said. "Thanks. June and I will be with him for the rest of the day. And Elsie. That was our daughter Elsie." Tim offered with a hint of embarrassment in his voice.

"There is another matter I would like to address with you–and I think it is best before your wife and daughter return." He obviously didn't know I could still hear him from where I waited outside the ladies room, even though I faced them both and had my arms crossed.

Tim raised his eyes briefly to mine and focused on the doctor's words, "Ernie has had quite a few hospital visits over the past couple of years. Normally, I would see this with a child who is somewhat accident prone or heavily involved in sports or has a rare medical condition. But, with Ernie, the reasons are more exotic. Looking at his chart and records, I am a bit alarmed."

"Well, yes Dr. Mills," Tim was a bit agitated. "As his parents, we are alarmed as well. Ernie has had more than his share of challenges, but we have always taken him here or to Dr. Reynolds. You must know Dr. Reynolds?"

Dr. Mills nodded.

"No one seems to know exactly what is happening or if Ernie's problems are related," Tim said. "Lots of tests. But no real diagnosis. But he is doing much better and before today, he hadn't been in the hospital emergency or the doctor's office for almost a year."

"I see," Dr. Mills said. "Well. I just thought it important to mention. I'll follow-up with Dr. Reynolds. There is a distinct possibility that Ernie passed out *before* he fell off the swings. Who was with him when it happened?"

"Really, he passed out?" Tim was alert. "Well, he has had these energy issues in the past, so we assumed one re-occurred and he couldn't hold onto the swing and fell off. My daughter, Elsie, was with him when it happened. She should be back in a minute, I think. They just went to the bathroom to wash off the soda. Poor kid hasn't had any lunch, so she went to the vending machines."

"Well, as I said, Ernie may have passed out first," the doctor said. "I suggest you speak with Dr. Reynolds and have your daughter relay the incident in detail to him. As I said, I'll share today's episode with Dr. Reynolds too."

Dr. Mills rose, offered his hand to Tim and quickly retreated to the reception desk. He made a short comment to the nurse and strolled out of sight into the hospital corridors.

After Dr. Mills left, I poked my head into the restroom to see how Elsie was cleaning up. I was relieved that he hadn't waited around for us. He didn't seem like a very understanding fellow. Tim stood by the couch while we approached. He wore one of his judgmental, are-you-kidding-me? expressions but didn't say anything. I knew I was in trouble.

"I know, Tim, this was serious," I said, cutting him off at the pass and reaching for a hug. "And I'm sorry if Elsie embarrassed you... okay so we both embarrassed you. But I had already seen Ernie and knew he was fine. Besides, sometimes in tense situations like this, there's a thin line between laughter and tears and something had to give."

"Uh huh," he said, not budging. "You noticed I didn't suffer from that dilemma?"

"So, is Ernie ready to come home now?" I dodged that bullet.

"I'm not certain he thinks Ernie should be in any home with you two!" Tim couldn't help but grin.

"Here, have a Snickers bar," I handed him the candy. He took it and looked beyond Elsie while he opened the wrapper.

"Elsie. Clean that mess up and let's get going. Ernie's here." He took a big bite and strolled toward the reception desk.

Elsie and I looked behind us and sure enough, Ernie was there with a nurse.

"Yeah Elsie, clean that up," I headed straight for Ernie. Ernie broke free from holding the nurse's hand and ran into my arms. We hugged tightly before he switched to his dad's bear hug. When he stood back a step and saw the Snickers bar hanging from Tim's mouth, his eyes lit up.

"Wow, where you get Snickers bar? I want one."

"Okay buddy. Go see your sister over there, she must have another one—or you can have mine, I only took a bite."

"Elsie. I go over to Elsie." And off he went. He stopped in front of his sister, hands tucked into the back pockets of his shorts, hung his head and said something we couldn't hear. She grabbed him and hugged him close. Then they both sat on the edge of the couch and looked over Elsie's feast of snacks and soda.

"Are you sure he should be eating that stuff?" I asked Tim. "I mean he should never be eating that garbage anyway, but because of the accident?"

"Yeah the doc said he was fine," Tim said. "He did say there was a slight chance of concussion in accidents like this, but they didn't see any signs. Just wants us to keep an eye on him…and that's it."

"Excuse me Mr. Gallagher, I need you to sign Ernie's release papers." The nurse stepped out from behind her desk. She reached out her hand to draw Tim toward the counter.

After papers were signed, we gathered up our children and what was left of the bounty, headed for the car and then home.

Ernie had beaten another round of mishaps and the family was back to *our* normal. At the dinner table we found out that Ernie had actually had a seizure, not just fainted from lack of energy while on the swings.

Tim asked Elsie and Ernie if they remembered exactly what had happened. Ernie said he didn't remember anything except being on the swings and then waking up in the grass.

Elsie was more helpful. She told us that she saw Ernie drop from the swing while it was barely off the ground. He went to his knees and tried to stand up but began to shake. Then he fell forward and into the grass and shook more violently, but it only lasted a minute. He had stopped by the time she had reached him.

In the commotion that followed, no one had thought to ask her about it; we all assumed Ernie fell off the swing while high in the air because all Elsie said was that he fell off the swing. Elsie didn't know what a seizure was.

We had all acted on what appeared to be the obvious to us with the information we had at hand.

We brought this new information to Dr. Reynolds a few days later during Ernie's scheduled visit. He confirmed the likelihood that Ernie had experienced a seizure, although *why* was still a mystery.

It wasn't until a few weeks later, when Ernie had a seizure in front of Tim and me in the living room, that we understood that his seizures could recur unexpectedly and without reason.

CHAPTER FOUR

FAME AND REAL LIFE

Just as I got off the phone with Tim who was getting Elsie from school, I heard a commotion outside. I looked through the peephole and saw a lot of people at the end of my front steps.

Reporters.

My first thought was, *How did Tim avoid them?* And more to the point, Why didn't he warn me?

I took a deep breath and opened my front door to get to the driveway and my car. A dozen anxious reporters and several camera crews leapt to attention. There were lights and lenses pointing in my face while I stood on my front stoop.

I was a news story and nothing was going to stop these protectors of the fourth estate from invading my privacy–uninvited–or losing out to a competitor. People love heroes and like it or not, I had been branded one by the officer on the scene and by this group of life observers.

Apparently, it took a while for someone to recognize me and for the press to run me down. Likely, it was my EMS friend who had supplied my name–not, I was certain, in a mean way, but as a matter-of-fact. He needed to write his reports as did the officer who spoke with me who also took notes.

However it happened, the proverbial cat was out of the bag and hissing in my face at my front door.

"How do you feel being a hero?"

"Did you know Kalea before you saved her life?"

"Will you be visiting her in the hospital?"

"Are you medically trained?"

"Did you fear for your own safety?"

"Did you try to get her parents out?"

It struck me that this was the first time I had heard the little girl's name. Knowing her now as Kalea, made what had happened more personal to me. I was grateful the reporter unwittingly provided that information, but I had neither the time nor desire to answer their questions. I had escaped them once before and I was more determined and motivated to do so again.

"I'm sorry, I have to go," I said. "I don't want to answer any questions." I elbowed my way through reporters and cameras.

"Elizabeth Cochrane, KBTV news." One of the more aggressive, self- assured reporters introduced herself as she pushed a microphone closer to my face while she and her camera crew blocked my path. "June," she said conversationally, "you're a hero and people want to know about you."

June, huh? So now we are on a first name basis.

"Listen lady, the only thing you or anyone need to know right now is that my son is in the hospital and I need to get to him. Now."

I pushed her microphone aside and strode right at the cameraman who blocked my way.

My last statement seemed to do the trick and the crew gave way, along with the aggressively friendly reporter. Some of the other reporters continued to hurl questions at me as I entered my car.

By now a large group of neighbors and passersby had joined the party. They were scattered on my front lawn, the sidewalks, and much of the street. I eased the car out of the driveway honking madly before I could finally get on my way toward the hospital and Ernie.

My bad driving habits had returned; I had no trouble exceeding the speed limit where I could. I needed to get there fast. I remembered our emergency trip two years ago on another visit to University Hospital where Tim had made it in 18 minutes.

Just before I arrived at Brinker, I got a call from Tim. It seemed to be a day for bad driving habits; I picked up my cell phone from the seat divider. Do we ever really learn?

"Hey, are you there yet? What did the doctors say? How's Ernie?" "I'm just pulling up now, Tim. There were a ton of reporters parked outside the front door when I tried to leave, *and* a mob of neighbors. I had to practically fight my way out of there."

"What were the reporters there for? Did they hear about Ernie? Is something really bad happening?"

"Geezus, Tim, no," I said, marveling at his short memory. "They were there because of the thing this morning with Kalea. I have to go. I'm in the parking lot heading for the emergency entrance and I don't know my way around here. I'll call you back."

I left Tim probably scratching his head a bit. We don't know anyone named Kalea. But even with the confusion at my front door, hearing her name stuck in my head. It seemed disrespectful and uncaring to call her "the little girl." She was a person with a name.

It took only seconds to get to and park in the emergency section of the hospital. I really didn't need to concentrate on where I was so much as I just needed to get off the phone and stop any distractions from getting me to Ernie.

The emergency waiting room was, thankfully, not as crowded as I had feared it might be; I went to the front desk immediately to get the attendant's attention.

"Hi, I'm Ernie Gallagher's mom. He was admitted just a bit ago?"

"Actually, he was admitted over an *hour* ago," the 50-something-year- old attendant said waspishly.

"Yes, well the school called me but my phone was in the other room and...and...I didn't hear it, so...I came as soon as I got the messages..." She had me on my back foot, and I heard myself stammering.

"Uh huh," she interrupted. "I see from our records that your son, Ernie, has been in the emergency room *quite* a few times before this."

What the hell was she talking about? Who the hell is she? Some front desk clerk should not be treating me like this.

"Um, no, he has never been in *this* hospital," I said, trying to remain polite. "Can you please just tell me where my son is and what is happening?"

She placed her freckled hands in front of her and folded them on the desk. She looked coldly at me and said, "I work with the social worker assigned to your account." *Wait. What? Social worker? My account?* "Your son is being examined by doctors. He seems fine other than bruises on his arm, and he is being checked for concussion. The doctor will be out shortly to speak with you and then we will examine your case."

I took in everything that she said, and I had a lot of questions. But all I wanted at that point was to be with Ernie. I'd tackle the rest later. "What room is he in? I want to be with him." I also wanted nothing to do with this social-whatever and her obvious insinuations. I wanted to see my son.

"You are not allowed to see him now," she said dismissively. "The doctor will be out shortly and then we can talk."

"Excuse me, but I don't want to talk to *you*," I said. That monster that appeared earlier with Tim was starting to wake up after its brief doze. "You are not a doctor and *certainly* not my son's doctor. I want to know where he is and if you can't help me, find someone who can."

There is something about certain people who are put in a position of authority and adopt an attitude of superiority that they know more than anyone else around them. That just sets me off. Especially when it comes to my loved ones–whom they know nothing about.

"Miss," she said, obviously ignoring my married state. "There are plenty of seats in the waiting room. The doctor will be out shortly."

"I don't think you get it lady," I could feel my fangs and claws extending. "I have a right to be with my son while he is being examined. I do not need your condescension *or* your *permission...*" Then my phone rang.

"Oh good," Miss Snippy said. "You have your phone with you now."

I couldn't believe she said that. I looked at her in disbelief and it took all my strength not to give in to my instinct to throw my phone at her. *What a little snot*, I thought as I answered the phone while glaring at Miss Helpful.

"Hello? June, are you there?" Tim's familiar voice gave me a bit of strength.

"Yeah, I'm here."

"So, what's going on with Ernie? Did you see the doctor yet? Are you with Ernie?"

I turned my back before barking loud enough for her to hear, "No. Some *smart-ass receptionist* won't let me back there to see Ernie."

"Huh? What do you mean? Is Ernie okay?"

"Yeah, he's fine. They're checking him for a concussion just in case. This annoying receptionist-cum-social worker of some kind says she's in charge of our account or Ernie's case or something. I doubt she knows the difference. She is so obnoxious, and I don't have the patience for her right now. I just want to smack her."

"Okay, so try not to do that and calm down a bit. So long as Ernie's okay, that's all that matters. Probably just some routine person they bring in because Ernie was admitted from school. I'm on my way and will be there in a few minutes."

"What? No. You have to stay with Elsie. I told you!"

"Okay, okay. June stop yelling at me. Give me some credit. Ginny came by after dropping the carpool kids off and offered to take Elsie home with her. She can hang out there and do homework and watch

TV with Beamer...um, Brian."

"Ugh. Beamer." Brian got his nickname because all he talked about were cars and especially BMWs. He was obsessed. "Okay. Well Ginny is great and Elsie likes her, so...yeah that's fine. Hurry up and get here so you can calmly deal with Miss Know-it-All."

With Tim on his way, I decided not to push things any further with the receptionist—or whoever the hell she was.

I sat in a row of seats near the window with my back to her so that I wouldn't have to see her smug face. I studied my cell phone apps for something to do. Tim was right. I did tend to go quickly overboard with my reactions when challenged about my kids. I couldn't help it. Mother's instinct. Fight first and then worry about what you said or did later when it didn't matter to your child's safety or well-being.

That was my somewhat flawed philosophy anyway and I was sticking to it. Tim, on the other hand, brought the same calm and discipline he applied to accounting and as he does to most situations. He looked at both sides of the balance sheet and tried to make them equal. He was the calm and I was the storm in these situations. Good cop, bad cop or whatever analogy you want to make. And it worked for us. I brought a certain passion to life and he brought reason. Not exclusively: either of us could be passionate or reasonable depending on the situation.

I decided to call Ginny to thank her and also to check in on Elsie. Ginny, as usual, was gracious and waved her gesture off as no big deal. She said Brian—she never called him Beamer—and Elsie did their homework and were binge-watching a TV show.

Elsie and Brian were nearly 13; I worried about what they would choose to binge watch. Ginny anticipated my thought and told me they were watching *Once Upon A Time*. We watched that show together at home; it had good family plots mostly and was just mature enough for young teens to find interesting. And it had some nice things for some of us adults too—Captain Hook!

Satisfied Elsie would be fine, I started to hang up, but before I could, Ginny offered to feed Elsie and let her stay overnight if need be. Ginny was a true friend. I was glad she was also my neighbor.

Tim arrived shortly after and found me near the window. He bent over my shoulder and gave my right cheek a kiss. I looked up at him but didn't say anything.

"Hi hon," he said. "Any word from the doctor or...anyone?" He subtly nodded toward the emergency desk.

"No. I've just been sitting here fiddling with my phone and trying to stay calm. Go talk to her and find out what is happening."

Tim paused. He looked at me and then at the woman at the desk, then back at me and finally decided to approach the emergency desk. I switched seats so I could see the desk. When he got there, the first thing I observed was his handshake and his posture, which suggested ease. I leaned forward to eavesdrop on their conversation.

"Hi, I'm Tim Gallagher. My son, Ernie, was admitted a while ago—he had a seizure at school, and my wife hasn't been able to see him or get any update on his condition. Can you tell me what room he's in? He'll be very upset that his mom and dad are not with him–and scared. We never leave him alone when he comes to the emergency room."

"I can tell you the same thing I told your wife," the woman said, nodding in my direction. "The doctor will be out shortly and..."

As if on cue, the doctor pushed open the door and approached Tim at the desk. He must have known we were out here; maybe the receptionist called him while my back was turned. I jumped up quickly and walked over to join them.

"Hi Mr. Gallagher, Mrs. Gallagher." He shook our hands. "I'm Dr. Grinsby. As you know your son Ernie had a seizure in school and was admitted by ambulance to the emergency room. He's doing fine, just a bruise on his arm we think from when he fell during the seizure and some scrapes on his elbows and a forearm. Again, most likely from the fall. But we like to be thorough and check these things out."

"Where is Ernie?" I asked for what seemed like the hundredth time. "I want to see him."

"Well, Mrs. Gallagher, he is in an examination room, doing fine. We are just finishing up our examination..."

"Yes, I know. I get it. Where is he? I need to be with him." *Why didn't these people get it? Why was it so hard to let me see my son?* "He shouldn't be alone all this time," I pleaded with just enough passion for Tim to interject.

"Doctor, Ernie gets scared when he comes out of one of these seizures. To be here in the hospital and not have his mom with him just makes it worse. If she could just peek in on him and let him see her that would be helpful."

"I am actually *not* asking for permission," I butted in. I'd had enough. "We're the child's parents, legal guardians, whatever. And we want to see him *now*."

"June..." Tim said.

"Mrs. Gallagher, we just need a few more minutes..." the doctor said.

"Is there something you aren't telling us?" I took a step closer to the doctor. "Is he physically not well or not recovered?"

"Well, no but..."

"Then you don't *have* a few more minutes." I was really holding back on all that I wanted to say. "Either bring my child out now or bring me to see him." I was calm but insistent. I didn't want any misinterpretation that could be construed as me wavering or in any way ready to give in.

"June...the doctor is trying to explain the procedures," Tim said.

"I get it Tim," I responded, "and *I* am explaining that I have a right to see my son and to take him out of here because there is no treatment being done."

Just then the self-important receptionist/social worker rose from behind her desk and looked past the three of us toward the entrance doors.

"Ah, here she is," she said as she came out from behind her desk and approached the woman who walked briskly toward us. The receptionist intercepted her and they briefly spoke just out of range of our hearing before approaching us.

The desk-lady fairly simpered as she introduced everyone. "Dr. Grinsby, this is Beth Myers, a social worker. Beth, this is Dr. Grinsby...and *these* are the Gallaghers." She flicked her hand in our direction.

"I thought *you* were the social worker?" I said to Miss Know-it-All, not acknowledging this new woman.

"No, I am the admittance specialist," she corrected me with sugar-on- top. "Beth...Ms. Myers, is the social worker assigned to your case."

"Hi Beth, I am..." Tim held out his hand. I saw this as just offering credence to this charade whose only purpose—as far as I could see—was to keep me from my son.

I interrupted the pleasantries. "I'm confused. My son was treated. Dr. Grinsby says he's fine. We are standing in the lobby of an emergency room, talking to two people who have nothing I need or my son needs, *and* we are being kept from seeing him. We want our son... *now*," I said as firmly as possible without exploding.

"Mrs. Gallagher," Ms. Myers said quietly, "I understand your frustration and I apologize for taking so long to get here. I was at University Hospital across town when I was contacted by Ruth here."

"But I don't get why you are here at all." I crossed my arms.

"Let me explain," she opened her arms as if to usher Tim and me. "Can we get out of the hallway and sit over there by the window?" She gently guided me by the shoulder toward the same row of seats I had just abandoned. There was something calming about Beth. She didn't condescend or seem judgmental. So, I acquiesced and followed, as did Dr. Grinsby, Tim...and Ruth.

"Ruth, we won't need to take any more of your time for this consultation." Beth stopped Ruth from joining us. I'm sure I saw a brief look of displeasure move across Beth's face. When we reached the windows, Beth, Tim and I took a seat while Dr. Grinsby remained standing.

"Mrs. Gallagher..." Ms. Myers began.

"June," I offered, not understanding completely why I was controlled enough to offer that. "And this is my husband, Tim."

"June and Tim." Beth settled in her seat, crossed her legs at the knee, folded her hands, and started again. "Whenever a child is admitted to the hospital system, especially as an emergency, certain protocols are initiated. The hospital staff are trained to look for any signs of mistreatment or injures that might be repetitive or outside the norm—any signs of abuse."

"What?" I interrupted. "We have *never* abused Ernie. He's a typical boy who gets scrapes and cuts and yeah, he has seizures that no doctor can figure out *why* and sometimes they result in a bruise..."

"June, I know. I know," Ms. Myers said, leaning forward. "No one is accusing you of anything." She lightly touched my knee and looked directly in my eyes as she spoke. "Again, this is just procedure and once it gets started, we have to see it through and do all that 'i' dotting and 't' crossing stuff that is required to release your son. Dr. Grinsby, you indicated on the phone that you didn't see any unusual bruises or signs of mistreatment. After concluding your examination has that opinion changed?"

"Noooo,'" Dr. Grinsby said. "But I can't say why the Gallagher's son had the seizure. That would take a lot more testing and frankly that is out of my area. But the child seems upbeat and healthy with some good old-fashioned boys-being-boys scrapes and maybe a lump or two from falling during the seizure. I will need to take a deeper dive into his long medical history to understand if there are any unusual patterns...but there is nothing in this examination that is out of the ordinary. I thought I explained that to Ruth but apparently she didn't understand and called it in anyway."

"Ohhh, I see," Ms. Myers said. "Ruth called it in. Okay. Well doctor, thanks for the report and sorry for taking you from your busy work.

Would it be all right for June and Tim to go back and see their son?"

"Sure," he said. "Follow me and I'll take you back there. Then I really must see other patients." He turned to Tim, not making eye contact with me. "You can actually take Ernie home if Beth is okay with that. You just have to sign the release papers at the front desk."

"Tim, you sign the papers," I said. "I'll go get Ernie."

"Mr. Gallagher, I need you to sign some other paperwork as well and then we'll be all set," Ms. Myers said. "I apologize to you both. I know this must be very upsetting. But my job is to look out for the children and sometimes that can seem invasive."

Ms. Myers rose and offered her hand in turn to both Tim and me. And just like that, it ended.

I was happy to have this nightmare over with and ready to take Ernie home. I didn't harbor any ill-will toward Ms. Myers. She seemed to be genuine about her job and her approach to it and sensitive to how people might perceive her inquiries.

But I was determined not to go back to this hospital—ever; I made a mental note to inform Ernie's school to *never* have him sent to this place...or to Ruth.

Ernie was, as anticipated, overjoyed to see me pass through the curtain in the examination room. He leapt off the table and ran into my arms. I gave him the biggest hug.

"Hi sweetie!" I said and held him tight. "How is my big brave boy? You had me so worried." I inundated him with Mom kisses and rumpled his hair.

"I'm okay, Mom," he said. "Ew," he squirmed and laughed at my sloppy kisses, wiping his face with his hand. Then he suddenly teared up. "What took you so long to get here, Mom? I been here for hours." *Sniffle.* "And they don't tell me what happens. Said I had a seizure like 'duh no kidding, like I never had one before." Another sniffle.

"I am so sorry sweetheart," I said and pulled him close again. "I was here but they wouldn't let me come back here to see you because they knew I would squeeze you to pieces and they didn't think you were ready for that." He laughed because I was truly squeezing him to pieces.

"Can we go now Mom?" He said, pulling away and looking for his clothes. "This place stinks. Belinda's not here." Belinda is his favorite nurse at University Hospital. "And–I'm really hungry." Those last three little words said, *I feel fine, Mom, and am back to normal.*

After he dressed, I raced Ernie to the lobby which drew looks of ire from some staff. We raced right past Tim on our way out to the car.

"Hi Dad, bye Dad," Ernie waved as he scooted by. "We're going to IHOP."

A beaming Tim joined us as we high-tailed it out the door.

***

I decided to take the next day–Friday–off. My quick departure from the media mayhem at my front door did just enough to discourage all but the most insistent of reporters. They had adequate footage of me and the accident scene to make the local television news and the papers anyway.

I was, like it or not, living my 15 minutes of fame and I had no desire to extend it to seven or eight hours at the office and with clients. My concern and attention now was for Ernie, whom I wanted to keep out of school this day too. But Ernie would have none of that. He didn't like being treated differently even though he knew that in areas of health, he was. He was a trooper; my brave little man. Off to school he went.

So, I spent Friday first taking the coffee-stained rug to our cleaners who then recommended another place who specialized in "cases like ours." Then off to the local Crate and Barrel for a *new* favorite coffee mug. I chose one that was more attractive mechanically than aesthetically. It had a large enough handle that my two fingers could slip easily in and out and was still nicely balanced.

During my browsing through Crate and Barrel, I was twice spotted as the "lady who saved that little girl." Two women approached me separately although I sensed others recognized me or thought they should. Apparently, people do watch local news.

One woman who looked to be about 40-ish said, "Excuse me but, aren't you the lady, oh, um…Mrs. Gallagher…who pulled that little girl from the burning car? God that was horrible. And her parents died…so sad. You are so brave to have done what you did, and every mother is thankful for someone like you. You know…"

"Kalea," I interrupted with little emotion and even less desire to engage. The woman stopped midstream and looked at me questioningly. "Her name is Kalea."

"Oh. Well, I don't remember them mentioning her name. Anyway, I just wanted to say…that was very brave." She shuffled off toward another department. A few moments later it happened again while I looked at place settings.

"Hi," came a younger women's voice, "I really don't mean to intrude." I looked up and saw that she was maybe 30, a few years younger than me. "You *are* Mrs. Gallagher, the woman who saved the little girl, Kalea, from the burning car?" I nodded while looking at the serving dish in my hands. "I never heard anything about how your son is and I…well just wanted to say I hope he is okay."

"Yes, thank you," I said. "He's fine." I didn't take my attention away from the dish.

"Well, that's good," she said politely. "Just wanted to ask. Bye."

I knew that I hadn't reacted well to either person. People just want to say something; to recognize a human moment and acknowledge that there are good people and good things that happen along with tragedy. In a way, they want to say *I know you* and *I approve of you* and maybe, *I feel something with you.* I looked toward the young woman before she was out of hearing distance.

"Hey," I said loud enough for her to hear. She turned. "Thank you. Thank you for asking about my son. He has seizures sometimes, but he is home now and going to be fine."

The young woman smiled, walked back to me and handed me her card. "If ever…" she began and let that comment hang between us as she walked away. I looked at the card and recognized her name. She was the aggressive reporter from my front stoop. Without her cameraman and microphone, and because of my strong desire to avoid *really* looking at people, I hadn't recognized her.

Before this interlude, I hadn't considered the mob of reporters at my front door as individual people. Certainly not people who had feelings for anything beyond getting their story. I still wasn't certain her concern wasn't a reporter's ploy to grease the wheel a bit before pushing for an interview, or if she was genuine. Something about her seemed *real* though and I decided to give her the benefit of the doubt. I put her card in my purse.

I determined to get out of there and out of public view until my moments of fame dissipated. I left without the mug and headed for the Starbucks drive-thru. Just because I didn't have a new mug didn't mean I couldn't enjoy a cup of coffee. The drive-thru ensured privacy so I wouldn't be recognized–I hoped. When I had secured my cappuccino, I headed home.

While I drove, my thoughts wandered among mundane things at first, like how I could never have my normal favorite black coffee at Starbucks. Their coffee seemed always over-roasted and tasted bitter and burnt which is why I was at Dunkin' Donuts the day of the accident; they had great coffee, lousy donuts.

Then I thought about Ruth's caustic comment, *"I see your son, Ernie has been in the emergency room quite a few times before this."* Funny, I hadn't thought about her since leaving the hospital.

But now that there was just myself for company, my mind had time to wander and contemplate yesterday's events and to confront my strong reaction to Ruth.

She *was* right. Ernie had been to the emergency room on several occasions for various reasons. Just not to *that* hospital. We always took him to University, though oddly, we had never met Beth Myers before.

I supposed that in the land of social spies, there is a mass complex of computers somewhere, filled with digital information about everyone who ever entered either of those hospitals and that ever-vigilant Ruth had access to that information.

During this conversation with myself, Rational June tried to convince Passionate June that this type of hospital system was needed; there are abused children in emergency rooms across the country and someone needs to look out for them.

I knew this was an important job and that Beth and yes, even Ruth, were part of those front lines of child protection. I just wished the job went to someone other than Ruth. Right then, Rational June retreated to her happy place while Passionate June made an audible "Eghh" with a snarly face. Our conversation ended when I pulled into my driveway.

Now that I was home, it was time for Take Two of "coffee and my corner of the couch with my friends." Even though I was drinking a fully-caffeinated cappuccino, I was certain I would nod off and take a much-needed nap–just an hour would be great–soon after I'd finished it.

I hadn't slept well the night before; too much excitement and worry and anger rattled around in my head–along with crash images–to just shut my eyes and sleep.

Tim, on the other hand, took about five minutes before he was off and snoring, which just added to my frustration and insomnia. It was his accountant brain at work again: In his mind, Elsie was home tucked in bed. Ernie had an episode but hey–he's fine now, at home and asleep. June is finally not yelling at me or anyone, and dinner was good. Work tomorrow, sleep tonight. All adds up to–lights out.

I envied his ability for separation and putting things into neat little boxes. But I HATED his snoring.

I looked toward the coffee table, and out of habit for the crossword puzzle. I was surprised to find it there under the newspaper. I never got around to throwing it and the stained bills away and had left them in a pile at the far, dry corner of the table.

When I lifted the newspaper, the crossword was face up and legible, although stained and wrinkled from the spill. I smiled. "Couch, coffee, crossword." I used my comforter for support to prop myself in the corner; I had left my down pillow upstairs and was too settled to retrieve it when I remembered. I took a sip of my cappuccino and glanced at *1. across: Eagle's claw –five letters.* Easy, TALON.

I looked at *1. down,* now that I had the 'T': *Impatient –five letters.* TESTY.

Ha, ha very funny Mr. Crossword. A smirk stretched my mouth. And then the phone rang. And it was the land line again. Not my cell phone which was right in front of me on the coffee table.

"Are - you - freaking - KIDDING - me?" I shouted. I was tempted to just let it ring but after all that had happened the day before, I decided against that idea. The phone rang again.

"Yeah, Yeah, I'm coming! Take a chill pill." I rose slowly and carefully placed my coffee on the table. Success. The cup sat stable on its bottom. The phone kept ringing. I headed to the kitchen and managed to answer just before whoever was on the other end hung up.

"Hello."

"Hi, is this June?" Although her voice was familiar, I wasn't going to budge until I knew who it was.

"Who is this?" I didn't want to be caught off-guard by some nosy, tricky reporter.

"Hi, this is Principal Mary Patterson from your son Ernie's school, may I please speak with June?'

"Oh. Hi. This is June. Is everything okay? The doctor said Ernie was fine to return to school today."

"Well, he had difficulty breathing during recess and then he got very sick to his stomach and we have him in the nurse's office," she said. "The nurse also said that he has a very unusual type of well– vomiting. The nurse is wondering if we should get him to Brinker Hospital again..."

"NO!" I shouted, then toned it down. "*No*, don't do that. I am leaving right now and will be at the school in five minutes. He goes to University Hospital. Dr. Reynolds. Don't send him to Brinker or anywhere. I'll be right there." I hung up.

I raced into the living room and glanced longingly at my near full cappuccino sitting on the table. I couldn't enjoy it in peace but grabbed it anyway and rushed back out and into my car and off to Ernie's school.

I knew what the "unusual vomiting" meant. I also knew what it would mean if Ernie went anywhere else but to University and Dr. Reynolds. The fallout to come was especially clear to me after the incident with Ruth and Beth, and I didn't want a repeat of *that* episode.

I had seen this happen with Ernie before; although the fatigue the principal described was more worrisome. That hadn't happened in some time.

CHAPTER FIVE

ANOTHER EMERGENCY

The drive to Ernie's school was short. It was another brisk October day and, if not for the emergency at hand, I would have slowed down and taken my time to enjoy the brilliance of the New England foliage that colored maple trees lining the route.

This time the colorful trees passed my windows in a crimson and yellow blur. I entered the school lot a mere five minutes after leaving home.

The brick school building had a large section of windows in the front, a portion of which outlined Principal Patterson's office. This gave her an unobstructed view into the parking lot. By the time I had parked and walked toward the entrance, she stood at the school's front door. There was an air of seriousness about her. She forced a smile with taught lips.

"Hi June."

"Hi Mary," I said–trying to look around her. "Is Ernie in the nurse's office?" I made a move to get around her and go into the building. Mary caught me by my forearm before I got more than two steps in that direction.

"We don't have Ernie here, June. I'm sorry, but we had to send him on to the hospital."

I stood silent for a moment while I processed that. I couldn't decide which question to ask first–*Which hospital? Why? You couldn't wait five minutes? Did he get worse?* While I stared at her, Mary continued.

"We just can't take responsibility for a student when they need emergency help, June." She dropped her grip of my arm. "We have to take necessary steps for the child's health and safety. For Ernie, that meant getting him to the hospital as soon as possible. We just don't know with Ernie–there have been so many...episodes."

"Which hospital?" I ignored what she said. I decided that to know where he went was the more immediate concern. A professional diagnosis was unlikely to come from Principal Patterson.

"We were able to get him to University hospital, but we had to call for a private ambulance company," she said.

That likely meant uncovered expenses which we didn't need; but I took the news with relief knowing Ernie would be in the capable, knowing hands of Dr. Reynolds and not some stranger at Brinker–and not admitted by Ruth!

"Thanks Mary, for doing that," I said quietly. I turned around and made a quick sprint to my car.

"I hope Ernie is all right," she called out. "Please let us know as soon as you can..."

That was all I heard before I slid into my Jeep, turned the ignition and headed out of the school lot.

It was now near 2 pm so traffic was only moderate; rush hour in our little suburb would not begin for another two hours, and even then the only affected area was the short part that required being on the Interstate.

I made the trip to University Hospital in about 20 minutes which gave me just enough time to consider all of Ernie's past ailments and what he might be suffering from now. Certainly, some of what Principal Patterson told me–the vomiting and energy drain–was not out of the ordinary; nor did it warrant any particularly new worry.

But I kept going back to Ernie's difficulty breathing and the terse tone in the Principal's voice when she said it. It would not be unusual for Ernie to take himself out of a playground game because of fatigue. But when he did, it was unusual for him to have breathing issues, at least nothing he complained about; he just lost his energy to move, along with losing some basic coordination.

Along the way, I telephoned Tim by using my new hands-free Bluetooth gadget I had installed. He was in a meeting. I hadn't any real information to share with him, so I decided it was best to leave a message with the receptionist to have him call me rather than pull him out of the meeting. As far as I knew, this would be a quick trip–another temporary scare that the school elevated to something more serious.

University Hospital parking lot was full. Apparently, Friday is a good day to take an afternoon off from work to make a hospital visit or schedule a doctor's appointment–and this Friday was particularly popular.

Parking spaces were limited, especially with so many spaces reserved for compact cars, not my mid-size Jeep. I made several spins around various aisles before I eventually found an open spot that would fit. However, I had to do battle with an SUV that sped toward the same spot, coming in the opposite and wrong direction of the parking lot arrows. When I saw what he was up to, I gunned it and steered into the open space, leaning on my horn the entire way.

We nearly collided head-on but I got the nose of my car into the spot before the guy going the wrong way did, and he had to concede–the space was mine! The defeat didn't sit well with him. Despite the fact that he was in the wrong, he let me know how much it displeased him with several clever hand gestures and some nasty words which were easy to lip read through my rear-view mirror.

I was tempted to send some of my own special love his way, but I didn't want to encourage more reaction from Mr. Wrong Way Driver. So I sat on my hands and smirked.

When he was out of sight, I re-parked my car at a proper angle so that the people next to me would have access to their cars without slamming any doors into mine. Then I slid out and walked toward the hospital main entrance.

I walked through a few hallways toward the emergency room area. I'd been here before. This had been my life for several years now: getting phone calls or witnessing events at home that led Ernie and me to this emergency room.

On occasion, ours would be a planned visit to a different part of the hospital for various specialists' examinations and tests. Whatever the reason, it had become almost routine to be here. And for Ernie too. As much as these trips were becoming integrated into my life, Ernie must have felt as though this *was* his life; that he lived in two places: his home and the hospital.

Any time we spent away from this place became part of our family's most treasured moments. Even if some of those moments were spent rehabilitating Ernie or helping him cope with his limitations, we celebrated them.

During Ernie's first three years, birthdays were private family affairs. They included Elsie, Tim and Tim's parents if they were in town. Well, except for his second birthday.

On Ernie's second birthday, my good friend Laura from work came with her son Jeremy who was the same age as Ernie. But that didn't go too well. Jeremy was a healthy, rambunctious two-year-old who could walk and throw toys and was very active. He wanted to play with Ernie, but Ernie still crawled and had his sudden naps and couldn't keep up.

That birthday celebration was sad for us to witness and kind of miserable for Ernie. I think Laura sensed it too. She didn't balk when a birthday invite didn't come for them the following year. She continued to send invitations to Ernie for Jeremy's birthday parties. Sometimes Tim and I brought Ernie over and stayed just long enough to leave a present, have some cake, and have a few minutes of small talk with Laura and a few other parents.

With all the other kids around, it wasn't awkward for Ernie to be quiet; he seemed to enjoy watching other kids play while he sat on the floor or in my lap.

But when he got to age five and had made improvements with his strength and entered school, we went all out.

His sixth birthday was during his first year in school, which was kindergarten because we had to hold him back. We held a big party in our large back yard complete with a bouncy ball cage, a clown, pony rides, and a magician. Looking back, it was a bit over-the-top, but Ernie had been through so much and had made such good progress, we wanted to share him with everyone; we wanted Ernie to have a real party.

We invited his entire kindergarten class of 30 kids and parents. Thankfully, only 17 of them accepted; I don't think we actually had enough room in the yard to host them all. It was a huge success. Soon Ernie was getting reciprocal invitations, most of which we accepted.

But now, here I was looking for my son again in the all-to-familiar surroundings of this hospital emergency room about to embark on yet another journey with Ernie's unknown illness.

That was the worst of it all. We were never told what Ernie suffered from. We got bits and pieces of things, but never anything that solidified it all under one medical roof. Without that, there never was any specific treatment aimed at the root cause of Ernie's ailment; we always treated symptoms as they showed themselves.

**

The emergency room area was packed and alive with activity. The reception area was full. The line was long. Some dropped off newly completed admissions forms at the desk, some complained about how long they had been waiting to see a doctor, and others tried to get any nurse's attention to find out what was happening to a loved one.

Every one of the worn and faded pastel chairs were taken, the couch was fully occupied, and two big chairs were each being shared by two or three small children.

Ugh. This was not a scene I wanted to be part of, nor one I had any patience for. There was no other option but to get in line and wait my turn. I hoped I could get back to see Ernie right away and not have to fight for a place to park my behind while I waited.

Beyond the reception desk, behind the glass-paned doors that lead to the curtained-off emergency beds, I could see a lot of movement from green hospital gown-clad doctors and nurses going back and forth between exam rooms. An occasional electronic device was wheeled in front of one of them as they made their way to the next emergency.

As I observed the scene and impatiently inched my way closer to the reception desk, one of the glass paned doors was pushed open. A nurse stood in the doorway and scanned the crowd, paying special attention to the line near the desk.

I recognized her. It was Belinda, the nurse who often was on call when Ernie was admitted; Ernie had come to be on a first-name basis with her. Belinda was always upbeat and kind with Ernie; she had a soothing effect on him.

Belinda was attractive–she was a 30-something, tall African-American woman, with a broad smile that immediately put everyone she encountered at ease. Anyone observing her at work could tell she was well thought of by doctors and other nurses. Although she had an easy way about her, she also had an air of efficiency and confidence.

Our eyes met. I nodded in recognition and smiled at her. She didn't return the smile. Her eyes fixed on me. She headed toward me with a determined pace.

The smile froze on my face. I took one step out of the line toward Belinda, letting people behind me take my place. My heart raced. Something was not right–Ernie was in trouble.

Belinda reached me and grabbed my arm just above the elbow. "June, Ernie's in trouble." She stood close to me. I stared at her looking for a sign that would tell me that "trouble" was a broad term containing holes full of hope in which I could take comfort. That sign did not come. Belinda led me away from the reception area mess and into a corridor.

"June, Ernie came in with very shallow, uneven breathing and an erratic heart rhythm," Belinda said. "His vitals were all over the place. There is also indication that his kidneys are shutting down.

What was Belinda saying in nurse speak? Was she saying that Ernie is dying? My son is going to die?

"Oh my God," I finally spoke. Fear dropped over me like a heavy, black curtain. "Oh my God, Belinda. Is Ernie going to…is he going to be…all right?"

"Ernie is in the best hands June, and he's a fighter. We have him in the IC unit and are trying to stabilize him. He has a ventilator. We're monitoring his heart and kidneys and brain function. He's unconscious right now. I can take you to the IC Unit waiting room but I'm afraid you can't see him yet. I'm sorry."

"I have to call Tim. He needs to be here."

"Why don't I take you to the IC Unit waiting area and you can call him from there?" Belinda took hold of my left hand and guided me forward to the elevators.

She held my hand until she had seated me in a waiting room chair. I felt like a child. I wasn't certain if she thought I might run if she let go or if she thought that I might faint before I made it.

"June, I'm going to go back in with Ernie now," she said. "I'll come back or send the doctor out when we know anything new. Call Tim." She turned and walked quickly away.

I sat there doing nothing; I tried to clear my head of the negative feelings that had invaded my thinking. After another moment of stillness, I dug my cell phone out of my purse and tapped the phone icon. When the number pad came up, I froze again. I wondered if this call would be a prelude to a more horrible message I would later need to relay to Tim about his son. *Why was I calling? To alert him that Ernie was in the hospital, but nothing further to report? To tell him his son might be dying and to get here right away?*

That was it. That was what I *didn't* want to say. What I didn't want to think, and why I couldn't touch those numbers on the pad that would lead to Tim's voice. I didn't want to say the words and give them recognition; to say anything that might bring words of death from my mouth that would give them life.

A second later, a cold shiver shook through my body and out into the ether. The tremor took with it my ugly thoughts and negativity that had invaded my soul. And, in the next instant, I awoke. I was clear-headed and positive now; certain of the call I would make and more certain that Ernie would pull through this latest episode of being, well, Ernie.

I tapped Tim's number on the phone pad and waited. The receptionist answered on the third ring and informed me that Tim was in a meeting, could she take a message, or could I call back?

She was a temporary receptionist just brought in while Jerry, the regular receptionist, was on vacation. She didn't know my voice; when I said it was June calling, that didn't register either. I explained I was Tim's wife and that there was an emergency with his son and could she please get him out of the meeting. There was a moment of silence. I imagined she was balancing my emergency with having been told not to interrupt the meeting. She asked me to "hang on" and then put me on hold. A few seconds later, Tim was on the phone.

"June? What's up? Is Ernie all right? What happened?"

"Ernie got rushed to the hospital again from school. He's with doctors now–Belinda is with him–and things are okay but he has different symptoms and it's a bit more serious. I think you should come to the hospital."

"Wait. What do you mean it's a bit more serious? Is it serious or not? And how serious? I'll slip out of this meeting early if I have to."

"Yes. You should meet me at the hospital. He's going to pull through fine, but he is unconscious now. He'll need you here when he wakes up. You need to be here."

"Is there something you aren't telling me June? This doesn't sound right."

"No. I don't have all the answers because like I said, the doctors are still getting things sorted out. Tim, please just come be with Ernie. And me."

"Okay. I have to get someone else to step in for me tell the clients in the meeting that I have a family emergency. I'll be there as fast as I can." He hung up.

I put my phone away and paced the floor. I was certain that Tim wanted to hear the best of what I said so he went along with my calm while knowing there was something more to this than one of Ernie's "normal" episodes.

The windowless Intensive Care Unit waiting room was about one-third of the size of the emergency room area. But it was quieter. Pacing this floor meant taking fifteen steps one way, then reversing direction, and heading back to my starting point. This was the older wing of the hospital which hadn't been upgraded in years–except they did manage to have enough left-over plastic pastel chairs from the emergency room to outfit this one. Ten paces into my shuffle, Tim called to say he was on his way. He wanted to drill me for more information, but I cut him off short and told him there was nothing new, just get here.

After forty-five paces with four pauses to use my phone to scan the Internet, Belinda came back. Her face was brighter. I tried not to take any false hope from her expression, but it did put me a bit more at ease.

"Okay," she said without preamble. "So, Ernie seems to be out of the woods. His breathing is normalized and he woke up briefly before dozing off again. We are still monitoring his kidney function and he's still on a ventilator, but he's looking better."

I cried.

All the false calm I had felt was just a mask my face adorned to protect me from showing the horror I felt inside. Now, the shield was torn off and the pure emotion behind it was on full display.

I hugged Belinda, catching her by surprise and nearly knocking her over. She didn't know exactly how to respond–my wet eyes smudged the breast of her green gown with dark mascara. She said, "Whoa" and patted my back. I briefly lingered in her hug before recognizing how awkward this was and took a step back.

"Oooh, I'm so sorry Belinda. I...I just...I don't know what..." I attempted to explain my actions.

"That's okay honey," she said. "I'm a mom too, so I get it. Just caught me off guard is all." She smiled while she spoke, chasing away my awkward feeling. I smiled too while I wiped away my remaining tears with shaking fingers.

"Gotta get back to the patients, but you can come look in on Ernie now for a few minutes. Follow me."

Belinda led me down a hall to Ernie's room. When I entered, I saw Ernie looking so small and helpless, lying there with tubes in his mouth, saline delivery tubes hooked into his arm, and heart monitoring machines with wires tracing back to Ernie's chest. The little guy looked so vulnerable and weak, but I managed to concentrate on the news that he was doing better, not on the intimidating sight in front of me.

I walked to the side of the bed that was clear of most of the machines. I leaned over him and kissed his forehead. The ventilator hummed with a regular pattern although it seemed that it wasn't doing all of Ernie's breathing. I reached down to take my son's little hand in mine. It felt cold. I brought my other hand to cover his and rubbed some warmth into it. Ernie opened his eyes.

He strained to keep his eyes open and was only able to offer me slight slits to smile at. He looked as if he wanted to speak, but with the ventilator engaged and as weak as he was, nothing came out.

"Hi sweetie," I whispered. "I'm here, baby. Momma's here.

You're doing fine honey. Just a little scare. Daddy's on his way too."

I wanted to comfort him as fast as I could, seeing that he was too weak to keep awake for long. I thought I saw him attempt a smile but realized I was likely creating it out of hope. "I love you Ernie," was the last thing I said before he closed his little eyes completely and drifted back to sleep.

A nurse entered the room to check readings on Ernie's various machines. She saw my exchange with Ernie and waited. Now she gently suggested that I leave to let him rest.

I looked at her, then down on my sleeping son. She was right. Rest was all that could be offered now. But I took comfort in knowing that he got to see that his mom is here; that would mean lots to him. I patted his hand once more, leaned in to kiss his forehead again, and then gently placed his hand to his side. As I left, I stopped in the doorway to look back at him and pray that all would be okay.

When I returned to the waiting area, two new visitors had joined me. They each had a Styrofoam coffee cup in hand and sat together at one end of the row of pastel seats. They didn't seem aware that I'd entered the room.

They were an older couple, I guessed them to be in their late sixties or perhaps the man was seventy. They each wore concern deeply etched across their faces. Both were neatly dressed, but not overtly so; their attire suggested financial comfort. She had an expensive Coach purse in her lap and a silk scarf accessorizing her neck and equally well-designed shoes–appropriate for her age but still stylish. They were not something anyone could buy at Shoes R Us.

The man was dressed in a comfortable, neat ensemble of khaki pants topped with a light blue button-down shirt covered with a navy blazer. They seemed to me to be out of place here–as though they should be waiting for an usher to show them their seats at a Broadway theater not waiting tensely in an ICU at the local hospital.

On the other hand, I was dressed in my typical stay-at-home-mom outfit: dark blue gym warm-up pants, an oversized, faded red t-shirt, and my ever-ready gray sweatshirt tied around my waist. Oh, and Nike performance sneakers. Looking at the three of us, I would be the one who seemed to be in the right environment.

Life's chaos doesn't cast its players by looking at our checkbooks. I *shouldn't* have been surprised to see this well-dressed couple in a similar situation as me. And I also shouldn't have been swayed by my own bias to assume otherwise.

I moved to the row of plastic seats and chose a yellow one on the opposite end of the row from the couple. I thought they would like their space as much as I wanted mine. They didn't seem to notice me at all as I sat there. They said nothing to each other. They alternated between staring into their cups and taking small sips of whatever was in there.

I wondered what calamity had brought them to be with me here in this ICU waiting room, though I knew from their expressions and from my experience of what this place was, it could not have been good. People who are called to this room need miracles for the people they love—or they at least need an answer to their prayers that would give hope. I knew that too well. As I gazed at this couple, I couldn't help but feel for them; I added my own prayer to whatever Godly appeal they may have been silently uttering.

CHAPTER SIX

A MESSAGE FROM GOD

There was nothing left for me to do now other than to wait for Tim and for any updates on Ernie's condition from Belinda or the doctor.

So, I waited as patiently and hopefully as possible. I called Ginny to see if she could pick up Elsie from school and take her home with her. There was a hesitation before she agreed, and I got the sense that it wasn't about any inconvenience. There was something in the way she repeated "again" when I explained that Ernie was in the hospital again. She sounded almost judgmental.

I thought, at first, that she was going to refuse to help so I waited for her to offer an excuse. But when I added that he's in the ICU, that new fact triggered a different reaction. Ginny quickly agreed to take Elsie, tossing off her inconvenience with, "Oh no worries, happy to have Elsie. I hope Ernie will be okay."

I said "Thanks," and hung up. I was relieved that Ginny would take Elsie, but the odd tone of her initial response lingered; I wondered if I had taken advantage of Ginny's kindness on too many occasions. Perhaps I had strained the relationship by taking her for granted.

After that brief call, I texted Elsie to let her know what was happening without going into scary details. I assured her that Ernie would be fine. The routine of hearing Ernie was at the doctor's office or in the hospital combined with the fact that I texted the news, kept her from asking too many questions.

When she was 11 years old, Elsie was one of the first kids in her school to get a cell phone. It wasn't something I was in favor of or thought was a necessity for a child until after a few emergencies with Ernie. Then I changed my mind.

Our family life had become too unpredictable to believe we could have any kind of normal routine. It was necessary for us to have immediate contact with each other; it was not a luxury.

Elsie was under strict guidelines for using her phone, and I didn't allow her to download a bunch of apps. She had music and a couple of not-to-horrific games, and that was it. She understood that the phone was a tool and not a toy. The phone did have Internet access which was a little worrisome, but I trusted that Elsie had good common sense and that she valued our open and frank conversations about dangerous people and things on the Internet.

I also threw in a healthy dose of threats to take the phone away from her for any infraction—just in case her common sense lapsed.

With those two tasks completed, there was little else to do except sit and wait or pace and wait. Pacing would need to be cut to fewer steps if I didn't want to impose on my two companions. So I opted to sit.

I thought about calling work. But truthfully, I was increasingly less involved there while Ernie became more susceptible to emergencies. Only a handful of active clients were still assigned to me. I worked fewer hours than ever and spent more time caring for my kids and the house and keeping my family on track.

I could see where this trend was leading. And I knew it wouldn't be long before I was completely indoctrinated into being a stay-at-home mom—a soccer mom. I chuckled at that last part. If Elsie outgrew her attraction to soccer, which was very likely, I could at least drop the soccer mom part of my title. Go Elsie!

This wasn't at all how I had imagined my life progressing. I loved my kids and my husband, but I also loved being challenged at work and being in an office environment. Working among professionals—and being one myself. But if giving all that up was the trade-off for Ernie being healthy and happy and leading a normal childhood…I would gladly accept this deal.

I didn't sit for long before the waiting room solitude was interrupted by a doctor speaking quietly to a nurse as they entered the waiting area. He removed his surgeon's cap and tucked it into the front pocket of his scrubs shirt.

The older couple recognized the doctor and rose to meet him, but the doctor stepped forward and was at their side within a few quick steps. He gestured for them to sit back down. The non-detachable seats made it nearly impossible to have a face-to-face, intimate conversation, so he crouched on one knee in front of them.

Tim burst around the corner looking harried and pale. He was relieved when he saw me at my end of the row. He practically ran to me and threw himself into the chair next to mine–giving me a start–as half of the row of chairs inched backward with a screech. He looked over his shoulder briefly to see if he had affected the group at the other end of the row. They did not react.

"Geez, Tim," I whispered. "Nice entrance."

"Oops. Sorry. Is Ernie okay, any new news?"

"Yeah, I got to see him for a couple of minutes. He barely opened his eyes and went back to sleep. But he saw me and I talked to him. He knows we're here and I know that means the world to him. He's still being monitored, but Belinda said he is stable and breathing better and out of the woods. He's on a ventilator and other monitors, but it looks worse than he is. Most of it is precautionary. Just waiting for the doctor to come out and tell us more."

"Oh, thank God. I was really worried after your phone call."

"Is that why you looked so pale when you came in?"

"Well, yes. And well, no," he said sheepishly and examined his fingernails. "Not exactly. On my way through the hospital, I was emailing work from my phone and not paying attention to where I was going. I took the elevator the wrong way and got off on the wrong floor.

"I walked right into the chapel before I looked up...and Christ,

June. I froze and started to hyperventilate. I thought maybe you had directed me there and didn't want to tell me something. Then I realized I was just in the wrong place."

Before I could respond to Tim, the unmistaken sounds of crying, accompanied by a garbled voice, came careening out of the couple's corner. Tim and I tried to pretend not to hear them or to react, but their cries were too painful to ignore. The doctor and nurse had left.

Tim broke first and looked directly at them. Then I did. The woman's cries echoed their sadness throughout the waiting room then were muffled when she buried her face in the man's chest. Her words tore at us as they drifted our way, "Why did God have to take him now?"

Tim grabbed my hand that was resting on my knee closest to him; he held it tightly. We didn't say a word. We sat there in silence, two visitors to someone else's tragedy, observing a scene we both knew could have been our own; relieved that it had passed us by.

In that moment, I recognized them; not as stylish, unknown people who were out-of-place, but as two familiar, vulnerable people facing the same life and death realities that we all share. Tim reached into his back pocket for his handkerchief, and dabbed tears from his eyes. Then offered it to me. I took it, wiped my tear-filled eyes, and blew my nose into it.

The nurse who had entered the waiting room with the doctor, came in and gently led the couple, still entwined in their embrace, out of the waiting area toward the ICU rooms.

Tim and I sat hand-in-hand for a few more minutes before I offered his handkerchief back. He took the wadded-up mess, unfolded it in his lap and then looked at me.

"Did you do laundry this week? 'Cause I'm gonna need a fresh handkerchief."

Incredulous, I looked at him. He held up the wrinkled handkerchief with the tips of his index finger and thumb and looked like he was about to say "Cooties!," like one of the kids. It was streaked with mascara and damp from tears and my runny nose stuff that came with them; that's why I half folded, half bunched it up.

I almost laughed. "Why don't you buy some new ones instead of using that faded old piece of cloth?" I teased.

Tim's comment was just enough to help us break the overwhelming sadness in that room and bring us back to a less tragic reality. We both needed it and sent a smirk to each other. He reached out and squeezed my hand again, then rolled the handkerchief into a ball and shoved it into his back pocket.

Tim's phone buzzed in his sport coat pocket. While he checked it, I took my phone from my coat pocket to see if Elsie had sent a message.

"Work?" I asked absentmindedly while I checked messages.

"Huh?" he said distractedly while he looked at his. "Oh, yeah. Just something I am cc'd on. Nothing important. That car dealership new client wants us to file an extension." He dropped his phone back into his pocket.

Belinda came into the waiting room. I scanned her face to see what news she might bring before she reached us to give an update. I breathed easier seeing her pleasant expression; I took that as a good sign.

"Hi Tim, good to see you," Belinda said, reaching out to shake his hand, and nodding at me. "So, Ernie is resting comfortably. No change in his condition, but he seems to be relying less on the ventilator and his brain function is in the normal range. We're moving him to a better room tomorrow. Not much for you folks to do here or anything to wait for. The doctor will be better equipped to give more news tomorrow morning. You should probably go home and get something to eat and some rest and come back tomorrow."

"Can we go in and see him now?" I practically pleaded. "Just for a minute? He might open his eyes again and see Tim, and...I can't just leave him."

Belinda smiled. "I can walk you back there. He has opened his eyes now and then so maybe...Come on, follow me. But only for a minute."

Tim and I followed Belinda back to Ernie's room. I was prepared for how Ernie would look but for Tim, this was his first taste of the seriousness of Ernie's latest health episode and how it had manifested itself. I walked right up to Ernie's bed while Tim stood at the doorway taking in the site of his son's condition. He turned as pale as when he had entered the waiting area earlier.

I kissed Ernie's forehead then sat on the edge of his bed and took hold of his little hand. "Momma's here sweetheart. Are you awake? Daddy is here too."

I looked at Tim, who had ventured to the foot of Ernie's bed, and gestured with my head for him to come stand by my side. I rubbed Ernie's hand gently while I spoke to him. "Hey Ernie. You're doing fine. The doctor said you will be in a better room tomorrow and then we can spend more time with you."

Tim joined me. "Hey big guy. Daddy's here. You gave us quite a scare there, buddy. But you're doing great now."

As if on cue, Ernie opened his eyes. They were bigger now than the slits he had managed earlier, and I swore that I saw the same smile I had imagined earlier. Ernie looked at me and then his dad. He was definitely awake and cognizant and not just reacting to stimulation from one of his machines.

Tim and I gave Ernie the biggest smiles we could muster. I brought his hand to my face and kissed it and then caressed my cheek with it. Tim squeezed in between me and the head of Ernie's bed. He leaned over and kissed his forehead, then moved back.

It was difficult to see that Ernie couldn't respond with anything more than his eyes. As hard as it was for us, I imagined it must have been even more frustrating for Ernie. Even if he *could* muster the strength, he could not speak through the ventilator that had invaded his mouth.

We felt useless. We couldn't even offer him a hospital sippy cup or bring him anything. All he could do was lie there and breathe—more on his own now than with the ventilator. All we could do was stand there and look at him with love in our eyes—and hope that was enough.

Ernie looked one more time from one of us to the other, then closed his eyes. The little guy needed sleep. Tim and I took that as our cue to depart.

I placed Ernie's hand on his tummy and kissed his forehead again.

Then I stepped aside so Tim could add his kiss.

"I love you honey." I don't know if he heard me, but they were my last words to my son for the day. We headed for the doorway and out into the corridor.

It was after 5 pm now and I had not eaten since breakfast. I felt fatigued from the long day. But I wanted to remain at the hospital in case Ernie woke up again.

Tim convinced me that there was nothing we could do and that it was unlikely Ernie would wake up before morning. We should go home, eat, and sleep and come back early the next morning.

So, we left. Tim's car was in the opposite direction as mine, so we parted ways just outside the hospital entrance. Tim headed for our favorite take-out pizza restaurant to get dinner. I made my way, a bit absent mindedly, to my car. I needed to go to Ginny's house to pick up Elsie.

All I could think about was Ernie and his sad little face and all the machines attached to him and how much I loved him. My mind was not involved in the insignificant task at hand. When I reached my car, I removed my keys from my purse and unlocked the door, but I hesitated before getting in. *Shoot. Ernie doesn't have any balloons or cards or anything to brighten his room.* I thought.

I turned back toward the hospital to get something at the gift shop and then stopped short when I remembered. "Ugh. You can't have balloons and things in the ICU rooms. I'll pick something up tomorrow when I know he'll be in a regular room." I didn't care if anyone saw me talking to myself. I pivoted to return to my car.

I took one step forward and saw it. Or them. I had two flat tires. Both in the rear. In my initial slumbered walk toward the car, I had failed to see them. Now, there they were, as plain as day. I stood there in disbelief.

"Un-fucking believable!" I yelled. "That stupid...uggghhh...son of a bitch slit my tires! It must have been him. All because he went the wrong way and I got the parking spot! Un-freaking believable!" I kicked the flattened tires.

I was tired and stressed and pissed off as all get out, so kicking the tires wasn't enough. I lifted my set of keys with the "Best Mom Ever" heart-shaped gold pendant attached and whipped them straight at my car.

It seemed like a good idea at the time—right up and until the keys hit the back of the car. The pendant scraped along the trunk, leaving a noticeable mark, before the keys bounced into the air and careened off the back windshield. They continued their journey onto the ground, then slid along the cement surface, and under the front of the pick-up truck parked next to me. They finally came to rest on the edge of a nearby water drain. Or at least I hoped they were *on* the edge and not *in* the drain. I couldn't see because of the big truck tire wheel that blocked my view. I couldn't believe what I had just done and witnessed. I was flabbergasted.

I stood there with my mouth open. I wondered, *Is this what they mean by a message from God?*

After taking a minute, to reflect upon my situation and to look around to see if anyone had witnessed my key-throwing, potty-mouthed diatribe, I took a deep breath and told myself everything would be okay. *Just relax, June. You will find the keys, call Triple A, get the tires repaired and all will be fine. Probably be fixed before the pizza is even ready. Don't let this a-hole guy get the best of you* (as if it wasn't a bit too late for that).

Re-fortified and determined to make that lemonade one hears so much about, I set to task one. I walked over to where I had seen the keys slide toward the drain, still hoping they might be on the edge, and that they hadn't actually dropped into it. I discovered that the pick-up truck partially covered the drain. Obviously, the owner misread the Compact Cars Only sign thinking it said, Yeah Compact Cars for Everyone Else, But *Your* Big Ass Truck Will Fit."

Breathe!

It was dark out and I couldn't get a good view of the drain looking from the front of the truck. I would have to crawl behind the driver's side massive front wheel, under the truck and look into the drain. I groaned. Luckily, I wore my "I might be going to the gym" outfit. I was dressed for just this occasion.

I crouched down and peered under the truck, hoping for a magical hand to jump out at me holding my keys–that was the type of "message from God" I hoped for. Of course, I realized that was not about to happen, so I slunk down to my belly and crawled under the truck toward the drain cover.

As I crawled along, my loose-fitting gym sweats began a trip of their own–off my waist and down my behind. The truck body was fairly high off the ground, compared to a car, but still did not allow enough room for my quick reaction. Startled, I reached for my waistband. I lifted and turned my head in that direction, banging my head on the undercarriage of the truck. "Shit!" I yelled. "Shitty, shit, shit, shit," I mumbled as I rubbed the spot on my head–it really smarted.

I must be quite a sight, I thought as I continued to rub the bump on my head. My legs were sticking out from under a parked truck with sweatpants in a position to challenge any plumber, my face was down on the ground, and mumbling was emanating from my mostly motionless body. If my head didn't hurt so much, I would have laughed at my own pitiful circumstances.

Lemonade, June. Lemonade. I crawled toward the drain cover, pants be damned.

I discovered that if l bent my knees, the little I could, and lifted up my bottom, then, as a partner to that motion, slid my top forward, I could complete one full crawl–sort of like an inchworm.

Keeping my arms folded under my breasts, while attempting this maneuver, kept me from scraping anything. I made the inchworm move, three or four times, before I made it to the edge of the drain.

I saw it! A shiny something sitting on the far side of the drain, between slats that stop large objects from sliding into the sewer system. *Please let that be my keys* I prayed.

I reached forward, gently cleared the leaf that partially hid the object, and...it was my keys. *YES! YES! YES!* I shouted inside my head, and then let one last "**YES!**" out of my mouth and into the fall air. "There is a God", I loudly proclaimed."

Unbeknownst to me, the man who owned the truck had finished his business in the hospital and had opened the driver's side door about to climb in when he heard the proclamation, "Yes, there is a God!" coming from under his truck. Startled and confused, he cautiously closed his front door and bent down to get a look.

I heard his door click shut and froze. I thought the truck was about to pull out with me beneath it. "SHIT!" I panicked and grabbed at my keys. I knocked them into the drain. "**SHIT!**" I yelled louder.

The man got to his knees and peered under his truck. When he saw me and my slightly exposed derriere, he chuckled. "Lady. What the F are you doing under my truck?"

"I'm looking for my keys," I said sheepishly. I began my crawl back out, reversing my inchworm technique, and emerged to the full view of the owner. He held out his hand and helped me to my feet.

I mumbled, "Thanks," while hitching up my sweats. He was a 40-something guy, fairly average looking with a strong face and rugged hands, dressed in a uniform that suggested he worked in a trade.

I looked closer and realized that he was dressed like...like a plumber. I glanced at his truck again and noticed the sign *Liquidator Plumbing –Sewers, Cesspools and Drainage Specialists.* I just stared at it.

"Ma'am," he said. I looked at him and wondered if he thought I was a lunatic escapee on the loose in the hospital parking lot. "How the heck did you lose your keys under my truck? And did you find them?"

I stared at the truck and the man a few seconds longer before I responded.

"Well," I said. "It's kind of a long story. And yeah, I found them. But when I heard your door shut, I got nervous because I thought you were going to run me over, and I knocked them into the storm drain. So...nope I don't have them now." I shrugged trying to pretend this was a no big deal kind of thing that just happens to people.

The plumber looked around to the front of the truck where he could see the part of the drain that his truck wasn't hiding. I think he kind of felt sorry for me. There I was, standing in my workout outfit now covered in oil stains and street dirt and whatever else collected near that drain. My face was streaked with dirt and my hair had clumped where I banged it on the greasy undercarriage of the truck. I also looked like crying was an option I was considering.

"I'm gonna move my truck and then we can see where your keys ended up." The man said looking at me pitifully. He jumped into his truck, backed out, and pulled into an empty spot that had opened up in the next aisle. After he backed out, I stepped over to the drain to take a look. I could see my keys on a cement ledge just below the drain slats. I was so relieved that they hadn't fallen deeper into the drain and out of sight and reach. The plumber joined me at the drain and I pointed to where my keys sat.

"Ahh that's lucky," he said and headed straight back to his truck. I just stood there, feeling "lucky," while I waited. He came back with a silver pen-like object in his hand. He took another look into the drain, assessed the situation, then pulled on one end of the "pen" and extended it to about three feet. He knelt next to the drain and inserted the tool between the slats toward my keys.

As he did so he explained, "It's a magnet on the end that should be strong enough to snag the keys, so I can pull them out." He was right. He hovered the magnetic end over the keys, then gently touched them and they clung to the tool. He slowly and deftly pulled the tool up and out of the drain, with the keys firmly attached. He grabbed my keys, stood up and handed them to me.

"There ya go," He smiled.

"Thank you," I fairly gushed. "Thank you so much. You're a life saver." I was sincere in my compliment. At that moment he was my hero.

"I wish I had a couple'a extra tires for you. You got Triple A or someone to help with that?" He pointed out the flats.

"Oh Yeah. Yes, I have Triple A. I was in the hospital visiting my son and some jerk sliced my tires. I'm going to call my husband to come get me while Triple A tows the car."

"Ahh that sucks. Had that happen to me once before. If it's one tire, ya got a spare, ya know? But when they do *that*...it's really lousy. They do that scratch on the side too?"

He leaned over and ran his finger over the fine scratch. I hadn't thought it was that obvious but looking at it now, it was fairly long and noticeable.

"Um, no that was there before." I lied, too embarrassed to reveal the truth.

He turned to me and asked, "Are you sure you'll be okay?"

"Oh yes. Thanks. Now that you got my keys for me I'll be fine." I suddenly felt conscious of how disheveled I was and how desperate I must have appeared, so I tried to make light of it all. "Nothing some clean clothes and a bath won't fix...and maybe a glass of red wine." I said with a forced chuckle.

"Oh yeah, I hear that. Headed to meet the crew for a beer myself. Well, you take care and good luck with everything. Oh and, don't forget your purse over there."

"I won't," and suddenly remembered that I had dropped my purse near one of my flat rear tires before I went looking for my keys. I shouted after him while I grabbed my purse. "Wait! Hang on a minute!"

He stopped and looked back at me just as he opened the front door of his truck. I jogged over and handed him a scrunched up $20 bill I retrieved from the bottom of my purse —mad money I threw in there in case I forgot to put my wallet inside.

"Let me at least buy the first round," I offered.

"Oh no, that isn't necessary," he said, looking a little embarrassed. "I was glad to help."

"Please. I insist. It's the least I can do, and it will make me feel better. It's your Knight's reward." I smiled and forced the bill into his hand.

"Heh. Geez. Well, okay if you put it that way. I'll tell the guys the first round is on a pretty damsel in distress I rescued." He laughed, pleased at his wit. I liked his subtle compliment to me.

"You do that Sir Knight," I gave a little curtsy. The Plumber Knight mounted his truck and drove off.

I felt a bit better about my situation now. I went from having two flat tires and no keys, back to just two flat tires—in a matter of minutes.

With some sort of twisted logic, I figured I'd gotten ahead of the game and that made me smile. I also realized that I still had to call Tim, to tell him that he now had to pick up Elsie, call Triple A to get the car towed, and then get me home.

It occurred to me that I would have been better off just staying in the ICU waiting area close to Ernie, like I wanted to do in the first place. Then I considered how this was all Tim's fault.

After all, if he hadn't insisted we should leave, I would...still have two flat tires...yes, but I wouldn't have had the whole key-losing episode, my car trunk wouldn't be scratched, my clothes would be clean, and I wouldn't have a bump on my head. And, I wouldn't know about the flat tires, so I wouldn't be upset just sitting in the waiting area being blissfully ignorant.

Then again, if *I* hadn't barged into that open space and cut off the guy who slit my tires, and if I didn't fly off the handle and throw my keys, I wouldn't have a scratch on the trunk of my car, dirty clothes, or a lump on my head...so I guessed blaming Tim wasn't going to float.

I shrugged my shoulders and took inventory of myself. I decided that I would go back to the waiting area and make calls from there. Tim could bring me a slice of pizza after he got Elsie, and he could take care of my car situation when he got here.

I tried to rub the grease off of my top and pants but no luck. My sweats were dark blue though and they didn't show the dirt too obviously, so I could make do there. I took off my sweatshirt top and tied it around my waist by the sleeves. It was a bit cold with just my baggy T, but I would soon be in the warm hospital. I headed for the entrance.

I remembered that there was a restroom just inside the lobby where I could wash my face and hands and comb the dirt from my hair. Maybe, with just a little lipstick touch-up, I would be presentable enough. I headed straight for the ladies' restroom and cleaned up. Satisfied with my effort, I made my way back to the ICU waiting area. Even though it was empty again, I still chose to go back to my same yellow chair that I occupied earlier. I called Tim to explain the change in plans. He answered his phone on the first ring.

"Hi," he said. "The pizza will be ready in about another five minutes so I'm almost on my way home. What's up? Did you get Elsie?"

"Yeah, about that," I said, twisting the arm of the sleeve around my waist. "You know the guy I told you about who tried to cut me off and take my parking space?"

"Um, noooo you never told me about that."

"I didn't? Oh. Well this guy tried to cut me off when I was parking at the hospital and he got mad because I got there first. And anyway he was going the wrong way. So, he flipped me off and said some nasty things, but I just ignored him."

"Okay, babe. Is this leading somewhere? 'Cause I'm sensing another spilled coffee episode and I just don't want to interrupt when my name is called to get the pizza."

"Ha, ha very funny Tim, and yes this is going somewhere. Listen… So, when I got out of the hospital to get in my car, I had two flat tires.

This moron sliced them for revenge. So I need you to call Triple A and get the car towed to wherever you take it to get repaired. Then I need you to go get Elsie. Then come get me at the hospital and bring pizza. We can all eat here."

"Seriously? And how do you know it was the same guy?"

"Yes seriously, and I know because…it had to be him. Who else would be so mean? Anyway, will you just take care of the car and get Elsie? I'll let Ginny know you're coming."

"Okay. Fine. Get the pizza Tim, fix the car Tim, go get Elsie Tim, bring the pizza to the hospital Tim. I should get a job with that new car service company…Uber."

"That's a great idea hon, but they don't serve our area yet. Meanwhile you can practice by doing these little things for your wife. Oh, and Uber doesn't fix flat tires."

"Oh, good one," he remarked. "Okay wifey, I'll get right on all that."

"So annoying," I teased. "Bye."

I couldn't help the quizzical look I was wearing when I hung up. Tim seemed to take everything in stride and with humor and wasn't the least bit annoyed. I expected more push-back or questioning or exasperation at the cost of having to replace the tires in addition to the emergency ambulance bill we were going to get. *Something.* But he didn't offer any of that. Maybe he was just that relieved that Ernie was getting better and his joy, compared to the misery of *my* little mishap, was far more empowering.

Whatever the reason, I wanted to hug him for being so good about it and for not adding to my stress.

I called Ginny to let her know that Tim was coming to pick up Elsie instead. She told me that Elsie was lying down in Brian's bedroom. Apparently, she had one of her migraines and it was pretty bad–enough so that she asked to lie down in bed–which for Elsie is a big deal.

Elsie would rather silently suffer if she knew she would be home soon and in her own surroundings and in her own bed, than appear needy or vulnerable in front of others. I knew Elsie would have been embarrassed to ask for something as personal as lying down in someone else's bed–even if it was her best friend Beamer's.

I asked Ginny to wake Elsie when Tim arrived–even if she had managed to fall sound asleep. I told her that Tim had a particular medicine that Elsie needed to take.

She would have to be woken up eventually anyway or stay the night and put Beamer out of his bed if Ginny offered that. Elsie would be mortified if that happened and would be upset at Tim and me–she would rather suffer through the migraine.

Because Tim was handling everything else, I decided I would sneak into Ernie's room for a visit until Tim and Elsie arrived–and the pizza; I was starving.

I walked down the corridor toward his room and was met by the same nurse who was adjusting Ernie's machines during my first visit. Belinda had gone off duty and I didn't know this nurse. But I was hopeful that she would let me at least sit with Ernie for a bit.

Before I could ask, she gestured toward Ernie's room and said, "Go ahead and sit for a while. I'm sure it will be okay." I smiled and thanked her; I tiptoed into his room and stood by the side of his bed.

All the machines were doing their job: monitoring his heart rate and pulse, helping him breathe, solutions dripping into his arm. And the imposing kidney machine doing its thing.

A minute later, the nurse came in with a small stool and offered it to me. I took the stool with a smile and placed it near the bed. I sat on the stool and realized it was in its lowest position; I looked like I was in a little kid school desk chair.

"It adjusts if you just turn it one way or the other to go up or down," The nurse informed seeing my predicament. Then she left.

I turned the seat clockwise a half turn, the only direction it would go, and it unscrewed itself with an obvious squeak. I didn't want to wake Ernie, so I tried the seat again; still a bit too low. I risked the squeaking once more and gave the seat another half turn with a little more pressure lifting up and that did the trick. I took his hand in mine and talked quietly to him.

"Hi honey. I'm back again. Just waiting for Daddy and Elsie to come get me. I didn't want to leave but they don't let us stay here too long so if I'm not here when you wake up don't be worried–I'll be here soon."

I knew he likely couldn't hear me. I really didn't want my voice to disturb his rest; though selfishly I hoped he might open his eyes again and see me. I sat there with his hand in mine and just let my mind wander.

I looked at my son's precious face and thought how beautiful he is, even pale. I thought about how handsome he was going to be when he grew up. Now, he looked like a pale cherub, slumbering after a hard day of angel mischief.

I leaned over and stroked his cheek. It was so soft. I remembered how fierce his eyes could be when he was doing one of is dare-devil feats like standing on his bike seat while gliding down the sidewalk. I wondered if, now with those eyes closed tight, *is he reliving one of those magical times too?*

I thought of how hard he tried to play ball with other kids and how draining simple tasks could be for him; how at times he would sit out games and just watch.

I remembered the first time he hit a T-Ball after his long recovery from his first crisis–how proud he was and so pleased with himself. I recalled the many times I watched him in the backyard playing catch with his dad; Tim was ever-so-patient and encouraging with every throw.

I wandered through my memories and I wondered...*When will my Ernie get well? When will he be able to be in school in his right grade with other kids his age? When will we finally figure out this mystery that has hold of his body? When will it let go of him? Is my little boy always going to be sick or will he outgrow it? I want him to have a normal life and experience everything other kids take for granted. I just want him to be well.*

It was a lot to take in. My lack of food and the stresses with the car and my keys and seeing Ernie like this, combined with all the reminiscing and questioning, was too much.

My eyes filled from my never-empty well of tears; they streaked down both cheeks unhindered. Within seconds, I was a mess and slobbering into the sleeves of my sweat top tied around my waist. I tried to take a deep breath and recover but was unsuccessful. I really didn't want Ernie to wake up and see me like this, so I turned my sweat top around my waist and put my whole face in it to muffle my sobs and catch my tears.

A hand gently touched my right shoulder and I jumped. I hastily wiped my face, trying to erase my emotional outburst before looking toward the source of the touch.

It was the nurse who had allowed me into the room and brought me the stool. She handed me a small box of Kleenex. She looked at me tenderly. "It's all right. I would've been surprised if I *didn't* find you this way. It's never easy to see your baby like this."

I made a small, "Yeah" and nodded my head in agreement. I dabbed each eye with a tissue, then blew my nose. "Thank you," I said and handed the box back to her.

"You hang on to that for a bit just in case," she said as she refused the box. "I have a bit of a break right now. I'm going to go down to the vending machines and get a soda. Why don't you take a walk with me; stretch your legs and maybe get something to eat?"

"Oh, thank you," I said, and sniffled. "That is really nice of you. But, umm, Tim, my husband, is on his way and he's bringing me some pizza."

"Well, that sounds better than one of those I-was-fresh-yesterday tuna fish sandwiches from the vending machine. I can tell you that much."

I laughed at that. "Oh my God, that is *exactly* what my daughter Elsie calls them. Only she says, "Mmm, yummy!" Afterward.

We both shared a quiet chuckle.

"Well, why don't you just come for the walk? We really should leave Ernie alone now and it would be nice to have the company."

"Oh," I said. "Well, in that case yeah, I'll come with you." I thought it was the least I could do after the kindness she had shown me. But more likely, it was she who was doing more for me by getting me out of the room and putting my mind at ease.

We walked along the corridor toward the elevators and rode down to the cafeteria level where the vending machines are. The cafeteria was closed for sit-down service during renovations–thus the vending machine meals. It was nice to have a conversation with someone about nothing in particular.

"So, tell me what kind of pizza did you order?" She asked as we walked along.

"Oh. Ya know, I don't actually know," I said. "Tim is taking care of that. But I think he knows what Elsie, that's my daughter, and I like. Though with Tim ya never know." I said with a slight tease in my voice.

"Oh, you don't have to tell me about that," she chuckled. "I asked my husband to bring me dinner here one time. You know what he brought me? Popeyes–*his* favorite fast food chicken that he knows I can't eat because it gives me terrible heartburn. In our twelve years of marriage, I never asked him to bring me dinner again." We both had a good laugh. "'Course, I kind of wonder if that wasn't some sort of plot on his part. Now that I think about it, maybe it was a conspiracy to get out of ever having to bring me dinner again; he's more clever than I thought…Nah." That really made us laugh.

The walk and the light conversation was doing the trick. I felt better and a bit more upbeat. When we reached the vending machines, the nurse wasted no time making her selections. She fetched a few of the quarters from her clenched fist and dropped them into the coin slot with exacting precision; as though she were an integral part of the machine. A snickers bar landed at the bottom with a thud. She moved to the next machine and threw a few quarters into the slot and a can of Sprite came smashing down with a *thunk*. She retrieved it and then the Snickers bar. I was impressed by her lack of indecision and her commitment to that Sprite and Snickers bar. She caught me staring.

"I know," she said defensively. "It's a can of sugary soda that causes all kinds of bad health issues, and I'm a nurse and should know better, *blah, blah blah*." Her grin told me she wasn't offended. "Well, this is my little treat to get me through the night and I don't care if it's a crutch and bad for me. It does my spirit good and that's a big benefit. And let me tell you, we have doctors and nurses here who still smoke and some who could stand to lose thirty pounds or so...and have you ever had the food in *this* cafeteria? Don't go looking inside a hospital for examples of good health habits."

I smiled back, and said, "Actually, I was admiring how determined and certain of your choice when you walked up to the machine. You have inspired me to have a Coke when I normally would have a Diet Coke...I need a treat too!"

We shared a hearty, guilt-free laugh. And then, I bought a Coke. I needed something to go with the pizza anyway.

I felt at ease with the nurse; as though I were talking to an old friend. Then I realized I didn't even know her name. But before I could ask, we had arrived back at the ICU waiting area where Tim and Elsie were hovering over the opened pizza box. The nurse tipped her can of Sprite toward me and made her exit. Tim looked up as I approached. He returned the slice of pizza he had selected to the box and gave me a hug. Then he stepped back and took my face in both hands.

"You okay, babe?"

I nodded, tucked my head into his chest and melted with his arms around me. I held him tight for a moment then broke the embrace and stepped back.

"Yeah, I'm okay. Just, stuff–ya know?"

Tim nodded. We sat on each side of Elsie. She had closed the pizza box without taking a slice. I put my unopened Coke on the seat beside me.

"Hi sweetie," I put my arm around her shoulder and pulled her close in a sitting-down hug. I felt her forehead and asked, "How are you feeling? Is your ache gone?"

"Mom," she swatted my hand from her forehead. "It's a migraine, not a fever. You can't feel it by doing that."

"Oh right. Sorry. I forgot." I couldn't remember when she started calling her ache a migraine. Was this the first time? Or was I missing part of her little signs of growing up? "Were you asleep when Daddy got you?"

"Sort of...not really. I was nodding off when they ripped me out of bed."

"Ripped you out of bed?" I said with a grin, trying to lighten her mood a little. "Sounds a bit dramatic. Sorry, honey but you know how P-d off you would have been if we left you there for the night."

"Okay, Mom. I get it."

"Okay, well eat something," I said. "Maybe it will help your mood."

"Really, Mom? That's all you got? Eat something and *oh it's your mood?*"

"Geez Elsie," I said gently. "Don't snap at me. I'm just trying to help. I'm sorry. Do you want to lie down in my lap and close your eyes?"

"No, Mom; that won't help what's wrong with me."

I looked at Tim for help. His mouth was full of pizza. He threw me a "don't ask me" look. When he finished swallowing, he offered his two cents.

"She was fine in the car," he said. "Just really quiet–other than asking about Ernie–and rubbing her tummy while she looked out the window."

I turned back to Elsie.

"Honey, what's wrong? Do you have a stomach ache?"

"Ugh!" Elsie groaned and looked at her dad looking at both of us. She stood up, grabbed my hand and pulled me out of the room. At nearly 13, she was close to my height and pretty strong. "Come on, Mom."

"Wait! Where are we going?" I trailed behind the human tow truck. I turned back toward Tim who had just taken the last bite of his pizza and was contemplating a second slice.

"Can you guys get me a Diet Coke while you're up?" Was all Tim had to offer to the scene in front of him. That man could be so single-minded no matter what was going on around him. Elsie led me to the elevators.

"Elsie," I was trying not to get irritated back at her. "Where are we going?"

"We're...going to get Dad a Diet Coke and one for me too."

The elevator door opened, we got in and Elsie punched the down button. Elsie was silent during the short elevator ride but didn't let go of my hand. At one point she looked at our entwined fingers and then looked up at me and gave me a cheesy grin.

The elevator stopped and the doors slid open. When we exited the elevator, Elsie looked furtively around for any strangers who might be lurking about. Other than the two people who were standing at one of the vending machines considering their options, the room was empty. Rather than leading me toward the vending machines and her waiting Diet Coke, she guided me to a private, corner cafeteria table where we sat facing each other, knees touching.

"Okay, Mom." Elsie finally spoke. "So, um. I got it."

"Huh?" I looked at her, puzzled. "You got what?"

"You know...IT."

"Oh God, Elsie. Is this going to be a twenty questions thing? I just don't have the mental bandwidth for that right now."

"*Mom,* I got IT! Hello?" She paused and stared at me so intently I thought her eyes might bug out of their sockets. I finally got—well, *it.*

"OMG honey. You mean you got your *period?*"

"Geez Mom, say it a little louder—the people on the fourth floor didn't hear you." Elsie rolled her eyes.

"Ohhhh, sorry honey. I'm just so happy for you. Is that why you were lying down at Grace's? Oooh, shoot, did you have your emergency packet in your back pack?"

"No. I mean yes. Um no. I was lying down because I had a bad migraine, but yeah, while I was lying down it happened. And yep, I had my emergency pack with me." Elsie beamed. I leaned across and gave her a huge hug.

"Oh honey, that is amazing. Did everything go okay? Were you able to use the tampon or did you just go with a pad? Or is that too much info to tell me?"

Elsie blushed but answered, "I tried the um, tampon, but it was kind of difficult at first and not being home and everything...I just used a pad."

"Oh, well that might take some practice. But I'm so proud of you that you were ready and could handle everything. Did you tell your dad?"

"No. That seemed icky somehow. You can tell him if you *have* to."

Icky. My little girl was becoming a woman, but things could still be described as icky.

I loved her so much and never felt closer to her than at that moment. I was so happy I had taken the time to talk to her last year about sex and periods and boys and girls—even though she giggled, blushed, and laughed at me when I said the word *penis.* For the most part, she was mature about it and intrigued and asked good questions. Thankfully, someone had invented Google, so I got a lot of advice from other women who had experienced this talk before. It really helped.

"Okay," I said, "I will tell him. He knows what periods are honey; you know that I'm still a woman right? I mean just because I'm your old, old mom..."

"Oh, brother. Yes, Mom."

"Sooo, were you mad at me 'cause I had to be at the hospital and not there for you?" I asked gently.

"Well, um no," Elsie said, ducking her head down so that her bangs swung forward and hid her eyes. "I mean, I feel bad for Ernie and I was worried about him. It's just. It's just that this was supposed to be a special day for us to share together." She tilted her head back up and looked in my eyes.

I looked into my beautiful daughter's eyes and thought for a minute. I remembered that we had made plans that when this day came, we would buy popcorn and ice cream and have a binge *Harry Potter* night. Elsie probably thought I had forgotten. But I hadn't–life had just thrown us both an unexpected curve.

"You know what?" I said and grinned.

"What?" A slow grin spread across her face.

"The very nice nurse told me we had to let Ernie rest now and visiting hours are over. Dad has pizza so he's a happy camper (Elsie chuckled).

He has to stay here and meet the Triple A people about my car anyway, sooo we can take his car, stop for ice cream and go home to watch *Harry Potter.*"

"Really? Popcorn too? We're supposed to have popcorn."

"Geez," I said and laughed, "did you write this down a year ago or something? Was a contract signed?" She was beaming and laughed at me. "Yes, popcorn too!"

"Cool!" She said and jumped to her feet. "Come on...old Mom...let's go!" She practically ran toward the elevator without me.

"Don't make fun of me or I will make fun with how fat you look after you eat ice cream and popcorn all night," I shouted after her.

By the time I reached her we were both giggling like school girls. All we talked about on the way back to the waiting room was what flavor ice cream we were going to get. Elsie insisted she should choose for both of us because it was her special day. But I pouted so she decided we could each chose one flavor. Elsie chose Ben and Jerry's Phish Food and I selected pistachio, my favorite.

She asked one other question.

"Mom, can I go in and see Ernie?" Her demeanor quickly changed; her focus went from her special day to the biggest thing on her mind—her sick brother.

I put my arm around her and said, "I think it would be better to just let him rest, honey. He won't be able to see you 'cause he's asleep." I didn't want her to see him with all the machines and tubes and looking so weak. She had seen Ernie in the hospital before and witnessed the horrible incident with the swings a couple years ago, but this was different.

This wasn't Ernie spending a few hours in an emergency room. This was life-threatening and complicated, and her brother would be in the hospital for a while. It was better to let her have her special night; we could all visit Ernie in the morning or she could come after school.

We arrived in the waiting room but there was no Tim. Elsie looked into the pizza box and saw *four* slices missing.

"Oh my gosh, Mom. We won't be the only fat ones!" She said poking fun at her dad. "Sure glad I didn't want pizza, 'cause there are only six slices in a box and Dad ate four!"

I looked into the box too and quickly grabbed a slice. "I'm glad you don't want any too. 'Cause I'm starving." I stuffed a slice into my mouth.

"Oh my gosh Mom–that is disgusting!" Elsie laughed at me and snatched the last piece.

We stood and leaned over the empty pizza box while we ate to catch anything that slid from our mouths as we chewed. Tim walked in.

He didn't miss a beat. "Nice mother and daughter eating-from-the-trough-moment. It's tableaus like this that inspired Norman Rockwell."

Elsie had no idea who Norman Rockwell was, but she got the pig and trough reference. We nearly choked.

"You should talk, Dad. Four slices?"

"Yeah, Tim," I added swallowing my last bite. "You're the head pig in this litter."

It had gotten so late that Elsie and I now thought everything we said was funny. We were high on ourselves. Tim rolled his eyes and looked at us as he would any pair of silly girls and gave a slight guilty-as-charged smirk.

Tim hadn't brought any napkins, so I wiped my greasy, cheesy mouth on the sleeve of my sweat top that was still hung around my waist. Elsie, who held the empty pizza box in one hand, gave me a quick glance and then snatched the sleeve closest to her and wiped her mouth before I could smack her hand away. My swat missed her hand and I hit the box, sending it flying onto the floor and landing upside down. It was empty of pizza, but the remaining crumbs were plentiful, and they spilled all over the floor.

That was too much. Elsie and I we went into a ridiculous laughing fit.

Tim's phone chimed. He shook his head as he pulled the phone from his pants pocket. He had a brief conversation.

"That was triple A," he said while sliding the phone back into his pocket.

Elsie and I laughed again. I don't know why. We were just funny that way. Tim rolled his eyes. "Triple A is here; they need me to come down and show them where the Jeep is and sign some papers. I'll text you when we're done to come meet me at my car. I'm parked next to yours."

Tim backed toward the elevator looking at Elsie and me as he went. "Oh, and thanks for the Diet Coke." He never misses anything; he had to get his little dig in. Well, we did forget his drink so, I guess we deserved that one.

Elsie looked at me like "Oh yeah, *you* forgot the Diet Coke." I gave her a *don't even blame me* look back.

"Tim, wait!" I called before he could push the elevator button. "There's been a change in plans."

"Ahhm, beyond getting Triple A to tow the car and go home, I didn't know there was a plan," he said.

"Well, there is now. Elsie and I are going to have a *Harry Potter* party night, so we need your car to go get ice cream and popcorn before we go home."

"Excuse me?" Tim tilted his head and looked at me like I'd lost what was left of my marbles. "A *Harry Potter* party night on a school night?"

I actually hadn't thought that far ahead, but now that Tim mentioned it, I had an answer. I can be quick on my feet when I need to be.

"She is taking the day off tomorrow to make certain her migraine is over." *Brilliant!* I thought.

Tim looked perplexed. He knew this didn't make sense. Elsie would never binge watch TV during a migraine episode. But rather than argue, he offered a different version of our plan.

"Yeah, okay," he said, holding the elevator door open. "So, since Triple A is already here, we'll all go down together. I'll sign the papers for them to tow the Jeep, then we can all go to the store and get your party favors. That way, I don't end up taking a cab home."

Elsie and I looked at each other. There was no arguing with that logic. I wondered why we hadn't come up with that solution and then figured it was because we didn't know when triple A would arrive. That had to be it.

"Okay, sounds like a plan," I said. "Let's go. But wait a second while I just peek into Ernie's room and say goodnight."

"Me too," Elsie chimed in.

"No honey," I said and waved her back. "You go with Daddy, they won't let us both in. Hurry up and I'll meet you at the car."

"Ugh. Okay, but say goodnight to him for me too."

"I will honey. Promise. And for Daddy too."

"I said goodnight earlier," Tim said. "That's where I was when you guys came back from not getting me my Diet Coke. I snuck in to give him a kiss and tell him I loved him. But you can say goodnight for me again."

"Oh good!" I said, pleased that he'd been in there. "And a nurse let you in or did you really have to sneak in?"

"Rowena? Yeah, she was great. I had to cut my visit with Ernie short, but she was really understanding." He was getting tired of holding the door open while it kept bumping his arm. "Okay Else, let's get this party on the road." They slipped into the elevator and out of sight.

Rowena? He spent maybe a minute with her and knew her name already. I spent 20 minutes with her, crying and bonding and...and I never even asked her name. But that was Tim. He could introduce himself to anyone and start a conversation, whether or not he knew them. He never bothered with the idea that maybe they didn't want to talk to him. He just went ahead; even if he got rejected for any reason, it didn't stop him from trying again the next time. Never phased him.

It helped that he had one of those minds that could remember everything about a variety of subjects; sports, movies, historical events, and things we did together –the day and year and what we did. That could be both fun and annoying depending upon the conversation. I envied him that gift.

But, at least now I could go say goodnight to Ernie and give Rowena my thanks.

I tiptoed around the corner toward Ernie's room. I figured I would run into Rowena before I got there—and I did. She walked with me into his room and told me to cut it short so Ernie would not be disturbed.

I thanked Rowena—referring to her by name—for her understanding and our walk. When she left the room, I said goodnight to Ernie and, as had become my custom, kissed his forehead.

CHAPTER SEVEN

I'm Hungry, Mom

My thoughts were with Ernie while I descended the elevator and walked out of the building toward Tim's car.

Ernie still looked so frail; I was worried. Yes, he had made improvements, but with no official diagnosis or *reason* for what happened, I felt uncomfortable by the thought that he could just as easily relapse.

I shook my head hoping that this negative thought would leave my mind as I did so. When I reached the parking area, the Triple A tow truck was exiting the lot with my car following behind on two wheels and Elsie and Tim were in the car with the engine running. I cleared my head of what remained of my worrisome thoughts of Ernie. Tonight, would be about Elsie. She needed this closeness with me. With all that happens with Ernie, that puts everyone else's needs on hold, I needed to make certain that she got it.

When I opened the door, I saw that Elsie had parked her bottom in my seat. She looked up at me with an impish grin. "I called shotgun but, umm...you weren't here to hear me soo, um...you lost."

"Get your bum out of my seat and get in the back," I said, trying to look stern.

"No, but Mom!" she argued, not budging her bottom. "I called it and this is my special day—remember?"

I paused, looking down at my smugly smiling child, then shrugged my shoulders. Tim's Miata doesn't have a back seat. It has space for a bag of groceries if you move the front seats up close. Tim had his seat so far forward his knees were touching the steering wheel. Elsie was in an equally uncomfortable position in her seat. I could only be grateful it was a short trip and that Tim would be forced to drive slowly. I climbed into the back and prayed the police wouldn't pull us over for having too many *groceries*.

Tim, who really didn't want to wade too far into this mystery mush, turned around to look at me. He stared for a moment, waiting for an explanation. When I didn't offer anything up, he turned around, shook his head slowly, and backed the car out of the parking lot and headed toward Stop & Shop.

When we finally got home, I took the goodies into the kitchen while Elsie ran to the couch and jumped into my corner. Tim shook his head again and said, "I think I'll just go upstairs and read in bed. Goodnight Elsie. Glad to see you're making a speedy recovery."

"Goodnight, Dad." Elsie responded then added two fake coughs and a moan. "I think I should be better in a day or two."

"Good night darling," Tim said when he came into the kitchen. He embraced me from behind and kissed my cheek. I stopped my duties as popcorn maker and ice cream scooper for a moment and enjoyed the closeness. He held me a little tighter, nuzzled my neck, and whispered, "Mmmm. I love the smell of grease and dirt on a woman."

I shoved him back a bit, hiding my grin, before responding. "Well, *that* would explain your high school girlfriend."

"Ohhh, nice one, He said appreciatively. "I'll have you know she was a real hottie." Tim gave my butt an affectionate swat.

"Ouch! Yeah, well I looked her up on Facebook and you should see your old hottie now."

"Ha. Really?" He wasn't even mildly intrigued. "Okay love. Don't stay up too late you two," he called while he passed the living room.

He trotted upstairs and I got back to my party duties. Tim was so much fun to tease. Normally he took my bait and I could get a rise out of him. But sometimes he just shrugged my barbs off and got all

114

kissy-huggy. Sometimes he fired right back. But mostly he was gentle about teasing and let me have my little victories.

When the popcorn finished doing its thing, I got two bowls out of the cabinet, two spoons from the silverware drawer, and the ice cream scooper. Then I got a big bowl from out of another cabinet and poured the popcorn into it. I saw that I managed to get almost every kernel popped which brought a smile to my face.

Now for the circus act: I hugged the popcorn bowl with my left arm, piled the two ice cream bowls on top of one another, threw the spoons inside the top bowl and cradled the cold ice cream in there as well. Using my chin to help balance everything, I grabbed that pile with my right arm, pushed it against my chest, and headed toward the living room.

When Elsie saw me approach the couch with this display of food and dishes barely balanced in my arms, she went right back to giggling.

"A little help please!" I said when the bowls wobbled. Elsie sat up and reached for the popcorn bowl.

"Noooo!" I panicked. "I got that. Take the bowls and ice cream before I drop them on you."

"Geez, okay Mom," Elsie said. "Don't panic, you got this." She giggled again. Then, she grabbed the bowls containing the spoons and ice cream in two hands and set them on the table in front of the couch. She sat back down. I stood there, still cradling the popcorn bowl, staring at her, plopped in *my* corner of the couch, with *my* comforter still partially wrapped around her.

"No way honey!" I said, shaking my head and putting one hand on my hips for emphasis. Your day is not special enough to take *my* corner of the couch. Move."

"No, no Mom, wait. Okay, so I can squeeze into the corner and you can sit next me, and we can both use the comforter."

"Uh...no." I said firmly. "I will sit in MY corner and *you* can cuddle next to *me* and we can share MY comforter. Now move."

Elsie studied me to see if I would crack. When I didn't, she huffed and moved over. I sighed with delight while I sank into my now-warmed-up-spot. My girl immediately slid closer to me, practically on top of me, and we wrapped ourselves up in the comforter. Two peas in a pod.

Only trouble was, one of the peas needed to dish out the ice cream.

That duty fell to me.

When we each had a bowl of our favorite ice cream in hand, and the big popcorn bowl was safely nestled between us, I grabbed the remote, pulled up Netflix, and ordered a three-movie bundle of Harry Potter. Our special night together began. My little woman-girl and I, faces smeared with ice cream mustaches, were creating a simple, warm memory to stay with us forever.

***

Elsie made it through two Harry Potter movies before she succumbed to sleep. She'd been trying to keep her eyes open for the last hour of *Harry Potter and the Chamber of Secrets*. Even the sugar rush from ice cream couldn't win over her heavy lids.

She slumped onto my lap. I stopped the movie, shut off the TV, and then gently moved her head from my lap and moved her sideways onto the couch.

I stood carefully, cleared the dishes off the table and put them into the kitchen sink. When I came back into the living room, Elsie looked so peaceful. I hated to disturb her, but I knew she would be more comfortable in her own bed.

"Elsie, honey. The movies are over. It's time to go to bed, sweetie."

"Hrmmn —did we see them all?" Came her very sleepy response.

"Almost. We can watch the next one another time."

"Another special day?" She mumbled. Her brain worked fine even if her mouth was a bit slow.

"Maybe just another special hour and a half or so. Come on honey, let's get to bed."

Elsie sat up and swung her legs onto the floor. She collapsed into my shoulder and nuzzled me.

"No, no sleepy head. Time to stand up and get your little legs moving. Come on, let's go." I stood and practically dragged Elsie to her feet. Once up, I took her by the shoulders, turned her toward the stairway, and guided her forward as though she were a wind-up toy.

When I saw her begin to climb the stairs on her own, I went to the front door to check the locks. I turned off all the downstairs lights and made my own lumbering attack on the stairway; I was exhausted too, and my bed was calling to me.

By the time I had arrived at the top of the stairway, Elsie had already made it to her room. From the lack of any light pooling under her doorway, I determined she must have just managed to make it to her bed and throw herself onto it before passing out.

I quietly opened the door to our bedroom expecting to find Tim neatly tucked under the covers, fast asleep. Instead, I found him only half covered in the sheet, with his blanket kicked to the edge of the bed in a lump, and an open book lying across his face. He still had one hand on the book's spine holding it in place.

His bedside light was angled in a way that illuminated only his head. As he breathed out, the book would rise slightly, then return to its previous position when he inhaled. As I watched the rise and fall of this literary moment, I wondered if Tim might think *this* tableau worthy inspiration for a Norman Rockwell.

I contemplated taking a photo with my phone to tease him with later but figured, better let sleeping Tim's lie. I slipped into the bathroom for a quick shower to finally wash off the grime I had collected from my adventure crawling along the underbelly of the truck.

The shower, and my heavenly almond soap, did wonders to relax and prepare me for bed. I slipped my naked, scented body into a pair of my favorite cotton, baggy pajamas, slid into bed carefully without disturbing Tim, and laid my head onto my cool, fluffy pillow. I sighed deeply.

I was ready for what I hoped would be a good night's sleep. Then, Tim began to snore into his book. Not little puffy wisps of air, but big, loud, sitcom-like snores.

Why now? I wondered. Why just when I am at peace and ready to slip away into dreamy sleep?

I sat up. I was determined to remain calm and deal with this. I would not let his snoring take me from my pleasant place. I needed sleep and to be awake and alert the next day for Ernie. No matter what else was going on that night, Ernie was never far from my thoughts.

I decided that if I reached over Tim's body and shut off his light, that might be just enough commotion to wake him naturally –sort of –and cause him to turn on to his side, stop his snoring, and let me to go back to my pillow and the waiting sweet dreams.

I reached over him with my right hand and placed it on the bed beside him and then, turning further inward across his body, I stretched my left arm out and found the switch on his light. Just as I turned it off, Tim tossed his book onto the floor, threw his arms around me, and rolled me over onto my back, landing on top of me.

I was completely taken by surprise and let out some sort of half-screech while my heart raced.

"Gotcha now," Tim said and smiled. He gently took my face in both of his hands, looked into my eyes, and gave me a long, passionate kiss. When he broke the kiss, I tried to speak. I wanted to know if he had lost his mind scaring me like that. But he shushed me before I could get a syllable out, buried his face in my neck and began to give me half kisses, half little bites. I let out a bit of a nervous giggle and, when Tim switched his face to the other side of my neck, I managed to get out my question. "Tim. Tim what are you doing? It's late."

"Elsie had her special day," he murmured. "And now you are going to have your special night."

His mouth was right back on mine covering my lips with insistent kisses. He moved down to the center of my neck and continued to kiss, lick, and nibble me. His right hand found my pajama top buttons. He deftly undid my top and his mouth found first one, then the other breast. He applied the same mix of nibbles and licks and kisses there before he moved on to my nipples.

I gave myself up to him. I stopped thinking or caring about what he was doing or why and I most definitely forgot about peaceful sleep. I closed my eyes, emptied my head of reason, and let the sensations Tim's deft attentions were causing me sweep over me and take me to a much better, pleasant place.

Tim continued his ministrations for what seemed like hours. He did things to my body with his hands and mouth and tongue, I thought he had forgotten how to do. Some were things that he had never done.

I didn't know and I didn't care. I just basked in waves of pleasure and the orgasms that floated to the surface with them. I was inside and outside of my body at the same time. The final, phenomenal release left me contented from my head to my toes and, after letting out one final moan, I curled up into a fetal ball.

Tim pressed in close, next to me, and wrapped his arms around me. I knew instinctually, by the way he held me, he wasn't looking for reciprocation. He really did just want to give me something special.

"I love the smell and taste of almonds even more than grease," Tim teased in a whisper. "And I love you. Sleep tight, babe."

He kissed my cheek and rolled over to his side of the bed to sleep. I think I fell asleep before Tim settled onto his side. It was the best slumber I had had in weeks—maybe months.

When I woke the next morning, and made my usual good morning stretch, I was grinning from ear-to-ear. In fact, I think my entire body was grinning. I sat crossed-legged on my bed, feeling refreshed, alive, and energized; I was ready to take on the world.

Tim had given me two gifts, both of which I treasured. I put this memory into a special keeping place in my head and in my heart. Sometimes, I knew Tim so well, but there were other times, I just couldn't figure him out. This was one of the latter, but I was just going to have to grin and bear it as best I could.

Tim came out of the bathroom freshly showered, shaven, and with a damp towel wrapped around his waist.

"Good morning sleepy head," He greeted me while he headed for the dresser for clean socks and boxers. "Did you have a good night and sleep okay?" He glanced over his shoulder at me with a grin.

"Yeah," I deadpanned. "Yeah, it was okay." I was teasing him, as was my natural response, but by the time I had gotten off the bed and reached the bathroom door, I decided I was feeling something quite different this morning. I poked my head out the bathroom door. "Actually, babe...it was the best sleep ever," I said before slipping back into the bathroom and the shower.

I couldn't see Tim's face, but I imagined he was wearing a very wide grin. He might have had it for a long time, because when I got out of the bathroom and made my way to my underwear draw, he was still smiling.

Tim completed dressing in his gray suit and blue shirt then began to fiddle through his mess of hanging ties draped over a coat hanger after his tie rack broke.

He looked puzzled; ensemble coordination was never his strong suit.

I walked over, took a quick look, and pulled a blue and gray striped tie from the tangled mess. I held the tie up to Tim's face and said, "This one."

He smirked and put it around his neck. He stood for a moment before tying it, looking at me with that strange quirky smile before continuing to work on the tie.

I gave him a raised eyebrow response, shrugged my shoulders, and went to my closet to pick out my ensemble for the day.

I reached for my black skirt, from my office work days, when it hit me why Tim had looked at me the way he did. I hadn't put on my exercise bra and non-descript "daily" panties. Without any thought,

I had chosen a matching set of turquoise panties and bra from my Victoria's secret collection.

I was also about to put on my "professional woman" attire rather than my usual soccer mom outfit.

Wow I thought. *Is this left over from last night? Just exactly what had Tim touched?*

My cheeks flushed. Whatever drove this morning's empowered, desirable-woman feeling–no matter how fleeting it might be–I was going to see it through, make the most of this day, and revel in how it felt.

By the time I finished dressing and made my way down to the kitchen, Tim was pouring a bowl of cereal for himself and Elsie, who, to my surprise, was dressed and raring to go.

"Well, good morning!" I said, pulling out a chair and sitting at the table. "What got you up so early?"

"Hi Mom. Um…it's 7:30 and I go to school this early *every* day."

"Oh, so you're going to school then?"

Elsie shot me a look and then glanced at her dad.

Cough, cough, choke. Elsie said, "Um…no Mom; on second thought I couldn't possibly make it to school today."

"Oh, don't you hate it when those migraines get into your throat and sinuses like that?" Tim mocked. He sucked down a spoonful of Cheerios. Elsie giggled. I thought, *Oh God, not another day of Miss Gigglepuss.*

"So, why *are* you up so early?" I persisted.

"I'm going with you to see Ernie," Elsie announced.

"I'm going to take you guys there and spend the morning with you and then go to work. They should have your car ready and bring it to you at the hospital before noon," Tim added in between spoonful's of cereal.

He got up to get another bowl and plunked it down in front of me. He nodded at the cereal box. "Here, breakfast of champions."

"Um...thanks. But that's Wheaties."

"Huh?"

"The breakfast of champions is the Wheaties slogan not Cheerios," I said.

"Oh. Really? Huh. So, what's Cheerios then?"

With perfect timing, Elsie and I responded in unison. "Breakfast of Fatties."

We looked at each other and giggled at our shared cleverness. Yep, it was going to be another day with Miss Gigglepuss, egged on by me.

"Well," Tim interrupted, "Eat up you two, so I have company."

"Yeah Elsie, have another bowl," I threw at Elsie as I watched her over-stuffed mouth expel milk down her chin. "I think I'll wait and get coffee at the hospital. Or no, we can go through the Starbucks drive-thru on the way."

"Good idea," Tim said. "I can get coffee too."

"Awesome! And I can get a Chai Tea with whipped cream!" Elsie beamed.

"No," I said, shaking my head. "You can get an orange juice because we are out of it, and also because you had enough sugar yesterday to last a week." I responded with a matter-of-fact tone that left no wiggle room for argument.

With the breakfast routine finished, we packed into Tim's car, me in my normal "shotgun" seat and Elsie in the back, headed for Starbuck's and then on to the hospital.

The closer we got to the hospital, the quieter we were. We each had enjoyed our special night, and we were now back to the uncertain reality of what was happening to Ernie; and the question, *Would he be out of ICU and coming home soon?*

***

When we got to the ICU waiting area, several people were there already, taking up most of the seats. Elsie and Tim leaned against a wall while I went to the nurse's station to ask about Ernie. Belinda was back on duty and greeted me with a warm smile.

"Hi June," she said. "How are you?"

"Hi Belinda. Well, I'm good if Ernie is?" I responded hopefully.

"He is," she said, "But he is not here. We moved him this morning to a regular room, semi-private. His breathing is normal, vitals are good, and his kidneys seem to be functioning...one is lagging a bit, but we think this is temporary."

"Oh my gosh that's great news Belinda. Thank you!" I nearly gushed all over her I was so relieved and appreciative."

"Best news is, he's awake and hungry," Belinda's words lit up my heart.

"He's awake? Oh my—yes, hunger is a great sign. Nothing rules Ernie like his stomach. Can he eat? Can we get something and bring it to him?"

"Well. He is still weak and because of his potential head trauma and his kidneys still lagging a bit, we are limiting food to liquids and intravenous feeding for now. But check with the attending doctor and nurse and see when he might be able to try some real food."

"Oh okay. Poor little guy probably won't like that. He'll be begging me for IHOP pancakes."

Belinda smiled. "I'll take you down to meet his doctor. I'll have to rush right back up here—we had a couple of overnight bad cases and are pretty swamped this morning."

"Okay, yeah. I saw the waiting area was pretty full. Tim and Elsie are just around the corner, so we can get them on our way to Ernie."

"Great!" she said. "Follow me."

Belinda headed toward the elevators, I trailed behind her, slowing only to wave at Tim and Elsie to follow. They caught up at the elevator. I explained that Ernie was out of the ICU and in a room on another floor, and repeated what Belinda had told me about his condition. I could see relief in both their faces as they listened to the report.

When we reached the second floor, Belinda led us into a hallway and veered left toward the patient rooms and the nurse's station. We stopped while Belinda spoke to a nurse and then turned her attention to the three of us.

"The doctor is with another patient, but I'm going to see if I can get her attention and bring her out," she said. "Ernie is in room 217 which is down the hall and to your left. Why don't you go in to see Ernie and I'll bring the doctor to you."

"Yes. Good. Cool." Came the chorus of responses from our little huddled group. We went immediately in search of room 217 while Belinda headed off to find Ernie's doctor.

Being in a semi-private room meant that Ernie could have a roommate. It also meant that we could not go rushing in and be loud. Well, we failed miserably. We were so excited to see him that we just rushed to his side without thinking. I was particularly comforted when I saw that nearly all the machines were gone and tubes removed from Ernie's body. He still had a saline bag attached and monitors for his vitals, but nothing else.

Ernie was sitting up, propped by pillows when we walked in. The TV was on. Elsie, being the quickest of the three of us, got to his side first, sat on his bed and gave him a big hug.

"So, bro, like lookin' pretty good there." She said in her *cool sister* imitation as she wiped away a tear. "Thanks, Else. I'm hungry."

Tim was next to reach Ernie. I lagged behind to take in the room and compose myself.

"Hey big guy. You gave us a bit of a scare there buddy." Tim kissed Ernie's forehead. "Nice to see you awake. You ready to get out of this joint?"

"Yeah, Dad. I'm hungry."

Tim moved aside to make room for me as I approached to sit on Ernie's bed. I leaned forward, gave him a hug, and held him. I lost my composure and the tears flowed. When we separated, I had streams of dark, zagged mascara lines running down my cheeks. Ernie teared up too.

"Oh honey, I am sooooo happy to see you." I grabbed him again. Tim offered me a handkerchief over my shoulder and I used it first to wipe Ernie's eyes and then my own. I put the handkerchief to Ernie's nose and said, "blow." Ernie, as weak as he was and as emotional as he was to see us, steadied himself against my motherly intervention. "I don't blow Mom."

That sent Elsie into hysterics. "God, I hope not little brother!"

Ernie laughed too. They had their own communication wave-length that had developed the older Ernie got. Tim and I looked at each other with mirrored smirked faces.

"Mom. I'm hungry." Ernie broke in with his now familiar theme. "All they give is ginnygerale and Jello. And I can smell bacon cooking!"

"I know honey. I'm sorry," I said. "But the doctor said you can't have real food yet. But soon. When they let you out."

"And then we can go to IHOP and get two breakfast for me?"

"Yeah buddy, then we will go to IHOP and eat them out of pancakes," Tim promised.

"And eggs and bacon," Ernie added.

"And eggs and bacon," Tim agreed.

"Can I come too?" Elsie asked. "'Cause all I ever get for breakfast is Cheerios." Ernie laughed and Tim and I just looked at her. "I'm just sayin' Mom. Would be a nice change."

I turned my attention back to Ernie. "How do you feel honey, other than being hungry?" I felt his forehead for fever. "You look really good."

Okay, so I told a little motherly lie. He looked pale and weak and so very thin, even though he had only been in here two days. But compared to how he had looked when all the machines were hooked up to him just yesterday, he appeared great.

"I'm tired Mom. Head hurts a little bit. And those places where tube things were. And I'm hungry." He said again with an impish grin.

"Wow, okay bro. We get the hungry part already." Elsie rolled her eyes.

"That's your boy Tim. Doesn't fall far from the tree." I teased nodding at Tim's slight paunch.

Belinda walked in while we were enjoying the light moment. "Well, I see you are all doing pretty good." Then she looked toward my daughter. "You must be Elsie?"

Elsie nodded her head, acknowledging that Belinda got her name right. "Elsie, why don't you keep your brother company while your parents step out to talk with the doctor for a moment?"

"Okay." Elsie moved away from Belinda. "Oh hey, Mom. Can you come here first?" Elsie was trying to be secretive.

"What Elsie? I don't want to keep the doctor waiting."

"Can I have some money?" She whispered in my ear. "I want to go down to the gift shop and get Ernie some balloons."

"Oh," I said, a little surprised that it wasn't vending machines loot she was after. "Yeah. Good idea. But don't take too long away from Ernie." I turned to Tim. "Tim, give Elsie some money, please."

Tim thought for a brief moment, then reached for his wallet and pulled out a ten-dollar bill and handed it to Elsie. Elsie stared at him with her palm up holding the money. Tim, familiar with this routine, opened his wallet again and fished out a $20 bill to add to Elsie's begging hand. Satisfied, Elsie turned to Ernie and said, "Back in five bro." And she was off, rushing past Tim and me and nearly knocking Belinda over when she ran out the door with a whoosh.

"Guess she's on a mission," Belinda said. She led Tim and me toward the nurse's station. We headed slightly past the reception desk and toward the back where there was a small office/meeting room.

The room was packed with boxes of files, surrounding a little round table with two chairs. A doctor sat in one and rose to meet us as we entered. She was a smallish woman who appeared to be Indian. She had a stern face with a studied look that was impossible to read. We all squeezed into the room while Belinda made introductions.

"Tim, June, this is Dr. Chawla," Belinda introduced us. "She is in charge of Ernie's care here. Dr. Chawla, these are the Gallaghers."

"Hello Mr. and Mrs. Gallagher," Dr. Chawla said. She didn't offer her hand for us to shake but got right to business. "I have news about Ernie, then you may ask your questions."

"Ernie had an issue of what we call MODS," she said matter-of-factly. "Multiple Organ Dysfunction Syndrome. His heartbeat was erratic and stopped for a few seconds. His brain activity was not normal, thus causing his seizure. His breathing slowed and then stopped. He is also suffering from kidney failure. This is most unusual and concerning because these symptoms all happened nearly at the same time. We have stabilized most of the conditions and believe his kidney function has returned, but we are still monitoring that."

Tim and I stood there, dumbfounded through all of this explanation. We had no idea of the extent of what Ernie was going through and had never heard of MODS. Somewhere in the doctor's summation was the good news that most of Ernie's condition had been stabilized, and that there was hope his kidney function had returned as well.

But we now had questions that went beyond how Ernie is to why this happened. Tim jumped in first. "Dr. Chawla. What is MODS? And is Ernie going to be okay?"

"Yes," the doctor responded, folding her manicured hands in front of her. "We believe he will continue to improve, but we will keep him here for a few days or more–depending on his kidney function. We have moved him out of the ICU and he will remain in his current room if all continues as it is. It is really astonishing that his recovery has been almost as fast as his body's breakdown. This is most unusual, but not completely unheard of."

"Oh I see," he said, although I could tell he didn't really, and neither did I." So, this MODS is it?" The doctor nodded in affirmation. "Is this the disease Ernie has that he has suffered from for years? We have never had an actual diagnosis before and we haven't known how to treat him or who specializes in this disease…this is the first we have heard about anything approaching a reason for Ernie's illnesses."

"No," Dr. Chawla said. "MODS is not the cause of his conditions or what I have seen in looking at his records. It is the result of something else."

My turn to pipe in.

"What something else?" I asked shifting my weight from one leg to the other. "Every time something happens to Ernie there is another *maybe it is this* or *maybe it is that* or *Ernie will outgrow it*…there has even been a suggestion that Ernie was poisoned somehow."

My last statement drew a change in Dr. Chawla's expression for the first time. She looked taken aback –like my great aunt about to give me one of her "tsk tsks" after an exaggerated story I told as a child.

"I cannot say for certain," she said cautiously, "but I believe his issues stem from a molecular disorder of some sort–an abnormality in his DNA or the mitochondrial DNA or such. That is why so many different illnesses have appeared and why some have happened all at one time."

Now it was our turn to be taken aback. Tim and I looked at each other, each with our own quizzical expression etched across our faces. We didn't know exactly what the doctor meant, but we did know that she was offering something no one else had ventured. To us laypersons, it sounded plausible because she was at least proffering something that *she* deemed logical and potentially definable. Something we might investigate further. Dr. Chawla continued.

"This is not my field, but I do have a recommendation for you. Dr.

Blackwell is new here at the hospital. She is a medical geneticist and a pediatrician. Belinda will give you her contact information. I think it is best that you wait until we have your son ready to be released, then you can see Dr. Blackwell as an outpatient if there are no more immediate complications. I must go now."

She looked at us as if to give us one more chance to ask questions. When we didn't say anything, Dr. Chawla left the room.

That left Belinda to fill in details about Ernie and to get us Dr. Blackwell's information. And, it left Tim and me to wonder if we were finally headed in a direction that would lead to answers about why our son kept getting sick.

"I'm going to write down Dr. Blackwell's number for you," she said. "Then, you might as well go back in with Ernie. I'm certain that the more alert he is, the more bored he will be with this place–although he may just fall asleep without much warning."

"Oh yes. That would be great," I said. "And you're right. He will get very anxious about going home. And going to IHOP." After Belinda handed me the phone number, I continued. "What happens next with Ernie?"

"Well, it looks like the plan is to keep him here a couple more days to make certain everything functions normally. Then you can take him home. He will likely still be too weak for school for another week or so, you might want to make arrangements for homework."

"Okay, good idea," I said. "Thanks Belinda." Belinda left us. Tim and I went back to Ernie's room.

Ernie's eyes were closed when Tim and I returned to his room, but as soon as we got near the bed, and I resumed my sitting position, he opened them and gave us a smile. The TV was still on and tuned to the weather channel. Ernie liked to watch the weather reports and especially any natural disasters like hurricanes or tornadoes. It wasn't that he liked to see destruction or loss of life or anything morbid like that, he was just in awe of the power of nature and how little control man had over it.

"Hey big guy," Tim said. "Now that I know how great you're doing, Daddy has to get to work. Will that be okay? I'll leave work early and come see you again before the end of the day, okay?"

"Yeah okay Dad. Elsie and Mom keep company me. And get me something to eat." Ernie giggled.

"Yeah okay buddy. Good luck with that part. Love you. See ya later today." Tim then kissed Ernie on the forehead and turned to leave. He stood for a bit and stared at me with a questioning expression before he headed for the door.

"Tim, wait." I called to him as I rose from Ernie's bed. "Honey, I'll be right back. I just want to say goodbye to Daddy." I told Ernie before following Tim out the door.

"Hey, what's up? You have been in an odd mood since yesterday. Nice, but odd." I questioned Tim gently.

"Nothing, I'm fine," Tim said. "Just happy Ernie is doing so much better is all."

"Tim. I get that you are relieved as we all are, but I know you. Something else is going on."

Tim gave me his shy, little boy grin before answering. "Well, I didn't want to say anything yesterday because it was Elsie's Big Day–which by the way, no one has yet told me why. And today, all we could think about was Ernie. So…no biggy, but there hasn't really been an opportunity to tell you that we signed that big client we have been working on for months."

"Oh my God Tim, that is great news." I gushed as I gave him a big hug which took him a bit by surprise. In his mind, he must have downplayed the whole thing as it took second and third place to everything else that was happening around him at home. I felt a bit sad for him that he couldn't just have walked in the door after work, made his announcement and celebrated with his family.

"Tim, I am so proud of you, honey. You worked really, really hard on this and I know it means a lot to you and to the firm and well, to us."

"Yeah, and to the hospital bills we should be getting soon," Tim offered sarcastically.

"Well yeah, them too, silly man. But hey, tonight, when you get home, you and I and Elsie are going to celebrate with champagne." I said beaming. "And who knows, maybe it will be *your* 'special night'." I said with a wink and a tone that dripped with sexual innuendo.

"Haha...ha well, in that case, I am definitely leaving work early." Tim closed the conversation with that and a kiss on my cheek. Then he turned and walked out of the room putting on his overdone sexy man walk for my benefit, which made me laugh. I watched him all the way to the elevators to see if he would keep up the walk even though strangers might see him. He did. That made me turn red and laugh harder.

When the elevator doors opened, Elsie poured out nearly running over her dad.

"Ohhh, hi Dad. Bye Dad. See ya later." She said loudly as she continued her uninterrupted journey, flying past me, and back to Ernie's room. Tim held out his hand palm up as if expecting Elsie to come back and turn over some change from his thirty dollars. Her trip to the gift shop was apparently so fruitful that she had spent the entire amount. The elevator doors closed Tim inside, empty-handed.

I stood there feeling proud of my Tim. Proud of his accomplishment. Proud of how he handled his responsibility as the main provider for his family since I couldn't really work much lately. Mostly, I was proud of how unselfish he is and the wonderful dad and husband he turned out to be. In that moment, life felt good. Then I thought about his sexy walk and laughed again.

My little moment was interrupted by Elsie's loud giggling accompanied by Ernie's weaker but just as enthusiastic giggling. I was grateful that Ernie didn't have a roommate. I was also eager to see to see what Elsie had bought with Tim's $30. The last time Tim forked over money to Elsie and sent her on a shopping spree, she practically emptied the vending machines and returned with an armful of junk food. I hurried inside to witness Ernie taking inventory of each item

Elsie presented to him. Laid out on Ernie's bed, was a hoard of silliness that consisted of stuffed animals, greeting cards, slippers, an empty photo frame, a metal mini license plate that said *Ernie*, and bubble gum. I was actually amazed that she could get so much stuff for only $30. I figured she would buy one of those mylar balloons that said get well Ernie or some such thing and that would be it.

Elsie presented each item to Ernie, one at a time, with an explanation of what they were for or why he needed them. I came in during the slippers presentation. What I missed, I later learned, was the presentation of the larger stuffed animal. It was a kangaroo with a small pouch in the front. Elsie had stuffed a snickers bar into the pouch while I was still outside the room. "Quick", she told Ernie. This is for later, so put it away before Mom comes back." She later confessed to me.

When she presented the slippers, she told Ernie, "Okay so, you know you're going to have to get up to pee eventually so, yeah, these will keep your feet from getting cold and dirty from walking on this icky floor." They looked like the cheap free slippers hospitals sometimes give you, but Ernie thought they were the cat's pajamas.

"Okay, so this frame is for my picture," Elsie continued, "so you have me with you, ya know. I'll bring a photo back later or tomorrow and put it in for you. This license plate thing is to put on your door at home in case you forget which room is yours—or something like that. And this card was my favorite one. See the bunnies? Okay, I'll read it to you first then you can read it."

And on it went. Elsie demonstrating each little gift with her explanation and Ernie hanging on her every word and giggling with each presentation. The whole affair took only 20 minutes but by the end of it, I could see Ernie was tiring. His energy became suddenly drained and he got quiet.

"Elsie honey," I said gently. "I think Ernie needs to take a nap now. We should let him rest a bit."

Ernie tried to perk up and keep us from leaving. "No, Mom I am waked. Really." He said trying to overcome the heaviness in his eyelids and beat the drowsiness that was settling in.

"I know, honey. But really you should get some rest. Elsie and I will still be here when you wake up. We won't go too far. I promise. Elsie, let Ernie have two of his gifts and put the rest in the bag for him to have at home. There isn't any room on the little table and we don't want them to get lost."

Ernie chose the kangaroo, with the hidden Snickers bar, and the empty picture frame which made Elsie smile. "Picture tomorrow Else," Ernie said pointing to the empty frame.

"Oh yeah, you got it, bro. Most important thing." She was all seriousness as she piled the rest of Ernie's loot into the gift store bag.

I kissed Ernie's forehead. "Love you honey. And so happy you are doing better. You rest so you can get even stronger and we can take you home okay?"

"K, Mom."

Elsie and I stopped to look back at Ernie before we left the room. His eyes were closed, and his rhythmic breathing told me he had already drifted into sleep.

CHAPTER EIGHT

AN IMPORTANT NEW FRIENDSHIP

As it turned out, Ernie only remained in the hospital for another two days. Elsie went back to her school schedule and Tim to his work routine, but on weekends, we all spent as much time as possible entertaining Ernie.

His strength improved each day and when he was finally released, his kidneys were in perfect working order, and all his vitals were in the normal range. He did have one slight episode of vomiting during the first day in his semi-private room. Apparently, he ate some kind of solid food that was too much too soon to agree with his sensitive stomach. When confronted with what he ate, Ernie was stoic in his refusal to spill the beans. Elsie, when questioned, simply snickered.

When we got Ernie home, though he had improved tremendously, he was still too weak to go back to school. He could get out of bed and come downstairs to eat or watch TV and made an occasional trip to a store with me. But taking on the regular routine of school and friends and staying alert during class was still too much.

A week after he came home was Halloween. I knew he would fight to go out and 'trick or treat' with his friends and I just couldn't take that away from him. I agreed to let him go but limited his efforts to a five-block radius—I figured that was far enough to gather candy to last a week.

Elsie was teetering on being too old and too cool for trick or treating, but she didn't want to disappoint Ernie either. And, I suspect she saw having to "go with her brother", as an excuse to get one more

Halloween under her belt, before it became completely passé.

Elsie went as a pirate and Ernie was a fluffy yellow cat. We had to go to three different costumes shops to find what Ernie wanted. But, it was worth it to see how pleased he was when he put the costume on. They had a great time and got a lot of candy.

Tim and I helped ourselves to a couple of Hershey's bars. After that, Ernie took his bag of goodies to bed with him to keep an eye on it. Elsie, who was more of an ice-cream and popcorn person said, "Go ahead fatties," and left her bag with us.

Ernie had already missed an entire week of school; and as he recovered further, it was obvious he would miss at least one more. I visited his teacher to get all of his assignments and to make arrangements for weekly lesson plans. If needed, we were prepared to hire a tutor to come to the house and keep Ernie on track with his school work. We were determined not to have to keep him back another grade or have him feel disadvantaged when he did return to class.

Tim was right when he sarcastically predicted that hospital bills would come after landing the big client. They started arriving soon after Ernie's release. And then they came some more.

They were in the thousands of dollars. As comprehensive as Tim's insurance was, it would cover only a portion of the total costs. That left us to pay several thousand dollars' worth of charges on our own. And we still had to take Ernie to this new specialist, which likely would involve more exotic tests and expenses.

This meant that Tim's earnings from the new client would be mostly eaten up by bills and not put aside for college tuitions as we had hoped.

But I counted our blessings—we were fortunate to be able to get through this financially when many families would not. It meant some belt-tightening; no family summer vacation to Disney World as we had promised, no new car to replace my aging Jeep, and no other luxury purchases.

We curbed dining out, gym memberships, and clothes shopping

that was not a necessity for the kids. We were determined to not dip into our savings or retirement accounts unless absolutely necessary.

We knew that we could approach Tim's parents in an emergency. They lived comfortably and could afford to help out. But that would be an absolute last resort.

At the time, his parents were traveling Europe and didn't know about Ernie's recent hospital stay. They were also mostly absent during all of Elsie and Ernie's lives. We would get phone calls asking how the kids are, birthday cards and presents or money for the kids, phone calls asking if Ernie was okay, and once a year, an actual visit from them. But they were hardly candidates for the world's best grandparents and I resented them for that.

Because I lost my mother who would have adored Ernie and Elsie and insisted on being in their lives, I was particularly sensitive to the lack of interest Tim's parents seemed to have in their grandchildren. In his own childhood, Tim had experienced a similar detachment from his parents. He merely said that this is their way, and this is how they are. But he believed that we could count on them when needed. I preferred to make certain that we didn't "need."

On the second Saturday he was home, Ernie came bouncing down the stairs. He was dressed in jeans, a t-shirt and sweatshirt, and he displayed an unusual amount of energy. Elsie, was up suspiciously early for a Saturday. She had to "study" at a friend's house. I remembered having some of those emergency study sessions with friends. I hoped hers were as innocent as mine.

I was accustomed to Ernie coming downstairs slowly, wearing his pajamas, and sitting at the kitchen table expecting me to wait on him and offer a variety of breakfast choices from eggs to cereal.

But on this particular Saturday morning, he energetically strode into the kitchen and went straight to the refrigerator. He grabbed two eggs, milk, and the bacon package and placed them on the countertop. With a slight smile he turned to me and said, "Breakfast Mom. Please."

Then he returned to the refrigerator, grabbed the orange juice and set it on the kitchen table. He got a napkin, fork, and a glass and set them on the table, then plopped into his regular seat and poured a glass of juice.

I watched with astonishment. I stared at him as though he had two heads. He gave me a huge toothy grin and then gulped down half the glass of juice.

"Are you okay Ernie?" I had to ask. "Yep. Just hungry."

"Okay honey. That is a lot of breakfast considering how little you have been able to eat since you got out of the hospital. Are you sure you want to have eggs and bacon? I don't want you to get sick, honey."

"Sure Mom. I like eggs and bacon."

"Yeah right. Okay. Two eggs and bacon coming right up." I said giving in to his request. I should have been accustomed to Ernie's energy swings. Through the years, I had seen this before where he would be tired one day or for several days, barely able to function, and the next day telling me about his soccer game with kids at gym. But this was such a distinct and stark change—it was almost alarming.

"Scrambledid eggs Mom. Not the eggs with the juicy eyes." Ernie reminded me referring to over easy fried eggs, which he did not like.

"Aye, Aye Sir." I gave a mock salute. Then I went about the business of making Ernie's breakfast. It was a labor of love, really. Ernie's upbeat mood had infected me too; while I prepared his bacon and "scrambledid" eggs, I hummed.

Then I began to sing. John Lennon's *Beautiful Boy* from Mr. Holland's Opus. I didn't know all the words but when I got to a few I did know, I sang them loud and directed my attention to Ernie. "Life is what happens to you when you're busy making other plans, beautiful, beautiful, beautiful, beautiful boy; beautiful, beautiful, beautiful, beautiful Ernie."

Ernie loved my attention, if not my singing voice. He laughed and made a goofy face each time I turned his way.

This was another one of those life moments that is too precious to share with someone outside; it might be tossed off as, "Oh that's funny," or "Oh that's sweet," and then forgotten. It was nothing that would change the outcome of anyone's life.

But I remember, during one of my turns to sing to Ernie, making a deliberate pause to memorize his face–and this morning, I made a little mental movie to play later. When and why, I wouldn't know for some time.

Ernie finished his breakfast and plopped himself in the living room to watch TV before his tutor, Charlotte Brown, arrived. She would be there at 9:30 which gave Ernie just 30 minutes of TV time.

I disappeared upstairs to finish dressing. I didn't put on the business attire of the other day, but I did choose a pair of brown slacks and nice cream blouse–no gym outfit–but no "Secret" underneath either. The doorbell rang as I made my way downstairs.

"I'll get it!" I shouted, thinking that it would be Charlotte a bit early. When I opened the door, I was surprised to see Elizabeth, the aggressive reporter and woman who had asked about Ernie while I was shopping.

"Oh!" I gasped in surprise. "Sorry. I thought you were my son's tutor."

"For your son's sake, I hope not." Elizabeth quipped. She had the same pleasantness to her demeanor that she had at the store when she asked about Ernie's health. "It's just me, Elizabeth, the nosey reporter who tried to grill you after the car accident incident."

"Yeah. Yes," I said wanting to be a bit more proper and on my guard. "I remember you –from the Crate & Barrel." I decided she deserved that nicer reference.

"I wanted to talk to you about a feature I am filming. Before you slam the door in my face, look around." She turned and gestured to my empty yard and driveway. "See? No cameras, no crew waiting to pounce. Just me, talking to you."

I hesitated. Elizabeth was being a different kind of aggressive– conciliatory and somewhat self-deprecating. I was still on guard, but there was something about her approach—and about *her*—that was warming me up.

"Well, my son's tutor is coming soon, but you can come in and we can talk in the kitchen." I offered as I held the door open wider.

Elizabeth stepped in and waited while I closed the door behind her. I turned and led her toward the kitchen. Ernie had already hopped off the couch and met us in the living room. He thought it was his tutor. He and Charlotte had been working together over the past two weeks. Ernie was very fond of her; I think he considered her as much a play pal/friend as he did tutor. He was disappointed when he saw Elizabeth.

"Well, hello there. You must be Ernie?" Elizabeth inquired as she squatted her 5'7 frame to get closer to eye level.

"Yes. You not Karlote. Okay. Bye." Ernie bluntly replied then retreated to the living room.

Elizabeth followed me into the kitchen, grinning from her encounter with Ernie.

"My gosh, he is adorable," she said. "And what a card! I would hate to interview him—he's all business."

"Yeah he's—he's special."

"He looks like he's doing well?" Elizabeth half asked, half stated.

"He has his days," I said as we awkwardly stood facing each other.

"Today he's full of energy. Coffee?" I was being gracious but also changing the conversation away from Ernie and his health status. I wasn't prepared to invite this stranger into my family's personal details.

"Coffee. Yes. Thanks. Black, please." I gestured to the far end of the table and Elizabeth took a seat.

"My husband makes the coffee at 7 am and he makes it like espresso," I warned. "I strongly suggest you consider adding milk."

"I like it strong, so no worries there," Elizabeth assured.

I poured each of us a cup of coffee, leaving room in mine for milk. I grabbed the milk from the fridge, stirred some into my cup and then set the carton on the table, along with our coffees. I took the seat opposite Elizabeth and continued to swirl my coffee.

She got right to it.

"Listen, June," She wrapped her hands around the mug. "I know our first encounter was a bit terse and I was that annoying person from the press. But that's my job—sort of people want to know about other people—especially those of our neighbors who do extraordinary things.

"And, like it or not, what you did last month was extraordinary And, whether you consider yourself a hero or not, what you did was heroic. Other people determine who is a hero; it isn't a title you give yourself.

"We look at people's actions, who, moments before they acted, are just like everyone else. And we see someone we want to be; we hope we could be. But somewhere in us is that little bit of doubt. As people, we have to say *'bravo!'* to those who overcome their doubt and risk their own safety to help a complete stranger."

Elizabeth was on a roll. She stopped momentarily, to take a large sip of coffee.

"And when people...Oh my *Gawd!*" She nearly spit the coffee onto the table. "That is...wow that is really..."

"Awful?" I offered. I slid the milk and my spoon across the table to Elizabeth. She looked at me.

"No. I have had awful before. This is way beyond that." She laughed while smothering her coffee with as much milk as she could fit. I laughed and offered, "Sugar?"

"Oh my God yes. Please," Elizabeth replied. We kept laughing while I went to get the sugar bowl.

And there it was.

That moment when a friendship is born. Not when it becomes a solid relationship, but the time that you remember when it began. Something I had read before came to mind out of nowhere. Part of a Ray Bradbury quote: "We cannot tell the precise moment when friendship is formed. As in filling a vessel drop by drop, there is at last a drop which makes it run over..."

For Elizabeth and me, those drops in the vessel were nearly as literal as they were metaphorical.

I brought the sugar bowl and set it in front of her. When I sat down, I took a chair closer to her so that we wouldn't have as much of a barrier between us. I was relaxed now and genuinely smiling–we both were.

"Okay," Elizabeth started over. "I get it. You hate this hero crap and exposing yourself and your family to strangers. I really do get it. And I'll leave it alone after this–but hear me out. Personally, I am just really, really intrigued by what makes ordinary people act in very unselfish ways. See how I avoided the hero word? People in general have the same or similar fascination. We want to know how this person came to that place, why they did what they did, and how it affected them. And on the other side, we are all curious to know how their behavior influenced the people or person they helped. As a journalist, I want to explore this and share what I find with others. It's, well–this is just good stuff."

"Ugh." I grimaced. "Okay. I understand all that. But what would this involve IF I said okay? What do I have to do? And I must have ground rules that can't be ignored."

"Ok," Elizabeth said, leaning forward in excitement. "All you have to do is spend a few hours with me–maybe three times–and just answer questions. *I'll* bring the coffee."

"Hmmm." I thought about it and drummed my fingers on the table. "Two things. No, three. One–my family and especially my kids stay out of it. Two, don't make me sound like a hero or anything uncomfortable like that. Three, make it cappuccino. AND, I will talk it over with my husband Tim and see what he thinks too."

"I can do all of that," Elizabeth flashed a megawatt smile. "Can we just have the background that you have two kids and a husband–just as background descriptions, no deep dive? I will stick to the facts of what happened and how it affected you. So, some personal feelings *do* need to come into it. But I don't even need to use your full name."

"I guess that's okay. I don't know how much of it I remember exactly. It was just a month ago, but it seems like ages now. And I really don't want the local press to dredge this up again. What are you going to *do* with this interview?"

"No local press. You and I will just talk, no one else around. You can take your time remembering things. I'll be honest, some of this might be difficult to recall–the scene and everything–but I need you to trust me that I will go easy and be a shoulder when you need one. I'll submit the interview to a major network and hope to get my foot in the door as a big-time reporter. It's a huge job opportunity for me to go from a small town into a bigger market. I have gone as far as I can with the local station. Oh, and there are three people I will interview including you, so you won't be alone in the piece."

"Yeah, bringing all this back up is not a pleasant idea to me," I said honestly. "The only person I talked about all of this with is my husband, Tim. I'm not certain about reliving this–so just know that I might not do it after all. I really do need to talk with Tim and think about this before I make any decision. I really would like to help you–make up for serving you that coffee at the very least–though in my defense, I did try to warn you."

"Oh yes, you definitely owe me for that. I really do understand your concerns." She pushed her half full cup of coffee away from her. "Well, I should get back to the office. Time to prepare for tonight's broadcast." She rose.

"Okay." I rose from the table. "And I will let you know one way or the other by the end of the week if that works?"

"Yep, that's great. You have my number?" "Yeah, surprisingly, I kept your card."

"Oh, I *am* impressed."

"In case I needed something to wrap my chewed gum in." I couldn't help myself. As soon as the words came out, I wondered if I had assumed too much about the feeling of growing friendship.

"Don't worry, I have 500 more," Elizabeth replied dryly. She handed me two more. "Just in case." She smiled, and we walked toward the front door.

When I opened the door to see Elizabeth out, there stood Ernie's tutor. Her hand was raised, index finger pointing toward the doorbell. She jumped and clutched her chest making an audible "Shit" as she did so. Elizabeth and I looked at each other with big smiles while Charlotte stood there with an expression of embarrassment.

"Sorry, Mrs. G!" Charlotte said. She was 17, serious, and the top student in her high school. With Ernie, Charlotte could act serious or silly, depending on the situation. She seemed more herself–more like a normal teen ager. But using swear words–especially in front of grownups–was strictly against her persona.

"It's okay Charlotte," I said, still laughing. "We gave you quite a scare. Ernie is in the living room pretending to watch TV but anxiously awaiting your arrival. And there's juice and soda in the fridge, so help yourself." I added as Charlotte passed Elizabeth and me on her way to the living room.

"There's coffee too," Elizabeth chimed in with a guilty smirk on her face.

After saying goodbye again, she headed toward the street and her car. Humor is something that can bond me to someone quickly, more than any other single trait, I think. And sarcasm is my downfall. I liked Elizabeth for sharing those traits with me.

Ernie and Charlotte got right to studying after Ernie gallantly brought a glass of juice for her. I think Ernie had a little crush on his tutor. It's sweet; I didn't tease him about it or suggest it to anyone else, especially Elsie. Although she loved her brother, she would certainly have busted his chops about it.

I went to my office nook in a corner off the dining room and set about doing the books for one of the few clients that remained in my care–a bowling alley. One perk they offered was coupons for free games and shoe rentals on any Tuesday night for my entire family.

I opened my client's file and thought about this added benefit. I sighed and thought, *So, this is what it's come down to. From art gallery opening invites and free theater tickets, to Tuesday night bowling coupons. I've arrived.*

I felt a bit snobbish to think that way. The bowling alley was a big deal to the owner, and to him, his books were just as important as any big client. His gesture of bowling coupons was kind and generous. Still...it was *bowling*!

After those thoughts cleared my head, I shrugged my shoulders and got to work on my client's books. In the background, I could hear Charlotte giving Ernie lessons in math accompanied by serious discussions about fractions and factors, interspersed with a few giggles.

Time slipped by before I realized how long I had been sitting at the computer. Charlotte stood at the entryway to the dining room saying goodbye to me.

"Oh my gosh Charlotte! Is it time already?"

"Yes, Mrs. G, it's noon. I would stay later but my mom and I are going to lunch and making plans about college visits. And I think Ernie is starting to droop a bit."

"Oh right. Yes, he is probably all fractioned out." I smiled.

"Well, we were doing *grammar* just now." Charlotte responded in her factual manner. I think that quality might be what drew her to Ernie.

"So...do you have colleges picked out to visit already? This is such an exciting time for you and you are such a smart girl–you'll probably have your choice of schools." She waited while I wrote a check for her tutoring time.

"Not exactly. That's why my mom and I are having lunch. The competition for top schools is pretty tight even with *my* grades and scores. Being accepted also depends on my essay, which has to be compelling…and whether I can get a full scholarship or a partial scholarship. A lot goes into the whole process and I may only get one offer–you never know."

"Right." I stood and handed Charlotte the check. "Well, good luck with it all. I can write a recommendation if you need one." I offered, feeling a bit inadequate about suggesting that a mostly stay-at-home mom reference would be valuable.

"That would be great Mrs. G.," she said. "I *am* including all my community outreach efforts in my applications and tutoring a child with learning disabilities, like Ernie, is a big part of that. Even though, technically this isn't strictly altruistic."

"Okay. Well let me know. I'll see you next Saturday?"

"Yes, and Monday and Wednesday after school unless that has changed?"

"Oh right. No. That hasn't changed. I will see you Monday then," I acknowledged.

We had been easing our way toward the front door during this exchange. When we arrived, I opened the door, said a final goodbye and thank you, and Charlotte made her way outside to her waiting mother.

I returned to the living room to check on Ernie. It was just after noon and I figured he might like lunch. But he was fast asleep on the couch, TV blaring on a cartoon channel. His school work and books were scattered across the coffee table. I decided to let him sleep while I finished my work and then wake him in about an hour for some lunch.

Tim came home at around 1:30 after he'd put his big client's taxes in order. He peeked into the living room before making his way to the kitchen. I was busy making tuna for lunch for Ernie and me, assuming Ernie would soon be awake and hungry. He set his briefcase on the kitchen table then came up behind me to kiss my neck.

"How's our boy? He looks wiped." Tim made his way to the refrigerator in search of a beer.

"He's fine. Charlotte was here for about three hours, so I think she wore him out. I'm about to try to wake him up for lunch."

"Who's Charlotte?" Tim asked as he retrieved a beer from the fridge.

"It's his girlfriend. She wiped him out. Poor kid likes older women." I teased. It was a more fun response than continuing to remind Tim who Charlotte was every time he asked.

"Atta boy!...So, you mean Charlotte his tutor."

"Nothing gets by you," I continued to tease. Tim just smirked into the neck of his beer bottle while he took a sip and made his way to the living room to see Ernie.

Sometimes the way we communicated felt as though Tim and I were in the middle of a family sitcom. Someone on the outside might see our banter as crude and disrespectful, but to us, it's just the natural way we like to tease–or maybe the way I like to tease Tim–and he enjoyed the attention.

I came around the corner to announce lunch just as Tim was about to go through his wake-up routine with Ernie. I leaned against the door frame and watched.

Tim put his beer on the side table then sat next to Ernie on the couch. He put his face close up to Ernie's and stared at him. This was a little game they played whenever Tim had the chore of waking Ernie up for school. Tim would put his face closer and closer to Ernie's until either Ernie woke up, or their noses touched, and the resulting tickle would shock Ernie awake.

Most of the time Ernie was already awake and pretending to sleep before their noses touched. When Tim touched their noses, Ernie giggled awake and Tim tickled Ernie's rib cage mercilessly until Ernie cried "Uncle!" It was impossible for Ernie to go back to sleep after that.

It worked this time too. Tim got closer and closer to Ernie's face until a tiny smirk spread Ernie's lips and widened his cheeks. Then, Tim went in for the kill: he touched his nose to Ernie's until Ernie woke up laughing. He wrapped his fingers around Ernie's ribs and tickled him. The more Ernie squirmed the more Tim tickled until Ernie was so exhausted from laughing that he could barely breathe. Once Tim stopped and Ernie recovered, he sat straight up on the couch, looked toward the kitchen and shouted, "Hey Mom! I'm hungry!"

Right on cue. "Off the couch and into the kitchen table if you want your lunch, Mr. Giggles!"

"I eat and watch TV...with Dad." Ernie pleaded.

"You eat in the kitchen and Dad can come too and keep us both company." I had our sandwiches made and placed at the table along with a glass of apple juice for Ernie, a diet Coke for me, and a pickle for each. Tim had eaten lunch at the office and was content with his beer. I took my seat and waited.

A few seconds later, the two of them came out of the living room. Tim was leading Ernie by his shoulders, steering him like a race car. They sat in their usual places. Ernie wasted no time in grabbing the first half of his sandwich and stuffing a large bite into his mouth.

"Could you try and eat with your mouth closed, Ernie?" I pleaded as I watched tuna fish and bread combine in a mash inside Ernie's open mouth. Ernie widened his mouth and gave me a fuller view of its contents. "Ernie! Tim, say something; he knows better and that's disgusting."

"Come on Ernie. Listen to your mom. That *is* disgusting. But, that's a nice-looking tuna sandwich you have. You both have. Funny, I don't have one."

I gave Tim the "look."

"If you do that in front of Charlotte she'll dump you." Tim admonished, in his own inimitable style.

I thought that was a stupid response; it exasperated me when it actually worked. The rest of the lunch Ernie ate with a closed mouth, chewed, and swallowed quietly before taking another bite.

Tim could barely remember who Charlotte was and I never suggested that Ernie had a crush on her. How did he know what to say to Ernie? I wondered how much of Tim's ignorant bliss routine was just an act.

The rest of the day was wonderfully uneventful. Elsie was gone most of the day Saturday and had a sleepover at a friend's house Saturday night. I made Tim's favorite pasta dish for dinner–Carbonara–which Ernie and I like too. Ernie watched TV with Tim and me–or rather, we watched TV that Ernie chose, *Despicable Me*; a movie Tim and I may have enjoyed as much as Ernie.

By the end of the movie, Ernie could barely keep his eyes open and went to bed without a fight. It had been an eventful day for him. It was only 8 pm when Ernie went up to bed, which meant that Tim and I actually had some together time before we could call it a night ourselves.

We both had red wine with dinner–a Barolo that one of Tim's clients gave him. It was an expensive bottle and we enjoyed it even though neither of us had an educated palette to appreciate its vintage.

I poured each of us another glass and settled into Tim's side to cuddle while he searched TV channels for something new to watch. It was nice to have quiet time and to be able to talk about whatever.

Tim absentmindedly asked if I had called the specialist that Dr. Chawla had recommended for Ernie. I said that I had and that I was able to make an appointment for Monday morning.

We talked about how good Ernie looked today and how much energy he had and how remarkably he seemed to be recovering from his MODS event.

We talked about Elsie and how well she was doing in school and the friends she had made–how much more confident she was becoming. I shared with Tim the reason for our special day. He wasn't surprised and had surmised as much on his own. He said that he loved that Elsie and I had that bonding and he loved how close we were. He even admitted that he liked our silly times when we laughed at his expense–or just anything at all.

149

We talked about the mounting bills and how we were doing with hospital payments and what might come down the road with a specialist and how our savings were doing.

None of our talk was romantic or trivial. But none of it was overly serious or detailed. It was pleasant to sip wine with and make a quick inventory of life together—with a noticeable bent toward the opinion that things were going along okay.

I changed the subject to Elizabeth's visit and the interview she wanted with me.

"So, I had a visit from Elizabeth late this morning," I said nonchalantly. "You don't know her. She's the TV reporter who was in my face at our front door right after the accident thing."

"Really?" Tim drew back a little to look at me better. "What the heck did she want? I thought you said you were yesterday's news and we were done with reporters hanging around our house."

"I was. And I am, but...she wants to do a special about three different, ordinary people who performed extraordinary feats—her words not mine—and what drove them to do it, stuff like that." I took another sip of wine.

"Did you slam the door in her face?"

I laughed. "No Tim. Actually, I never told you, but I also ran into her at the Crate & Barrel right after the front door thing. She was very polite and asked about *Ernie*—nothing at all about the accident or my role in it. And she gave me her card."

"So, you let her in?"

"Yeah, I thought it was Ernie's tutor..."

"Charlotte." Tim piped in as though remembering her name now proved he had never forgotten it.

"Ugh. Yes Tim, Charlotte."

"I have a great memory hon. It's also just very short." Tim gave me a big smile.

"Am I going to be able to finish this story or do you have twenty more silly comments to make?"

Tim sipped his wine.

"So, I thought it was *what's-her-name* when the doorbell rang but it turned out to be the reporter, Elizabeth. She caught me by surprise. I decided to let her in and see what she had to say. Then I offered her some of your coffee." I deliberately waited now for Tim to add a comment, knowing he would be unable to resist.

"Oh, so you slammed my coffee in her face. Good one!"

I laughed. Even though I knew it was coming, I had to laugh.

"She took one sip and said it was the most disgusting thing she had ever tasted," I giggled at the memory of her face. "That's when I decided that she had good taste, was straight forward and...well, and I liked her."

"Well, I'm ecstatic that my coffee could bring you a new friendship."

"I told her that I would think about the interview but that it couldn't involve the kids or you or any intimate details about our family. She agreed. And I told her that I wanted to talk it over with you first. See what you thought."

"Oh boy. You are seriously considering doing this?"

"Yeah. But mostly because it is three different people and not just me...and Elizabeth was upfront that this would help her career if it went well and she acknowledged some of this could be tough. I don't know. I just, sort of trusted her. She didn't say anything about it, but I got the feeling that it might involve Kalea, the little girl I saved, and having us meet. I know I don't talk about that or any of it, and I have never wanted to have an awkward, meet-the-girl-you-saved moment, but now I think maybe it was rude of me not to. And maybe I should meet her, acknowledge her–if she wants that."

"And other than a cursory, *Hey, these are my incredible kids and this is my handsome husband,* we're out of it?"

"Definitely."

"Well, then I think you should do what feels best."

I gave Tim a look of disappointment at that comment, which he correctly interpreted and continued.

"Babe, I'm not saying that as a copout or from being disinterested. I'm being sincere. My concern is for you and our family's privacy–and you covered that. I don't think any of us can make this decision for you. I wouldn't council you one way or the other. If this feels right to you and you want to do it, then go for it. I support your decision. I would just advise to stay on your toes and not be too trusting of this new 'friendship'…just in case."

"Okay." I took my last sip of wine and set the glass on the table. Then I turned into Tim, wrapped my arms around him, and stretched my head up to give him a big kiss. I looked into his soft brown eyes and asked, "Do you love me?"

I was pretty sure of his answer, especially after the way he just expressed his support, but I liked to hear him say it from time to time even if I had to prompt him.

"I love you like Ernie loves his tuna fish sandwich," Tim said. Before I could complain, he pulled me into him and whispered in my ear, "I love you more than the sunrise."

I melted.

That was what Tim had said to me the first time he said, "I love you."

It happened when we were camping out with a bunch of college classmates, hoping to catch a glimpse of the Lyrids meteor shower which occurred every April. The event was said to be easy to see in North America and the moon was supposed to be slight and a non-factor. None of this mattered. To most of us college students, camping out in a large open field was an excuse for an all-night party.

Tim and I stayed up searching the night skies for meteors and talking until dawn between drinking, making out, and a fair amount of semi- public fondling. It was a romantic scene in its way.

When sunlight crept over the horizon, we were both awake but feeling sleep-deprived and in need of coffee. We had classes to attend in a few hours.

As the tip of the sun reached just above the crest of the ridge of hills in the distance, it created a beautiful halo effect of orange-yellow mist. I sat on the grass in a makeshift lotus pose, admiring nature's prism. Tim crawled up behind me and pulled me back into his lap, rocking me gently back and forth.

"I really love this sunrise. It's beautiful." I said staring straight out over the field as he held me. Tim moved my hair to one side, kissed my neck, and whispered in my ear, "I love you more than the sunrise."

And I vomited.

I had had way too much to drink along with crappy hotdogs to eat. Add no sleep. And Tim was rocking me. My stomach also wasn't ready for the nervous reaction of being told "I love you."

Tim and I had been together almost a year, so his declaration wasn't completely out of the blue. It wasn't that I didn't want to hear it. I really *did* want to hear, but wasn't expecting it at that moment. I also wasn't sure *if* he meant it or *how* he meant it and well, I was a young college girl who was uncertain about when I wanted anyone to say that to me.

In other words, I was a stomach full of nerves and cheap sangria and something had to come out of my mouth in response. My body chose retching.

Instead of being dejected by my response or angry or moody, Tim gently rubbed my back and offered me his handkerchief. I couldn't look at him; I was so embarrassed. I gingerly took his handkerchief to wipe my mouth.

When I finally found the courage to look Tim in the face, I found him patiently looking at me. He said, "Does this mean you love me too or you want to think about it?"

I flung my arms around his waist, holding him to me as tightly as I could. We didn't speak.

I didn't say it, but I loved him too. With my sarcastic sense of humor and its importance that I place in life, how could I not love a man who responded like that? Whatever doubt or logic I harbored for *when* I should love had vanished.

When we pulled apart and I looked up at him, I could see he was confused and maybe even a little hurt. I cupped his face in my hands.

"I have to shower, drink a ton of coffee and get to class," I said. "After class, I am going to take a nap. Then, you are going to come over around 9 pm with something light for us to eat. Then after we eat, I am going to give you a chance to show me just how much you love me—and maybe I will show you back."

I stood up and left him sitting there with the strangest look on his face. I don't think he knew what had just hit him.

But he showed up at my dorm room at 9 o'clock sharp with two chicken Caesar salads and two Diet Cokes. We ate without much conversation at my cloth-covered steamer trunk that doubles as a makeshift table; we mostly gazed at each other as though we were studying for hidden meaning in our expressions.

When our salads were done, I told Tim to gather up the trash and take it to the bin down the hall. When he returned, I locked the door behind him and smiled. I led him by the hand the few paces it took to reach my bed.

We spent the rest of the night saying I love you without speaking a word.

Our very first "I love you," went from a gastronomic catastrophe into a passionate, romantic memory that we both cherish.

***

After I recovered from Tim's sweet, reminiscent "I love you," I took the near-empty wine bottle and our two glasses into the kitchen, set them on the counter and quickly returned to him. I had decided two things during my short trip: one, I was going to do the interview with Elizabeth, and two, I was going to take advantage of an early evening together and give Tim a night to remember.

I offered Tim my hand and said, "Come on big boy, I've got something I want to tell you in the other room." Tim took my hand as he rose from the couch. He followed as I led him upstairs and into our bedroom. When I brought him in and shut the door, he said, "So, what is this..." But I cut him off.

"Shhhh," I placed my index finger on his mouth and played seductively with his lips. "This is going to be a silent conversation...sort of...like we had in my dorm room that night. I want to see how big I can make your grin this time." Tim blushed and stumbled back onto our bed when I gently pushed him backward.

I climbed on top of him and gave him sultry kisses on his neck, nibbled his ears, and then came back and smothered his mouth with mine. This was going to be *his* "special night" and I was going to make certain he remembered it for a very long time.

CHAPTER NINE

SOLVING ERNIE

Elsie came home Sunday morning looking as though she had spent a long night with her friend binge-watching television shows without anyone suggesting a bed time.

Ernie was up early again and seemed to be doing well. He stayed in his pajamas, as was normal for Sunday mornings. And he was hungry. Tim had gotten up before me; I stopped him at our bedroom doorway before he could disappear downstairs. "Hey. You going out to get breakfast?" I knew what he was doing, because it was what we always did on Sundays. But I wanted to see if he had *that* smile on his face. I wasn't disappointed.

Maybe his smile wasn't as full-blown as it had been during our college days, but it was enough to send me back under the covers for five more minutes of savoring a warm glow before beginning my morning routine.

Tim came home with bagels, lox, and two kinds of cream cheese: plain and chive. Elsie, who had climbed the first three steps up the stairs toward her bedroom and sleep did a quick U-turn when Tim came home with the bagels. I guess she decided that sleep could wait.

There was only one kosher deli in town where we could get *real* bagels and it was a 25-minute drive away. No one in our family missed Sunday bagels, especially not for something as trivial as sleep.

That was the beginning to our lazy Sunday. Not much else exciting happened. Elsie napped, Tim read, Ernie played with his toy soldiers, and I did the Sunday crossword. Correction, I attempted the Sunday crossword. Everyone did their own thing for lunch, except Ernie who insisted I make him a "tuna fish sandwich." Later in the afternoon, I went shopping for the week ahead and for Sunday's dinner which was a pork loin roast with potatoes, fresh green beans, and salad.

After dinner, we played a rousing game of Spit. Ernie often lacked the energy to play at the speed needed to win this maniacally fast card game, but that Sunday he was as alert and as quick as the rest of us.

We all slapped cards in the middle of the floor, accusing each other of cheating, smacking hands while we tried desperately to put our own card down ahead of the competition, and racing to empty our entire pile of cards before everyone else.

The room echoed with our screams of success and failure while we sat on the floor wildly throwing cards about. We played four rounds; Ernie won once, and Elsie won every other time. Tim was the worst at the game—slow reflexes—while I was too distracted, still trying to think of 38 down from the crossword puzzle. Elsie was lightning fast. She also cheated more than anyone else. At least that's what Ernie claimed.

Despite the heavy competition and the many accusations of rules violations, everyone laughed as much as they accused, and we all had a fun, exhausting time of it.

Bed time came early; Elsie had school and Ernie and I had an early appointment with the specialist. Tim was coming to the doctor's office with us before he went to work from there. He was as anxious as I was to hear what this new doctor had to say about Ernie's condition.

It was a good weekend Tim and I agreed as we laid in bed and talked before turning the lights out and cuddling together for a few minutes prior to welcoming sleep. Tim turned on his side, facing away from me, to begin his journey into dreamland while I nestled my head into my pillow, ready for...I got it! Thirty-eight down! I got it!

I jumped out of bed, turned on my phone light, and ran downstairs to the living room. I lit up the coffee table with my flashlight app and grabbed the crossword section of the paper that was neatly folded in half. I found 38 down, "Supreme last name" –I entered Ginsburg for Ruth Bader Ginsburg.

I was smug. Then I looked again and realized the correct answer of Ginsburg meant two of my across answers that intersected with it were wrong. There it was; the thrill of victory and the agony of defeat with the stroke of a pencil.

Deflated, I trudged back upstairs to bed. Tim was already snoring. I climbed into bed and tried to get the wrong crossword answers out of my head. I don't know how much time I spent on that effort, but I do know I was exhausted when the alarm went off the following morning.

Monday morning was filled with the usual stuff. Tim was up first and readied for work. When he was out of the bathroom, it was my turn. Elsie and Ernie were still under their covers, blissfully unaware it was morning.

Tim strode into the hall and knocked on Elsie's door repeatedly. He was looking for a sign of sluggish life, which came from the sound of an odd language that combined "Yeah" and "Okay I'm awake" into "Yeahmkaywake."

Satisfied, Tim moved on to Ernie's room, opened the door and began his face-into-face tickling routine which brought Ernie to giggly life.

We all eventually gathered in the kitchen and prepared our individual breakfast choices. Normally this meant cereal with fruit for Ernie and Elsie, toast and coffee for Tim and coffee and fruit for me. But this was also Monday, and on Monday mornings everyone headed for the bagel bag for leftovers with cream cheese and their place in line at the toaster. I was always last. I made everyone have juice in the morning–usually orange juice.

After breakfast, Elsie headed outside to walk to the bus stop with her friends. Ernie, who was still in his pjs, went upstairs to brush his teeth and get dressed for the doctor's office. We still had about 30 minutes before we had to drive to the hospital, so I went back to my crossword to try and fix my mistakes. Tim answered a few emails on his phone.

Ernie took his time getting ready. I yelled upstairs more than once while Tim waited and paced in the laundry room. I told him to go on ahead and we'd meet him there. We had to take separate cars anyway, so Tim could continue to work after our meeting.

Five minutes after Tim left, Ernie came down wearing a long-sleeved, green plaid shirt–with red shorts. He looked like a Christmas ornament.

"Ernie, what are you wearing?" I asked incredulously. "It's November, and it's very cold outside."

"Wearing shorts and a shirt Mom. I'm hot."

"Honey, you won't be hot when we get out of the house," I reasoned. "And, well, you might want to save that outfit for Christmas. Besides, if you're hot, why the long sleeve shirt?" Ernie looked down at his outfit as if he was seeing it for the first time.

"Come on, let's go pick out something less…colorful."

I rushed Ernie upstairs and put him in a pair of beige slacks and let him keep the plaid shirt. He liked it and because we were now running late it made our exit faster.

The trip to the hospital was quicker than I anticipated because we missed the rush-hour traffic. I was able to make up enough time to arrive on schedule. Tim waited in the lobby when we came in and was now pacing *that* floor. By the time we met him mid-stride in the far end of the waiting room, Dr. Blackwell had come out to look for us. She must have been given a pretty good description because she walked right up to us without hesitation.

"Hello," she said, extending her hand. "Mr. and Mrs. Gallagher… and Ernie right? I'm Dr. Blackwell."

"Please, call me Tim," he said while he shook her hand. "Nice to meet you doctor. This is my wife, June…say hello to Dr. Blackwell, Ernie."

"Hello." Ernie said quietly. He looked down at the floor, his hands in his front pockets.

"Why don't you follow me to the back where the main building connects to the medical center?" She gestured to the side and moved toward the hallway behind her. "That's where my office is. I would have had you meet me there, but people often get lost trying to find it on their own." She led our little group out of the waiting area and toward the back of the hospital.

She seemed pleasant enough. Tall and thin, with dark hair that she wore at chin length and bangs that partially hid a large forehead. She appeared to be in her late thirties or early forties, but there were no particular features that stood out to give away her age other than a few fine lines around her blue eyes.

The walk to the other building and Dr. Blackwell's office was not long but it did involve a lot of turns and confusing signs and I could easily see how someone would get lost. I appreciated that she had come to meet us and save us that embarrassment.

When we entered her office, she went behind her desk to her big black chair. While she sat, she motioned for the three of us to take two of the seats in front of her. Ernie stood next to me, half leaning onto my chair.

"Should I get another chair for Ernie?" The doctor offered.

"What do ya think buddy?" Tim asked. "You want to sit on my lap?"

"No. I stand."

"You sure?" Tim questioned. Ernie nodded.

Now that that was settled, we turned our attention toward Dr. Blackwell. We expected an explanation of what was wrong with Ernie or at least, what she *thought* was wrong.

"Okay then," Dr. Blackwell began. She leaned forward and clasped her hands together. I noticed her nail polish on both index fingers was slightly chipped. "Let me tell you a little bit about me and then what I think may be going on with Ernie. Okay?"

Tim and I nodded.

"First, I think this might be above Ernie's comprehension but it's good that you are including him because it's less scary when kids take part and understand. I'll try to make this simple for Ernie as much as I can. But Ernie," she spoke directly to him, "You may ask as many questions as you want—and you folks as well." She turned to Tim and me.

"Along with being a pediatrician, I am also a medical geneticist—so I have a combination of practical application mixed with genetic research. I have a particular interest and specialty in the research of mitochondrial disease and the related functional disorders. I have spent a lot of time in the lab as well as in the field and am one of a handful of doctors who recognize and treat mitochondrial disorders.

"Dr. Chawla told you that Ernie may have a disorder related to his DNA or mitochondrial DNA. You likely said "uh-huh" not really knowing exactly what she may have meant."

Again, Tim and I nodded. I was beginning to feel like a bobble-head doll. Ernie had quickly become bored and plopped himself in my lap.

"I think we lost him already, doctor," I patted Ernie's knee. "But please go on. I'll let you know when you lose Tim and me too." I smiled.

"Sure," she said and smiled back. "Let's talk about mitochondrial DNA otherwise known as mtDNA. If you remember your high school biology, you might recall that our bodies have two sets of DNA. There is the DNA we all read about in connection with inheriting traits and tracing our ancestry, and then the mtDNA that is rarely mentioned. The mtDNA or mitochondrial DNA, is in nearly every cell of your body. The mitochondria supply your body's cells with the energy they need to function." Dr. Blackwell looked at Ernie. "Ernie, can you lift your arm for me, please."

Confused, Ernie looked at me. "Go ahead honey." He lifted his right arm.

"Good. You just used energy for your muscles to do that. And those muscles got their energy from your mitochondria." Ernie kept his arm in the air until I reached over and helped him lower it.

"Now Ernie, what did you have for breakfast?" Dr. Blackwell asked.

Once again Ernie looked at me. "Go ahead Ernie, tell her."

"Um, I had bagel with cream cheese. The cream cheese with green things. I put bagel in toaster. But before I put cream cheese on it or it melts and makes a mess and Mommy yells at me. I had orange juice too." Mr. Literal was enjoying telling on his mommy yelling at him.

"Well, that was informative," Dr. Blackwell said smiling. "Most kids just say, 'I had cereal' or something like that. You might have the makings of a scientist there Mr. and Mrs. Gallagher. So, Ernie, where do you think that bagel with cream cheese—with the green things—is now?"

"Um, in my stom...tommy." Feeling his oats, he added, "and then my poop."

"Ernie!" Tim admonished, embarrassed. I stared straight ahead.

"Huh, it's okay, folks," Dr. Blackwell chuckled. "I'm a pediatrician, I hear it all. And yes Ernie, you are correct. It goes into your stomach, through your intestines and eventually, it's poop.

"Ernie, do you know what makes you have the energy to digest that food and move it along?" he shook his head no. "Your mitochondria."

She finished her conversation with Ernie and directed her attention to Tim and me.

"The mitochondria provide the energy for almost everything your body does, from the simple act of muscle movement to digesting food and activities in your brain. Because mitochondria are involved in so much of what your body does, if it goes wrong, if there is a mutation in your mtDNA, it can affect any number of body functions. It can and usually does affect several functions in the same person."

The doctor paused to let this information sink in. "Following me so far?"

"Yes," Tim and I said in unison.

"Just by looking at Ernie's records–and I will want to examine him at some point–I see he has suffered from seizures, bouts of unusual vomiting, very low energy, developmental issues, and the most recent and serious MODS. All of this points to a good possibility that Ernie has a form of mitochondrial disease. But we will need to do more involved testing to be certain."

I looked at Tim, Tim looked at me, we both looked back at Dr. Blackwell. Then I spoke.

"Tim, why don't you and Ernie go look for something to drink in the vending machines? I would like a cup of coffee. Doctor?" I had serious questions to ask that I didn't want Ernie to be a part of.

"No coffee for me, thank you," she said. "But why don't we have Ernie go to the little waiting room right next door where my nurse is and he can do some coloring books or read." She assumed my intentions.

"I'll take him and be right back. Just right next door?" Tim asked. "Yes. Out and immediately to your right."

Ernie jumped off my lap and followed Tim who returned within a couple minutes.

"You must have a lot of questions," Dr. Blackwell said when Tim returned. "So, fire away."

"Well, the most important question is, will Ernie be okay?" That was first and foremost on my mind.

"I can't say with Ernie how involved his disease might be right now," Dr. Blackwell said kindly. "I can say that many people, mostly young children, live and are living with many of the same symptoms that Ernie has displayed. They learn to live with the disease and manage it."

Tim seemed okay with me taking the lead in the questioning, so I continued.

"So, Ernie's mtDNA? Is messed up somehow and can't be fixed? And it might attack his stomach or make him have a seizure or stop him from being active? And we have no way of knowing where it will attack him or when?"

"It isn't an attack like the flu or an infection, although infections can complicate things," Dr. Blackwell said. "Think of it more as mitochondria are running around Ernie's cells, trying to give him energy in different places, but some of these mitochondria can't do what they should–so the cells they *should* feed with energy are left hungry and can't do their job correctly. That is over-simplified but you get the point."

"Is there any treatment, anything Ernie can take to help his mitochondria work?"

"Unfortunately, this is a very new area and not much research has been done beyond myself and a handful of others. Most doctors and hospitals don't know what mitochondrial disease is and others go as far as to even deny its existence. Funding for what I do is very difficult to come by.

"I do have a treatment, a cocktail of sorts, that has shown some good results for many patients. Often the best results are for children who have one or two of the lesser symptoms such as cyclical vomiting syndrome, recurring migraines, and low energy. The more complicated cases need more research."

"And Ernie," I asked. "Is he one of the more complicated cases?"

"Well, again, I have to examine him and go over his history and yours and send him for tests to be certain that it is his mtDNA that are affected. But yes, it sounds that way right now."

"This explains why we get looks from the school principal, some of the nurses at certain hospitals, and have even had it suggested that we poisoned Ernie...accidentally of course," I said.

"I'm not surprised," Dr. Blackwell said. "That is not uncommon among parents of children with mitochondrial disease. The kids get rushed to the hospital one day and the next they seem perfectly fine. Or they come into a hospital having been vomiting for a week or more at a time and every test is run with no result. Kids with recurring migraines go to the doctor and complain–and again, they are not diagnosed with anything, and often not taken seriously. I have had several patients' parents regale me with stories of being told their kids are suffering from emotional distress or physical abuse, suggesting the parents are to blame, or at least seriously involved in their child's suffering."

"Well, we came close to that with this ridiculous woman named Ruth at Brinker Hospital," I said, looking at Tim for agreement. He nodded. "So, you want our history? Like parent's cause of death or current health issues, that sort of thing?"

"Yes, and yours in particular, June."

"Mine? Why mine?"

"Most of the functional mitochondrial diseases are maternally inherited. Others are inherited through DNA and can be from one or both parents. That is why ladies in our support group refer to themselves fondly as Mito Moms. Because mtDNA is passed on through them."

"I see," I said, but didn't like what I had just heard. It sounded like *I* was responsible for Ernie's sickness although I knew that was not what Dr. Blackwell was saying. "Well, I don't know how much help I can be. Both my parents are gone. My mom died of a heart attack when I was about 15 and my father was killed in a car accident while I was a freshman in college."

Then Tim spoke up.

"My parents are still alive and really don't have any health issues beyond medications they take for blood thinning or cholesterol. A few aches and pains, and my father had surgery on his back a while ago."

"Well, I'm going to give you a questionnaire to take home and fill in as much information as you can about your parents and your grandparents," Dr. Blackwell said. "Also, you have a daughter...Elsie?"

"Yes, but she doesn't get sick like Ernie," I said. I'm sure I sounded defensive.

"Well, June," Tim cut in, "she does have migraines, has since she was very little." Tim looked first at me and then at the doctor. "And that was on your list of disorders I think, doctor."

"Yes, it is," she said. "And it is very common for all or some of the children in the family to have a form of mitochondrial disease—or it can skip children in the same family. Each child's symptoms can be vastly different."

"I've had migraines my entire life, as far back as I can remember," I volunteered. "I've learned to deal with them; they seem to have lessened over the years." I didn't really want to make any connection between Elsie's and Ernie's health problems and mine.

"All of that information, along with Ernie's doctor and hospital records, strongly suggests to me that he has a form of mitochondrial disease," Dr. Blackwell said. "In the case of some developmental disorders, such as Ernie's speech and learning inefficiencies, I might have recommended a chromosomal microarray (CMA) blood workup. But given how many other areas of Ernie's health are affected, I am of the opinion that he should undergo a muscle biopsy."

"A muscle biopsy?" Tim asked. "What will that involve?"

"Well, as I said, it is not the normal first course of action, but given all the information I have on Ernie, I think it is best. The tissues with the most mitochondria are the kidneys, liver, brain, heart, and skeletal muscle; this makes muscle the most viable candidate for testing. It involves taking a small piece of muscle, usually from the patient's upper thigh, and sending it to a lab to analyze. There is no permanent damage to the patient although it will leave a small scar several inches long." The doctor continued.

"That sounds invasive and a little scary," I said. "Will it hurt him? And will you be doing the biopsy?"

"It is a minimally invasive procedure with little risk. There is always the risk of infection, but we can manage that well enough. Ernie will be locally anesthetized for the procedure, so no it won't hurt. Maybe a slight tugging at the site or some similar feeling, but in and out the same day—with a bandage and maybe a little limp for a day while he heals. You can be with him the entire time and that may help because he needs to be very still during the procedure. I will give you a pamphlet you can take that answers all your questions about what happens before, during and after.

"And, no, I won't be doing the biopsy, but I can schedule it to be done here. The sample will need to be sent to a lab and the results can take several weeks to come back. It isn't cheap. I say that to prepare you. I don't know what your insurance coverage is, but I would be prepared to have some portion of the testing or the procedure voided by insurance."

"Well, yeah," Tim said and reached for my hand. "We've been through a small mountain of bills with doctors and hospitals and insurance claims, so we know the drill. But if this is what you think we should do, then we want to do it. It would at least give us a starting point, a name and reason for Ernie's difficulties."

"Yeah, I agree," I added, squeezing Tim's hand back. "If Ernie *does* have this mitochondrial disease of some sort, at least we would know what is going on and not be in the dark and feel like we are helpless and alone."

"Speaking of that, I want you to know that you are not alone," Dr. Blackwell said kindly. "I have many parents with children who have mitochondrial disease; they meet and talk from time to time. There really are not many other places for people affected by this disease to go, so I have patients from all over the country. There are support groups and a national mitochondrial group where you can get a ton of information and support.

"But first, let's get the test results and go from there," Dr. Blackwell said putting a period to the discussion. "I'll schedule the biopsy for as soon as I can and let you know when–likely next week. I'll coordinate with the lab. Meanwhile, I would like to have Ernie in my office for an examination. I would like get back the questionnaire my nurse will give you before the biopsy, along with any medications Ernie takes or allergies he has, etc. It's all in the questionnaire. We need to have all of that on record for the surgeon and also for my records.

"All right then, why don't you get Ernie? My nurse will get you what you need and schedule Ernie's examination appointment." Dr. Blackwell rose and stood placing her hands in each corresponding lab coat pocket.

Tim and I stood too, and took turns shaking her hand while offering our thanks. We left her office and made our way to Ernie. When we got there, Ernie was finishing one of his unique crayon renderings.

"Hi honey. Ready to go?" I asked.

"K Mom. Just finish one part." Ernie didn't look up from his drawing.

"Let me see honey," I said, moving toward him. "What are you coloring?"

"Wait! Not yet." He covered his drawing with his arm.

"Ah, we kind of have to go big guy," Tim said.

"Okay, done." Ernie announced and put his yellow crayon down. He handed the coloring book to me.

"Oh wow, that is a cool looking dinosaur!" I said. Then I shared the image with Tim.

"Cat." Ernie said matter-of-factly. "Fuzzy yellow cat."

"Wow, really?" Tim said with disbelief. I elbowed him in the stomach.

"Ouch, er, umm, oh yeah. A yellow hairy cat that just saw a dog and is—umm his hair is standing on edge. Pretty cool Ernie." Tim did his best to recover. I stared at the drawing with my own look of disbelief.

"No dog. Just a cat." Ernie said again. "I take it home to show Else." He ripped the page along the perforated line and placed the rest of the book back in the magazine rack next to his chair.

I felt bad for the little guy, but he seemed oblivious to our reaction and certain that Elsie would want to see his latest artistic endeavor. She must have a way of reacting to Ernie's artwork that was special.

I made a mental note to be there when Ernie presented his "cat" to her, so I could see for myself how she did it.

The nurse, who remained seated and quiet during our little Rembrandt's presentation, got up and handed me a folder.

"This is all the information for Ernie and the questionnaire for you folks to complete," she said. "I put a note in there for Ernie's examination appointment with Dr. Blackwell which I've scheduled for next Tuesday at 3 pm."

I took the folder and perused its contents quickly. I thanked the nurse, gathered Ernie by his bony shoulders, and headed him toward the door, Tim leading the way. When I reached the doorway, I stopped and turned back to the nurse.

"Do we come right back here for Ernie's examination appointment?"

"No," she said with a smile. "You can let the receptionist in the main entrance know you are here; I will come get you both."

"Oh. Okay," I said, relieved. "Well, thanks. See you Tuesday."

CHAPTER TEN

MEETING KALEA

After we left Dr. Blackwell's office, Tim drove to work while Ernie and I headed for home. I had some food shopping to do and managed to convince Ernie to go with me, but only after promising lunch at IHOP once the shopping was complete.

When we arrived home, Ernie helped me bring in our grocery bags and then made a dash for the couch and the TV remote. He plopped himself down in a corner of the couch; before I was through putting away the five bags of groceries, he was sound asleep.

I figured he was worn out by the doctor's visit and the shopping; we walked every aisle of the store in a semi-methodical way, assuring I didn't miss anything on my mental list.

My kids naturally hate food shopping, but for Ernie with his low energy issues, this outing was particularly grueling and tested his resolve. I could see him fading when we got to IHOP; he nearly fell asleep in the booth before he was revived by the smell of bacon teasing his nose when the waitress placed his plate in front of him.

He nodded off several times on the drive back home from the restaurant. He would wake when the back wheels of the car aggressively attacked a pothole in the road or from my foot weighing heavily on the brake as I navigated the slow-moving traffic in front of me.

Charlotte would be arriving soon enough, so I decided to let Ernie sleep now and be awake and alert for his lessons. He would rejoin his classmates the following Monday and I wanted him to be and feel as prepared as possible.

With Ernie napping on the couch, I figured I had free time to straighten the kid's rooms and tidy up our bathroom before Charlotte arrived. Ernie was fairly neat and since I had been in his room this morning to help him change, I saw that it only needed minor care.

I began with Elsie's room. With the vacuum cleaner in one hand and a can of Pledge in the other, and a roll of paper towels tucked under one arm, I headed upstairs. When I opened Elsie's bedroom door, I saw what can only be described as bedlam.

There were clothes everywhere. Used glassware appeared on every surface of furniture: bed stands, dresser, extra sitting chair, and there were dishes stacked on top of each other on the floor in front of the dresser. Some of the dresser drawers were half open with various articles of clothing peeking out, giving the dresser a colorful smiley face effect.

I looked toward her bathroom. *Not even going there*, I thought. I took one last look around, left the vacuum cleaner in the middle of her room, threw the paper towels and pledge on her unmade bed, and left. When Elsie got home, she would get an earful and one hour to make her bedroom and bathroom spotless!

I looked toward Ernie's door then shrugged my shoulders and figured bed-making could wait another day. I remembered the pamphlet Dr. Blackwell's nurse had given us and thought I would use this free time to look it over and maybe even begin to tackle the questionnaire.

The folder was still on the front seat of my car where I had left it before grocery shopping. I went outside to get it and made my way to my makeshift little office space off the dining room to read the pamphlet.

Dr. Blackwell had cautioned Tim and me to wait for the biopsy and a confident diagnosis of what was causing Ernie's health issues before we jumped into any research of what she thought the root cause might be—mtDNA issues. But I couldn't help myself and within a minute of sitting in my chair and turning on my computer, I was typing mitochondrial disease into the Google search bar.

There were a surprising amount of entries for a disease that is so rare. Many were clinical research documents too complicated for me to grasp, or links to health sites that had information about the disease in generality. But two entries stood out: Mito Action and UMDF for United Mitochondrial Disease Foundation.

I clicked on one and then the other to get a general sense of what each might offer. Both seemed to be designed to speak to average people like me who were coping with the disease. The UMDF site focused more on research and treatment on a national basis, and Mito Action was geared more toward general information, support options, and personal stories.

Both sites had presentations of what mitochondria are, how they work, and how they can affect the many functions of the body. This was what Dr. Blackwell told us, but these sites presented me with much more detail and so many more variations of how mitochondrial disease can manifest itself.

I was fascinated. I wanted to read every page. The more I read, especially the personal stories from parents and children dealing with this disease, the more I was convinced—without the need for a biopsy—that Ernie was suffering from some form of mitochondrial disease.

I stayed at my desk reading, soaking up as much information as I could for what seemed like only minutes when in reality I had been reading for more than two hours. I was so engrossed in my education that I hadn't even noticed that Ernie was awake and watching television. He doesn't turn the volume down during his cartoon studies, so I was really surprised that I hadn't been aware that he was awake until I heard him yell, "Door Mom!"

I looked at the clock on my computer, it was 2 pm—time for Charlotte to arrive for Ernie's tutoring. I pulled myself away from my computer and made tracks for the front door fully expecting to let Charlotte in and go straight back to my reading.

But, it wasn't only Charlotte at the door. When I opened it, I was greeted by Charlotte, followed closely behind by Elizabeth and two men; one carrying a camera and the other holding metal boxes of some sort of equipment and a long pole with a large, fuzzy looking end—a microphone.

Charlotte said, "Hi Mrs. G!" I stared at Elizabeth and company, so Charlotte simply made her way past me and toward the living room where she knew Ernie was waiting. Elizabeth stepped forward.

"So, we are filming the first part of your interview today; and by the look on your face, I am going to guess that you forgot?"

"I...well...did we schedule something for today?" I was confused.

"Yep. I left you two messages on your phone. Told you the day and time and said call me back if this is a problem...otherwise I'll see you then." Elizabeth stated.

"Oh my God," I said. "I never got the messages. Shit. Stupid phone. I don't know why it didn't make that alert sound or ring or vibrate or something."

"Hm, me neither but well...here we are." Elizabeth said with a hopeful grin.

"Uh, yeah, here you are," I agreed. "Well, come in I guess."

I stepped aside and let Elizabeth in and waited for her crew to follow. I now saw a fourth person, a woman, carrying a case. I shrugged and closed the door behind her.

The foursome headed toward the living room where Ernie had returned to his spot on the couch next to Charlotte. He had already brought two glasses of juice and put them on the table. We all entered the room and just stood, each of us looking from one to the other waiting for someone to take the lead. It was Elizabeth who finally spoke.

"So, June, this would be a great place to film the interview, but I see Ernie and his tutor have dibs on the room."

I was still in a state of unpreparedness, so it took me a few seconds for everything to register.

"Ernie, can you and Charlotte take your things into the kitchen and use the table there to work? Mommy needs to use this room."

"Sure Mrs. G," Charlotte said and gathered her books.

"You gonna be on TV Mom?" Ernie asked looking at the camera and strangers in his living room.

"I hope not,'" I said. "God I hope not."

Ernie followed Charlotte to the kitchen, holding the two glasses of juice.

"June," Elizabeth said, "This is the crew: Roger on camera, Dillan is the sound guy and Maggie is your makeup artist."

"You mean we're actually going to do this *now*? I didn't expect there would be a crew. And I'm a mess. I would have had my hair done and makeup and..." I hoped to dissuade her.

"No worries. You look fine...or you will when Maggie gets through with you." Elizabeth added with that smart-ass sarcasm that drew me to her initially.

"Uggh. I hate you," I said, only half joking. "What about my clothes?" I was in my third or fourth day of ever-lessening business attire and was quickly morphing back into soccer mom look. Fortunately, today was Ernie's doctor appointment so I had managed to put on a nice pair of slacks and white blouse.

"Love the slacks, nix the white blouse...doesn't play well with the camera. Got anything light blue to go with the dark blue slacks, or beige...?"

"Ah, sure I have a light blue or can I just put a blue sweater over the white blouse?"

"Eh, could work but the blue blouse would be better."

"You know you haven't even asked me if this was okay to do now."

"Phone."

"Huh?"

"Hand me your phone," Elizabeth held out her hand. I gave her my phone, skeptical about what she was up to.

Elizabeth took my phone and studied it before explaining.

"You see this little tab on the side?" She showed me as I peered at it. "If this tab is down like this, it turns the sound off. Have you dropped your phone recently?"

"I don't know. Probably."

"Well, you did. And when you do, it can easily move that tab to the off position without you knowing it. So, when I called twice your phone didn't ring and you didn't check for messages either. So upstairs you go and change your blouse. Maggie will be ready for you when you come down."

I stared at Elizabeth for a minute. How dare she tell me it was *my* fault and tell me what to do...then I went upstairs and changed my blouse.

When I came back down, Elizabeth had arranged the couch so that my comforter was moved somewhere else and the pillows were neatly fluffed and placed two in each corner. She borrowed another cushion from the big living room chair to place behind my back so that I wouldn't sink into the couch and look as though I was slouching. Roger, the cameraman, already had his camera set up and pointed to the place where I would sit.

Dillon, the sound guy, had his boom mic hooked up to the camera with wires into one of his metal boxes; he was doing sound checks.

Maggie had brought a dining room chair into the living room and directed me to sit there while she worked on my makeup. After about twenty minutes, she had done the best she could do with what she had to work with—my words—and we were ready to film.

Elizabeth directed me to sit on the couch in my "place." She would sit off camera in front of me and ask questions. I was a nervous wreck. I wasn't certain about this entire thing and now the reality of it had come without warning with no time to prepare mentally. All that ran through my head was the plethora of information I had just read about mitochondrial disease.

"So June, let's do a sound check. Just respond to me in your normal voice and look at *me*, don't look at the camera. We are just having a conversation." Elizabeth saw my nervousness and the far-away look on my face and gently brought me back to the matter at hand.

"Maggie, get June a glass of water in case her mouth gets dry. Ernie can tell you where the glasses are." Elizabeth was in complete control now.

"Here we go with a test. Hi June. Tell me what kind of car do you drive?"

"What kind of car do I drive?"

"Yes. It's a sound test, not a congressional inquisition." Elizabeth joked.

"Fine. I drive a Jeep Cherokee that is eight years old and needs to be replaced. It's white with a tan interior and it gets terrible gas mileage. What kind of a car do *you* drive?"

"I ask the questions. Roger, camera okay?"

"Roger," he said. I should have expected that but it made me laugh. "Shouldn't he be the sound man?" I suggested. I couldn't stop myself.

I was on the verge of hysterical, nervous laughing. Elizabeth and everyone else ignored me. Roger probably got that response a million times. But hey, it was his fault for answering "Roger."

"Dillon—all good?" Elizabeth continued.

"Roger," Dillon couldn't help himself either. Now everyone grinned. "I knew I should have done your interview first," Elizabeth said and rolled her eyes.

Maggie came back into the room with a glass of water and placed it on the table in front of me but out of sight of the camera.

"Cute kid you got there. I think I like him," Maggie said as she backed away from the couch.

"Thanks, I think…What did he do?"

"Nothing," Maggie said. "I asked him if I could have a glass of water. He just looked up and said yes and then went back to what he was doing. So, I asked him if he could *get* me a glass of water. When he hesitated, I changed it to would he please get me a glass for water for *you*. And he did."

This brought a chuckle from cameraman Roger.

"Yeah, he should come with a warning sign for strangers," I said. "He isn't being fresh, he's...well, he's just a very literal kid."

"Okay. So, let's get the interview started." Elizabeth resumed control. "June, one other thing. We talked about you meeting Kalea and her aunt, so I have asked them to come by."

I stared wide-eyed at Elizabeth.

"Before you freak or throw me out...we did talk about this and you agreed it was about time and would be a positive thing for her and for you."

"Oh my God. Elizabeth! I am not prepared for *any* of this and now you throw meeting Kalea at me? Are you going to film that too?"

"Yes. I know, I know. It's a lot to deal with. Remember I told you some of this would not be easy. But June, they are just as nervous as you are and well, people want to see this special connection...the human side of what your actions meant."

I looked around the living room and then at the dining room and kitchen before responding.

"I would have cleaned the house if I knew they were coming." I was resigned to the fact that this was going to happen now and aware that I had agreed–even if I had no evidence of agreeing to doing it today.

"Your house looks fine."

"Yeah well, don't let them see Elsie's bedroom."

"Umm... Okay, we weren't planning on that," Elizabeth said reassuringly with a touch of sarcasm. "We will just film you three meeting for the first time and then they will join you on the couch for a few questions—and that's it. So, you ready to begin the interview?"

"Yeah. Okay. I guess so."

"Good. Guys let's record everything and then we'll edit in the intros later."

The camera light went on, the sound man held his boom overhead and Elizabeth began the questioning.

"June, tell us a little bit about you—your work, family life…just a little background."

"Well, I'm an accountant—or I was. I am a part-time bookkeeper now and full-time mom."

"And did the accident have anything to do with you changing career goals?" Elizabeth's voice came out from behind the lights.

"No, that happened a while ago. It was family things."

"Tell us about your family…"

That is how the interview continued. Elizabeth asked questions and I answered them. When I had a hiccup with words or thoughts, we would stop so I could re-group, and Elizabeth would repeat the question, so we could re-shoot it.

At the beginning, the questions were fairly innocuous, work, kids, husband, how long I had lived in the neighborhood…just background information that was not too invasive as Elizabeth had promised when I agreed to do the interview.

Then the difficult question came.

"June, can you walk us through that day? Take us from being at work consulting with clients on tax issues and taking a quick break for lunch, to the accident. What happened? Take your time, I know recalling this can be difficult."

And she was right. We had to stop a few times for me to compose myself, though I knew some of those dramatic parts would be left in. At one break, Maggie had to run into the kitchen to quiet Charlotte

179

and Ernie; the sound of their energetic tutoring was carrying into the living room and onto the recording.

Another time, we had to stop because Elsie came home from school. She walked into the living room and was spellbound to see her mom sitting in front of a camera, all made up and lights shining in her face with a microphone hanging over her head.

As soon as I saw her I went into outraged mom mode, partially spurred on by the emotion of retelling that day. Ignoring the fact that we were filming, I set out to reprimand Elsie about her room.

"You get upstairs, pick up your clothes, make your bed, straighten out your dresser drawers, dust, and bring all those dishes downstairs! And don't make any noise...we are filming." I loudly scolded her as I rose from the couch.

"Geez okay, Mom. Prima donna much?" Elsie said loud enough for me to hear.

I sent Elsie a glare that said more than words and she made a hasty retreat up the stairs as fast as her little legs could take her. Then I returned to the couch and saw Elizabeth and the crew staring at me.

"I hope you got that little bit of real family life on film!" I quipped sending everyone into a much-needed moment of laughter.

"You should come by my house and record us!" Roger offered. "I've got *three* teenagers!"

"That was pretty real, but I promise we will cut it out. Maybe just share it on social media." Elizabeth teased.

The doorbell rang just then.

"I'll get it," Maggie piped up and scurried out of the room toward the front door while we picked up the interview with the end of my story.

When we were done, Elizabeth checked with the cameraman and looked at parts of what was just filmed as she had done on and off during the process. Satisfied, she looked back to me.

"Well, that looks like it's going to be really good, June. You're a natural and the last part especially was very impactful." Elizabeth made her way over to the couch and sat next to me. She took hold of my hands which I had folded neatly in my lap.

"So…I am pretty certain that is Kalea and her aunt Lashay at the door. I know that this is a private moment and we are invading that privacy. But just let it be what it is. Forget about us. This is about you meeting the life you saved. Okay?"

I nodded slightly.

"Okay. We all set crew?" Elizabeth changed her focus to Roger and Dillon, each of whom gave a thumbs-up. Then Elizabeth turned back to me. "Take a deep breath. Let's bring in your guests."

Maggie, who had been leaning into the room to eavesdrop for her cue, lead Kalea and Lashay into the room. I rose from the couch and stepped out from behind the coffee table to greet them. My heart was pounding. I didn't know what to say or how to act. You can't rehearse something like this—not if you're human.

Lashay guided Kalea into the room by her shoulders and they stopped just in front of me.

Kalea looked beautiful. She was in a pretty blue dress with dainty white flowers, black patent leather shoes with a bow on each, white socks, and a light blue, flowered hair comb neatly holding back the bangs of her long, curly brown locks. She looked as though she had stepped out of a children's fashion magazine. Her head was slightly lowered as her aunt eased her closer to me.

I knelt to be on eye level with her. I was about to speak—what I was going to say I didn't know—when Kalea raised her head and brought her deep, doe brown eyes into contact with mine. I said nothing. Kalea said nothing. We weren't being shy; we were both too emotional to speak.

My lips quivered as my heart tried to find the right words. Tears escaped from Kalea's beautiful eyes, and my own tears followed.

Kalea threw her arms around me and I hugged her close. Together, we sobbed. At that moment, there was no one else in the room. There was no camera or cameraman, no soundman, no Elizabeth. Almost as Elizabeth had instructed, we had forgotten them.

Kalea cried into my ear. "Thank you. Thank you for saving my life."

"I'm so sorry that I couldn't save everyone, Kalea. I'm so sorry." I wept in response as Kalea and I continued our slightly spasmed embrace. "I'm so sorry I couldn't save your parents." I softly spoke through my tears, giving the "everyone" an identity that was so painful to acknowledge.

We stayed in our moment out of time for another minute, waiting for our emotions to subside when we could join the rest of the world.

When we finally pulled apart, I tried to wipe Kalea's tears with my sleeve, and used the other sleeve for my own eyes—without much success. I looked up helplessly to the others in the room. They were all crying.

The cameraman's head was hidden by his machine, but I heard him sniffle. Dillon, while maintaining his grip on the microphone boom with one hand still placed overhead in just the right spot, was trying subtly to wipe his eyes with the other. Maggie stood with her arms crossed and a stream of tears running down her cheeks. Elizabeth clutched her notepad, digging her fingernails deep into the cardboard cover as she tried to be stoic and above the emotion. Of course, she failed the unhuman test and had to wipe her eyes more than once.

Finally, Kalea's aunt Lashay, a mess of tears herself, stepped forward and handed Kleenex tissues to each of us; she was the only one who was truly prepared for the effect of this meeting. When I accepted my tissue, Lashay embraced me.

After a few seconds, she stood back but held onto my arms just above my elbows and looked me in the eyes to make certain I was listening to every word.

"Elizabeth told us you hate hearing this, but you *are* our hero. Kalea and I will always remember you and celebrate you and what you did."

Lashay was so sincere that she brought about another round of tears while I hugged her back.

During the entire scene, I was oblivious to what was going on around me. I didn't notice that Ernie and Charlotte had come out of the kitchen and into the edge of the living room to see what was going on. Elsie, who was too curious to miss the excitement in the living room, had risked her mother's ire to sneak back downstairs and witness me meeting Kalea and her aunt.

And all three were affected by the emotion they witnessed. Ernie walked up to me and gave me a big hug.

"Luv you Mom," he said, with tears in his eyes. Then he headed back toward Charlotte and the kitchen. When he got about even with Elsie, who was standing in the hallway now, he stopped and walked back. He stood in front of Lashay, who was still holding the box of Kleenex. Ernie held out his hand. Lashay figured it out pretty quickly and handed Ernie a tissue.

"Three please." Ernie requested.

Lashay counted out two more tissues and placed them into Ernie's hand. Satisfied, Ernie walked to Elsie and handed her a tissue. Then he walked over to Charlotte and handed her one. Finally, he brought the third one to his face and loudly cleared his sinuses. He walked with Charlotte back to the kitchen.

Kalea, who was still at my side, held my hand and smiled up at me through her red, swollen eyes. The sweetness of the scene combined with its humor, had temporarily transformed the heaviness that had engulfed us all. It took a while, along with nearly the entire box of Kleenex, before everyone was composed enough to sit on the couch and return to the interview.

CHAPTER ELEVEN

MY BRAVE LITTLE MAN

Elizabeth seemed pleased with the interview with Kalea, her aunt Lashay, and me. When we wrapped, I had everyone come into the kitchen for a cup of coffee–freshly made *my* way.

Charlotte had left by then and Ernie had retreated to his room for a nap. Elsie, I figured, was busy cleaning her room–hope springs eternal.

The entire event took about three hours which meant it was just after 5 pm when we finally broke. It was close to the time when Tim would come home. I walked Elizabeth and the crew to the door and said my goodbyes to Maggie, Roger, and Dillon. Elizabeth lingered after the others had headed to the van. Kalea and Lashay remained in the kitchen.

"June. Thank you. This meant a lot to me, but I hope too that you got something good out of it." Elizabeth gave me a big hug.

"Yeah, all-in-all, I'm glad I did it," I said, hugging her back. "I'm glad I met Kalea. I think we both needed that. I was trying so hard to ignore the emotions and avoid reliving everything. I wanted to down-play the entire event. Especially, I wanted to avoid feeling as though I failed Kalea by not saving her parents too. I didn't know how to face her with that…that feeling of being responsible for their deaths. But, Kalea…she is such a beautiful young girl. And I felt that the minute our eyes met. I knew she understood my pain and that, in a way, I shared hers. Sounds silly I guess, when I say it like that."

"No. No it doesn't, June. And we all witnessed it. Some moments… just are. They don't need words or explanations or judgments. They just need to be left alone. I think this meeting put a period to one sentence in Kalea's story and to yours. It will always stay with you and her, and that is how it should be. But part of it has a special ending."

"Were you a therapist in an earlier life?" I moved to my comfortable place of sarcasm to avoid another gush of emotions.

"No. But I was a psyche major in college. So…" Elizabeth shrugged with a grin. We gave each other one more hug goodbye. Just as Elizabeth reached the front door of the van she looked back at me, still standing in the doorway.

"Call me. We'll have lunch," she said, then realized how trite that sounded. "No, seriously. I would love to get together…soon! You have my card and numbers."

"Yeah okay," I said. "I can probably pry the gum off one of them." I was pleased with my humorous self. But I knew lunch with Elizabeth was something I would look forward to, and that I *would* call her.

When I returned to the kitchen, Lashay was getting Kalea ready for them to leave as well. I felt sad when I saw them preparing to exit my life. It didn't seem right that someone whom I had shared such a connection with was about to be a memory.

I stood for a moment, taking in the two of them, determined to make one of my little movies to play back in my head whenever I needed. That is how I kept special moments close to me, to remind me of the loving moments in my life that would get me through the rougher ones. This was one of those moments.

"Well, June," Lashay said. "I have to get Kalea back home and get dinner on for her and my other two darlings." She sounded exhausted.

"Oh my gosh. Dinner? Isn't that what husbands are for? You know, call them and say 'Hey sweetie, can you pick up dinner on the way home?'" I joked, but I had forgotten all about the time and dinner.

"Honey, I used that one last night. It won't float two nights in a

186

row," Lashay quipped bringing out a chuckle from both of us. "Kalea, say goodbye to Mrs. Gallagher."

Kalea ended our meeting as it had begun. She walked up to me, this time head raised and eyes looking up at me and gave me a big hug as I crouched to meet her. I hugged her back not wanting to let go. When I did finally release her, she looked at me with those penetrating brown eyes and said, "I love you, Mrs. Gallagher."

I took her little face in both hands and said, "Oh, Kalea. I love you too." I kissed her forehead the same way I did my own children.

"You know what, Kalea? You are going to grow up to be an amazing person and have an incredible life. And I hope I get to witness some of it." I said, barely able to contain my emotions.

I stood and exchanged hugs with Lashay. I knew that our lives would most likely take different paths, but I hoped that I might be thought of on major events in Kalea's life. *I would love to share some of those*, I thought.

Lashay led Kalea down the hall and out the front door. All that remained were final goodbyes and thank yous and just like that they were gone. I felt a rush of emptiness as I stood behind the closed front door of our house. A big Chapter in my life had been given an ending. Although I was grateful for that closure, I was equally sad that someone beautiful had left me.

It didn't take long before my solace was interrupted. Elsie stomped down the stairs, thumping the vacuum cleaner behind her. She passed by me with barely a look and continued to the laundry room where we kept the vac. As I watched her, all I could think of was, "Did she actually use the vacuum cleaner?" Because I didn't recall hearing it. When she returned from her laundry room trip, I confronted her before she could make her way back upstairs.

"So, is your room all nice and clean now? 'Cause if it is, I'm ready to go inspect it."

Elsie gave me a blank stare, followed by an exaggerated hug. "I love you so much, Mommy." She said with a cheesy grin.

"And I love a clean room. So, is it?" I asked which broke her mood and her grip on me.

"I don't know…is dinner ready Mom?" Elsie had turned to being snippy now which brought out another of my threatening looks.

"Okay geez. Fine. I just have to finish the bathroom and then do my homework." Elsie blurted out and then ran up the stairs. When she reached the top, her bravery returned. "Maybe I can get some dinner after *that*." She ran into the supposed safety of her room and closed the door. At least she knew better than to slam it.

My daughter is barely 13 and already the transition from sweet Elsie to ugly teenager is happening, I thought. Before I could continue considering all that "that" might mean, Tim's car pulled into the garage. I met him at the doorway to the laundry room.

"Hey," he said and gave me a peck on the cheek before continuing past me and into the kitchen. I followed him. He laid his briefcase on the kitchen table and then helped himself to a beer from the fridge. With the refrigerator door still open, he held the beer bottle up, considered it for a moment, and then put it back without opening it. He continued to stare into the refrigerator, looking as if he expected something wonderful to jump out at him, then closed the door and headed back my way.

I looked at him curiously.

"What?" He said. "I decided that I had more of a scotch day than a beer day so…yeah." He headed toward our little bar cart along one of the walls in the dining room. I just watched him while he grabbed a glass, let out an irritated moan and walked past me toward the kitchen again.

"Forgot the ice," he smiled and gave my cheek another little peck on his way. After he dropped two cubes in his glass, he headed back to the cart and poured a couple fingers of scotch He returned to just in front of me, took a sip of his scotch and sighed.

"Sooo. What's for dinner?" He asked enthusiastically.

"I love you so much Tim," I said giving him a cheesy grin before I threw my arms around him. I knew it hadn't worked for Elsie, but this was Tim–not me, so I thought maybe?

"And I love dinner," he said, his voice dripping with sarcasm, "which I assume has no chance of happening."

"Oh God. This family is so....predictable." I said releasing my hug. "Come sit on the couch with me and you can tell me about your "scotch" day and I can tell you about my day and why dinner is going to be late or...delivery."

I grabbed Tim's hand and led him to the couch. I took my corner seat and patted the space next to me. I was attempting to be as warm and inviting as my comforter and smiled lovingly at him. Tim looked at me with his puppy dog expression. Then a smirk broke through. He shook his head and said, "You are something else" while he plopped down next to me.

"So, tell me about your day?" I suggested.

"Uhmmm, well, actually," he began, "It was pretty typical. Just a lot of meetings and number crunching so I thought a scotch would clear my head better than a beer. Nothing really out of the ordinary. Besides, I would rather hear about your day and how I am going to get dinner out if it eventually."

I got up from the couch and went straight to the junk drawer in the kitchen. I pulled out a stack of take-out menus and then went to the stairway and yelled up to the kids.

"Elsie, Ernie...come get your dinner...quick! Elsie wake Ernie up if he's asleep." Then I went back to my spot on the couch.

"Here is dinner." I said as I handed Tim the stack of menus. "I recommend the Greek place. They're faster and healthier." I added going back to my sweet, loving smile. "Oh wait, before you make dinner, could you get me a glass of white wine? There is some open in the fridge and I don't want to have to get up again."

I usually knew when and how far I could push Tim and when to back off. Sensing his good mood, I thought I would have a little fun.

He looked at me and did what he always does when he thinks I am some sort of alien creature: he shook his head, smirked, and then did what I asked. He left the menus behind and while he was gone, I sought out the Greek restaurant menu and held it, putting the rest of the stack out of the way on the table. Tim returned to the living room closely followed by Elsie and Ernie. Ernie looked groggy and a little pale. Elsie had her, "I am so over you Mom" expression on her face.

"We're having Greek delivery," I announced. "So, everyone take turns and circle what you want on the menu. Then, I am going to tell you all about my interview today while we wait for the food." I grabbed a pencil from the rectangular basket on the table and handed the menu and pencil to Ernie first. No one said anything. Instead, Ernie and Elsie clumped together to read the menu while Tim sipped his scotch and waited his turn.

After everyone had circled their selection, Tim called in the order. Ernie took a seat on the couch next to his dad and Elsie sat on the floor in front of Ernie, leaning against the couch.

"Okay, so we are all ears and waiting with bated breath," Tim proclaimed. "Tell us about this interview."

Ernie looked at Elsie. As weak and sleepy as he still was, he managed a little giggle when he told Elsie, "Ewww, Daddy said he has stinky breath."

Even though Elsie was still in her early teenager mood, she couldn't resist her brother's interpretation of his dad's words. "He said we all have stinky breath and you have the stinkiest," she teased him, grinning.

"No, Mommy has stinkiestest breath," and off they went into Silly Land.

"Ughh, okay you two," I interrupted. "Can this family have a nice conversation? I have something important I want to share with you all. Do you want to hear about the interview or not?"

"You mean the interview you did with the TV people who I saw you with where you were a star and yelled at me in front of everyone?"

Elsie took her shot. I didn't glare at her. I gave her a look of disappointment and hurt and didn't respond.

"Okay," she said, suddenly apologetic. "Sorry Mom. I want to hear about it...really."

"I saw some, Mommy. Heard some. And the little girl." Ernie piped in.

"Well, I am really intrigued now. I definitely want to hear all about it." Tim joined in with encouragement, sensing this was a family talk moment that we needed to have, and something I wanted and needed to share.

"Okay. So...where do I start? Last month there was an accident..."

While I told the story, Elsie and Ernie became more focused and involved in it, asking questions when they had them. Tim had heard most of it before and Elsie knew some of it, but much of it that was new—especially to them—was my sharing the feelings I had then and now. I edited out the gory details of the accident and concentrated more on the events afterward and especially on the interview and how it felt to finally meet Kalea.

Ernie was fascinated, and he loved the idea that his mom was a hero. He had seen some of the interaction with Kalea but he didn't know how everything connected and why I was so sensitive with her. Elsie, being more like me, was taken in by the emotional impact of it all and softly cried during the part about meeting Kalea. Tim was very quiet during my telling about meeting Kalea today and at one point reached for my hand and gave it a slight squeeze.

When I finished, we all sat in silence, interrupted only when the doorbell rang. It was good timing and brought everyone back to a lighter reality. I stood up quickly and announced, "Food! I'll get it. Tim, you and the kids set the table. Okay?" I headed for the door.

"I'll help you get the food Mom," Elsie offered.

"Okay, grab my purse off the kitchen counter," I instructed her.

Tim and Ernie went about setting the kitchen table while Elsie grabbed my purse and met me at the front door. She grabbed the two big bags of food from the delivery man while I got the cash from my purse and paid him.

I closed the door and turned to walk toward the kitchen. Elsie stood in front of me and, when I was close enough to her, she threw her arms, weighted down by the bags of food, around my waist. She gave me a nice hug, then she stepped back and looked at me with slight traces of tears rolling down her cheeks.

"I love you, Mom," she said. She stood looking at me for a minute. "That's all." She shrugged her shoulders then she turned to deliver the food to the kitchen. I stopped her for a moment.

"Wait, Elsie. Umm, did Ernie show you his new drawing he made at the doctor's office?" I asked wanting to answer my earlier curiosity.

"Oh yeah," she said and grinned. "It was great. A big yellow cat. He was fuzzy and cute. Why do you want to know?"

"Oh nothing. I just wanted to make certain he showed you and that ummm, well, you liked it." I said fibbing a little. I really wanted to know if she saw a cat right off or if Ernie had to tell her.

"We should get a cat Mom. I think Ernie likes them. He draws them a lot and they're always different but kind of the same, ya know?"

"Oh yeah, yup," I continued with my little fib, wondering still how Elsie saw cat when Tim and I saw dinosaur or some other creature. Then I realized this was just another way that these two connected within their special relationship. I hoped they would always be this way; always there for each other and always connected.

But I also wondered if Ernie would be prepared for Elsie's continuing journey into "teenager-ness" and the potential separation from her "uncool" family. Would we become irrelevant? I only hoped that for the two of them this would be a short-lived period and that they would come out the other end as best friends.

***

On Tuesday the following week, Ernie had his examination with

Dr. Blackwell. She found nothing that was contrary to her thinking about the mitochondrial disease diagnosis, but nothing definitive either; which was her expected result.

Ernie was deemed fit for biopsy, so it was scheduled for that Thursday. Dr. Blackwell figured that would give Ernie enough recuperating time to ready him for his return to school the following Monday. That was also Thanksgiving week, so he only needed to attend Monday and Tuesday before school was out for a long weekend.

Meanwhile, she would send Ernie's blood to a new company that offered molecular sequencing of DNA and specifically mtDNA, to test for markers for mitochondrial disease. This was fairly new and the results could take a very long time. And yet they still might not be specific enough. But the doctor thought it was a good step to take with a potentially significant benefit.

Thursday was a low-energy day for Ernie. Tim had difficulty rousing him from sleep, so it took me a few trips to his room to get him moving. I felt bad dragging him out of bed like that, but this test was too important to reschedule.

If Ernie was a bit nervous, he didn't show it. Ever the trooper, he only asked a few questions.

"Mom," he said while he buckled himself into the back seat and I eased out of the driveway, "how long it will take? Do I stay in hospital? Will it hurt?"

I told him he would be coming home with me right away after the procedure and allayed his fears about any pain. He brightened a bit. I told him they would do something so he couldn't feel what was happening, and that there would just be a little sting like when Elsie pinched him. And, I told him, I would be there with him the whole time. I think that pleased him more than anything.

When we got to the hospital, everything went as planned. Dr. Blackwell's nurse met us in the hospital lobby and took us to the room where the biopsy would be performed. Because this was an out-patient procedure, there was no need for an operating room: we were ushered into a patient exam room. There we were met by Dr.

Blackwell and the doctor who would perform the procedure, Dr. Phillips. After a brief introduction, Dr. Blackwell began to explain what would be happening.

"So, Ernie," she said, stooping a little to look in his eyes, "this will be very quick and simple and you won't feel much of anything. Then you can be off back home right away. Okay?"

"I will be pinched," Ernie corrected, tightly gripping my hand.

Dr. Blackwell pulled her head back slightly then gave Ernie a smile. "Yes, you might feel a little pinch, but nothing a big, brave, boy like you can't manage." She reassured.

"K."

"Can I stay with him?" I asked.

"I don't see why not..." Dr. Blackwell said and looked toward Dr. Phillips.

"Yes, that should be fine. In fact, if you stand facing Ernie with your back to the procedure, that will help him keep his focus on you and keep him still," Dr. Phillips suggested.

I nodded and smiled at Ernie, giving him a wink.

"Ok Ernie, we need you to take off your pants and hop up on the bed here," Dr. Phillips said.

Ernie looked at everyone in the room before giving me a shy look of embarrassment. Dr. Blackwell got it immediately.

"Ernie, you can go into that bathroom," she gestured to the other closed door in the room. "There is a robe hanging on the back of the door that you can put on. It will be kind of huge on you, though. Do you want your mom to go with you and help?"

"K," Ernie said. He looked at me and then led me by the hand to the bathroom.

Ernie took off his pants, handed them to me, and then pulled on the huge robe. He looked silly standing there with all this material hanging around his feet. It made us both grin. I tied the sash around Ernie's waist then rolled the excess of robe into the sash, so that it stayed out of the way enough for Ernie to walk back into the exam room. He climbed up onto the bed without any help.

Dr. Phillips asked Ernie to lie down, then pushed the robe further up Ernie's right leg, exposing his upper thigh.

Dr. Blackwell gently touched my back and pointed to where she wanted me to stand. "June, if you stand over there with Ernie, facing him, I'll go to the other side and act as nurse today." Dr. Blackwell said as she moved to Ernie's left side.

I took my place close to Ernie, with my back to Doctor Phillips, blocking the procedure from Ernie's view. I brushed Ernie's hair off his forehead then held onto his hand while I smiled at him, making him as comfortable and secure as possible.

"Ernie," I am just having Doctor Blackwell rub some liquid on your leg, so you might feel something cold." Doctor Phillips began as he readied for the biopsy. "Then you are going to feel just a slight pinch. This is medicine to make your leg feel a little numb. After that, you might feel a little pressure, but nothing will hurt. If it does, let us know. So just stay as still as possible and it will be over before you know it."

Dr. Phillips was business-like but had a comforting tone to his voice. He made everything seem very matter-of-fact no big deal, which was just what Ernie needed. Me too.

Shortly after Doctor Phillips' last statement, I felt Ernie tense just a bit and his hand squeeze mine for a second.

"Pinch, Mom," he said.

"Yah, just a little though, right? Are you keeping your leg still?" I smiled and did my bit to make it no big deal, too.

"Yeah."

A couple minutes later, I heard the two doctors mention scalpel and knew they would be doing the small incision. I was told this could feel like a strange tugging, so I kept Ernie occupied with me and with staying still until I heard Doctor Phillips say, "Okay. That went nicely. Good sample. Let's put a couple adhesive strips over the area, I don't think we need stitches for this."

That was my cue that it was over. And I let Ernie know as well. "All done honey. Just need to finish putting the band aid on and we're off –right doctor?" I said directing my voice toward Doctor Blackwell.

"Yep," Dr. Blackwell said. "All done, Ernie. You did great." Ernie beamed at her.

"Okay folks," Dr. Phillips said. "I'm going to get this sample over to the lab. Dr. Blackwell will give you instructions about changing the bandage and anything else you need." He gave a quick wave and a smile to Ernie and was off before we could thank him.

"Okay Ernie, you can go get dressed now," Dr. Blackwell said. "Mom, let's help him down off the table and then you go with him to change. Ernie, you might feel a slight tugging on your leg when you walk for a couple of days. It's nothing to worry about, BUT, no rough-housing or running or playing sports for at least two or three days. Your mom will see to it."

Turning her attention to me, she said, "And June, change the bandage once a day and give my office a call if you see any lasting redness or swelling or anything that suggests the wound is not healing. We want to guard against infection. You can get the bandage material in our Pharmacy here. Any questions? Everything good Ernie?"

"K," Ernie said.

"Does he need to come back for anything…well, there are no stitches, right?" I asked.

"Right, no stitches," Dr. Blackwell answered. "But I'll have my nurse make a follow-up appointment for next week to just see that everything is healing well. You also need to stop by the reception desk before you leave to fill out paperwork for today's procedure. I'll see you two in about a week. We won't have the lab results back before then, though."

"Okay. Thank you, Dr. Blackwell. Say 'thank you,' Ernie."

"Thank you," he said.

"You are welcome Ernie, and you were very brave."

"K."

Dr. Blackwell tousled Ernie's hair, smiled at me, and left the room. I watched Ernie as he studied the bandage on his leg for a few seconds.

"Everything okay honey?"

"K. We get dressed now." He stretched out his arms for me to help him off the table.

I helped him get dressed and then he limped along beside me as we made our way back to the reception area. He sat, keeping his leg straight, while he waited for me to fill out the necessary paperwork.

Ernie continued his awkward walk as we headed for the car and home: his leg felt a little tight around the bandage he said, and his pant leg rubbed against his covered wound. He wanted to get home quickly and put on his pjs which were soft cotton and *very* baggy and would not rub. But, Ernie was also hungry. So, rather than head straight home, we went to IHOP because, as Ernie put it, "I get reward 'cause I was brave." How could I say no? I swear that kid would eat every meal at IHOP if he had his way.

***

We were planning to send Ernie back to school the following Monday, but Ernie became very weak over the weekend and by Monday, he had begun vomiting. It continued as it had in past cycles, and that meant we had to keep him out of school longer than we had hoped. As before, his episodes were not food-related and his heaving was dry and granular, as if his insides were projecting outwardly. Combined with his weakened condition, it was worrisome. We contacted Dr. Blackwell. Finally, we had someone to reach out to who was familiar with this type of cyclical vomiting.

Although she recognized it as another likely presentation of mitochondrial disease, she did find it unique that Ernie would go long periods without experiencing these particular symptoms.

We kept our appointment to check on Ernie's leg, and the Dr. added another examination for possible direct causes of his vomiting. She wanted to see if there was something more concrete than the illusive mitochondrial disease supposition. There was none.

Dr. Blackwell told us that she was concerned over how low Ernie's energy was and how much thinner he looked after just a few days. Although she had not received specific confirmation yet that Ernie had mitochondrial disease, she decided to put Ernie on a "mito cocktail" daily vitamin regimen. These energy-enhancing vitamins had proven effective for many of Dr. Blackwell's mito patients, specifically with improving energy.

The concoction was made up of key ingredients of Coenzyme Q-10 and L-carnitine along with B-vitamins and others. I was familiar with it from the hours spent at my computer reading everything I could.

So many vitamins meant Ernie would have to take as many as 50 pills every day, in high dosages, with some side effects. Tim and I needed to find a compounding pharmacist in our area who could combine the recommended vitamin regiment into liquid format, just to make things easier for Ernie.

The next day was Thanksgiving. I wanted to make my traditional New England feast complete with acorn squash, stuffing, and two kinds of homemade cranberry sauce; just as I had made the year before. But with all that was going on with Ernie, all I had time to make was reservations. We had a very festive meal at an old mill house turned restaurant. It was a nice evening; one of the few times we were able to go out as a family. We missed not having leftovers the next day, but we had so much to be thankful for that no one complained.

***

It took about a week to get the prescriptions, due to the high dosages and the instructions from Dr. Blackwell to the pharmacist. The pharmacist we found was about 20 minutes from Tim's office, so he became the official securer of Ernie's vitamins or as Elsie later named him, Ernie's cocktail waiter.

During that week of waiting, I put Ernie back on tutor sessions with Charlotte, anticipating that he would need yet another week on his vitamin therapy before he would be ready to attend school. Charlotte was happy to get the additional work and pleased to help her favorite student—as she put it.

I was pleased that Ernie wouldn't lose study time even if he did miss class time and would remain disconnected from his friends. I knew he missed playing with them and that saddened me.

I continued to pick up assignments at the principal's office from Ernie's teachers and delivered completed work back to the principal, who acted as compiler of everything.

Despite all of Ernie's set-backs, we had managed to keep Ernie back only one year. Now in second grade, we teetered on having him miss another year; but I was determined not to let that happen to him.

During Ernie's extended time away from school, I stayed close to home and took him with me when I had to go shopping or made a trip to the Starbucks drive through. Given his recent battle with low energy and vomiting, I was fearful that he might be approaching another MODS event.

Tim worked overtime as end-of-quarter corporate tax preparations approached. Most nights he didn't come home until after 7 pm.

Christmas and New Year's were approaching too, and after the holidays, he would be working on Saturdays, preparing his clients for springtime tax season. So, my time confined to the house was only going to get longer as the months went along if Ernie continued to need to stay at home.

Normally, during this time of year, Tim loved to putter around the house. He would spend time tightening all the loose kitchen cabinet handles, changing the smoke alarm batteries, or preparing the house for winter; he found this relaxing. As fall went along, his putzing would evolve to cleaning the gutters, raking and bagging leaves, and cleaning the garage. Tim would often involve Ernie in these little tasks as his special helper. It was fun bonding time with his dad for Ernie and he was especially helpful at diving into a newly raked pile of leaves that had been neatly gathered before bagging.

Tim wasn't overly fond of this activity, but he chuckled at how much fun Ernie had.

The best part for Ernie was Tim chasing him around the yard threatening him with the rake. Ernie would run in circles for a bit, his dad in hot pursuit, then find a pile of freshly-raked leaves and collapse into them. Tim would then grab handfuls of leaves and throw them on top of Ernie until he was completely covered. Ernie, short of breath but still in the game, would wait until he was smothered in leaves and then slowly rise out of them like a zombie coming back to life. He would stand straight up, arms extended unbent outward–like a Frankenstein monster–and walk toward Tim, growling and spitting leaves out of his mouth. Tim would feign horror and fear and run away screaming, Ernie walking ever faster toward him, acting more menacing with each step.

Depending upon how much energy Ernie had, this would eventually end with Ernie on top of his dad, the two of them laughing and pleased with themselves and their play.

Tim's reward for his completed chores and encounter with Frankenstein, was a cold beer and the afternoon sports game. During this time of year, there was always something on–baseball, pro and college football, basketball, or soccer; Tim was never at a loss for something to cheer for or against.

Ernie would join Tim on the couch, glass of juice in hand, and the two men would sip their brews and share commentary about each team's performance and the stupidity of refs.

As an observer to their vociferous bonding time, I learned that one thing all sports have in common is the ineptitude of the officials. The only thing that could drag Ernie away from watching sports with Tim was Elsie looking for something to do, such as coloring or watching some silly video on YouTube.

Now, with Ernie's health in jeopardy and still needing to recover, his bonding activities with his dad were limited; there would be no leaf- raking or Frankenstein moments. He would have to settle for yelling at the players and refs on TV.

I had barely any connection left with my office, and I wasn't taking on any new clients, so there was little or no opportunity to socialize even there. I only had two familiar places to get adult time—some needed "me" time. I wasn't looking for anything grand, just an hour here or there on the weekend to connect with a friend. Most of my college friends had move away or had families of their own. Some, I just lost touch with.

My two options were to spend time with Ginny, who had so often taken Elsie during one of Ernie's unpredictable emergencies; and Elizabeth, my new "friendly" reporter whose company I was learning to appreciate.

I decided to call Ginny and invite her out for lunch on a Saturday while I still had Tim at home to watch Ernie.

I wanted to go someplace nice and treat Ginny for all her kindnesses shown Elsie in our times of need. There was a great little bistro downtown known for their amazing brunch offerings. They had an outdoor seating area in the back, with a trellis vined with delicate white lights woven between the green of rambling ivory. The tables and chairs were white wrought iron with flower pedals intermittently placed as to not overwhelm the clean simplicity of the overall design. Heaters were placed inside a large awning that could be opened or closed on all sides, making the area usable all year round.

The menu had the bistro's take on brunch classics such as eggs benedict and corned beef hash along with some specialties like Italian panna cotta pancakes, Dutch pannekoeken with stroop, and English bangers and mash. Theirs was an eclectic menu where anyone could experiment or go for America's standard eggs and bacon and sausage fare. And they made a great Bloody Mary with a green olive, celery, and a crispy piece of bacon.

I called Ginny excited, thinking about how nice brunch with her would be and what a great treat–for both of us.

Ginny answered her cell phone after about five rings, just before the call went to voice mail.

"Ginny! Hi it's June. I am so glad I caught you."

"Oh, hi June." Ginny said. She definitely lacked my enthusiasm. "Listen," I said, pressing on anyway, "so, you have been such a doll watching Elsie all the time and I really appreciate it. And, ughh, it's has been so long since you and I just had a coffee or anything more than a wave across the street. God knows *I* could use some adult conversation time with a friend," I was babbling.

"Well, anyway I want to take you to Bella Famiglia for brunch on Saturday." I said anticipating that my invite to this well-known restaurant would garner *some* returned enthusiasm.

My sentence hung there for a moment or two as if I had just asked to borrow a thousand dollars. Finally, she responded.

"Oh. Oh, that isn't necessary June. I was happy to help." Her reply was flat.

"No. I know. I mean I get you were just being a good friend, but I want to do something nice in return, and like I said, I would enjoy your company." I rephrased my words slightly, thinking maybe I had just caught her off-guard with my gesture.

"Really, June you don't have to do that; and actually, I can't possibly get away Saturday."

"Oh. Oh, well it doesn't have to be this Saturday. How about next week?" I was disappointed. I really wanted to do it this week.

"Ah, well, I can check with Geoff, but I'm pretty certain he has family outings planned for us for the next few weeks. You know with the holidays coming up and family coming to town and stuff like that." Geoff is Ginny's ex-husband. I was surprised to hear her include him in holiday plans given their ugly divorce.

"Oh. Okay. Yes, I forgot about the holidays and everything." I answered with my own version of apparent disinterest.

"Well. Thanks for the call and happy holidays."

"Yeah. Yes, happy holidays."

As I hung up, I was taken aback. Ginny would normally have loved an invitation like this. She would have refused at first not wanting to make more of her deeds than necessary, but she would have been talked into it and excited to go. This call was like speaking to a stranger. I could have been selling time shares and gotten as much interest.

I didn't know what to make of it. I wondered if maybe she was having difficulties at home and didn't want to be around people. We were friends, but not best friends; maybe she didn't want me asking questions she couldn't answer.

Anyway, I decided to put the conversation out of my head for now and try option number two–Elizabeth. We had said we would keep in touch and even went so far as to mention a lunch date, so I thought this might be good timing.

I had put her number in my phone which was a good thing because I somehow managed to lose the cards she gave me, or they were buried too deeply in my pocket book to find. It took only two rings for Elizabeth to answer.

"Hi Elizabeth, this is June…" That's as much as I got out before she chimed in.

"Yes Junie, I know it's you, your name comes up on my cell phone. Welcome to the 21st century."

Her bright-voiced response was refreshing. She was teasing me, and I welcomed it.

"Okay, if you're going to make fun of me, there will be no free Bloody Mary in your future." I picked up our usual smart-assed banter.

"Oooh, free Bloody Mary? I'm in. When and where?"

"Well, we are going to Bella Famiglia and…Saturday?"

"Bella Famiglia? I love that place!" Her excitement made me smile and my heart feel better. "Oh and *best* Bloody Marys. What day? My mind stopped working after Bella Famiglia."

"You mean it stopped working after Bloody Mary. So, Saturday."

"Sat-ur-day…Sat-ur-day…" Elizabeth said while she considered her calendar. "I have a meeting on Saturday…ehhh the heck with him. I'll re-schedule. Saturday. Definitely. What time?"

"Is 11 am too early?"

"Yes, that is too early for my first Bloody Mary," she said with a laugh. Make it 12:30. And give us two hours. I have lots to catch up with you."

"Oh. Okay. I will make a reservation for 12:30."

"And try to get us outside in the patio. It's supposed to be warm Saturday."

"Wow. Any other demands for your free brunch?"

"Don't be late."

"Aye, Aye captain. See you Saturday at 12:30." I was smiling ear to ear and it felt so good.

"Great. This is going to be such fun!" Elizabeth said. "I thought I was going to have another dull Saturday. See ya then! Bye."

And that was that. Simple. I still had a huge grin on my face while I searched my phone for the restaurant's number. I wanted to make the reservation before I forgot or got shut out of the time Elizabeth wanted.

What a contrast to the conversation with Ginny. Where Ginny was dry and void of interest, Elizabeth was bright and excited and full of life. I still felt bad for how the conversation with Ginny went and it didn't sit well with me, but I needed Elizabeth and her zest. I looked forward to Saturday.

CHAPTER TWELVE

BELLA FAMIGLIA

On Thursday evening, Tim came home later than usual and informed me that he might have to work on Saturday. He was meeting with bookkeepers from the new "big" client ahead of the fourth quarter and end-of-year closing of the books.

Needless to say, I was not a happy camper. And I was not giving up my brunch.

"You cannot work on Saturday Tim," I told him in no uncertain terms.

"Whoa!" he said, looking at me as though some demon had entered my body. "Why not? I'll clean out the gutters when I get home. Ernie will help me. Right buddy?" Tim directed the last of his sentence to Ernie who was sitting in the kitchen with me. Tim sat next to me.

"No. Else and me ride bikes Saturday." Ernie corrected his dad.

"Oh."

"Tim. I don't give a shh…um…poop about the gutters." I said catching myself before I said the "s" word in front of Ernie. But hearing the word "poop" was much better for Ernie and it sent him into the giggles.

Elsie bounded down the stairs and into the kitchen, apparently spurred on by the sound of her brother's giggling.

"What's so funny?" She asked and plopped herself into the seat next to Ernie.

"Poop! Mommy said we have poopy gutters and Daddy wants me to help him clean them." Ernie continued through his laughter. Tim cracked up.

"Ohhh gross Dad!" Elsie scrunched up her face in disgust.

"Ughh, that is not what I said Ernie. I said I didn't care about...the *poopy* gutters." I answered using Ernie's exaggerated emphasis on the word 'poopy'. Then I laughed too. Ernie had a way of affecting everyone around him with his silliness. What really amazed me though, was how long of a response Ernie gave. It was one of the longest sentences he had said in a quite a while, and it needed no interpretation. Was this a good effect from his vitamin cocktails?

I mentally gathered myself and tried to get back on topic.

"Seriously Tim. If you work on Saturday, you *have* to be back before noon. I have plans and you need to stay with these two...adorable children." I added with mockery while flashing an exaggerated grin at Elsie and Ernie.

"What plans?" Tim questioned.

"Plans. Something I have to do."

"Well, how long will you be gone? Elsie can watch Ernie."

"We're going bike riding Saturday after breakfast." Elsie piped up.

"No, Tim, you can go bike riding with them both...and you two can wait for daddy to come home...*before noon.* I don't want Ernie outside without one of us." I insisted. "And that's only if Ernie has the energy to ride his bike." I added. I wondered again if Ernie's newfound energy was the result of his *cocktail.*

"I don't know if we'll be done by then. And, you didn't answer my question. What plans?" Tim kept prodding.

"Why do you have to know every little thing I am doing?" I said not wanting to hear some judgment about why I was going to be out and spending money on myself and a friend.

"Umm, because I'm your husband, and because you're telling me I have to stay home from work." Tim rose from his chair and knelt next to mine. "And because I wuv you." He said mimicking a child as he kissed my cheek and nuzzled my neck.

"Ewe!" Came the coordinated response from Elsie and Ernie.

"Yeah, Tim, ewwwww-uh," I said half kidding as I pretended to wipe Tim's slop from my neck. That made Ernie and Elsie laugh harder.

"Okay fine," I continued. "If you must know...I'm having brunch with Elizabeth."

I said it quickly, rose just as fast, and clapped my hands. "Okay kids, get the table set...dinner in five minutes."

I went to the cabinet to get the dishes out. Dinner had been simmering in the crock pot all day. It just happened to be one of Tim's favorites; beef bourguignon with vegetables. I had a French baguette warming in the oven and the makings for a Caesar salad.

When I turned back toward the table, Tim was still kneeling next to my chair. He gave me one of his, "are you kidding me?" looks. I smiled at him.

"Come on Tim," I barked, like a drill sergeant at boot camp. "The Caesar salad stuff is in the fridge. Chop, chop! Get on that salad."

I just kept going along as though everything was perfectly normal. The kids joined me, doing their respective table-setting chores. Tim didn't say anything. He slowly shook his head at me as if to say "typical"–and went about making the salad.

Tim had spent a year in college working part-time as a waiter. One of the restaurant's specialties was a Caesar salad which the waiters made at diners' tables to serve fresh on their plates. It really was quite good.

Dinner went without any further mention about my upcoming brunch with Elizabeth. I guess on a scale of importance it didn't rank very high. Elsie was unusually talkative and told us all about her day at school. She had to write a scene to act out as a pantomime and present it in class. She had to have a partner for the scene and she chose Beamer, Ginny's son.

Elsie nonchalantly told us that Beamer had hesitated for a bit, looking around the room at other available kids, before accepting an invitation to partner with the girl who he secretly fancied. By the time he had made up his mind, most everyone was partnered except for Cyndy, the shiest girl in the class...maybe the entire school. No one wanted to do a scene with someone who didn't speak.

Elsie said she was upset with Beamer and the other girl at first, but then seeing Cyndy standing alone without anyone to partner with, Elsie felt bad for her. So, she walked up to Cyndy and asked if she would be her partner. Cyndy smiled and agreed.

"Wow honey, I'm surprised about Beamer," I said, "but that was so nice that you asked the shy girl. She probably appreciates it."

"Yeah honey," Tim added, "That was a nice gesture."

"Not really," Elsie said and ducked her head while she poked at her salad with her fork. "I mean I felt bad for her and everything, but we were the last ones left so if I didn't ask her, I would be by myself. Besides, I figured, it's a pantomime. So, you don't have to speak. She just has to act something out with me with gestures. How hard can that be?" Elsie confessed before she took a long drink from her glass of milk.

"What's a panty mine?" Ernie spoke up not realizing what he had said. Tim and I burst into laughter. Elsie laughed so hard that milk started coming out of Elsie's nose. Ernie just stared at us looking sorry he didn't get the joke and couldn't laugh along, although he was amused at Elsie's nose-spurt.

"Oh my God, bro" Elsie chortled. "It isn't *panty mine.*" It's *pan-to-mime.* Say it...panto..." Elsie tried to get Ernie to learn the word without sending us all back into our laughing fits.

"You're a panty head, say it!" Ernie blurted and pushed back his chair with a loud scrape. He ran from the table and up the stairs to his room.

We looked at each other in amazement. Ernie had never reacted this way before. He either would laugh at himself or have no reaction at all. I started to push my chair back to get up and check on him. I felt somewhat guilty for my participation in the joke, but Elsie got up first.

"I got this Mom. I speak Ernie." Elsie said before she rushed out of the kitchen in pursuit of her little brother.

I looked at Tim, Tim looked at me. I shrugged my shoulders. Tim shrugged his shoulders.

"Don't look at *me*," he said. You and Elsie laughed most.

"I feel bad," I said. "Ernie never gets this sensitive about things."

Tim thought for a moment. He took a sip of his wine before responding. "Maybe he has always been this sensitive," he said. "Maybe we just assumed he wasn't because he was so quiet."

That was more insight than I expected or wanted at the time. It made me feel even worse because here was an idea that I possibly didn't really know my little boy well enough to understand his feelings. Had we been so involved with Ernie's physical health that we didn't take enough time to pay attention to what he *wasn't* telling us?

I didn't have an answer, but just the fact that I had the question made me decide that I was going to spend more time at home with him with an emphasis on talking and listening.

Tim decided this was a good time to push me on the brunch question. "So, where are you having this important brunch?"

"Ughh…" I muttered. "You have a one-track mind."

"So, somewhere nice?" Tim said matter-of-factly, ignoring my point.

"You're not going to let this go are you?" He shook his head.

"Fine. Bella Famiglia. Please pass the wine dear." I went back to my casualness about the whole "brunch thing."

"Bella Famiglia? Wow. *Un*believable." Tim was almost scolding me.

Then he changed his tone. "Actually, that's a pretty good choice. Can I come?"

"Nope."

"Honey, you know that place is not cheap, and we are trying to save money."

"I know. But Tim, I am at home all day every day with Ernie and scheduling his tutor, picking up his homework and delivering it back, doing all the shopping and laundry and cooking...I just need a few hours a week to spend with a friend." I said trying not to sound whiney.

Tim considered that for a minute.

"Yeah. Yeah okay. Good point. I get it. Just don't spend those hours at Bella Famiglia every week. We can't afford it!" He smiled at me.

Ernie and Elsie came skipping back into the room, holding hands. They stopped in front of the sink and turned to face Tim and I sitting at the kitchen table. Ernie had one hand behind his back. They didn't speak. They stood there, standing very straight and still, facing us.

When they were certain they had our undivided attention, Ernie moved his hand from behind his back and with a big grin, held up a pair of Elsie's undies. Elsie feigned being upset. She tried to grab the undies, but Ernie snatched them away before she could grab them. She tried again with the same result. Ernie pretended to laugh loudly at Elsie, pointing at her and mimicking huge guffaws until Elsie began to "cry."

This made Ernie stop laughing and stare wide-eyed at Elsie. Elsie pointed at the panties and then pointed at herself.

When Ernie didn't move, she did the series of gestures again. Suddenly, Ernie got it and he pretended to feel bad. He "cried," rubbing his eyes and wiping away fake tears. Then he handed the panties to Elsie.

They both stopped crying and grinned widely.

Elsie declared, vocally this time, "panty *mine.*" Ernie stuck out his tongue at us, and then the two of them joined hands again and skipped out of the room, and ran up the stairs, giggling as they went.

Tim and I were silent at first–stunned more like it–processing what we had just witnessed. Tim spoke first.

"Not the best pantomime I've ever seen but still…clever kids."

"That had Elsie written all over it." I answered.

"Yeah, but I thought Ernie was really good in his part."

"They mocked us!" I said, "and Ernie stuck his tongue out at us! We should be pissed."

"Oh yeah, I am so pissed at them for that." Tim tried desperately to hide the smile that was pushing out his cheeks.

"*Un*-believable Tim. You think that was funny." I tried to suck in my own smile. Before Tim could respond to me, we both burst out laughing.

"Oh my God, June, That, was the funniest thing I've seen them do!" Tim gasped.

"Oh, they were *so* getting revenge for us laughing at Ernie," I said. "And I can't believe Elsie gave Ernie a pair of her undies–and he held them up! Don't know how she convinced him they weren't full of cooties."

"I was just hoping they were clean ones," Tim said, tears streaming down his cheeks.

"Oh gross, Tim. You always have to take it that one step beyond! Now you ruined the joke for me."

"Sorry. I was just being…practical." Tim tried to weasel out of his inappropriate comment.

I ignored him. "I can't decide if we should call them down to scold them for being bratty or to tell them how good they were. I have to admit, it was a pretty clever way to get back at us for laughing at Ernie."

"Yeah it was really good," Tim said. "Did you notice how Elsie managed to get out of being part of the guilty party? I mean *she* laughed at Ernie the most."

"Oh yeah. She switched sides and came up with this clever little response, so she totally won Ernie over. She's quite the little manipulator when she wants to be." I grinned.

"Hmmm. I wonder where she gets that from? Tim rhetorically asked.

I tilted my head to the side and looked at him with one eyebrow raised, suggesting that he should stop wondering and go in another direction.

"We should call them down to finish dinner." Tim said taking the hint. "They didn't eat any salad."

"Well, we could have saved the salad if you didn't put the dressing on the whole thing and just put it in a cup or something, on the side. Like I always tell you. Now it will just get soggy."

"And, as I always tell *you*, that's not how I make my delicious, perfect Caesar's salad. You know I made these at a restaurant..."

"Blah, blah, blah, yeah while you were working your way through college even though your parents could have paid for it blah blah blah." I knew what his response was going to be from years of this routine. "Okay Mr. Waiter, let's see how good you are at busing tables. Clear the table and bring me the dishes." I said and rose from my chair.

Tim had his hurt puppy dog look on his face that was softened by a slight smirk. I couldn't resist. I took his face in my hands and kissed his lips. Then I headed for the sink. By the time the table was cleared and the dishes had been put in the dishwasher, Ernie and Elsie had ventured back downstairs and were plopped on the couch scanning television stations.

Finding a show to interest a 13-year-old *and* a 10-year-old, *and* their parents is not easy. Elsie often watched cartoons or other younger fare with Ernie–that doesn't appeal to Tim and me. We would have to wait until the kids went to bed to get an hour or so of adult television. Until then, we would just let the kids take control of the TV. Usually, Tim read and I did the crossword puzzle.

Tonight though, our family show, *The Middle,* was on so, we settled into our usual spots to watch it together. Although the show was a little bit mature for Ernie, he usually got more of it than we thought he might. And for the times, it was relatively tame.

No one brought up the panty mine performance. Tim did make one wisecrack during the show. Elsie noted that one of the kids in the show, who was strongly featured that week, was a very good actor. "Yes," he began with mock sincerity, "it's amazing how clever some kids can be when they really put their mind to it."

I lifted my eyes from the crossword puzzle just in time to see Elsie crack a sly grin without looking away from the commercial. Ernie ignored the remark. He was more interested in performing the commercial along with the actor on the screen: "Block, block, block, block" he stood and acted out a silly Old Spice commercial where the actor punched and kicked odor away. Ernie did this every time the ad came on. Sometimes, Elsie joined in and they battled odor together adding their own nuances–like smelling their own supposedly stinky underarms first and declaring "pee-ew!" before attacking their foe.

When the program was over, Tim ushered the kids to bed. Because Elsie was older, she went to her room to read for another hour. More likely she was going to sneak in a phone call to a school friend. Tim tucked Ernie in for the night and then we watched one of our "adult" programs until 11pm; nodding off before the show ended.

The remainder of the week went on much the same with each of us comfortably in our own routines, except for Ernie. He oscillated between having barely enough energy to get out of bed to begging me to ride bikes with him–if he wasn't having a vomiting spell or other issues. With Ernie, routine was not a common word.

***

By the time Saturday rolled around, I was more than ready for my brunch with Elizabeth.

Tim went to work Saturday morning which left me feeling a bit on edge wondering if he would get back in time. But, true to his word, he was home before noon. Elsie was "studying" at a friend's house and Ernie was bored. He had spent the morning anxiously awaiting his dad's return and whatever little project they would work on together. Basketball season had just begun too so that most likely meant "men time" in front of the TV with beer and juice and snacks. They were out in the garage fiddling with some project before lunch, so I said goodbye to an empty house.

I was dressed and ready to go early. It was an unusually warm November day; perfect for sitting in the outdoor section of the restaurant as Elizabeth had insisted. I was happy I had listened to her and made a reservation. I wore a pair of black dress slacks topped with a long-sleeved, orange blouse that had a mix of leaves and plants in shades of light blue, red, orange, and white scattered about. I paired the outfit with practical black loafers and decided to carry a white, cotton, button-down sweater, just in case the weather turned cool.

When I entered Bella Famiglia, a full 20 minutes early, I felt and looked festive. I did a quick scan of the inside in case Elizabeth was as anxious I was, but I didn't see her. I was about to turn and walk back out front to wait when I heard someone call my name from the doorway to the patio area.

"June! Out here!" Elizabeth called to me while waving her hands in the air like a drowning person.

Smiling, I waved back and made my way over to meet her just outside on the patio. Elizabeth wore a simple cotton dress which hung just above her knees. I admired the flower motif of bright reds and yellows which recalled images of spring but, given the warm day, seemed appropriate. A narrow black belt cinched her waistline. Her shoes were black, open- toed heels that were a conservative three inches. She looked lovely.

Elizabeth greeted me with a friendly hug. "I got here early and the table was ready, so I took it." She explained as we walked toward the back of the patio to our table. "I was afraid I would be late, so I left extra time to get here and…ehh well. I was getting antsy sitting at home all dressed and ready to go." She explained further as we took our seats.

"I see you weren't shy and waiting for me," I said as I scooched my chair in and nodded toward the Bloody Mary perched in front of her.

"Oh that? Pffft. I needed something to keep me company," she said with a pretend guilty grin.

The waitress came over and asked to take our drink order. Elizabeth held up her Bloody Mary to the waitress as evidence of her order already being filled. "I'll have what she's having." I instructed the waitress who smiled and then retreated to put in my drink order. Elizabeth took hold of her glass and was about to take a sip when I stopped her.

"Wait! You can't drink any more of that until I get my drink! We have to make a proper toast to commemorate the occasion." I practically shouted.

Elizabeth, startled at my loud, sudden reproach, put her drink down and regarded me with wide eyes. "Whoa. Sorry. I didn't realize that brunch was such a big event in your life." We both had a good laugh at my expense.

"Listen. You have no idea how boring my life is. Ummm, no offense. I mean how special brunch with you is." I said and had a little laugh at Elizabeth's expense. She good-naturedly joined me.

The waitress appeared with my drink. "They must make these things by the pitcher," I said. "She got back with this drink faster than if I had ordered water!" I lifted my glass and Elizabeth mimicked. The waitress still hovered, so I looked at her questioningly. She got the hint.

"I'll come back in a couple of minutes to take your order." She said and left a menu in front of each of us before she moved to another table.

"Okay so. Umm...well, to us and brunch and our new friendship." I offered up as a celebratory toast.

"To us," Elizabeth said. We clinked glasses and took a sip of our Bloody Marys.

"Ohhh, that is soooo good and soooo needed. This whole brunch thing is." I said after finishing a second sip of my drink.

"Well, I have some other reasons to celebrate." Elizabeth said with a bright look in her eyes that matched the tone in her voice. "But some of it you might not exactly like." She continued reducing the sparkle in her eyes to a mere stare and bringing the pitch of her voice to a less enthusiastic volume. Something had struck her thoughts in the middle of her excitement that seemed to take the joy out of her approaching announcement. "Hang on a minute...I have to go pee first." Elizabeth whispered to me then abruptly rose and dashed off toward the restroom.

I sat sipping my delicious Bloody Mary and eating the bacon strip that had now soaked up some of the spicy mix. I was curious about her news and anxious about what the supposed negative aspects could be. Elizabeth returned to the table with the waitress at her heels.

"Have you folks decided on brunch?" The waitress asked holding a pen in one hand and a small pad in the other.

"I'll have the lemon pancakes," Elizabeth told the waitress with some of her earlier joy returning to her voice. "And another Bloody Mary." She looked my way for approval. I smiled.

"And you ma'am?" The waitress asked me.

"Oh. Well, I was going to have the lemon pancakes too but you had to copy me..." I looked at Elizabeth mischievously. "So, I will have the...panty cooken."

I tried to pronounce the actual name of the Dutch pancakes but in my butchering of the word, I had done exactly what we had laughed at Ernie for doing. I cracked up at the realization of what I had just done and began to snort from my hysterics. Elizabeth and the waitress regarded me as someone who was high or drunk or maybe nuts. Once it was apparent that I had gathered myself enough to act in a rational manner, the waitress continued with my order.

"Pannekoeken," The waitress corrected me, stone-faced.

"Yeah that," I said, trying not to snicker. "And black coffee."

"Excellent," the waitress said half under her breath.

"Umm no, no. She'll have another Bloody Mary." Elizabeth corrected my order. "If she's going to be this silly, she needs a good reason."

The waitress looked at me and I looked at her.

"Okay, why not? Make it another Bloody Mary." I responded to the waitress' expressionless face.

After the waitress spun on her heels and left our table, Elizabeth wanted to be let in on my joke.

"Okay, so what the hell was so funny about Dutch pancakes?"

"Nothing really," I said as a big smile took over my face. "I called them panty cooken." Elizabeth still looked quizzical. "It's something Ernie said the other night when he tried to say pantomime and we all laughed at him and…Ohh never mind you had to be there."

"Say no more," Elizabeth said. "If it involved Ernie, I think I can imagine. That kid is funny without trying to be."

"So, what is this news of yours?" I wanted to get back to Elizabeth's earlier inference of an important announcement. I took another nibble of my bacon.

"Well," Elizabeth said, leaning across the table, "You know I sent the interview project we did to a major network as part of my resume and job interviews."

"Yeahhhh."

"Well. They loved it and I got the job!" Elizabeth leaned back and clasped her hands. She beamed with joy.

"Oh my God! Elizabeth that is great news. Really. I am so happy for you!" I said matching her excitement. We toasted to that, before I continued. "So, what exactly is this new job Elizabeth? What will you be doing?"

"Ughh, well, first off, if we're going to be friends you have to call me Lizzie. Elizabeth sounds so formal and well, old. Nothing like me," she said, batting her eyelashes.

"Ohh, okay. Lizzie. I like that. Dizzy Lizzie." I teased.

"Don't you dare!! I got called that in high school and if you do that, I will make you call me Mrs. Cochoran—wait, no you will know me as Lizzie Borden!" Elizabeth threatened with just enough seriousness for me to get the point and drop the teasing.

"Okay, okay! Lizzie. Really, I love that name, and I'm glad you asked me to call you Lizzie. So, what's the job?"

"I am going to work with the features editor and producers on the *Day Show*. I'll be helping to identify and do background shots and things like that for their feature stories."

"Wow. That is really great. Their show is seen by millions! Isn't that the only all women's morning news show?"

"Well, it's a combination of news and other more fun stuff that plays to the morning audience, but they want the features part to separate them from other offerings. Sort of a morning *60 Minutes*-type of show. And yeah, the three main segment anchors are all women. Might have been a little reverse sexism at play there in giving me the job... ehh but screw em." She laughed and shrugged her shoulders.

I raised my Bloody Mary –nearly empty now –to toast again. "Yeah screw 'em. Viva the all-girls network." I offered joining Lizzie's proclamation.

"So..." I said after we finished our feminist moment. "What was the bad news?"

"Well..., the job is in Chicago; that means I have to move." Lizzie blurted out.

All at once, I was crest-fallen. My emotions had roller-coasted from the pinnacle of Lizzie's exciting new job to the nadir of realizing that I was losing my new friend. My best friend, really. I didn't know what to say. The waitress brought our food while we sat in silence. I picked up my fork and poked at the pannekoeken in front of me that only moments earlier, I was eager to taste. Lizzie broke the silence.

"Listen. I know it seems like you are losing a friend but June, Chicago has two airports. We have cell phones now and modern ways to keep in touch." Lizzie was trying to ease my concern.

"I know," I finally responded. "I know. Really, I hardly know you. I mean we have hardly known each other very long and everything… but, I don't know, sharing so much of my life with you…there was just some special connection and friendship I felt and…well, who the hell is going to have panty cooken with me now?" I looked up at her and tried my best to smile and make light but had to stop mid-sentence to wipe the tears that had begun to form in the corners of my eyes.

Lizzie reached across the table and grabbed both of my hands in hers. "June…"

I stopped her. "You have to call me Junie."

"Looney Junie?" Lizzie smiled at me and I managed a sort of laugh. "Looney Junie and Dizzy Lizzie. See? We were meant to be friends."

We both laughed.

"Seriously June," I pretended to glare at her. "Err. Junie…I feel the same connection. And you *are* my friend. And I won't let what—a thousand miles or so? —change that. We will stay in touch and I will convince you to come visit me so I can show you Chicago. And I will be back here—I still have family here, you know. And you will still know that there is someone out there you can talk to whenever."

"It still sucks," I said, but brightened just a bit. "Oh eat your damn lemon pancakes before they get cold. I suppose this means you will be switching to deep-dish pizza."

"Oh definitely. Sorry, but you lose on that one." She released my hands and grabbed her fork.

The rest of the brunch was better; we continued our normal banter and lighter conversation. I thoroughly enjoyed the afternoon and our time together. When brunch was complete, we said our goodbyes in front of the entrance to the restaurant and hugged each other tightly. It felt good to leave Lizzie's presence with the warmth of her embrace lingering on me. Before I had gotten more than a few feet toward my car and away from Lizzie, I heard her shout to me.

"Hey Junie girl. I forgot. I don't leave for two weeks so, get your husband to babysit next Saturday. I'll pick the place. Bye!" And then she was off in a flurry of determined footsteps, the clicking of her high heels echoing our separation.

I stood watching her for a bit. I felt a little silly at how emotional I had gotten when I learned she was leaving. I didn't have many friends and it seemed Ginny was separating from me. The thought of losing this new friendship made me feel more isolated and alone. I determined, before continuing to my car, that I would spend next Saturday with Lizzie, no matter what. I would make the necessary effort to keep this friendship going—including figuring out how I could get time away to visit her in Chicago after she was settled. I also made a note to remember my mental camera. I wanted to take an image of a special moment from our next meeting to recall when I needed.

***

The week Lizzie left for Chicago, Dr. Blackwell received the lab results from Ernie's muscle biopsy. The test was negative.

I was so frustrated. We were no further along in giving Ernie's disease a name than we were before. Still, Dr. Blackwell was convinced that Ernie had mitochondrial disease of some variation so we continued the "cocktail" she had prescribed. Meanwhile, there was progress being made with genetic testing and Dr. Blackwell was optimistic that this testing might soon be available to us.

Ernie returned to school the Monday after my last brunch with Lizzie. His tutoring and my efforts at collecting his schoolwork, had kept him on track with his classmates but his health was still an issue. The "cocktail" Dr. Blackwell prescribed was having a positive effect on Ernie's energy level to some degree; he was active for longer periods of time and his vomiting issues seemed to have dissipated.

In the beginning, the doctor had pointed out that Ernie needed more than a week or two on the supplements and that she might have to make adjustments and consider other therapies as we went along. She was encouraged by his progress and counseled us to have patience. That was good advice, sure, but Ernie was still frail. Although I didn't want to disappoint him or risk keeping him back another grade, after the latest test results, I suggested that he stay home from school another week. I didn't want him to overtire.

Ernie would have none of that. Over that weekend he did his utmost to convince us of how good he felt and how much energy he had. He rode his bicycle every day that he could get Tim or me to go with him, he played on the swings, which made me nervous, and he roughhoused with his dad playing at MMA combat.

Ernie also found time to disappear when he thought no one would notice. Once I found him curled up behind the couch when Elsie and I came home from shopping. Tim had been busy around the house checking all the batteries in the smoke alarms, fixing a loose handle on a kitchen cabinet, and doing other similar odd-jobs—projects that Ernie would normally help him with. Tim had assumed Ernie went shopping with Elsie and me, and maybe that is what Ernie told him. But Ernie used that quiet time as an opportunity to take a nap out of view of his worrisome parents.

Even so, he did seem to be doing better. Tim and I reasoned that, if the first day or two was too much, we could always keep him home. We came up with a compromise: Ernie would go to school for half days for the first two or three days. If things went well, he could go to full days. Ernie protested at first, but after realizing that we were not asking for his permission, he determined that *some* time back at school with his friends was better than nothing, so he accepted our ruling.

The first two days of Ernie's experiment went well. I picked him up at school at noon and watched closely while he made the short walk from the school front door to my car. I wanted to see if I could pick up on any signs of fatigue or anything abnormal. When he got in the car, I gave him a kiss that he tried to fight off so no one in the school would see. Then I asked him how the day went. He answered the same way, "Good. I'm hungry."

I took that as a positive sign and a return to his usual state of mind.

He didn't talk too much about school and shrugged off most of my questions about his friends and classes and how he was doing with keeping up. He mostly sat quietly while I drove home.

On the second day, he told me that the principal called him into her office on his first day back. I pressed Ernie to find out why. He said she asked a lot of questions about home, about how he was feeling, about his accident on the swings and about his emergency hospital visits. He said another lady was there too, but he didn't know who that was. It wasn't one of his teachers. She also asked about Elsie and her migraine headaches.

I didn't like the sound of any of this. I especially didn't like having my son ambushed and interrogated by adults without me there. I wanted to know everything they said but, not wanting to upset Ernie, I let it go. I did take a little comfort hearing that all he answered was "good," or "fine," or, "Elsie is good." They clearly did not know my son if they thought they would get more out of him. As Elsie might say, "They didn't speak Ernie."

One certainty was that I would be making my own trip to the principal's office, unannounced, before the end of the week. I was going to perform my own interrogation.

By Wednesday, Ernie had difficulty getting out of bed in the morning. I also found out that he wasn't participating in any recess activities. He looked pale and was very quiet that night at dinner, not sharing anything from school or joking with Elsie as he normally would have.

Tim and I discussed keeping him out of school for the rest of the week, but Ernie insisted that he was just sleepy because school was new to him again. However, he didn't balk at extending the half-day plan for the rest of the week. In fact, he seemed to welcome the idea.

We decided to give Ernie another half day at school.

Elsie, on the other hand, was very talkative at the dinner table. She told us how she and her partner Cindy had given their pantomime in front of the class. Thankfully, it didn't involve panties.

They decided on two fishermen casting their rods into a lake. One of them, Elsie's character, made a big deal of showing off her new fishing pole and doing a very elaborate casting of her line while sporting an obvious smug expression. The other, Cindy's character, acted out having a simple rod that she cast into the lake with little fanfare.

After a moment, Cindy's character pulled in a big fish while Elsie's caught nothing. A moment later, Cindy pulled in another fish causing Elsie to get jealous. This went on two or three more times until Elsie turned beat red with anger while Cindy stood over a basket full of fish grinning from ear-to-ear.

Finally, Elsie catches hold of a big fish. She is ecstatic and beams a look of triumph toward Cindy. She reels it in, struggling to control the obviously huge fish.

When the fish was finally near the end of the fishing pole, Elsie handed her rod to Cindy, so she could take the fish off the hook. Suddenly, the big fish began to jump around and flap about while Elsie tried frantically to catch the slippery thing in her grasp. Alas, the slithering creature proved too slippery for Elsie and it flew out of her grip, into the water, and swam away.

Cyndy, still smug, looked at her basket full of fish, then back at Elsie. Elsie grabbed her rod back from Cindy, snapped it over her own knee and tossed it into the lake. With her nose high in the air, she marched off. End of pantomime.

Her classmates loved it. Shy Cindy had become an instant star and surprised everyone with her underplayed, well-timed comic expressions. The teacher gave Elsie and Cindy an A+ for their effort.

But one other thing Elsie shared at dinner was disturbing. She said that at lunch time, she had looked for Beamer to sit with. Most of the lunch room was segregated into girls and boys, because of the nature of boys and girls at her age. There were a few pockets of exception to this, and Elsie and Beamer belonged to that "club."

Elsie was enough of a tomboy to fetch the admiration of boys yet girly enough to have graduated from a love of Barbie, to sharing a secret crush on the latest TV hunks. Her normal lunch table was a mix of both sexes without any uncomfortable undercurrents or mean teasing; though there was occasionally some lighthearted banter of Elsie and Beamer sitting in a tree because Elsie spent so much time over at his house when Ernie was sick, and because they were neighbors and rode bikes together, and they studied together. None of the teasing was hurtful and both Elsie and Beamer laughed it off.

However, at lunch today, when Elsie tried to sit opposite Beamer at the lunch table, he waved her off telling her that he was saving the seat for Amy, another girl from their group. Elsie told us that she thought that maybe he had a crush on Amy, which was fine because she had no interest in Beamer other than as a friend. But when she asked if Beamer was coming over to her house later to study for tomorrow's math quiz, he squirmed a bit and then flatly said no, without any explanation. Elsie said she stood there feeling awkward and rejected until one of the other girls called her over to the other end of the table.

She told us that she confronted Beamer at his locker before their next class. She wanted to know if something was wrong and why he was avoiding her. She said that she tried to stay upbeat and teased him just a bit that maybe he was throwing her over for Amy. But the response she got was surprising and hurtful. She recounted their conversation:

"Umm, I can't hang out with you because of the stuff that's going on with Ernie and you." He told her as he tried to escape down the hall.

Elsie said she stepped in front of him. "What stuff? What are you talking about?"

"I...I don't know. You know, the stuff with your mom and Ernie and your sickness stuff. My mom just said they are looking at it and I have to stay away. That's all I know. I can't talk about it. Sorry."

Beamer stepped around Elsie and rushed toward their next class.

I was shocked to hear all of this. I tried to underplay it so as not to upset Elsie, who appeared to think it was because Beamer's mom thought Ernie and she might have some sort of contagious disease. I could see that she was hurt and confused.

Tim jumped in, more upset than I would have anticipated. "Honey, Ernie is not contagious with anything and neither are you. You have migraines for Christ sake! And whatever it is that Ernie has is not contagious."

"So why is his mom keeping him from me? I thought she was your friend, Mom."

"Yeah me too," I said with a soft judging tone before I continued in normal voice. "Maybe she read something on the Internet or something...or someone said something to her."

"Yeah, I always said she was a bit of an airhead," Tim threw in still annoyed. "You know, the elevator doesn't go all the way up..." He made a wide-eyed expression and circled his finger near his temple, which made Elsie laugh.

"Tim!" I said, "that isn't nice. Ginny *is* my friend and she has been very good to us and Elsie when we needed her help." But Tim wasn't buying it. There was something about Ginny that had always bothered him—he thought she was phony.

"Yeah, ok Mom. Well maybe you need to talk to your 'friend'." Elsie sarcastically suggested.

"Okay I will," I decided. "Probably just something silly. Probably, Amy is so jealous of you that Beamer made the whole thing up to get you out of the picture." I suggested half joking.

"Well, yeah I mean, I can see *why*." Elsie said while making a mock model pose and batting her eyes. That brought smiles to all of our faces, including Ernie who until then, had sat expressionless and removed from the conversation.

My quick look in Tim's direction told me he was still not convinced that this was all innocent. And, to be honest, neither was I.

Later that night, when Tim and I settled into bed, each buried in our own novel, he interrupted his reading to engage me on the topic again.

"I don't think that Beamer made all that up," he said without any introduction to the topic.

"Huh? All what?" I asked as I finished reading the last sentence in a paragraph in my book.

"That stuff with Ginny and what Beamer told Elsie. I don't buy it."

I put my book down and looked at him. "You know. I'm glad you said that. Because I don't think it was just some mistake or anything to do with this Amy girl either."

"You don't?"

"No. I meant to tell you this earlier tonight. Ernie was called into the principal's office and there was another lady there. They asked him all kinds of questions about his health, about home and Elsie…"

"Seriously? That is bullshit. That isn't even legal to put a kid through the Spanish Inquisition without a parent there. We need to go down to the school and give them a piece of our mind." Tim was getting worked up.

"Minds."

"Huh?"

"Never mind." I said before I realized everything that was wrong with my response. Tim gave me a quizzical look. "You're right. I'm going there on Friday so that Ernie doesn't have to deal with any potential repercussions before the weekend."

"Well, I'll meet you there. I want to make certain they get how upset we both are." Tim offered a bit calmer now. Tim didn't normally react strongly to things; he remained analytical in most situations. But, he saw this as an attack on his kids and his family. That was a line no one could cross without repercussion.

"You know," I added. "Ginny was very strange with me the other day too. Very removed. I invited her to brunch before I asked Lizzie–Elizabeth–and she was ice cold toward me and turned me down. She wouldn't even commit to a future date."

"Told you. Phony." Tim muttered.

"Tim, I think it is something more than that." I only half-scolded. "You know what all this reminds me of?"

"What?"

"It all has the familiar ring of one thing or person. Remember the questioning of our parenting and Ernie's hospital trips and the ugly undertone suggestion that we might be unfit parents?"

"Ruth!" We said at the same time.

"Okay," Tim said. "We need to get to the school and find out what is going on; tomorrow, not Friday. And you need to walk over to Ginny's house and confront her."

"Yeah okay. I will. And if this is coming from that busybody Ruth, we need to confront management at the hospital and maybe threaten them with a legal response."

"Yeah well, I know someone I can talk to about this," Tim said. "One of my clients is a law firm. I don't know all the partners, but they are highly recommended. There might be a legal course we can take, maybe just a letter...Ruth's accusation or insinuation might be considered libelous...especially if she is acting on her own. I mean, she wasn't even an actual social worker right?"

"I don't know," I said. "She was *something*. I don't know if this is coming from her, but it's coming from some organized effort. Why else was there another woman interviewing Ernie at school?"

"Okay," Tim said, his mind made up. "I am going to take off work tomorrow afternoon. You visit Ginny, and then we'll go together to the school when I get home. And then we can see what is really going on."

"I would have thought Ginny would come to me and ask if something was wrong or warn me if there was a rumor going around or anything like that. I can't believe she might be involved and being secretive." I said trying to understand what Ginny's reasoning might be.

"I don't know. But let's get some sleep and fix this in the morning." Tim said before he kissed me goodnight. He turned off his reading light, put his book on the nightstand, and rolled over.

Now that he had a plan and a compartment to put his worries into, he could sleep. I, on the other hand, was unable to think of anything else. I knew sleep for me would not come before more hours of worry. I grabbed my book and prepared for the long night ahead.

CHAPTER THIRTEEN

FIGHTING FOR ERNIE

On Thursday morning, Ernie was up early and dressed for school. I was the last one down, the result of my extra hours of worried reading. Even Elsie managed to get an early start without grumbling.

When I entered the kitchen, Tim was at the counter making coffee. Ernie was sitting at the kitchen table with his back to me, across from Elsie. I could see that he was wearing a pair of slightly faded blue jeans topped with a bright blue cardigan sweater with the collar of a gray cotton shirt accenting the back of his neck. He looked very preppy I thought to myself and I was amazed that he was so coordinated and ready to go.

But when he turned around to face me, I was shocked. He looked so very pale.

"Ernie, I think maybe you should stay home today."," I said. I came around in front to feel his forehead with the palm of my hand.

Ernie backed away from my touch and pushed my hand away. "I'm fine Mom," he said. "Just hungry."

"You look really pale honey. Tim, don't you think he looks really pale?"

Tim moved his head around to look at Ernie. Before Tim could answer, Elsie spoke up in Ernie's defense.

"Oh, he just looks that way 'cause the sweater is so bright. That color makes everyone look pale."

"Yeah, that is a pretty bright blue. He looks normal to me. I mean you know he always looks a little pale." Tim said before he turned back to the coffee maker.

"Well, how do you feel Ernie? Are you too tired to go to school today? I wasn't completely convinced.

"I feel good, Mom." Ernie was quick to reply.

"Well, then why haven't you finished your cereal?"

"Oh, that's his second bowl, Mom. But umm I guess he wasn't that hungry. So, nice outfit he's wearing though right Mom?" Elsie said jumping to Ernie's defense once again, quickly changing the subject.

"Umm yeah," I said and smiled at Ernie. "Yeah you look very preppy."

"I picked it out," Elsie bragged, sporting a big grin.

All through the short conversation, Ernie looked at Elsie for answers while he pushed back the cereal in his bowl to get at a spoonful of milk, which he slurped. That should have been a hint to me that something was not right.

It became obvious to me that Ernie and Elsie had spent the morning getting him ready and rehearsing his story. She must have seen how pale he was. Or maybe he had a vomiting fit that morning that Elsie witnessed. Ernie probably begged her not to tell because he wanted so much to go to school again. Because she didn't want to disappoint her little buddy, she came up with the "dressing to impress Mom" idea. The other parts were just her natural quick thinking. It worked because I gave in and didn't pursue the school issue any further.

"Okay Ernie," I relented. "Half day again. BUT if you feel sick at all you go to the nurse's office and have her call me and I will come get you. Okay?"

"K Mom," Ernie answered without looking up from his bowl.

Tim grew impatient with the automatic coffee maker and moved the glass pot aside to slip his cup under the liquid flowing from the machine. Once his cup was filled, he returned the pot to its place and joined Elsie and Ernie at the table. I then took my turn being annoyed with how slow the coffee was entering the pot. I repeated Tim's method with my own cup and sat across from him at the table.

"Hey buddy. Look at me." Tim told Ernie. But he got no response. "Ernie, look at me, I want to see how you look. Or you can just stay home I guess." Tim matter-of-factly threatened.

Ernie looked up from his bowl of now mushy cereal and stuck his tongue out at Tim. Tim didn't respond. Ernie retracted his tongue and gave his dad a big, cheesy smile.

"Yup. He looks normal to me. That's my boy!" Tim quipped.

Elsie, who was anxious to see if Ernie would pass this test, gave her brother a big grin, then popped up from the table.

"Bro, we have to go. The bus will be at the corner in like five minutes."

Elsie ran around the table, grabbed her brother by the arm and practically dragged him toward the front door.

"Wait! Elsie, I was going to drive Ernie to school," I shouted at their backs as they high-tailed it to the front door.

"It's okay, Mom. I got this. We're going to ride the bus together." Elsie shot back before she whisked Ernie out the door.

Elsie rarely took the bus. She usually rode her bike to Beamer's house and then they would ride on to school together. From there it was only about two miles to their school; Ernie's school was more like five miles but on the same bus route.

I wondered if she was taking the bus because of what Beamer had said and how he had treated her. Although I didn't really want Ernie going to school without me, he was with Elsie and...and sometimes as a parent you have to give in to some things. Every little sequence with your kids can't be a trial. Sometimes, you just have to let them be.

***

After Tim left for work, I was by myself with my thoughts. The more I went over the events with Elsie and Beamer, Ginny's odd behavior on the phone with me, and the meeting Ernie had to endure in his principal's office, the more I was certain that all these things were related and not a strange coincidence.

Although I had no proof, my intuition kept nagging me that Ruth was somehow connected to all of it. I felt better knowing Tim was going to contact his lawyer client for any background advice on how we should approach the hospital and what our options might be if Ruth was at the root of our perceived problems.

Until I had some answers to those questions, I decided to put off confronting Ginny.

I decided to distract myself by grocery shopping. I hoped the banality of picking out the best apples and scanning shelves for which toilet paper was on sale might replace the conspiracy theory that was taking shape in my mind.

It took me longer than normal time to finish shopping. I kept stopping mid-aisle, staring blankly at rows of canned soup and at the overwhelming number of yogurt options. I kept running the conspiracy through my head over and over, slightly varying the storyline but never the villain. I bruised more than one apple before I realized I failed at this multi-tasking attempt.

It was after 11 when I finally left the store with my cart full of grocery bags. Tim would be home within an hour. We would soon be on our way to getting answers.

I had to get home and put the groceries away and *then* sit for bit to gather my thoughts and shape my questions for the meeting at school and the hospital; I didn't want to leave either place wishing I had remembered to ask something I just thought of. And I needed a few minutes to bury my distaste of Ruth and to keep it in check before I spoke to her. I would need calm to get my questions answered. Tim would likely have his own questions as well, so I thought it would be good to take some time before the meetings to share our questions and approach to show a united front.

As I loaded my bags into the back of my Jeep, I had a brief moment of panic: I wasn't exactly certain what groceries had ended up in my bags. I got that feeling you get when you are certain you left something behind but can't remember what.

But, I had five full bags of food so I figured that if I forgot something, it couldn't be that important. The Gallagher's weren't going to be deprived from leaving it behind. I shrugged my shoulders, closed the trunk and got into my car.

I slid my key into the ignition and my phone rang. The Caller ID showed that it was Ernie's principal. I froze for a few seconds and wondered if she was calling to set up her own meeting showdown with Tim and me? Or worse, to tell me that something had happened to Ernie.

"Hello?" I answered with trepidation.

"Hi June. This is principal Patterson I'm afraid Ernie had an...episode...and we had to call an ambulance to take him to the hospital."

My heart stopped.

"An episode? What kind of an episode? What do you mean? Is he okay? Where is he?" Panicked, I rambled.

"I don't know, he collapsed again at recess and he didn't wake up, that's all I know. The paramedics took him." She answered with little emotion.

"Paramedics...where? What hospital?" I asked fearing what the answer might be.

"Brinker."

"Brinker? Oh my God no. I *told* you he can never go back there. He has to go to University. Why the hell did you send him to Brinker?" I was apoplectic.

"I'm sorry June. But that is where we were told to send him. His case is with Brinker child services there. And besides, that is where the ambulance company is engaged from."

"WHAT? What do you mean his case is there? Goddamit!" I shrieked and threw the phone down on the seat next to me, it bounced to the floor and disconnected the call. My worst fears were coming true. My Ernie was sick again, and he was going to Ruth.

I cursed and cried for several moments before fetching the phone from the floor. I wiped my tears and tried to regain my composure before I called Tim. He answered on the third ring.

"Hey honey. I am just going to make a quick client call and then I'm heading out," Tim explained.

"No. No, Tim. They took him. Ruth has him and he's sick again. We have to go *now!*" I tried to speak quickly and clearly, past my torrent of tears and frustration.

"Whoa! Hang on June. What do you mean Ruth has him? Where?"

"They sent him to Brinker again. The school did. He collapsed at recess and they sent him by ambulance to Brinker. I *knew* he didn't look right this morning. I *knew* I should have kept him home."

"June. June, you couldn't have known this would happen. Just get to the hospital. I'll meet you there. Are you okay to drive?"

"Yes."

"Okay. Take a deep breath and drive carefully. Ernie will be fine. He probably just had one of his seizures from being too tired. Just get there and I'll meet you; we'll figure this out. I am leaving now too. Okay?"

"Okay." I said somewhat calmed by Tim's logic. But I wasn't convinced that anything about this episode would be 'okay'.

***

I got to the hospital two minutes after Tim arrived. When I entered the lobby, I saw him bent over the reception desk, leaning on both elbows. He was apparently in an argument with someone behind the desk, who was hidden from view. I hurried to join him; when I got to his side, I immediately saw the cause of Tim's angst; and soon to be mine—it was Ruth.

On seeing her, I instinctively copied Tim's rigid stance. At my height, I had a much less intimidating presence than Tim. I didn't bother with any pleasantries—not even a hello to Tim. Anyway, he was too engrossed with whatever happened before my arrival to need one.

I went straight to the reason I was there; why Tim and I were both there.

"What room is our son Ernie in?" I said through clenched teeth, glaring at Ruth.

"She won't tell us," Tim said with a slap on the counter as he turned to me. "She says we can't see him and she won't give us any information." Ruth rolled her chair away from the desk, distancing herself from her two encroaching assailants.

Tim was more upset than I had ever seen him when confronted by illogical bureaucracy. Usually, he could calmly wade into the mess, find a path out and get to the outcome he needed.

But now, he had caught my anti-Ruth fire, and no amount of logic was going to interfere with that passion. She was the object in the way of being with his ailing son and nothing more; the same as she had become to me at our first meeting. I felt a bit apprehensive.

I worried that I had fired Tim up during our conversation the night before. I also worried that without my calmer half, I would have no one to talk me down from my normal and sometimes irrational response to anyone whom I saw as a threat to my kids. I needed his balance.

"You know what?" Tim continued after an awkward pause in which Tim and I exchanged glares with Ruth. "We don't need you. Come on." Tim grabbed my hand and led me toward the swinging doors leading into treatment rooms and main area of the hospital.

"You can't go in there!" Ruth shouted at us. This drew everyone's attention in the waiting area—as well as the security guard who was leaning against the wall near the doors.

We didn't stop. Tim led me straight through the doors and then said, "You go that way and I'll go this way. Text when you find Ernie." And we went our directed ways.

The security guard, a 65-year-old man who was likely doing this job part time, took no action to stop us. He followed us through the doors and just stood inside with his arms crossed and legs planted wide.

Apparently, Ruth wasted no time calling the security chief to alert him of two intruders inside the hospital emergency treatment area.

Shortly after Tim and I had separated, an announcement was made over the hospital-wide communication system, alerting everyone to our presence. It was in code, "Security, 315 to area 2. Security, 315 to area 2."

It didn't take a genius to know what or who the message was referencing.

I continued on my path and quickly checked the two curtained-off emergency beds before heading down the hall toward other rooms, whizzing past radiology, emergency surgery, and any other places that were unlikely to be hosting Ernie–or that I could not gain entry to.

Then my phone buzzed. The shorthand text from Tim said, 'Found him. Cops fnd me.'

I started to rush back toward the way I had come then abruptly stopped. *Better I don't draw attention to myself*, I thought. I knew *about* where Ernie was now and maybe, if security guards are busy with Tim, I could make my way to Ernie without being noticed. Then I heard behind me, "We got her."

Two security guards rushed toward me. My first impulse was to run, but I wasn't a criminal. I just wanted to find my son and I had a right to know where he was and what was happening to him.

The first security guard to reach me was civil. He was tall, about 40 and looked to be in very good shape. He placed a hand on my upper arm. "Ma'am, you are not allowed back here without permission. You need to come with us back out to the waiting area." I played dumb.

"What?" I looked at him wide-eyed. "I'm just looking for the right room where my son is. They said he is back here but I went the wrong way." I lied as convincingly as possible.

The second security guard pointed to the ceiling and a round, black globe attached there.

"Lady, we have you on camera and we know who you are. Either willingly walk back out to the waiting area with us or we call the cops and you get arrested." The second guard, a tall, skinny 20-something, said with much less care or civility than the first guard.

When I hesitated, the more aggressive guard grabbed my other arm and began to lead me down the hall.

"Don't you touch me. I have the right to be here and you *don't* have the right to keep me from my son." I said. I ripped his hand from my arm and stood my ground.

"Ma'am," the other guard stepped in front of the skinny one. "We aren't trying to keep you from your son. We're just telling you what the rules are. If you come out to the waiting area and talk to the folks out there, you can straighten everything out."

The older guard was much more physically intimidating but also more adept at dealing with people and deescalating situations.

"It's those people out there—one person—who is causing all this... this problem and keeping us from seeing our son!" I informed the guard with as much control I could muster.

"Listen," he said. "I got kids. I get it. But let's try to do this the easy way okay? You're no help to your son if you get arrested."

I stared at him trying, unsuccessfully, to find an argument to his logic. "I'll tell you what. What's your son's name?"

"Ernie. Ernie Gallagher," I answered.

"Okay. You go back to the waiting area with Jim, and I'll find Ernie's doctor and see if we can't get him to come out and talk to you. Okay?"

"Yeah, I guess so." I hesitantly replied.

"Great. Jim, walk her to the waiting area—without touching her—and I'll see what I can find out."

After that, I followed Jim out to the waiting area where I found Tim arguing profusely with Ruth. We were right back where we started. But Tim had texted he found Ernie.

"Tim!" I called. He stopped mid-rant and turned to look at me. I gestured for him to come over. I didn't trust myself to be around Ruth right now. He looked at me and then back at Ruth briefly before heading my way.

Most people in the waiting area seemed attuned to our drama. Though, when I glanced their way, they avoided making eye contact. When Tim reached me, his face was bright red. I led him to a corner of the room to avoid becoming more of the day's entertainment.

"What happened?" I quietly asked when we were sufficiently alone.

"That idiot woman. You were right. She is the cause of all of this. They won't let us back there to see Ernie and we can't take him out of here all because of *her*." Tim said pointing in the direction of Ruth. He was beginning to steam again.

"No, no, no. Wait yeah, okay...I mean you saw Ernie. Did you talk to him? Is he okay?"

"Yeah," he said, focusing his eyes on me. "I got about 20 seconds alone with him before the Gestapo dragged me out here. He's fine. He said he had a slight seizure, you know, passed out for a few seconds. He told them he was fine and just needed to sit for a bit and take half day maybe. But the principal said he had to go to the hospital and they threw him in an ambulance without calling us first."

"Okay, but he's all right? He looked okay?"

"Yeah. He was pale, you know, but he sat up when he saw me and gave me a big hug." Tim said as the redness began to leave his face.

"So, what's going on with Ruth over there?"

"She's being tight-lipped and kept saying when the doctor comes out, we will discuss Ernie's case."

"Crap. This isn't good, Tim. I think you need to call the lawyer now and get him down here. Something bad is going on here and we need help."

"Yeah. Yeah, I think you might be right. With everything that has been going on with Ernie's school and Ginny and Ruth and her 'case' references, this is not looking good."

Tim retrieved his phone from his suit coat breast pocket. Before he cold dial, the security guard, who said he would help me, came through the swinging doors with a doctor at his side. The guard looked around, found me, and then pointed to me. The doctor nodded at him, then headed our way.

"Tim, don't call yet. I think this is Ernie's doctor."

Tim looked up from his phone and saw the approaching doctor. But he had already dialed.

"Hello, you must be Ernie's parents. I'm Dr. Grinsby." The doctor introduced himself.

"June Gallagher," I said, "and this is Tim." I responded plainly as I took the doctor's hand. Tim, who was about to initiate a conversation on his phone, held up his index finger to the doctor indicating one minute and then turned away.

The doctor turned his attention to me. "So, "Ernie is doing well. Vitals are okay, he's a bit weak but nothing life-threatening at the moment. We're going to keep him overnight before we release him to social services..."

"Whoa, whoa, whoa, wait a minute. What do you mean release him to social services?" I interrupted. "Tim." I said turning to Tim who again held up his index finger while he continued his conversation.

Fuming, I turned back to the doctor. "We are his parents and demand that you release our son now!"

"I'm afraid in cases like this, as attending doctor, and given Ernie's history…"

"Listen, you have no idea what Ernie's case or history is. You are *not* his attending doctor you're just the guy who was here when he was admitted. His doctor is Dr. Blackwell and if he is not ready to be released, he belongs with her at University Hospital where she is treating him."

Tim hung up his phone and turned back to us. "What's going on?" Tim demanded.

"I was just informing your wife that we cannot release your son to either of you. Social Services has been called and they will oversee your son's case now."

"What case? I keep hearing the word 'case' but what case? Ernie doesn't even get treated here. He is being seen by a specialist for mitochondrial disease—and you have no clue what's wrong with him." Tim half explained and half yelled.

"Well, we don't see that idea as a viable reason for Ernie's many ailments, his speech problems, and multiple trips to the emergency room for various injuries," The doctor said, almost condescendingly.

"Excuse me," I interjected, "but Ernie has never had 'various injuries.' He has had health issues related to his disease…"

Now the doctor interrupted me. "He has had some head trauma, vomiting for no apparent reason, exhaustion from obvious lack of sleep. There are a lot of indicators, as Ruth has helped us to explain and to uncover, that indicate a need for Social Service interaction and intervention."

Tim was irate and not trying very hard to hide it now. "Doctor, you have no clue what you're talking about. Ernie fell off the swings in our yard *once*. All the other indicators are related to his mitochondrial disease and the swings accident was as well. You really need to talk to Dr. Blackwell, so she can explain this all to you."

"Yes. And Ruth is not a health expert or even a social services person. She's just a know-it-all busy body who's trying to cause trouble." I added.

"I'm sorry. This is not a matter of some unknown mitochondrial disease in my opinion; the matter is now in the hands of Social Services." The doctor stated defensively and then walked away. He stopped and turned back for a moment to declare, "And Ruth is now the Social Services liaison for this hospital."

I started after the doctor to insist he send Ernie out, but Tim clamped onto my shoulders and held me back.

I rounded on him. "I want our son back! We can't leave him here with them, and especially not with *her.*" I nodded my head in Ruth's direction.

"I know. I got through to the lawyer. He said he will make some inquiries and call us back tomorrow."

"Tomorrow? Tomorrow? Christ Tim! We can't leave Ernie here overnight. How do we know they won't take him somewhere else and not tell us? God, this is like a communist country. They can't legally do this, Tim. We aren't charged with anything–we haven't done anything. How can our son just be taken from us?"

"I don't know," he said, shaking his head. "But we need the lawyer's help, and he needs to get information first. I don't think they are taking Ernie anywhere tonight. We'll come here first thing in the morning and camp in this waiting room until they release him to us. I don't know what else we can do until then." Tim tried to comfort me with a hug. But I was too rigid with anger to be consoled that way. I crossed my arms.

"We need to at least be allowed to go see him and tell him we'll be back. And, he needs his cocktail today. That's the only thing that got him back to school and was making him better until today. And that's probably because he took on too much too soon. He needed more time on the treatment."

"We're probably going to have to go through the newly promoted Ruth to do any of that. Let's go and try to talk to her."

"No," I shook my head emphatically. "You go talk to her, Tim. If I have to be near that woman I will lose it. I swear."

"Well, I'm the one who was yelling at her today after the guards threw me out of Ernie's room. I doubt she's gonna want to talk to me or do me any favors, but okay. You stay here and I'll give it a try."

Tim took a deep breath then calmly walked over to the admittance desk where Ruth was engaged in a conversation with another of her potential victims. After three or four minutes, Tim got a chance to speak with her. I saw him go from standing relaxed at the desk using small, subtle gestures and speaking softly, to waving his arms around, leaning forward and yelling, all in the same span of time it takes to make a soft- boiled egg.

The last thing I witnessed was Tim throwing his hands in the air and shaking his head while he yelled at Ruth, "You won't have this job after our lawyer gets through with you and this hospital." Then he stormed back to me.

"Come on. We're coming back here tomorrow morning, with our lawyer, and we're getting our son out of this place."

Tim headed for the door and I followed as did all the eyes in the waiting area.

We had taken separate cars to the hospital, so there was no one to vent with during the ride home. Instead, I played all the scenarios over in my head that I could think of, trying to find the one that I could control and that would lead to the outcome I wanted—which was Ernie safe at home. But every mental path I took came back to working with the lawyer and hoping he could fight the bureaucracy that kept Ernie from us.

The one other person I thought might help us deviate from the anticipated course was Dr. Blackwell. If she could importune Dr. Grinsby to at least transfer Ernie to her care, that would get us access to Ernie while insuring he got the care that he needed. It seemed logical and reasonable to me. Yet I was somewhat reticent to believe that reason was going to be the driving force toward a favorable conclusion.

Nonetheless, I made up my mind and called Dr. Blackwell's office while I drove home. Her receptionist answered and informed me that Dr. Blackwell was out at National Institute of Health Sciences meeting in Washington, DC and wouldn't be back in the office until Monday.

Apparently, she and a handful of other mitochondrial specialists were making an appeal for research and diagnostic grants. The receptionist was excited to tell me about the potential if Dr. Blackwell was successful in securing the grants. I understood the importance of what the doctor was doing, but it would have no immediate benefit to my situation with Ernie–which was my singular focus.

I had to cut her short and ask her to make certain she had Dr. Blackwell call me the first thing Monday morning or sooner if she checked in over the weekend.

By the time I arrived home, it was near 2 pm. Tim had made the drive faster than I did and was waiting when I got in. So was Elsie, which surprised me. They were both seated at the kitchen table, deep in an animated conversation when I walked in.

"June," Tim said, "you have to hear this. Elsie, tell your mom what you just told me."

"So, I was called to the principal's office today...well, I mean. I was given a note in homeroom that I had to meet with the principal at 1 which would have been math class so...anyway, when I got there the principal apologized and said 'Never mind, go to math class 'cause yeah the lady we were meeting with got held up at the hospital.' So, um that's it. Oh, and I am having the meeting on Monday morning instead."

"Did the principal say what this meeting was about?" I asked. "No. That's all she said and then I left and went to math class."

I looked at Elsie questioningly and sat down. "Oh yeah, um, so math class had already started and then I got Dad's text that Ernie got taken to the hospital again so…I just came home."

"Don't you see June? Ruth, was the lady who was supposed to be at the meeting, but because we showed up at the hospital, she couldn't make it." Tim said with renewed vigor.

"Oh my God. And she must have been the lady in the meeting with Ernie, which is probably another reason why she didn't want us to see Ernie." I said catching Tim's fire. "Tim, this has got to stop. She has obviously stirred up a lot of talk and egged people on to make them think that our kids are mistreated. She's poisoned Ginny, Ernie's principal, people at the hospital she works at…and now they gave her some status as a Social Worker or something along with power she should never have. She isn't going to give Ernie back." I was astonished at my conclusion.

"I think you might be right, June. And worse, it seems like she might be after Elsie too." Tim added.

"You think so? Can she do that?" I said with panic rising in my voice.

"OMG Mom, no one can take me or Ernie away from our parents!" Elsie was scared.

"Oh no, honey, you're wrong," I said. "They won't let us see Ernie or even transfer him to his regular doctor's hospital. And this woman is out of control with power. You have no idea how invasive the government can be and how misplaced their authority is."

Tim grabbed his phone and typed in a number. "Are you calling the lawyer?" I asked.

"No, I'm calling my parents. If this is as out of control as we think it is, we need to get Elsie out of town. I'm not waiting for some lawyer." Tim walked out of the kitchen and into the living room to speak with his parents.

"Wait, is that even legal?" I yelled into the living room.

"I don't know and I don't care. I'm not having both my kids taken from me because of this bullshit." Tim yelled back. Then he said, "Hello, Mom?" Then his voice grew too faint to hear.

"Mom, I can't leave I have school and stuff." Elsie looked near tears.

"Honey, you can't go to that meeting on Monday. We don't know what will happen. Right now, we need to make certain you don't get swept up in whatever this is. The most you will miss is a week."

"Mom, a week is a long time, and I will have a ton of make-up homework. And I don't even like Grandma and Grandpa. I mean I hardly even know them. What are you going to tell school? I got a sudden illness and had to leave?" Elsie sounded desperate.

"I don't know honey, your father and I will figure it out." I reached out and took her hands in mine to reassure her.

Tim came back into the room. "That was quick." I said.

"My dad wasn't there and I just told my mom that we might need to send Elsie to them for a while and I would explain later. She said they were going to Italy next week for two weeks. So...I don't know."

"Perfect," I said. "They can take Elsie with them. We never ask them for anything and they never spend time with their grandchildren, so now they can."

"Italy? I love Grandma and Grandpa!" Elsie did an about-face. "This is a great idea, Dad!"

"Elsie this is serious. It's not a vacation!" I scolded.

"Umm yeah, okay, Mom...but Italy? It kind of would be a vacation. I mean for me anyway." Elsie corrected me.

Tim's phone rang; this time it was the lawyer. Tim put him on speaker phone and we took turns explaining all of the events this morning. He had a lot of questions about Ernie's illness, his hospital visits in the past, Dr. Blackwell's diagnosis, her contact information, and general background questions concerning Ernie.

He was also very interested to hear about the meeting Ernie had at school. We explained that we couldn't say for sure who the other person was at that meeting, but we were suspicious it was Ruth.

Then we had to explain who Ruth was. We also told him about the meeting Elsie was supposed to have today and why we thought that was probably Ruth as well. And we told him that we were fearful that Elsie was going to be taken away.

Then Tim let him know about our plans.

"So, Larry," he said, "theoretically speaking, what if Elsie didn't go to the meeting on Monday and was out of the country? I mean, could we be in trouble if they were trying to take Elsie from us and she disappeared?" Tim asked.

"Tim. Theoretically and in reality, don't do that. It isn't necessary, and yes, you could both get in trouble. What we need to do is find out who was at the meeting with Ernie. If it was Ruth, it is unlikely that she had the authority to call Ernie into a meeting like that without your permission or at the very least, notifying you.

"She must be a registered Child Protective Services (CPS) professional employed by the authorized agency. She cannot do anything as a hospital employee other than file a complaint to CPS with a simple phone call. CPS can interview a child without notifying you, but we can also put a stop to that. We will tell both Ernie's and Elsie's school to put a permanent note in their record that no such meeting is authorized.

"If CPS feels the case warrants further review, they may come to your house for the interview and once again you can refuse or allow it. I always advise refusal until and unless your lawyer is present. And CPS will likely get a court order to force such an interview if they deem it in the child's best interest. So, we need to discover the history behind that meeting.

"I also share your concern about Elsie, but I think the best way to handle that is to go to school with Elsie and show up at that meeting with her on Monday. Note who is there, and then politely refuse to let Elsie be subjected to the meeting. Then leave.

"What would be better is if you chose to hire me—or another lawyer–to represent you, and I highly recommend you hire someone for all of this immediately, and have your legal representative show up at the meeting with you. That will put them on notice that you are serious, and it will likely make them back off.

"There is more to taking a child away than just one Social Worker's opinion. When we nip that in the bud, we can concentrate on Ernie's case and see if they have drawn up any paperwork to justify their actions.

"Again, if this is just this Ruth person acting independently, the hospital will likely acquiesce rather than face a lawsuit. If not, then at least we will find out what is behind their actions and can make a plan to fight it. Does that all make sense?"

Tim and I said "Yes," and Elsie added her own, "Yep."

"So, Larry," Tim said and looked at me. "Yeah. I mean we need help with this and we would definitely like to hire you. You're the person who was recommend to us and working with you…I feel like we would be in good hands. June?"

"Yeah, absolutely. I agree." I nodded my head.

"Does this mean I'm not going to Italy–hypothetically speaking?" Elsie asked with mock innocence.

We just looked at her. We heard Larry chuckle in the background. "Why don't you two come to my office? Now would be good. We can sign the paperwork and I can get started on this right away." He suggested.

"Okay," Tim said and looked at me. I nodded. "Ahhh, yeah we can be there in 20 minutes."

"Great. See you then." Larry hung up.

"Okay, let's go." Tim rose from his seat at the table.

I turned to Elsie while I rose, "Elsie, do some of that tons of homework or clean your room or something. Don't just watch TV."

"Okay, Mom. But what about Ernie?"

"I don't know Elsie," I said patiently. "We can't see him or talk to him. I'm heartbroken, but your dad said he looked good. Tomorrow we'll show up with our lawyer and then we'll go see him."

"And bring him home?" Tears filled Elsie's eyes.

"Yes," I said, and bent down to kiss the top of her head. "And bring him home. Even if I have to steal him back." I said as my own eyes began to water.

"It's okay Mom. We'll get Ernie back. You got this." Elsie offered seeing the emotion building in me. She gave me a big hug and then stepped back wiping her tears from the corners of her eyes.

"Come on June. Let's get going and get our son back." Tim gently nudged. "Elsie, honey." He said and then stepped to her and gave her forehead a kiss. "Try not to burn the place down while we're gone." He teased easing her concerns with his humor; for a moment at least.

"Wait, let me make a mental note…'don't burn the house down.' Okay. Got it Dad." Elsie was quick to move to the lighter side Tim offered.

And then we were out the door and on our way to the lawyer and to getting our son back. Or so we hoped.

On our way to Larry's office, Tim and I didn't speak. It was as if we had buried our worry about Ernie not having his parents to comfort him for another day.

I felt helpless and afraid and angry all at once. All I wanted was Ernie back home or if need be, in the care of the doctor who knew his condition and cared about our son and also about our family. I didn't want him or Elsie in Ruth's hands and that of her cohorts in cold hospital rooms, a pawn in a gruesome self-serving plot. It was too much emotion for me to hold back much longer.

CHAPTER FOURTEEN

ARREST AND DEVELOPMENT

After meeting with Larry Greenbalt, we felt somewhat better. We now had legal representation and had already received advice that kept us from making a very rash decision.

But Larry couldn't help us with the immediate need to get Ernie out of the hospital.

For one thing, the weekend was approaching, which meant nothing was likely to happen from a legal standpoint until at least Monday. If hospital officials, via Ruth and supported by Dr. Grinsby, had caused CPS to file a case to remove Ernie from our care, Larry would need to see the report and obtain a court date to repudiate the claim. That was going to take a few days.

We couldn't accept that. If such an effort was being considered, that could take the CPS authorities up to 72 hours to complete. To us, that meant that we had a window to get Ernie out of the hospital–and that would mean doing it Saturday–tomorrow.

As far as we knew, and Larry agreed, doctors in the hospital could not perform any procedures or in any way treat Ernie without our consent–the exception being an emergency. Because the attending doctor told us directly, that Ernie was under no such threat, we were confident they had no legal standing to keep our son from us or to keep him in the hospital.

Larry agreed to meet us at Brinker Hospital on Saturday to press that case and see if this could be resolved amicably.

But Tim and I agreed that we were going to take Ernie home—amicably or not. Of course, that could mean dealing with security guards again; but we thought we might threaten calling the police and charging the hospital with kidnaping or something. Or we would just find a clever way to get past them and walk Ernie out with us.

We would have to make certain that our lawyer was not seen as being involved if it came to that. Our plan needed work, but our determination was secure.

***

Friday evening passed slowly. Sleepless hours of worry continued throughout the night. Not even my book or crossword puzzles could grab my attention long enough to induce drowsiness.

When I woke on Saturday morning, I had only wrested two hours of sleep. My bags were fully packed under my sore red eyes. *Thank God for makeup*, I thought while I smoothed concealer under my eyes and prepared to face the world. It's the one inequity with men that I was not anxious to march against.

Even Tim tossed and turned several times before finding sleep and, in the middle of his slumber, he began flaying his arms about and talking nonsense before settling in for the remainder of the night. Despite Tim's midnight battle with Ruth—I assumed—he was up by 7 am and probably working his way through his second cup of coffee when I came down an hour later. It was later than I had wanted my day to start. I wanted to be at the hospital by 8 am.

Elsie was still asleep, which was just as well because she would have insisted on coming with us. Tim and I both agreed it would be better for her to remain home while we fought what was sure to be the upcoming battle for Ernie. We didn't attempt to wake her.

Tim greeted me as I entered the kitchen with a thermos cup filled with black coffee.

"Come on," he said, moving toward the front door "Let's get going and get to the hospital before they can do any more damage. Larry is meeting us there at 8:30."

I took the coffee and followed Tim to his car which he had already backed out of the garage and into the driveway. I didn't say anything, just sipped my coffee, until we were in the car and on our way to Brinker Hospital.

"So, what's the plan when we get there?" I finally spoke. "Huh?" Tim mumbled. He was in his private world.

"The plan Tim. How are we going to handle this? Are we going to get Ernie even if they say no?"

"Yeah. Yeah, sorry. I was just running the whole thing through my head. I didn't sleep well last night."

I gave him an incredulous look but didn't follow it up with a verbal response.

"I think we should let Larry do what lawyers do," Tim continued. "But I think we need to have just one goal. I mean, I don't see a scenario where we leave Ernie at that hospital. Do you? Unless someone from CPS shows up and insists that Ernie stay and has the police with them...I just don't see how anyone at the hospital has any authority other than what they are assuming to have."

"Yeah, I think you're right." I took a sip of coffee.

"So, if Larry tells us that they have legal paperwork from CPS or some other reason to keep him, we have to just insist that we *see* Ernie if we have to leave him there while we fight it in court. Not what we are hoping for, but it might come to that. And, it's important that we at least get to see him, so he knows that everything is going to be okay."

"That isn't going to make me happy," I said. "But, I guess...yeah, the most important thing is that we at least see Ernie and get to be able to see him when we want."

Even with his night of interrupted sleep, Tim had mellowed in his response—to a degree—or at least blanketed it with reason. For me, accepting Tim's reflective reasoning was driven by exhaustion; but I knew that coffee, and more likely dealing with Ruth, would soon revive my passion. For now, I welcomed Tim's logic and calm and his less stressful approach.

"So," I said, twisting the warmed thermos between my hands, "what is the plan if there *is* no legality to stop us taking Ernie back, and it *is* just Ruth and others at the hospital overstepping their rights?"

"Well, if that is the case, then it's us against them and we can't let them pretend they have rights over our son."

"And so...."

"So...while you were getting ready this morning, I looked up the plans to the hospital online. I just found the basic layout, but one of us can enter the hospital through the normal visitor's entrance. It's likely that no one will stop us. We find Ernie, get him dressed and just walk him out."

"Okay...and how do we know exactly where Ernie is? What if they moved him from the room you saw him in? And how do we keep the guards from looking for us? Won't they be on alert when we show up at the hospital? And what if Ernie doesn't have his clothes? What if he is still too weak to walk?" I became enthralled with how much thought Tim had given his master plan. I wondered if it was a security guard that Tim had been fighting with in his dream.

"Well, I already put clean clothes in a bag in the back seat. If he can't walk, we just use one of the wheelchairs. No one pays attention to a parent wheeling a child who is dressed. We just have to sneak into his room and past the nurses' station."

"Uh huh. And how do we know which room?" I asked after looking in the back seat to see the shopping bag of Ernie's clothes.

"Okay well, we have to count on Larry getting you access to Ernie. I don't think they will deny that–just probably need to have one of them with you. When you know what room he's in, text me. I'll go up from the visitor's entrance. While they are watching you and walking you out, I sneak in and get Ernie."

"Wow, Tim. You are quite the little criminal. I had no idea. You have this all planned out." I said feeling quite proud of him. "Why won't they be looking for you?"

"Ahh, because I am going to announce–and you will back me up–

that I have to go to work. I will leave before you go in. So, they won't be thinking about me. And thanks for the compliment."

"What happens if we or you get caught?"

"Worst case scenario, I get in a fight with the guards. And, I don't know. But when I am down the elevator and out the door, you meet me at the curb and we're off. Nothing they can do."

"So, why don't we just call the police and tell them the hospital has kidnapped our child? I mean, if they have no case to keep Ernie."

"Because the doctor will lie and say it's an emergency and Ernie must stay there. The police will back the doctor and hospital and force us to go to court. No way we win in that scenario."

"This is getting really intense," I said and rubbed my fingers across the worry lines developing in my forehead. "But yeah. Yeah, if they have no right then they have no right. If Larry says there is nothing to give them legal right, then...we have to get Ernie out of there on our own. I'm in. But let's go over the plan again."

For the remainder of the ride, we went over all the various aspects of the plan and how it might play out–including what Tim would do if he got stopped by guards. He amended part of the plan to say that he would tell the guards our lawyer had secured Ernie's release and was already waiting downstairs with the police.

Tim was confident that he could get out the door before they could check any of that. He was also confident it would be a different set of guards on weekend duty, so they wouldn't immediately recognize us.

Finally, Tim told me it was imperative for me to stay calm no matter what Ruth or anyone said or did. I just needed to get permission to see Ernie, and then text him the room number. When I returned to the emergency entrance where Ruth sat on her perch, I could start a big scene to distract from Tim and Ernie's escape.

The more we talked about the idea, the more ridiculous and criminal it sounded. But it was either follow the plan or leave Ernie at Brinker with a doctor who doesn't recognize Ernie's disease, will deny Ernie his "cocktail" medicine, and treat him for God-only-knows-what.

And all this while Tim and I are investigated for child abuse—which will only confirm the doctor's inept diagnosis. We couldn't allow that to happen. Our child's welfare was at stake. Ridiculous, criminal, or otherwise, we were going forward with our plan if necessary.

We arrived at the hospital in time to meet Larry just outside the emergency room entrance. We briefly discussed what we would like to accomplish, leaving out our plan to sneak Ernie out. Larry agreed that the two primary goals were to make certain we had visitation rights with Ernie and force hospital officials to present factual reason for keeping him.

When we entered the waiting area, Ruth stood at her guard post, her left hand on her hip and a pen in her right fist. The index finger on her right hand pecked at a computer keyboard that lay just below the countertop.

Larry approached her first with Tim standing on his right side. I stood behind Tim, half out of site, holding the bag containing Ernie's clothes behind me, and trying to gain control of my breathing. I was nervous. More so over how I might lose control and force a conflict, than about the possibility that we would have to execute Tim's plan.

"Hello," Larry said, commanding Ruth's attention. "Ruth is it? I'm Larry Greenbalt. I represent Tim and June Gallagher." Larry introduced himself to Ruth without offering to shake hands. His introduction seemed to make her nervous. She glanced at Tim and then put her attention back to Larry.

"I would like to inform you that you are holding my clients' son, Ernie Gallagher, against their will. Further, you have denied them access to visit their son and in fact forcibly removed them from his room. Can you show me the order or report from Child Services or a court authorizing this action?"

"Well, errr no there is no report yet but Child Services has been informed and will make an assessment." Ruth replied with a slight stutter.

"So, then you have no authority with which to hold a child against their will or refuse the child's parents visitation," Larry stated, giving no room to wiggle. "Is the hospital administrator aware of your actions? Before we call the police for abduction and sue the hospital, we would like to make certain the administrator is aware of your policy."

Larry didn't pause for a response. He hit her with all the key words and threats without giving her time to think or to argue with him. "Please get the administrator down here now. In the meantime, tell me what room Ernie Gallagher is in. His parents need to see him—now."

Ruth was caught off-guard by Larry's fast-paced speech and almost arrogant assurance. She couldn't do anything but follow Larry's instructions.

"He is in room 213..." Ruth answered.

Larry nodded at Tim; he grabbed my hand and we made a beeline toward the corridor to the visitor entrance and the main elevators.

"Err, but the doctor...they can't go back there by themselves," I heard Ruth trying to stop us.

"Ruth," Larry said evenly, "is the administrator on the way? We really would like to keep this out of court and keep this hospital's name out of the newspapers." Larry threw at Ruth keeping her off-balance and her attention away from Tim and me.

Now that we both knew Ernie's room number and were headed there, we needed to alter our plan.

"Tim, we don't want to get Larry in trouble, I know—but now that we can just go to Ernie's room, should we just take him out of there and leave?" I asked while we rode the elevator up to the second floor.

"Well, I don't know. I think one of us should still go back down to see what's going on with Larry and the administrator. Maybe they just gave in."

The elevator doors opened, and we stepped out and stopped just in front of them turning in to each other so that we could not be easily overheard.

"Let's see how Ernie is doing first," Tim whispered. "Then I'll go back down to meet the administrator. I'll text you if it isn't going well. I think it might be less questionable if a woman is walking or wheeling their child out of a room than a man. Then, if we have to go to our plan, I will get Larry out of there and get the car and come meet you at the entrance."

"Okay...I guess."

We broke our huddle and headed for room 213.

When Tim and I arrived at Ernie's room, we were greeted by an unsmiling nurse. *Good grief*, I thought. We hadn't covered this possibility in our criminal scheme. I kept the bag of clothes behind my back and out of her view.

"Excuse me. Can I help you?" She asked sternly.

"Oh *hi*. We're Ernie's parents just checking in on him. They told us to come by this morning." I responded with every bit of fake cheerfulness I could muster as Tim and I continued into Ernie's room.

"I'm not certain you are supposed to have access without Dr. Grinsby's approval..." The nurse said, trying to verbally stop us.

"Oh, pfffff!" I said and waved my hand as if batting a pesky fly. "Oh my, no. Our lawyer is with your hospital administrator now. They are working out all this misunderstanding. I don't think Larry–that's our lawyer–is going to have to call the police?" I said with mock sincerity looking toward Tim.

"No. No. I don't think so. They were all smiling when we left and I think Ruth was getting everyone coffee." Tim added picking up on my ploy.

We were lying through our teeth and we knew it could all blow up in a matter of minutes. Best case scenario for us was that the administrator agreed with Larry and overrode Ruth and the doctor. Otherwise, our criminal activity was going to have to play out.

The nurse gave us a strange look that suggested she wasn't 100 percent sold on our story. But, I think the words 'lawyer' and 'police' were enough for her to let us be—at least until she could check our explanation with Dr. Grinsby.

We smiled at her as she left. I turned my body to face her as she walked out, making certain Ernie's clothes bag stayed hidden. We proceeded to Ernie's bed. Ernie was on his side facing away from us. I gently touched his shoulder and kissed his cheek. He slowly rolled over and rubbed his eyes with both hands, then looked at me.

"Mom?" He said in a groggy whisper and then offered me his outstretched arms. I dropped his bag of clothes onto the floor and took him into a deep embrace.

"Yep. It's me honey. And Daddy is here too. Ohhh, I love you so much I could squish you." I said tearing as I gave him an extra squeeze before breaking our hug and sitting on the edge of his bed. Tim stepped in and took my place and repeated the ritual, ending his embrace of Ernie with a kiss to his forehead.

"Hey buddy, we missed you. How you feeling?" Tim walked around and sat on the other edge of Ernie's bed.

It wasn't until we had both given our hugs that I noticed how gaunt Ernie was. Overnight he had gone from pale to ghostlike. When we hugged, his arms seemed sapped of strength.

"Can...we go...home? They say I go...not go home." Ernie struggled to speak and stared at me with pleading eyes.

"Honey, Daddy and I are going to take you out of here." I assured Ernie. "Can you get dressed if I help? And are you strong enough to walk?"

"No clothes, Mom."

"Daddy packed your clothes honey." I held up the bag.

Ernie smiled. "Okay. You help."

I turned to Tim and quietly said, "Tim, we didn't count on the IV drip and monitors. They'll know when we disconnect him."

"Yeah, I was just thinking about that. This is going to have to be a grab and go. There is no way they sign him out if the doctor gets here. This nurse will raise a stink, I'm sure. I don't know how much time we have. You get his pants, sneakers, and socks on. The gown will be enough for his top for now and cover his pants. If the nurse comes back, she won't notice. I'm going down to see how Larry is progressing. I will text you if we have to go through with taking Ernie on our terms. When I do, that means go *now*. Okay?"

"Yeah okay," I said. "I'm nervous, Tim. I know they have no clue how to treat Ernie, and without making something up, they really have no right to hold him. But it still feels like we are breaking the law somehow."

"Yeah I know June," Tim stood and walked around the bed and put his hand on my shoulder for reassurance. "But we are trying to do the right thing. If they're going to be adversaries for their own arrogant reasons, we are going to get our son out of here. Unless you want to keep him here and see how it goes?"

"No!" I nearly shouted. "No, no. We are getting him out. I wish Dr. Blackwell were here. I think maybe she could just get them to transfer Ernie to her care."

"Well, she's not so…"

"Okay. Go quick. I'll get Ernie dressed."

Tim grabbed my hand and looked in my eyes. "It will be okay hon." Then he left.

"Okay Ernie. We're gonna play a little game. Okay?"

"No. No game. Just go home." Ernie answered.

"Umm yeah, this is a game *about* going home. It's called 'sneak out of the hospital.' The first part of the game is to put your pants and socks and sneakers on, but you have to stay under the bed covers and don't let anyone see them. Okay?"

"Okay." Ernie was not excited about the game but didn't question any further. We got him dressed and back under the covers when the nurse came back into the room.

She checked Ernie's monitors briefly before speaking to me.

"I spoke with Dr. Grinsby," she said. "He should be here shortly, but said that Ernie cannot be released until he gets here. So, we'll have to wait until he's here."

I wanted to argue with her–to say, "That's what you think!" and grab Ernie out of bed right then and there. But I swallowed my reaction and smiled at her instead. I think that surprised her. I was fairly certain Dr. Grinsby's words were stronger than "Wait until I get there." The nurse contemplated my smile for a few seconds and then let the room.

Meanwhile, I figured that Tim had made it downstairs by now.

***

Tim

I left June and my son in the room and hurried to the elevator and down to the waiting area where we'd left Larry to intimidate that banshee Ruth.

When I arrived, Larry was sitting in one of the ever-present plastic chairs in the corner of the waiting area with Ruth and another woman. I guessed her to be the hospital administrator that Larry had told Ruth to get down here.

When I approached, their conversation stopped, and the other woman got up to leave. She didn't stop to say anything to me and seemed to be in a hurry to get somewhere else.

"Hey Tim," Larry said when I got to where he sat. I nodded at him and looked at Ruth.

"Well, I must get back to my desk," she said hurriedly. "There are patients and families waiting for me. If you'll excuse me." Ruth stated as she rose and then made her way back to what June calls 'her perch.'

"So, it doesn't appear to me that things went well or is it just my presence that made everyone leave?" I asked sarcastically.

"Yeah," Larry said with a chuckle. "No. The administrator is backing Dr. Grinsby's stance that Ernie is in imminent danger and cannot be released. I explained to her that his statement is contrary to what you were told yesterday by Dr. Grinsby himself. I reminded her that the hospital has no legal standing in lieu of an actual threat to the patient's life. She was insistent that we wait for Dr. Grinsby's arrival and meet again when he is here."

"Jesus, Larry. These people are something else. Nice move in getting us in to see Ernie though."

"Yessss, well, they want to end that too until Grinsby gets here," he said. "As soon as Ruth is done with the mob at her station, I have a feeling the upstairs nurses' office is going to get a call."

"Shit." I grabbed my phone and texted June. "Get out now." Then I turned back to Larry.

"Larry. Thanks for your help. I think June and I will take it from here today. No need for you to wait around for Dr. Grinsby." I explained to Larry rather hurriedly and awkwardly as I extended my hand..

Larry was a smart guy and I could tell he figured out what was going on without directly making mention.

"Tim," Larry said, ignoring my hand and putting his in his trouser pockets. He rocked back on his feet a little like an old-time preacher.

"There is tricky legal standing here; I am not certain, without Dr. Grinsby's direct input, what rights the hospital has–especially given that the administrator basically punted until Grinsby arrives. So, it may be that there is no official standing right now. Just know that could change now or…. later. And, yes, I think it is time for me to go."

He grabbed his briefcase and placed his hand on my shoulder "Good luck." Then he shook my hand. He turned and quickly left the hospital.

***

My heart began to beat rapidly when I got Tim's text. I knew I had to act fast, but I was scared that I would get caught and not certain what that would even entail or how I would react.

I made a quick check of the hallway from the doorway of Ernie's room. The elevator was about four doors down. Although we wouldn't have to pass in front of the nurses' station, we would be clearly visible from it.

As weak as Ernie was, we couldn't rush without drawing unwanted attention. I would have to curl him into me to hide him and help him along. But that wasn't our biggest challenge.

As Tim mentioned, the monitor alerts would sound the second I disconnected Ernie. I wondered what would happen if I just unplugged them? Would an alarm still sound at the nurse's station? I decided it was no more of a risk to do that than to turn them off or just disconnect Ernie. Unplugging became the new plan.

I returned to Ernie.

"Okay honey. Time to start the game. So first, I'm going to take the thing out of your arm. Then I'm going to run around to the other side of your bed and unplug the machines. Then I'm going to rush back here and take the sensors off of you."

I was talking to my son as if this was a fun adventure, keeping my voice light and almost childlike. "After I do that, you are going to jump out of bed and we are going to sneak out to the elevators. Sound like fun?"

"No. I hungry." Ernie said with all seriousness.

"Oh. Well part of the game is...is going to IHOP after we escape and maybe getting something to go. So, let's do this." I said trying to motivate him.

I took Ernie's arm gently. I skittishly removed the IV line. He gave a brief, low "ouch." Then I sat Ernie up in bed, so he could hop off easily. I ran around to the other side and unplugged the monitors. I listened for a few seconds. No alarms. But that was because the machines were off. It didn't mean the nurse's station monitors weren't giving an alarm.

I ran back to the other side of the bed, stripped the sensors from Ernie's body, helped him hop off the bed, yanked the ridiculous hospital gown off his body, grabbed his shirt from the bag and pulled it over his head, and then headed for the door with my arm wrapped around Ernie's shoulder.

Ernie wobbled just a bit when we started our walk but, after a quick check to see if he was okay, we continued. The elevators were in sight. I had to squelch my desire to grab Ernie up and run for it.

Normal. Just act normal and don't draw attention I told myself with each step. The floor was laid out linoleum or some such material, with each square following another, outlining a direct path to the elevators. I counted 17 squares to freedom. Ernie leaned heavily into me. I don't know if it was for comfort or support, and I didn't have the luxury of stopping to find out.

A nurse came down the hallway from the nurse's station and headed our way just before we passed the door to the last room—just before the elevators.

Shit, shit, shit. The alarms, I thought in a moment of panic. I stopped and pulled Ernie around to the front of me, knelt and then brushed his hair with my hand pretending to straighten it. "Oh my, your hair is a mess, honey." I said more for the nurse's benefit than for Ernie to hear. *Normal. I was being normal. I'm not a person sneaking a child out of the hospital.*

It worked. The nurse passed by us with barely a glance and headed for a room down the hall. Maybe the alarms hadn't sounded. Maybe she was heading to Ernie's room to check. I didn't wait around to see. Eight more squares and we were safe.

Ernie made a haphazard attempt at swatting my hand away from his hair.

"Mom. Go now. Tired."

"Okay honey, almost there." I assured him as I gathered him back up under my wing.

The nurse came back down the hall in a hurry. She was coming from Ernie's room.

"Excuse me!" She called. "Excuse me miss!" She called to me before stopping at the nurses' station to bark an order at someone I couldn't see behind the desk.

I grabbed Ernie in a bear hug and ran the last eight tiles to the elevator. I pushed the down button as soon as I reached it. "Come on. Come on damn it," I whispered.

"You squish me Mom," Ernie complained. But I didn't listen. I couldn't do anything to make him more comfortable now. The nurse was rapidly approaching us and the elevator door had not opened. I looked down the hall toward the stairway. We could take the stairs. But there was no way we would make it that far without having to confront the nurse.

Ding.

The welcoming sound of my savior gave notice just before the nurse caught up with us. I rushed inside the elevator, nearly knocking over two people who were trying to exit at the same time. I pushed the button for the first floor. The nurse, who had caught up with us at the elevator, let the couple come out.

"Excuse me, but you can't just take him out of the hospital without checking out and without the doctor's permission!" She put her hand on the closing doors while she spoke, stopping the doors from closing. But she didn't enter the elevator.

"I'm his mother and I can do anything I want," I argued while repeatedly pushing the close door button.

"This hospital is responsible for patients in our care and Dr. Grinsby has a do-not-release order on your son." The nurse insisted, still preventing the doors from closing. I put Ernie down and stood in front of him, protecting him from any attempt she might make to grab him from me.

"Yeah, well I have a lawyer downstairs who says Dr. Grinsby's orders are as useless as his...his doctoring." I responded in a fit of fear and passion, unconcerned with how much sense I made. "Now, please take your hand off the door." I firmly threatened as I reached to pry her hand from the door.

The nurse flinched and released the door, reacting to the threat of the crazy woman who was about to grab her hand. The door finally shut, closing Ernie and me into the relative safety of the elevator while it drifted down to our escape.

Ding. First floor.

The elevator doors opened. I kept hold of Ernie's hand and led him out of the elevator toward the hospital exit. We took the right turn from the main hall to the visitor exit doors as planned.

I stopped to look around for a bit. Everything seemed normal. People were coming in and out of the gift shop, pacing the lobby while on their cell phones, walking toward other parts of the hospital. Other people moved toward us and the elevators.

We walked determinedly toward the exit. As I got close, I could see the outline of what appeared to be Tim's car. I was squinting, through the glass door, trying to get a better look when *bam*! Two security guards came out of nowhere and stepped directly in front of us.

I abruptly stopped, letting out startled gasp.

"Ma'am you can't take that child out of the hospital." A short, stout, 50-something guard said, holding his arm and hand out mimicking a crossing guards stop signal.

I took a moment to get my breath back. I pulled Ernie closer to my side. "This child is my son, and I have every right to take him out of here." I said as I attempted to sidestep the guards. They moved in unison mirroring my action and stopped me again.

"Ma'am, we have our orders," he said. "You can't leave this hospital with your son." The same guard responded, this time with both hands wresting on his utility belt.

"I don't give a crap what your orders are!" I said. "This is *my* son. Get out of my way or I will call the police." My blood was boiling.

They didn't move.

By now a few people were watching the commotion we had started. I decided to take advantage of their interest and make this uncomfortable for the guards, hoping they might acquiesce.

"Help!" I yelled. "Help, these men are trying to steal my child from me! Please! Please call the police! They are kidnapping my child!" I screamed at the top of my lungs.

The guards fidgeted and looked around the room a bit nervously but didn't budge. All eyes were on us now. I took advantage of the guards' momentary confusion and took a step around one, moving toward the exit again.

"No you don't, lady." The stout guard said as he rushed to get between us and the exit door.

"Help me, please!" I yelled again to the crowd that was growing. I saw a few with cell phones out taking video and, I hoped that some were calling the police.

"Mrs. Gallagher, is this necessary?" I heard a man scold from behind me. It was Dr. Grinsby. Ruth followed closely behind.

"You tell these imbeciles to get out of my way or I will sue them—and you—and have them arrested!" I didn't care if people took pictures or video or anything. I didn't care what I looked like or how I sounded. I cared only that I get Ernie out of there and home or to Dr. Blackwell.

"Mrs. Gallagher, as attending doctor I have the right to keep your child here under an emergency situation." Dr. Grinsby said more forcefully.

"Stop it!" I yelled. "Stop the lies! There is no emergency. Ernie is able to walk with me out that door and that is what we are going to do."

A woman watching the situation escalate stepped forward. She looked to be in her late 60s. I noticed that she had an erect, proud posture and purposeful demeanor.

"I called the police," she said to me. Turning to Dr. Grinsby and taking in the guards and Ruth with her sweeping glance, she said, "You have no right to take this woman's child. Don't worry, honey," she patted my arm, "you don't do anything until they get here...and call your lawyer."

She gave Dr. Grinsby a parting sneer.

"Mrs. Gallagher, you see how unnecessary this is," the Dr. said. "You are making a scene. We have to take Ernie back to his room and then we can..."

"The *hell* you are!" I yelled again. This was my new normal. "You aren't taking my son anywhere. We're leaving."

I turned from Dr. Grinsby, and the now meek Ruth, and again lead Ernie around the guards. I got halfway around the stout one when he grabbed my arm with one hand and took hold of Ernie's with the other.

He pulled hard trying to separate us. Ernie, who had remained my silent shadow throughout the whole ordeal cried out, "Ow, ow! Mommy, he hurt me." I whirled around and instinctively slapped the guard hard on his face.

"Don't you *ever* put your hands on my child!" I screamed, this time not for affect but out of pure, beautiful anger. The room of onlookers uttered a collective gasp. The guard dropped both of our arms and took a step back. The other guard was frozen in place; I don't think he wanted to get involved in this scene.

I hooked my arm around Ernie, under his arm, and half dragged him on our march toward the elusive exit.

Out of the corner of my eye, I saw Tim enter the visitor lounge, led by two uniformed officers. What they must have witnessed, was me slapping the security guard then marching toward them.

To me, the police officers' blue uniforms looked similar to the security guards. They had badges on their shirts, utility belts with things hanging from them, black shoes–all things, that from my position, partially bent over dragging Ernie along, looked the same.

266

"Ma'am, stop there, we need to..." The new uniformed man began speaking. He sounded, eerily similar to the stout guard and was not that dissimilar physically. I interrupted him.

"Get out of my way!" I clenched my jaw and grit my teeth and fairly spit the words at him. Putting Ernie behind me, I thrust my body forward toward his shoulder. My arm was extended with my palm out. I looked up to assure my hand would find its mark and give the desired effect of pushing the guard back, off balance. It was then, at the moment my hand was about to strike his shoulder, that I realized this guard was actually a police officer.

I watched, in slow-motion disbelief, as my hand, encouraged by the weight of my forward- thrusting body, detached from any thought that could pull it back, continued on to the police officer's shoulder. My hand careened off his shoulder and caught him squarely on his jaw. The officer's head snapped back a bit and his teeth made an audible click.

I stood frozen. An open-mouthed and pale Tim stood motionless behind the officers. The room was silent. Then, in the next second, the other officer was behind me and grabbed my upper arms.

"Release the child and put your hands behind your back now," he said sternly. "You're under arrest for assaulting an officer."

"I'm sorry, It was an accident officer, I...I thought you were more security guards trying to stop me from leaving with my son. I'm so sorry." I tried to explain but without effect. The officer I struck stepped forward now. He was stunned by the unexpected blow but seemed to be suffering from damaged pride more than my punching prowess.

"We saw you assault that security guard and now you were going to assault another one. That's your defense? I don't think so. You're under arrest. Now let go of the child."

Tim stepped forward to speak to the officer I had struck.

"Officer, officer," he said, moving in front of me. "I'm sorry. My wife...these people are trying to keep our son without legal cause and we are just trying to get him out of here. She would never strike a police officer..." Tim pleaded.

"But she would strike security guards?" The officer dead-panned.

"No, no officer, that man was assaulting my son, practically ripping his arm off in trying to get him from me. I had to stop him." I added to Tim's pleading.

"Here's what I know. You slapped that guard, you knocked me in the face. You're under arrest. You can do all of your explaining with your lawyer in court. Now release the child or we'll add obstruction to the charges. And you", the officer said indicating Tim. "You get out of the way and step aside or we'll arrest you too."

That was it. This officer was not going to let a reasonable explanation, which seemed suspect to him anyway, change his mind *or* his sour disposition toward me.

I reluctantly let go of Ernie's hand. Tim stepped aside as ordered and I was handcuffed by the officer who had grabbed my arms. Dr. Grinsby stepped forward to take control of Ernie. He grabbed his little hand and began to walk away with Ernie in tow. Ernie gathered all the energy that remained in his overworked little body and yelled out through tears, *"Mommy!"* He kicked Dr. Grinsby's shin, hard. The pain caused Grinsby to release Ernie's hand and to hop on one foot as he rubbed his bruised chin. Ernie ran to me and threw his arms around my waist.

"Mommy!" He cried. "No hurt my mommy you...*panty head!*" He screamed at the officers. Tears and snot streamed down his face. It was the most horrible thing he could think of to call someone. I began to sob as well.

"It's okay honey. Mommy is okay." I tried to console. Tim stepped forward and knelt on front of Ernie.

"Ernie buddy," Tim choked on his words. "It will be okay. I'll take care of Mommy. No one is going to hurt her." Tim gently pried Ernie off of me and held him close.

Dr. Grinsby limped back to the officers and tried to take charge. "Officer, I am Dr. Grinsby. This child is my patient and needs emergency care. He cannot be taken off the premises."

Tim rose but held on to Ernie's shoulder, keeping him close at hand. "Like hell. He is *not* my son's doctor. And he is *not* treating my son for any emergency. He has no right to keep our son here and that is why we were trying to get away from these...*people*. Our lawyer met with them this morning and they could not present any legal reasoning for keeping our son." Tim argued firmly.

"I don't see the emergency here doctor," the officer said, looking at a teary-eyed Ernie. "The parents have the right to refuse treatment for their child. Unless you have a court order or CPS is involved..."

Ruth suddenly found her voice and stepped forward.

"Officer," she simpered, "CPS has been informed of the situation with the Gallaghers and their children and they are investigating."

"You have a report from CPS or a court order through them or anything I can look at?"

"Well, no it isn't here yet but by Monday we should have something."

"Okay, then on Monday, CPS can do their thing and make a determination, but until that happens, this hospital has no authority. I don't see...."

The officer stopped mid-sentence. Ernie began to shake. He was having a seizure.

"Ernie!" I called. "Catch him Tim! Oh my God Tim! Not now!" I said as I tried unsuccessfully, to break away from the officer's grip. I knew what this meant; it would give Dr. Grinsby all the authority he needed to keep Ernie under his control at this hospital. There was no way the officers would be convinced this was now not an emergency. My tears flowed more freely at this realization. We had lost.

Tim laid Ernie on the floor and supported his head. It was a mild seizure and lasted only a few seconds, but Ernie had lost consciousness. Dr. Grinsby stepped forward to check Ernie's vitals.

"Now you see," Grinsby directed at the officer. "This is an emergency and we must keep this child here and not in his parents' care. Ruth, call for a stretcher and let's get him back upstairs."

"Ernie buddy, it's okay. It's okay buddy." Tim whispered to Ernie as he rocked him in his arms. "Ernie has these seizures. It's part of what is wrong with him that this doctor doesn't understand or know how to treat. My son is already being treated by Dr. Blackwell at University Hospital. We need to get him *there*." Tim implored the officer trying to move him back to our side.

"Sir, I'm sorry but this isn't a matter for CPS anymore. Your son is obviously ill and needs immediate attention. We can't force them to let you take him away from here now." The officer tried to explain to Tim.

"You don't understand, we want to take him to *another hospital*. You can call them. Ernie's doctor is there Dr. Blackwell. She is treating my son for his disease." Tim tried desperately to convince the officer.

"I'm sorry Sir, but this is out of my hands now. You'll have to work this out with the hospital and whoever else gets involved."

The officer who had handcuffed me, began to lead me away. The other officer, the one I had struck, said he would take statements from everyone.

A few people in the crowd volunteered to step forward and give their accounts; more than one offered that they had video of some if not all of the events.

The stretcher arrived and Dr. Grinsby took Ernie back upstairs. Tim caught up with me outside the visitor entrance as I was being led out to the police car.

"June. I'll get Larry to sort this out and get bail. I'm sorry honey. I'm sorry you had to go through this."

"It's my fault Tim. It's my fault." I said through my tears.

"No, it isn't. It's my fault for this whole plan." Tim confessed near tears himself.

"Just stay with Ernie and make certain he's okay," I said. "I'll be fine."

The arresting officer put me in the back of his car. Tim stood and watched as the police car, with me stashed in the back seat, drove off. Then he returned to inside the hospital.

***

I sat in the back of the police car handcuffed like a common criminal. Up until that point, I had never been in the back of a police car; I had never been in trouble with the law. I cried most of the way to the police station, not from the shame of being arrested, but because of how I had failed Ernie.

Being handcuffed and stuffed into a cramped back seat of a police car, was only the beginning of the many humiliations I encountered from my first experience with being on the wrong side of the law.

Even my arrival at the police station was an ugly testament to my criminal status. It was nothing like walking into the police station for a traffic violation or parking permit.

In our town, criminals like me are driven to a back-alley entrance and ushered into the police station through a small metal door with an electrical lock that said, "criminals enter here"–not literally.

From there, I was walked, still wearing the handcuffs, through a dingy, narrow corridor, down an elevator, and into an interview room; the arresting officer constantly at my side. The only stop we made was a short one for him to place his holstered gun into a secure locker and out of reach of unsavory inmates like me.

My belongings were taken from me and put in an envelope.

Fortunately, the only items I had were my car keys and my phone.

The interview room was compact–big enough for two metal chairs and a metal desk. There was barely room for the arresting officer and me. When a second officer entered, a large intimidating man, I felt especially small. I was Mirandized just like on TV. But, unlike TV, I couldn't change the channel and make it all go away. I was officially being arrested.

I was offered a chance to explain what had happened at the hospital prior to my arrest or I had the option of remaining silent–maybe wait for Larry, whom I'm certain Tim must have called by now. Everything I said would go into their report. I had to think about this. *Was I going to say something I shouldn't? Would I be admitting to a crime?*

The large officer studied me as I considered my options. He nodded to the arresting officer.

"Bill, outside with me for a minute." Bill rose and followed him out of the room. About two minutes later, they returned. "Bill, you can take the handcuffs off her." The large officer said, and the handcuffs were removed. It felt good to get them off; my small wrists showed the red marks from the handcuffs wear. It also felt a bit less intimidating hearing the large officer refer to the other one as Bill. That humanized the situation for me somewhat. I was handed a form to sign to agree to the inventory they had made of my personal items.

"June Gallagher. So, are we talking or remaining silent?" The larger officer asked.

I wiped the dampness from my face that my tears had left on my cheeks and under my eyes. When I pulled my hands away, I saw the smudge of black on the ends of my fingers. *Great*, I thought with slight amusement, now *my face likely confirms my criminal status.*

I looked at the officer who was questioning me and responded. I decided the truth didn't need a well-rehearsed legal answer, but I knew Tim and Larry would advise me to be silent.

"Look officer...?

"Sergeant O'Neil"

"Sergeant O'Neil, I don't mean any disrespect and I am so, so sorry for hitting you, officer Bill. It really was an accident. I was trying to defend my son against the security guards. I thought you were one of them. But that is all I can say. I'm going to have to wait for my husband to get hold of our lawyer. Sorry."

"Okay," Bill said, "No, that's okay, that is your right."

"All right, Bill, process her." The sergeant directed and then left the room.

Officer Bill opened the door and indicated to me to go ahead of him out of the room. *Process her.* Those words echoed through my head as I walked down the hallway.

I was hoping they would just give me a stern talking to or something. I mean, I was not a criminal. Maybe I should have opted to talk, to explain. Maybe they would have just let me go. Now, I was going to be "processed."

Officer Bill led me back along the narrow corridor, through another electronically locked door and into the booking area.

This was a large room that was compactly designed to fit all the necessary elements for booking and holding us criminals. Everything was close together and visible for the most part. I saw several holding cells along one wall and another area behind glass where the holding area officers worked safely tucked away from what happened outside their enclosure. The holding cells were not very large, maybe three or four times the size of the interview room I had just left. They were made of concrete block on three sides and glass or some sort of plexiglass along the front. A metal bench was secured to the cement floor where one disheveled woman sat on one end of one cell. Another woman sat on the floor, muttering. A metal toilet was on the other end–fully exposed.

I tried to remember how much of my morning coffee I had actually drank; I also made a mental note to not drink anything else or even *think* about water. There was one cell for women and one for men–each of the same design.

I could only see partway into the cell holding the men and counted two occupants. One man was very skinny and looked dirty. He stood a few feet away from the brick wall at one end, picking at his pockmarked face. Another man was clean-shaven and neatly dressed in a dark suit. *He's like me*, I thought. *Probably just a simple mistake that got him put in here.* Then he rushed to the metal toilet at the end of the cell and heaved. I stepped back.

"Drunk driving," Bill said, following my gaze. He was waiting to surrender my package of personal belongings to the officer behind the glass enclosure.

The women being held could have been characters from a TV crime show. One was a youngish girl, 20 -25 maybe, and obviously strung out on some kind of drugs. She wore torn jeans and a dingy yellow man's t-shirt and worn-down sandals. She talked to herself and yelled at an imaginary person while pulling at her hair while she sat on the floor. Twice she got up and ran to the glass wall to yell at me, "I see you out there! I know you! I know what you are!"

She was frightening and yet, at the same time, almost comical in her drug-induced madness. Mostly, she was pitiful. I had never seen firsthand the devastation that drugs can have on a young person's brain. I wondered what episode in life could have driven her to this horrible, declined state of being so early in life.

I was fairly certain the other woman's crime had something to do a very old profession. She was possibly 35 and heavily made up. She had on five-inch, bright pink heels, a blonde wig, that had dislodged itself partially from her head during her arrest, and tight neon pink pleather pants and an equally tight light pink midi blouse. Both the pants and the blouse looked to have been deliberately chosen to be a size or two smaller than the woman's frame, leaving her fully on display—including her belly that hung over the too-tight waistband of the pink pants. I was relieved that I was not going in that cell with those two women.

After my envelope of belongings was handed over, I was led down another narrow corridor and into a tiny cement room with one glass wall that faced the officers work area from the other side. There was a stool to sit on and a wall-phone. That was it. The room was so small, to exit, I almost had to back out the same way I came in—I could barely turn around.

With each new step in this "process" I was feeling increasingly de-humanized. I had been handcuffed, led through the bowels of the police station to areas reserved for common criminals, read my rights, had my belongings taken from me, and now, I had come to the infamous "one phone call" part of being arrested.

"You can make three phone calls, using the phone on the wall," Officer Bill said, "but the calls must be local numbers." I took a seat. So much for TV crime shows.

"Um, I don't know my husband's cell number by heart–which was sadly true–or our lawyer's number. They are all programmed in my cell phone you took away." I explained.

"Okay," he said. "One of the officers will get your phone and you can tell them which phone numbers you want and they'll write them down for you."

Officer Bill gestured toward the glass enclosure. A female officer came over and I relayed, through an opening in the glass wall, what officer Bill had suggested. I asked only for Tim's number. She acquiesced and brought me his number written on a yellow sticky note. I picked up the wall phone receiver. I was careful not to press it to my ear or mouth to avoid making contact with whatever germs might have been left by the last user. I dialed Tim's cell number; he answered on the first ring.

"June! Are you all right? Where are you? Did they let you go? Do I need Larry to come down or do I need to bail you out?" Tim peppered me with questions.

"Tim, Tim slow down. I don't know what is going to happen. This is my one-phone-call-thing." I said trying to bring focus to the conversation. "I'm fine and yes come to the station to get me. Are you with Ernie now? Is he okay?"

"Okay, I'll come get you," he said, then, "No. No I'm in the waiting area. Ernie is still unconscious, but that's all I know. They aren't exactly being forthcoming with me. I'm going to come get you and then I'll go back to the hospital."

"Yeah, okay. We can demand they let us see him."

There was a long pause before Tim responded. "Okay umm I'm

leaving now. Do you need anything?"

"No. I just need to be out of here and with Ernie. Oh wait, what about Elsie?"

"She's home. She's fine. There's lunch stuff in the fridge and if we aren't back, I told her she can order take-out for dinner. She's worried about Ernie. I didn't tell her about what happened to you."

"Oh. Yeah better she doesn't know her mom is a criminal."

"June…"

"Okay I have to go get processed some more. Please come get me unless they let you see Ernie—then I can wait."

"All right. Okay. Bye."

I hung up the phone and turned my head toward officer Bill for my next instruction. He turned his palm upward and waved his fingers in toward himself and then out and then in again gesturing for me to come out of the phone booth.

Just a few steps away from the phone booth was the fingerprinting station. This police station was an early adapter of digital finger-printing. They don't press ink-covered fingers against a postcard-like paper. I put my entire hand palm-down on top of a scan; the machine took an image.

There was a smaller screen for just my thumbprint. Officer Bill explained that the new system was easier and more accurate, and that digital prints could be sent to the FBI for faster identification.

I supposed he told me all that because he was very proud of their new toy. But to me it was just another reminder that I was being arrested, no matter how fancy and fast the methodology was.

My last stop was steps away from the former main station. This was the dreaded mug shot. I stared at the camera for a moment before responding to Officer Bill's instructions about where to stand and where to look.

I had scanned Hollywood gossip pages online and seen tabloids at the grocery store check-out line before. I knew that these cameras could make Gisele Bündchen look ugly and menacing.

The only plus on my side was that I was sober and alert; I wasn't in some drug or alcohol-induced stupor like so many of the tabloid victims. Even though I wasn't a celebrity, I still couldn't help but feel apprehensive about my mug shot somehow getting out to the public and embarrassing Elsie and Ernie, Tim…and me.

Snap, my front view headshot was taken. "Turn to your right," officer Bill instructed. *Snap,* another image. "Turn to the other side." *Snap*. the final artful shot was completed.

"Okay. This way." Officer Bill said as he led me to the women's holding cell.

"*Crap!* I thought. *I am going to have to be in with those two women? Are you kidding me?*" As I stopped well short of the holding cell door and several steps behind Officer Bill.

"We're gonna run your information through the system," he turned around and looked at me. "Slow day, so it should come back fairly quickly. If everything checks out–no outstanding warrants–you get kicked loose and get a court date." Officer Bill explained taking note of my reluctance to enter the den of suspected sinners.

When I finally did enter, I turned immediately back toward him with a pleading expression on my face. But he closed the door and locked it, leaving me inside to cope with my two new colorful friends.

I turned around, taking in the cell's interior, trying to decide if I would just stand there, risk taking a seat on the bench, or find a corner to make my own. What I didn't want was to make conversation with my roommates, if I could avoid it at all. But, the young druggie wasted no time accosting me. She stood straight up from the wall she was sitting against and quickly walked toward me. At first I thought she might actually attack me because she didn't stop until her face was nearly shoved into mine.

"*Bullshit!*" She screamed into my face, exposing her putrid smelling breath to my unprepared nose. I put my hands in front of my face to block her from touching me.

"It's all *bullshit!*" She yelled at the officers in their walled-off area.

Then, to my relief, she retreated back to her spot on the floor.

"Don't mind her. That one's crazy out of her mind from too much heroin. But she's mostly harmless." My colorfully dressed roommate offered unsolicited.

I just looked at her. I didn't want to be chatty.

"Come have a seat if you want," she said, unperturbed by my silence. "I ain't gonna bite you. You gonna be in here for a while. No use trying to stand all that time."

I thought about it for a moment. Strangely, I didn't want to be rude to my new companion but, at the same time, I didn't have the desire to be chummy. I looked at an unoccupied corner where I could sit on the floor before I considered again the bench spot being offered.

I definitely did not want to stand for any length of time. I also had no idea of what nastiness might have been on that floor—so I opted for the bench. I walked over slowly and sat down as far away from my cell- mate as possible.

"So…" she said. "What you in here for? You don't look like most of the people I meet in here."

"Oh. Um. I hit officer Bill." I plainly stated.

"You what? You hit a cop? Ohhh honey. You gonna be in here for a loooong time." She said with a large laugh.

"It was an accident."

"Ah huh. Ain't it always an accident though?" She said continuing her chuckling. "I accidently got caught helping a nice man get some relief and he accidently offered to pay me for my kindness. Now we both in jail." She said nodding toward the cell containing the men. He must be someone in there I didn't see when I was first brought in.

"So, have you been through this before?" I asked. Chattiness was going to happen, whether I liked it or not, and I might as well get some information.

"Oh yeah. I've had lots of accidents." She replied with a grin.

"Um, how long does it usually take, you know before they release you?"

"Well, that depends," she said, scratching a spot on her wig with long, hot pink fingernails. "On a busy night, I might be in one of these cells seven or eight hours before Chester get my ass out of here. Couple of times overnight. And it depends if you got any other crimes they find on that computer or if you on parole...stuff like that. But today, if you as clean as you look, probly not more than a couple hours or less...of course...you did hit a cop...accidentally...so they might want to make some example of you. Might keep you all night."

I was silent. I couldn't be here all night. I had to get back to Ernie. I had no way of knowing how he was or if Tim could get him out. Did Dr. Blackwell get back? Did she get to see Ernie? Was Larry back at the hospital arguing for us or preparing a legal case at his office? My mind raced with these questions. I felt despair rush over me from being useless to my little boy who needed me. The beginning of tears formed in the corners of my eyes. I turned my face from my bench companion and wiped the wetness from my eyes with my hand.

"Here," my new friend said as she slid closer to me on the bench. She retrieved a neatly folded handkerchief from her ample bosom and waived it in my face. "You might want to put some spit on it and wipe those black trails off your face too," she said referring to the mess on my cheeks.

I hesitated but took the handkerchief. Being this close to her, I could see on her face the wear of a struggle-prone life. She was much older than I had thought. I guessed she was over 40.

"Thanks," I said and took the handkerchief from her hand. I dribbled some saliva onto the handkerchief and tried to wipe off the dried mascara river from earlier.

"Let me see that. You ain't got no mirror in here and you just makin a worse mess," she scolded as she watched me try to fix my face.

There was something almost motherly about her demeanor now that made me soften toward her and trust her intentions. I handed the handkerchief back to my cell-mate. She held it in front of my face and said, "Spit. And don't give me one of them shy housewife dribbles. Give it a good soaking."

I filled my mouth with as much saliva as I could muster and then sent it forth with force onto the waiting cloth. What would have disgusted me any other time seemed oddly appropriate here. I was desperate. I was in a jail cell with a drug addict and a prostitute...who was going to judge me other than me?

She mushed the wet cloth together before attending to my face with carefully placed dabs followed by gentle swipes down my cheek. After applying the same technique to both sides of my face, she firmly took my chin in her hand and turned my face one way, then the other before declaring, "Good. Now you look like your presentable self." She handed the handkerchief back. "You keep it. I got plenty of 'em. Girl's gotta be prepared, ya know?"

For the first time since I was arrested, I smiled. I regarded her for a moment. I saw her now, not as a prostitute in jail, but as a woman: a human being who was kind to a stranger.

"June," I said and extended my hand to her.

"June, like the month. Now that's a good name. Always sunny." She said as she took my hand in hers. "I'm Belinda. But my friends call me Lindie. I don't now why really. Someone just said it once and it kind of stuck." She grinned.

"Lindie," I repeated. "I like it. I have a good friend named Elizabeth but her friends call her Lizzie. I think they call you Lindie because it's happy-sounding and friendly...like my friend Elizabeth. You make people feel comfortable."

"Well, I think sometimes they might feel *too* comfortable if you know what I mean," Lindie said and let out a big laugh. I laughed with her.

We were beginning to get comfortable.

Before we had finished our shared laugh, Officer Bill suddenly appeared at the cell door. "June Gallagher, you're being released. Let's go."

I immediately brightened. I had been in the cell less than an hour, not the seven or eight hours or overnight sentence that hung over me. I practically jumped off the bench and headed for the door. I stopped just before exiting and looked back at Belinda.

"Lindie. Maybe you should keep this," I offered the handkerchief back.

"No. No you keep it and you give it to someone who needs it, like I did for you. They call that paying it forward I think." She said with some pride.

"I hope you get out soon," I said.

"Don't you worry 'bout me Junie girl. Chester gonna get me out of here soon enough."

And, as her last sentence trailed off, I stepped through the cell door and out to the main area. Officer Bill closed the door behind me.

"Will she get out soon?" I asked him.

"Her?" He asked nodding toward Lindie. Then he shook his head. "These women come from out of town mostly from everywhere. Passing through, usually from one city to another. They don't stay too long. They stand out too much in a small town and get arrested all the time."

"But she has a umm, boyfriend, or a...pimp–I hated saying the word in reference to Lindie–that will bail her out?"

"Chester?" he asked. I nodded. "Who knows? He's a drunk she hangs with. He might show up today, tomorrow. We don't know. This one can't come up with the $500 bail to get out so, there she will sit for 45 days. First time we caught her, but there was another one hanging on Chester's arm last week."

All of this conversation happened as Officer Bill got my belongings envelope from the police officers behind the enclosure and I signed for them.

"Okay, I'll walk you out. Your husband is outside near the main street entrance where we're headed, and he can meet you there if you want to text or call him."

Officer Bill then led me back through the door we had come in by. Waiting outside, was Sergeant O'Neil and another man who was dressed in a cheap suit. They were having a conversation which our presence interrupted.

"All set, Bill?" Sergeant O'Neil asked.

"Yep. Just walking her out to the street where her husband is."

"Mrs. Gallagher. You will get a notice for a court date. Make certain you don't ignore it." The Sergeant advised me.

"Okay." I politely answered. I wondered if we were supposed to shake hands or something or if I should growl and act tough, now that I was being released from the big house.

I followed Officer Bill back to the elevator and up to street level. "This is where I leave you, and where your husband can pick you up...out there." Officer Bill pointed toward the sidewalk in front. He stepped back inside the station, and just like that, my time behind bars was over.

I walked to the sidewalk and peered up and down the street looking for Tim. I didn't see him, so I called him. He was sitting in the car on a side street waiting to hear from me.

"Hey. You're out? Where are you?" Tim asked immediately after answering his phone.

"I'm in front of the station...actually just on the side before the main door."

"Okay. Okay. I'm going to do a U-turn and be there in two minutes." And he hung up.

Two minutes later, his car pulled up. I ran to the passenger door and opened it but didn't get in.

"Babe!" Tim said, leaning over to see me. "Thank God you're out of there. Get in and let's get going." Tim looked relieved and guilty.

"Give me your wallet."

"Huh? Oh crap do you have to pay bail? They told me no."

"No," I said, shaking my head and holding out my hand. "Just give me your wallet. Please, I don't have time to explain now. I need to get to Ernie, but I have to do this first. Or just give me the credit card."

"You can't sign my card June…not at a police station. They'll probably arrest you for forgery or something."

"Okay fine. Go park the car back where you were and come back. Hurry." And I shut the door.

Tim gave me "the look," and then put the car in gear and drove off.

Three minutes later he came scurrying back.

"Okay. I ran back. I had to park further away 'cause I lost the other space." Tim explained slightly out of breath.

"Okay. Come on. We have to go to through the front this time. And pay bail."

"Wait. So, you *do* have to pay bail?"

"Not mine, Someone else's."

"Who?"

"Someone who was in there with me and who has a good soul."

"Wait, wait, wait, wait. You want me to bail out a stranger because you think they have a good soul?"

"Yes. Tim, please. Just trust me." Tim looked at me blankly. "Tim, do we give money to charity?"

"Well yeah, it's a tax write-off."

"Okay great. Well we are going to make a charitable contribution. Not for tax reasons but because…"

"…because the person has a good soul." Tim finished my sentence for me. His expression and tone of voice told me he knew this was going to happen and he just had to accept it on faith. "Okay. Let's go do it and get out of here."

And that's what we did. We paid Belinda's bail and left. I was sure that Lindie would assume that Chester had bailed her out.

While Tim drove us to see Ernie, I imagined what would be happening inside the jail. I pictured her being ushered out the door, and the officer accompanying her handing over an envelope before he disappeared into the bowels of the police station.

In my mind's eye I could see Lindie studying the envelope, turning it over several times to look for any writing that might indicate who it was from. She opened it and pulled out a slightly spit-damp, mascara- stained, handkerchief–nothing else.

I could almost hear her hearty chuckle as we sped to the hospital: "*Well, I'll be Goddamned*"

CHAPTER FIFTEEN

Persona Non Grata

Tim and I drove straight to the hospital. He was mostly quiet during the ride except for the occasional inquiry into my time in jail. But, my attention had quickly turned from my humiliating experience in jail to my concern for Ernie, though truthfully, Ernie was never out of my thoughts. I had little desire to reminisce about my experience and even less appetite for Tim's attempt at humor. When he jokingly referred to my experience as being "hard time in the big house," I answered him with silence.

He responded with something else as we pulled into the hospital parking lot.

"June. You can't go into the hospital." He said, all hint of humor gone from his tone.

"What do you mean I can't go in?" I asked incredulously. "I am going to go see Ernie. I *have* to see him!"

"I know, but you can't. I didn't want to tell you while you were in jail and upset you more, but hospital security is under strict rules to not let you in."

"They can't do that. I have a right to see my son!" I argued as though it were Tim making the judgement.

"Yeah I know. But you assaulted the guards and a police officer, so they won't let you in."

"I defended myself and Ernie against kidnapping! I am going in to see Ernie and bring him out." I snapped open my seat belt, reached for the handle and opened the door enough to stick my leg out.

"June!" Tim shouted at me and grabbed me by my left arm pulling me back in. "If you try to enter the hospital they will call the police. You'll be arrested again. Is that what you want?" Tim rhetorically asked before realizing he was squeezing my arm forcefully and released it.

I sat motionless, stunned, and defeated by Tim's rebuke. Then I began to cry.

"I have to go see Ernie. I failed him Tim. I left him in there and he is all alone and...and he needs me...and I need him." I blubbered more than spoke through a river of tears.

Tim undid his seat belt, reached across the car and drew me into him as close as possible, my face resting in his chest.

"You didn't fail him, June. We didn't fail him. And we're going to get him back. We're going to get him back and everything will be okay." Tim gently assured and kissed the top of my head. I sat up and looked at him while wiping my tears from my face with the palm of my hand. I thought of Lindie and her handkerchief.

"What are we going to do, Tim?" I asked. I composed myself enough to speak quietly and with a marginally clear head.

"For now, I am allowed into the hospital but not to Ernie's room," he said. "Ruth elevated the case after...after we tried to get Ernie out and they...CPS has taken over now. But Larry is going to court Monday morning to get us visiting rights and then to challenge CPS and the hospital on keeping Ernie. We need Dr. Blackwell's help. She's the only one who can argue in court and to hospital officials about Ernie's mitochondrial disease. But she isn't back yet. Hopefully, first thing Monday morning. Her nurse knows what's going on and will make certain Dr. Blackwell knows as soon as she comes in."

I felt more helpless and useless as Tim's explanation of how things would proceed progressed. My child had been taken from me, literally ripped from my grasp, and there was nothing I could do about it. I had to rely on a stranger and the courts to get my child back to me.

I looked at Tim with pleading eyes, hoping he might have developed an alternative plan–a way to steal Ernie back. I didn't care if it meant being arrested again; nor had I assigned any logic to the idea. Tim read me.

"June." He cupped my limp left hand in both of his. "We don't have any other option. This time, we are going to have rely on Larry and Dr. Blackwell to get Ernie back."

After a pause, Tim continued. "I'm going to go back into the hospital and see if they will give me an update on Ernie's condition. Then I'll come right back and tell you what they say. Okay?"

I nodded.

"June. Please promise me you'll stay right here and not try to get into the hospital. Don't make this worse."

"Fine. I won't go in." I said in a dismissive manner.

Tim hesitated, staring at me and trying to read my face to see if my response was sincere.

"Okay, go." I said and shooed him with my hands. "Find out how Ernie is. I'm going to call Elsie so she knows I'm okay in case word has gotten out already."

Tim gave me one last stare, as though he might have something to say, but remained silent. He released my hand and exited the car.

I figured that what he could have said was that Elsie did know everything. My face was probably all over the local news stations with the story of my arrest at the hospital.

I found out later that Ginny had already called our house to ask Elsie if she needed to come over for a while. Elsie smartly declined.

.

I also found out that reporters had apparently made their way to our front door, but Elsie ignored them and pretended no one was home. I'm not certain Tim knew that tidbit or not, but he knew Elsie was already dealing with the effects of my arrest and chose not to tell me.

He also knew, and neglected to mention, that reporters were hovering outside the main entrance to the hospital. They were mostly from the local papers and affiliates of major TV stations.

So, of course, I didn't know this when I left the car to make my way to the hospital. I wasn't going to go in. I just needed to be nearer to where Ernie was and, in my mind, somehow, being at the front door of the hospital would make me feel closer to him.

I grabbed my phone, left the car, and headed for the front entrance.

On the way, I called Elsie's cell phone. She answered on the first ring.

"Mom. Oh my God, Mom. Are you okay?"

"Hi honey. Yes. Yeah I'm fine."

"Mom. Everyone has been calling and the news people are out front.

Are you still in jail?"

"No. No, I'm…sitting in your father's car at the hospital waiting for him."

"Mom. I can't believe you got arrested. You punched a cop? I can't believe it. My Mom went to the big house!"

Elsie's voice was more excited than concerned. She sounded like she had some big tragic story she was readying for her guest appearance on The Tonight Show.

"Seriously Elsie?" I was a bit miffed. "It was a big mistake…a misunderstanding and…and anyway it was just the local police station not some big prison. Geez! And I'm glad you're concerned for how *I'm* doing."

"Mom. Sorry. But I did ask how you were first and…well…you hit a cop! And everyone is talking about it."

"Who is everyone?"

"Well Ginny called and then tried to come over, and my friends at school, and a couple of Dad's friends from work. Then I just stopped answering the phone 'cause reporters were calling too."

"Oh my God. Okay well I'm sorry honey. Just...just don't answer the phone or open the door for anyone. And I mean *anyone*. Okay?"

"Yeah okay, Mom. When are you guys coming home? And what's going on with Ernie?"

"I don't know." I sighed. "Your father is in the hospital now trying to get an update. Ernie had one of his seizures and the doctor there dragged him off before we could get him out and to Dr. Blackwell and that's the last I heard."

As I spoke with Elsie, I wandered closer toward the hospital, not paying attention to what was going on around me or to how close to the front door I had ventured. Suddenly, a bright light shone in my face and a small group of people began to follow it in my direction. I held my hand over my eyebrows in an effort to dim the blinding effect of the light. That's when I recognized the group of people was a gaggle of reporters.

"Shit." I said aloud as I froze in place.

"Mom. What? What's going on?" I had forgotten I was in the midst of a conversation with Elsie.

I turned away from the quickening onslaught of the mob and speed-walked back toward the car.

"Nothing. Nothing's wrong. I have to go."

"Wait, what? Are you running? I thought you were in the car. Are the police chasing you Mom?"

"Oh my God no, Elsie. Turn your imagination off for a minute. I have to go. It's reporters. Just stay inside the house and don't open the door. I'll call you back later."

I made it to the car before the reporters caught up with me. I got safely into my seat and locked the doors. That didn't discourage this group though. A cameraman shone his light through the car window. Reporters blurted out their inane questions.

"Mrs. Gallagher, why did you hit the officer?"

"Is it true your son was being held against his will by the hospital?"

"Will there be formal charges against you?"

"When they arrested you, did they know you are the hero who saved Kalea from the burning car?"

"Why is your son not being released to you? Is it true he was taken away from you by Child Protection Services on charges of abuse?"

That last question sent me over the edge. I leaned over and tried to beep my horn and scare them off. It didn't work. Then I saw Tim's keys lying on the console between the passenger and driver seats, which I foolishly overlooked when I exited the car. Tim must have left them in case I needed to start the car for the heater or something. I maneuvered myself into the driver's seat, started the car and leaned on the horn. That made everyone jump back. I put the car in gear and sped out of the parking space leaving my stunned pursuers well behind me.

I had a feeling of déjà vu as I drove away. I never wanted to be in the spotlight for any reason and yet, here I was, running away once again from notoriety. But this time it was from something darker and more personal. I drove out of the parking lot and stopped at the side of the road about a half mile away. I called Tim.

"Hey. Everything okay?" He asked. "Yeah fine. Did you get to see Ernie?"

"No but they gave me an update. He's awake but only on and off. He's very weak. Nothing critical they can see but uh, he's being fed intravenously and getting some liquids that way and um, they are, you know, just monitoring everything."

"Yeah, nothing critical they can see because they're clueless, Tim," I said bitterly. "We have to get him out of there. He needs his cocktail. He was getting better with that and he needs all the energy he can get to fight whatever is wrong now. You know that Tim. And he needs Dr. Blackwell." I began to sob again.

"I know June. I know. We're going to get him out and to Dr. Blackwell.

I'm coming back out now."

"I'm not there now. I had to move." "Why? Where are you?"

"Reporters started harassing me and I had to get out of the parking lot." I explained through my tears.

"Okay. Okay. Just uhhh, drive into the front area of the parking lot and I'll walk out to meet you. Okay?"

"Yeah. Okay."

"All right. I'm walking out now."

"Don't let the reporters see you."

"No. I found another door; one of the nurses told me to use that one to avoid all that commotion."

Tim left by the hidden side door and found me where I had pulled over. Our drive home was mostly silent. Now and then one of us would express our own version of what was likely to happen now to get Ernie out and, more importantly, to get us in to see him.

Even with the update Tim received, we still were not certain if Ernie was just experiencing one of his episodes due to low energy or if something more serious was happening–like before when his system shut down.

We would have to wait until Monday morning when Larry had a hearing in front of a judge before we would know about visitation; and we would have to wait until tomorrow for Tim to go back to the hospital and get another update on Ernie's condition.

I avoided talking about the reporters and neglected to say that I had left the car.

We decided to order Thai food for dinner. Tim would pick it up from our usual haunt. While he was gone, Elsie helped me set the table for dinner while she peppered me with questions about being in jail and what she should tell her friends or teachers at school. I didn't get into a great amount of detail about jail. I didn't see the point.

I just told her, "Don't ever get arrested...unless it's for something good like protecting your family. And that's what you should tell your friends and teachers if they ask, 'My mom was protecting my brother.' Period. Then just ignore them if they keep asking more questions. And don't talk to the teachers or the principal or any strangers about anything else. Politely refuse and then call me as soon as you can."

"Is Ernie going to be okay, Mom? Are we going to get him back?" Elsie asked no longer concerned about her friends or teachers. Her eyes watered as she posed her questions and I could see she was genuinely scared.

I took a deep breath in an effort to steel myself against the emotions that would otherwise have mirrored Elsie's.

"Ernie is going to be fine, Elsie." I said and took Elsie's face in my hands. "He is in a hospital now, so he is getting care. He just needs to be with Dr. Blackwell so he gets the best care. She'll be back on Monday and then we'll see about getting Ernie moved. And tomorrow Daddy will go check on Ernie again." I released her face and hugged her close.

"I want to go see him tomorrow too." She said as she broke from my embrace and looked up at me.

"You can't, honey."

"Why?"

"Because...because the hospital won't let us."

"Why, Mom? *I* didn't get arrested."

"Elsie that isn't fair." I answered solemnly.

"Sorry, Mom. But why can't I go see Ernie with Dad even if they won't let *you*?"

I could see now that my approach wasn't going to work. Elsie was too mature and too inquisitive to be placated this way. I didn't have an answer. Elsie stomped into the living room and threw herself onto the couch.

I sat at the table running my finger and thumb along the same napkin crease over and over and pondered options. I finally decided that when her dad came home with the food, we would have a family session where Tim and I would explain everything we could about the hospital's role in keeping Ernie, about Tim and I trying to sneak Ernie out and why, about exactly how I got arrested and even about what happened while I was in jail. If Elsie was going to have to live through this, then she needed to know everything in order to be prepared—especially now that it seemed the press was involved. We weren't going to be able to shelter her.

When Tim came home, I sent Elsie out of the room on a made-up errand—upstairs to pack some clothes for Ernie. While she was gone, I talked to Tim about the idea of including Elsie on everything that was happening. He was against the idea at first, thinking, as I initially did, that we needed to protect her. But, when I mentioned the phone calls she had already taken and the likely questions she would get from teachers and friends at school, and how the press would now make everything that much more public, he agreed. "Better she heard the truth from us, than be surprised by the rumor mill and public accusations."

Elsie came back downstairs and into the kitchen, after placing the clothes she had gathered for Ernie on the living room couch. We had the Thai food laid out and plates and silverware on the table. We each dug in and selected our favorites from the plastic containers. Once our plates had been covered with Thai food and Tim had delivered a glass of diet Coke to each of us, Tim and I began our story of everything that had happened. We told Elsie about the plan we had hatched to get Ernie out of Brinker Hospital and why we thought it was necessary. Then we explained what happened in the hospital and how we almost got Ernie out and…how I got arrested. Elsie listened wide-eyed and asked very few questions other than seeking some explanation about the legality of the hospital keeping Ernie and why they could keep us from even seeing him. Tim and I did the best we could to explain something we didn't completely understand or agree with ourselves.

The story of my brief but memorable stay in jail and being "processed," amazed Elsie. She was especially interested in my interrogation–her interpretation of my interview in the tiny room–and cell mates. She asked if I was scared to be locked in with them. She couldn't imagine her mom being put in jail and fingerprinted just like she sees on TV.

But in the end, what was really of importance to Elsie was Ernie; was he going to get better and back home to us soon? All we could say was that we were working with our lawyer, Larry, on all fronts and that we were certain everything would be fine. We didn't say that we weren't really certain.

After 45 minutes, we had finished our family talk, but not the food on our plates. The three of us were too involved in conversation and too nervous about Ernie to do much more than pick at our meals. So, we stood and silently put cling-wrap over the individual plates and put them in the refrigerator for later when our appetites might return.

Tim grabbed a beer from the fridge and headed for the living room. Elsie and I each snatched a frozen yogurt pop and joined Tim on the couch. We were in unspoken agreement that some mindless television was needed to sooth our thoughts–for as long as that cure would work.

I moved Ernie's clothes to the chair and tucked myself into my corner with my comforter; Elsie plopped into the middle with Tim on the other side. Tim turned on the television once we were all settled. The TV was preset to the local news station which was the last thing someone had watched when it was turned off. When it came on, there I was, on camera, being chased by reporters from the front of Brinker Hospital and into Tim's car; the group finally descending outside the car window.

"Oh my God Mom, I didn't know they got to you at the hospital," Elsie said. "How come you ran away instead of you know tell them your story?" Elsie innocently asked.

"Yeah June. I didn't know they found you *outside* the car, at the front of the hospital either. How come you ran away?" Tim echoed Elsie's question with biting sarcasm.

"I'm going upstairs to read." He huffed as he rose from the couch, took one last, large gulp of his beer and then placed the bottle on the living room table. He took two steps toward leaving the living room then stopped and turned back to face me. "You are un-freaking believable." He said while shaking his head from left-to-right. Then he left.

Elsie looked at me for a reaction or possibly an explanation. I simply leaned over Elsie and grabbed the TV remote which Tim had tossed on the couch when he stood. "Let's watch one of our shows," I said while I switched channels to our menu of recorded favorites.

Elsie smiled, then scrunched closer to me. We stayed that way, sucking on our yogurt pops and watching our show. We didn't have our usual conversation about the characters in the show, nor did we laugh at places we normally would have. We were still in the throes of despair over Ernie; no TV show could offer us anything but small relief.

Elsie went straight to bed after our show finished. I stayed up and considered my crossword. I was killing time, hoping Tim would be asleep before I went upstairs to bed. I simply was not in the mood for a scolding or lecture from him. I deserved one, but I wasn't ready to volunteer for it.

Around 11:00, I made my way up to our bedroom. I stopped at the top of the stairs, staring into Ernie's empty room. A fearful melancholy washed over me while I stood there peering through the open door at his empty bed. I should be walking through that door to tuck in my little man and give his forehead a gentle kiss goodnight. But this night there would be no kiss; only a silent prayer that God would return my Ernie to me.

When I entered our bedroom, Tim was on his side, facing away from me; he appeared to be asleep. I picked up my pajamas that were laid out on my side of the bed and went into the bathroom to wash my face and brush my teeth and change into my pajamas.

After finishing with my bathroom duties, I turned to leave the room but stopped before I opened the door. The melancholy I had felt when gazing into Ernie's room, was still draped around my shoulders. The weight of emotion forced me to slowly sink to my knees and bow my head.

"Dear God." I began to softly pray as I clasped my hands together with intertwined fingers when my knees had steadied on the cold tile floor. "Please bring Ernie back to me. To us. I know I don't go to church or pray…ever anymore…I confessed pretending God didn't know that already. But my Ernie is so innocent and so good. He's been through so much in his short life already and he could use a break. I'm not asking for a miracle, just some help to get him back to us and to his doctor where he can get well. I know I shouldn't have acted so crazy at the hospital but God, I just wanted my Ernie to be safe."

At this point, the tears started to flow. I must have been a pretty pitiful sight. Kneeling on the bathroom floor in my "Pooh Bear" pajamas–a birthday gift from my kids–praying to an unseen deity, tears running down my cheeks. But I didn't care. I knew that humbling yourself before God was how you were supposed to pray, and I needed help. I needed someone, something bigger than Larry and the law to put my faith in.

"Please God, just help me get Ernie back," I continued. "And, I promise I will be a better Mom and person. Amen." I finished with the customary bargain then wiped my tearful face with the sleeve of my pajama top.

I rose from my penitent position and walked into the bedroom where I discarded my blouse and pants to the dry-cleaning hamper. Then, I lightly settled into bed. I turned off the light on my side table, gently turned around and then lay facing Tim. He started to snore. I turned in the opposite direction and prayed for sleep.

****

Sunday morning, Tim was up early again, well-rested and downstairs by the time I dragged myself through my morning bathroom and dressing routine. I could hear he and Elsie downstairs chatting, probably over breakfast.

Sleep had evaded me again and the dark bags under my eyes were beginning to show the effects of multiple restless nights.

I dallied only long enough to inhale a half-cup of Tim's black coffee before uttering a hearty "let's go" to Tim. There was no conversation between us about last night. He was sullen and gave me the "silent treatment."

We were off to the hospital to try and get in to see Ernie, or at least to get Tim visitation. Elsie insisted on going too and managed to convince Tim that Ernie would want to see her and that she could sit in the car with me if she couldn't see Ernie. Tim seemed to brighten at the suggestion that someone would help keep me in the car; away from the front door and any gathering of reporters.

We piled into my car and drove off just as two news crew vans approached. It was 8 am; I guess they hadn't figured on us escaping early on a Sunday morning. We didn't wait around to see if they were going to sit at our front door or follow us. Tim drove quickly down the street and out of their view. We got to the hospital 20 minutes later. It was a quiet drive, each of us lost in our own thoughts.

Tim went inside while Elsie and I waited in the car at the far end of the parking lot. Tim used the secret side door again to avoid potential reporters. Elsie played a game on her phone, while we waited, and I used the time to take a much-needed nap.

When Tim returned, 20 minutes later, he took his seat behind the wheel and relayed what had happened inside. He said Larry was in deep conversation with Ruth as he entered. Tim stood off to the side until Larry was done with Ruth and the two had a chance to speak. Larry had arranged, by way of some convincing legal threats, to get us all visitation rights. They came with conditions: they had to be monitored by hospital staff, each visit could total no more than an hour, and there could be only three visits per day. Larry explained that on Monday morning, he would be going to court to lift all restrictions and to get Ernie released; if not home then to our preferred hospital.

"Wow, Tim. That's great news about visitation even if it's a bit limiting." I said feeling energized.

"Well, when Larry saw the press scrambling after you, he figured he better fix as much of this as he can before it becomes too much of a zoo and the hospital takes charge of the PR aspects; they could sway opinion their way." Tim explained.

Now, I became concerned.

"Wait. Does visitation include me too? The hospital was pretty adamant about me being arrested and everything."

"About that...Larry made a couple of calls to the station," Tim said. "They aren't pressing charges and there won't be any court date. Apparently, the sergeant who interviewed you when you were brought in recognized you; he was there when you saved Kalea. Well, the prosecutor was talking to the sergeant when you were being let out. He remembered the story too and apparently figured, what was the point of prosecuting a hero for what could easily be argued as an accident–an accident that happened in the heat of the moment when a mom was trying to save her sick child. Good luck with that case. And, anyway, the officer that you hit didn't have the stomach for pursuing something this minor. He took enough ribbing from the rest of the cops at the station."

"That is incredible news!" I threw my arms around Tim's neck and gave him a huge hug. I broke the embrace and continued. "I guess this hero thing had some unexpected bonuses."

"Yeah, well, hero or not, Larry did suggest you stay away from the press and use the phrase 'no comment' when dealing with them. No need to draw more attention to our case. Larry said we might want to use the media later if it becomes necessary. Oh, and try not to hit anyone else. That advice is from *me* not Larry," he teased, pleased with himself.

"Really, Tim?" I asked without a hint of humor.

Unphased by my scornful retort, Tim, went on. "We're going to push the time-table on this and we should have Dr. Blackwell give him a call. Larry will need to have her prepped to testify if things go that way."

"Okay, I'll call her Monday morning. Is that everything?" "Umm, yeah pretty much."

CHAPTER SIXTEEN

A Small Victory

It took me about a second to jump out of the car after giving Elsie a commanding "Let's go!" She and Tim were nearly as quickly out of the car as I was and were soon on my heels as we jogged toward the hospital main entrance. Tim's phone rang.

"It's work." He called after us. "I have to take this, but I'll make it quick." He stopped to deal with the caller.

"Come on." I said over my shoulder to Elsie then continued my jaunt toward the entrance. Suddenly, I stopped, just before I reached the entrance. "Shit." I said louder than I intended to.

"Mom, what?" Elsie asked nearly running into me. "There are a couple of reporters standing at the door." "Where? How do you know?"

"I recognize them from before. The tall guy. Okay so, we're just going to walk in like nothing is happening. And if they ask anything just…just don't answer. Just walk straight ahead. Okay?"

"Yeah okay."

"Okay. Take a big breath and let's go."

Tim still had not caught up with us. It was too late to tell me to take his secret door.

I took Elsie's hand and we casually marched into the hospital. One reporter tried to intercept us, but I quickly put him off when I held up my hand and simply said, "Nope." The other one, the tall guy, was bolder, and followed us into the hospital anyway.

"June, can we get a statement about your arrest and why the hospital is holding your son." He asked as he walked alongside us.

"Nope. Sorry. No comment." I answered without breaking stride. He wisely gave up before Tim reached us. I sensed this "story" they were trying to pursue was about to give up as well and that brought some relief.

"Hey," Tim said as he reached us. "Reporters?"

"Yep. But just the two and they gave up pretty easily," I said.

"You didn't say anything did you?" Tim asked, all prickly again. "'Cause Larry just said we should say 'No comment'."

"Duh. No, Tim I didn't say anything. Give me some credit." I answered defensively.

"Yeah okay. Self-control isn't exactly your strong point." Tim reminded me which brought a giggle form Elsie. I cocked my head and swore at both of them with a steady glare, which silenced them both.

"So, let's go see Ernie." I said as I broke my stare and began to back toward the hallway toward the elevators, waving my hand at Tim and Elsie to join me.

Tim stopped me with a barked command. "Not so fast. We have to check in with Ruth before we go up. Visiting hours don't start until 9am."

"Ruth? Seriously?" I groaned.

"Yeah seriously. We have three rules; we can only go three times during visiting hours, we have to be accompanied by someone from the hospital, and we can only stay an hour combined." Tim reminded me to my dismay.

"Umm so it's 8:35 now and we have 25 minutes to wait, so yeah," Elsie said as she looked around the lobby. "I call the big chair." And she was off. She threw herself into the big, comfy chair in the waiting area across the way from where we stood.

Tim and I followed less enthusiastically and plopped ourselves on the couch. And we all waited impatiently. Elsie did whatever it is that teenagers do on their cell phones, Tim answered emails from work, and I got up and paced the waiting room floor trying desperately not to glance Ruth's way. After the twelfth look at my watch, accompanied by an equal number of times getting on and off of the couch, it was finally 9 am.

"Okay, time to go. Come on." I said with renewed energy as I headed quickly toward Ruth. I didn't look behind me to see if Tim and Elsie followed. Ruth must have seen me coming toward her station because she had managed to pick up the phone and avoided any eye contact with me.

Normally, I would have welcomed the snub. But today–this morning–I was driven by one thought, *see Ernie.* And nothing–not Ruth, not the security guards, not God Himself–was going to keep me from my son. I stood tall, firm, and strong at Ruth's desk and stared directly at her. She must have snuck a peek or maybe she just sensed my presence because she turned her back to the wall behind her.

When Tim and Elsie joined me, all three of us stood, staring at the back of Ruth's head.

"So, what's going on? Is she calling to get a guard or someone to take us up to Ernie's room?"

"Shhh, Tim. Ruth is on a very important call and we mustn't interrupt her. We need to just be patient." I responded with a mocking tone intended more for Tim and Elsie's benefit rather than Ruth's ears. As much as I wanted to insult her, I knew that this time I'd better hold my tongue.

Tim ignored my snarky remark with his usual head-shaking. Elsie thought it was hilarious and snorted out a laugh. After about two minutes passed with our trio of statues planted in front of Ruth, Elsie decided she'd had enough.

"Hi, can you tell me which room my brother Ernie Gallagher is in?" She said very loudly to Ruth who was still speaking on the phone or pretending to. "No? Okay no worries. I can find it on my own.

Thanks." She announced even louder to the ignorant Ruth. And just like that Elsie headed straight for the hall that lead to the elevators.

Ruth, who was not as oblivious to our presence as she acted, suddenly became animated. She rose from her chair, dropping the phone and leaving it to dangle from its cord.

"Wait. Miss. You can't go up unaccompanied." Ruth shouted after Elsie who was about to disappear into the hallway. Ruth looked my way with a half-pleading expression.

I shrugged my shoulders as I responded. "She's got a mind of her own that kid."

Tim, who usually did not partake in my antics, mimicked my shrug when Ruth looked his way. Then Ruth took off after Elsie shouting, "Miss! Miss!" as she went. Tim looked at me with bewilderment.

I smiled and said, "I guess this means Ruth is taking us to Ernie's room."

"Yeah, I guess so." He responded. We followed Ruth side-by-side. "I don't know where that kid gets these ideas from." Tim added wryly as we walked.

"Yeah me neither." I answered challenging the rhetorical nature of Tim's question. And then…I beamed.

Tim and I reached Ruth just as she caught up to Elsie standing at the elevators.

"Miss, you cannot go up alone to visit. You must be accompanied." Ruth scolded Elsie who was repeatedly pushing the up arrow with determination in each depression.

"Why don't you take us Ruth? I mean since we're all here now and it is after 9 am. And that way you'll know everything is being done right?" I said with syrupy sweetness.

Ruth stood there sputtering while the elevator chimed the arrival of the next car. When the doors opened, Elsie and I wasted no time stepping inside. We smiled at Ruth as though she were our best friend. Tim, who was a bit slow to catch on, suddenly got it and stepped inside with us.

"Ughh here Ruth let me hold the door for you." He offered to a dumbfounded Ruth.

"Well. Well yes. I suppose it would be best for me to take you up... this time." Ruth stammered as she accepted Tim's invitation to board the elevator. "But next time, we...we have to have a nurse or security take you up."

"Of course, Ruth. We really appreciate your help." Tim responded now fully-engaged and enjoying the role play.

"What floor?" Elsie asked Ruth with a big smile.

"Two please." Ruth answered sounding as though she had willingly joined our little family game.

The ride seemed longer than normal and proceeded with awkward silence. On occasion, Ruth turned back to regard our trio. We forced a smile at Ruth whenever we caught her gaze. She answered with her own forced grin. As we exited the elevator, a flurry of activity rushed passed us.

Two nurses were making a determined journey toward a room to our right. They were followed closely by a man pushing a cart with a machine mounted on it. The caravan nearly ran into us. We pressed our backs to the elevator doors that had closed behind us. Tim pulled Ruth back by her arm just as she was about to step in front of the cart. The flustered Ruth stood motionless for a moment. After gathering her wits, she made a few steps in the direction of the parade of nurses.

She turned back toward us and sternly said, "Wait here." We froze in our spots.

Ruth disappeared into the room where the commotion had headed. Over the hospital intercom system, we heard. "Dr. Grinsby to two-oh-four. Dr. Grinsby to two-oh-four. Stat."

We had no idea what was going on.

I suggested to Tim that this would be a good opportunity to find Ernie's room. We could have an extended visit while Ruth was busy elsewhere. Tim agreed and the three of us headed in the opposite direction Ruth took. We decided that Tim would search the rooms on the right side of the corridor while Elsie and I searched the rooms on the left side.

Elsie and I peeked into our first room...no Ernie. Tim did the same on his side and again no Ernie. As we met in the corridor before checking our second set of rooms, the elevator doors opened, and Dr. Grinsby emerged and ran down the hall and into the same room where Ruth had disappeared.

None of us said anything but we knew whatever was going on in that room, must be serious.

We resumed our search of the rooms. At our second meeting in the hall, Tim shook his head no at Elsie and I and we returned the gesture. Before we could look into the next set of rooms, Ruth suddenly appeared outside the room where Dr. Grinsby had gone. She frantically waved at us with both hands as she walked quickly in our direction, using an awkward tip-toed, run-walk technique. We immediately ceased our room searching excursion and waited for Ruth to reach us.

Her face looked odd–with squished cheeks, wide-eyes and pursed lips –kind of like a caricature of herself. When she arrived, she froze for a minute and considered each of us before she spoke.

"We...we should all go back down to the waiting area." Ruth suggested in a tone that was half statement and half question. "Yes. Yes, that is what we should do." She continued in a more certain voice and she turned around to walk to the elevators assuming we would follow.

"Whoa...whoa whoa whoa!" I called after her before she had taken more than two steps. Ruth stopped and turned back toward us.

"We came up here to see Ernie, and we are not going back to the waiting area." I said firmly. "Remember?"

"Yeah. I don't understand. What's going on why can't we visit our son?" Tim questioned.

"I'm, I'm sorry. Yes. Yes, you will, you can...we just need to talk downstairs." Ruth was stammering as she had earlier when we invited her on to the elevator.

A nurse hurriedly left the room where the emergency was happening. The elevator doors opened and a doctor hurried out and headed toward the room the nurse just left. Silently, Ruth followed the action with her eyes before she spoke again.

"We really should go downstairs," Ruth said quietly.

I studied her face as she spoke. It was covered with worry and her voice, normally stoic and pointed, carried the undertones of uncertainty. I considered her actions, the way she looked at the room where the emergency was happening and especially, the way she was trying to hurry us downstairs. A chilling realization washed over me.

"Wait. Is Ernie in that room?" I asked looking Ruth directly in the eyes. She didn't respond. "Is that my son's room?" I pointedly repeated the question.

"Yes," Ruth surrendered.

I gave Ruth a blank stare then took off running toward the room. "But you can't go in there." Ruth shouted after me trying to take command without the verve to do so.

Tim followed on my heels. Elsie remained behind, frozen with fear.

***

Tim and I barely got into his room before we were ushered out by the nurses and doctors attending to him, who threatened to call security. I pleaded with them to let me see Ernie but to no avail.

At one point, Tim physically restrained me from going back in while reminding me that being thrown out of the hospital, or worse—being arrested again—wouldn't help Ernie. I knew he was right. But being right or logical or anything other than determined to see my little boy was just not who I could be at that time. I was more scared than ever for Ernie. It took all of Tim's strength to drag my 5'6" frame out of the room. It took 30 minutes of a combination of pleading, scolding, and understanding for Tim to get me to calm down and retreat to the waiting area with him and Elsie to wait for the doctor's report.

I was a mess and it didn't go unnoticed by Elsie. She always mirrored whatever I was feeling. We had all been through medical emergencies with Ernie before, but this one brought a chill to me that I had never experienced. I couldn't explain it. A mother's intuition–connection to her child perhaps. But something deep within me knew this episode was going to have consequences for Ernie beyond a short stay in the hospital followed by a complete recovery.

When Dr. Grinsby entered the waiting area an hour after we arrived, he took Tim and me aside to explain the situation, recommending that Elsie stay in her chair alone.

I turned toward her and called for her to join us.

"We aren't keeping things from Elsie. She has been through everything with Ernie and, well...she has a right to hear." I explained to the doctor. Tim nodded in agreement.

"Mr. and Mrs. Gallagher," Dr. Grinsby said, nodding toward Elsie. "Your son is resting comfortably now. He had an episode where his organs shut down..."

"MODS." I interrupted.

"Uhh, well, yes." Dr. Grinsby confirmed. He looked startled that I knew what that was. "He stopped breathing, his heart stopped, and we suspect his kidneys have stopped functioning. We are running brain function tests now. We stabilized him and we just have to wait and see. He's on a ventilator, heart monitor, and an IV; and we will probably put him on dialysis if the tests are as we suspect."

"Can we see him?" I asked quietly while my insides turned over. This was his second bout with these same symptoms in a short period of time; I knew that made this time all the more serious.

"Well, he is in a coma right now," Dr. Grinsby said."

"A coma?" Tim asked with surprise.

"Well yes..."

"Is that why you are running brain tests?" I asked. "He's going to come out of it though right? Like he did before." I was looking for some positive sign from Dr. Grinsby's diagnosis.

"Well, Mrs. Gallagher, we never know precisely with this sort of thing. Your son is having brain synapse issues which we believe are causing his organs to malfunction. But it could also be that his organ failures, especially lack of oxygen to the brain, are causing the coma. As a result, we have to look for swelling in the brain. Of course, there is the possibility that your son hit his head when he fell during... eh...during your confrontation with the police...and he has swelling from that. So, of course, if we can figure that out and take some of the stress off of his system...many times the patient's brain heals itself without direct surgery or other intervention...and well, we just have to see. We have moved him to Intensive Care for testing and monitoring."

"Uh huh," He just had to slip in that he thought I was responsible. Not him and his illegally holding Ernie, or the security guards over-zealous response; it was the parents' fault or in this case, one particular parent. "So, you don't know what is causing Ernie's MODS or the coma?" I was trying hard to suppress that horrid feeling that had invaded me earlier, along with my resentment of Dr. Grinsby's suggestion that I was to blame. I wanted to concentrate on getting this doctor to see that Ernie needed special care...at University Hospital with Dr. Blackwell.

"Well, err no, this is very complicated..." he stammered.

"And you've never seen this before, right?" I continued to bait the doctor with unusual calm.

"Well not this exactly..."

"Right. Which is exactly why Ernie needs to be at University Hospital with Dr. Blackwell. She is the only one who understands what is happening, has seen this before with others, knows Ernie, and can offer a treatment."

"Mrs. Gallagher, your son is getting the best treatment available, the doctor said defensively, "but until we can identify what is happening to him, we can hardly begin to treat him. We have to keep him stable and work on one thing at a time..."

"That's my point. You don't know what you're doing because you have no clue what is wrong with Ernie. Dr. Blackwell does and *we* do. He has Mitochondrial Disease." I was getting really agitated; Tim could see this and rightly predicted how far I would take this.

"Dr. Grinsby," Tim stepped in calmly, "We have been through almost this same exact thing with Ernie before. No one knew why this happened to him or many other things like seizures and no energy and development issues; there was a lot of stuff all together that puzzled everyone. Only Dr. Blackwell had experienced these types of symptoms in other patients and recognized that Ernie likely has Mitochondrial Disease. Isn't it in Ernie's best interest to send him where there is an expert in the field? Doesn't that make sense?" Tim explained with his usual reliance on logic.

"Frankly, while I understand your concern, there is no recognized expert in the area of Mitochondrial Disease. It's a far-reaching diagnosis for a group of disorders—and your son could be suffering from any number of diseases or other circumstances."

I was getting to the end of my rope. Loudly, I said, "Just because you don't know anything about it doesn't mean it doesn't exist. And what else is supposedly causing Ernie's problems?"

"Well, there could be...he could have brain malfunctions that are causing issues, poisoning or malnutrition...we really need to do more testing before we go wildly into some unknown area," Dr. Grinsby said.

"Oh. My. God. Great. So, Tim and I are poisoning our son Right back to "Ruth Syndrome." I was a second away from a full-on verbal attack.

Tim stepped in front of me before I could continue my assault.

"Look doctor, it's obvious to me you're not going to relent and see what is best for Ernie," Tim said "So, we're going to have to go to court to get our son out of here and into the place we see is best for his treatment. Okay? Tomorrow, we're going to do that. Okay? But for now, we just want to see our son. So that's what we're going to do." Tim took Elsie's hand and nodded to me to come along as they headed for the elevators. The doctor said nothing.

I thought Tim would just placate the doctor, but his words and manner were far more aggressive. He had lost his patience. I briefly looked at Dr. Grinsby before following behind Tim and Elsie. From behind me, I heard Dr. Grinsby's voice, "Ten minutes—no longer. I'll let someone at the nurse's station know."

While we walked to Ernie's room, I put my arm across Elsie's shoulders and explained to her that her brother was going to look strange; probably a little pale with a lot of wires and machines hooked up to him and that she shouldn't be worried. He would be asleep and just dreaming until he's ready to wake up.

Elsie nodded that she understood. I think she was placating me while embracing her own need to push her real concerns aside, in order to face what she was about to see. She had seen Ernie recovering in the hospital before, but usually when he was on his way to recovery. This would be very different. Her brother would look more vulnerable and seriously ill than anytime she had seen him.

Just outside of Ernie's room, we stopped and Tim took hold of Elsie's shoulders, turning her toward him.

"Ernie is a real fighter and brave kid, Elsie," he said, looking into her eyes. "Nothing phases him, and he has made it through this before. He's going to be fine. He's going to wake up when he's ready. And you know what? The first thing he is going to say is, 'Mom, I'm hungry.' Tim said as he smiled down at Elsie then embraced her. When they broke, Elsie wiped a tear from her eyes and attempted a smile.

Then the three of us entered Ernie's room. Inside, a nurse read various machines and made notes. She moved to adjust Ernie's IV drips.

Elsie, being brave for her little brother's sake, stepped in front of Tim and walked right up to Ernie's bed, ignoring all the wires and machines. She sat on the edge of his bed, leaned over Ernie ever so carefully, and gave his cheek a kiss. "Yo little bro," she said in the same tone she would have used if he had been wide awake. "You gotta wake up 'cause umm, yeah, IHOP is having a two for one special and like it ends soon so...yeah, we gotta get there. I'll wait until you wake up and we can go just you and me. Okay? Okay, beast!" That was a new expression Elsie had picked up somewhere. We guessed it meant "great."

Elsie kissed Ernie's cheek again and then stood, making room for me to take her place. I sat and leaned into Ernie and kissed his forehead. I took his hand and spoke to him while I caressed his cheek.

"Honey, Mommy and Daddy are here, and Elsie. But you know that 'cause she just talked to you. We love you honey; we'll be here when you wake up. We just want you to take your time and get better so you can come home. But don't sleep too long okay? We want you home with us. Oh, and Charlotte will come help with missed school work again, so you don't have to worry about that. Okay honey? Okay. Love you to pieces." I fought back my tears as I gave his forehead one more kiss. Then, it was Tim's turn.

Tim mimicked much of my routine, kissing Ernie's forehead and holding his hand while he spoke to him. "Hey big guy. It's Daddy. Duh. Listen, I was looking at the lawn today and it needs mowing. But I decided that you are old enough to drive the mower. So, I'm going to teach you how to do that when you get home. That's pretty cool right? Oh, and I have a couple of little projects I can't do without my special helper so, I'm kind of at a loss without you. So, you know, get better; but don't sleep too long 'cause the grass will get too long. Okay buddy. I love you and we'll all be here when you decide to wake up."

Tim finished his soliloquy as he had begun it, with a kiss to Ernie's forehead.

Ernie squinted open his eyes, looked straight ahead and, with a soft, weak voice said, "Beast." Then he went right back to sleep.

The three of us were stunned. We looked wide-eyed at each other before we looked at the nurse. Tim sat back down and took hold of Ernie's hand. "Ernie. Ernie it's Daddy are you awake buddy?" He said as he tried to get Ernie's attention. There was no response. I squeezed in front of him and made my own attempt. "Ernie. Hi honey Mommy is here. You awake sweetheart?"

Again, there was no response. We all looked at the nurse again who had now come closer to the opposite side of Ernie's bed. She watched Ernie's monitors for changes for a few seconds and then turned toward us.

"Well, that was surprising," she said. She pushed the call button to summon the doctor. "I've heard of this happening, but never seen it before. Sometimes, a patient in a coma can be aware of what is happening around them but still be sort of stuck inside their self. Then they wake up for a minute and go back to sleep. I think that normally it is just a movement of a limb or a blinking eye type of reaction. I have never seen anyone wake up and speak...and have it be a response to a conversation around him."

"Ernie must have heard what you said, Elsie," I said, growing excited. "Tim—he used Elsie's word, 'beast'—which she has never used with him..." I turned to my daughter, "have you Elsie?" Elsie thought for a moment and shook her head no.

Dr. Grinsby entered the room during the last part of our conversation and made his way to Ernie's side. The nurse stepped aside to make room for him. He opened Ernie's eyes one at a time and flashed his little pen light into each pupil. He regarded the monitors for a moment before addressing the nurse.

"So, what happened here? Did he move?"

"No," I interrupted. "Elsie told Ernie that she would take him to IHOP for a "beast" breakfast. She's never used that word before. Then Tim told Ernie he could ride the lawn mower when he got out. And Ernie opened his eyes for second and said 'beast', then he went back to sleep."

Dr. Grinsby looked back to the nurse for affirmation. "Is that right?" "Yes, doctor. I didn't pay attention to all of their conversation with him, but that's pretty much what happened."

Dr. Grinsby briefly looked at Ernie then regarded Tim and me. "Well, that's odd. To have wake/sleep intervals isn't a normal course for most coma patients. But...it isn't entirely impossible or unheard of. It may be that he is experiencing something other than a coma or perhaps his coma is aligned with the other oddities of his condition. I'm going to have the neurologist come by again and take a look as soon as he is available. He might have more input on this. But...right now...everything looks unchanged and stable. His breathing is shallow but doesn't need intervention right now. Heart rate is...low and a bit weak. It's looking like we will need to get dialysis started with possible tube feeding if he doesn't wake up today or tomorrow...so, things are still very serious."

"But...Ernie waking up, even if for a second and understanding what was going on around him, doesn't that bode well for him to completely wake up soon?" Tim was hopeful.

"Well, not necessarily," the doctor said. "But it might suggest that he is at least trying to. Right now, it's more important that his brain takes over his other functions more fully; waking may happen more quickly once that happens. It's early yet, so I really don't expect him to be awake this soon."

Dr. Grinsby then left the room. Elsie, Tim, and I stood for a moment staring at each other and Ernie, in silence.

"It's time for you folks to leave now. We'll let you know if there is any change." The nurse directed us. She took one last look at Ernie's monitor then walked to the door and ushered us out.

Before we left, I moved back toward Ernie's bed and kissed his forehead again. "I love you sweetheart."

The three of us left his room and stood in the hallway. Tim looked contemplative, I was teary-eyed, and Elsie was white as a ghost. We had not heard the words of encouragement we were seeking, and it hit us hard.

"Let's go downstairs and get a cup of coffee or hot chocolate and wait." Tim suggested barely audibly. He headed for the elevators. Elsie and I followed in a zombie-like death march, each step somberly announcing the numbness we felt inside. The fearfulness that invaded me earlier, had returned full-forced and it seemed to now have infected Tim and Elsie as well.

***

We spent the remainder of Sunday either in the hospital waiting area or making trips to Ernie's room as often as we were allowed to. The staff got lax with us as the day progressed, letting us in more frequently and without a guard dog. I assumed they realized that even crazy June was not going to drag her son out of Intensive Care. We ate dinner in the cafeteria although no one had much of an appetite and took naps on the couch or sitting up in chairs. There was no change in Ernie's condition the entire day. When we left after 9:30 pm, we were all mentally exhausted. We got home and headed straight for bed.

I wanted to talk to Tim about the strategy for court tomorrow morning. I was still resolute in my belief that Ernie needed to be at University Hospital and under the care of Dr. Blackwell. But, by the time we finally crawled into bed, I had lost all my energy and so had Tim. He was lying on his back staring at the ceiling. I adopted a fetal position facing away from him, trying to hide my tears. He moved next to me. He said, "Ernie is going to be okay. He has to be. And we'll get him out of there." He gave me a kiss on the cheek and spooned me close to him. I lay there, crying softly, thinking of my wonderful little boy and praying Tim was right.

There would be no sleep.

CHAPTER SEVENTEEN

Fighting For Ernie On Two Fronts

The following morning Elsie went to school while Tim and I drove to the hospital. Elsie wanted to come with us, but we didn't want to keep her out of school; we promised to come and get her after her last class, so she could see Ernie. We reasoned with her that he might be out of the coma by then and she could spend more time with him.

We arrived at the hospital too early for visiting hours, so we decided to split our efforts—I was to remain at the hospital to see Ernie and get updates on his condition; Tim would meet Larry at the courthouse to get the status on the briefing.

I spent my time pacing the waiting area floor, again waiting for 9:am to arrive.

***

Tim

I got to the courthouse early enough to meet Larry outside and accompany him into the courtroom. I had to sit in the observer's section and wait until our case was scheduled to be heard. This would just be a preliminary hearing and the best outcome we could hope for was the judge would see that Ernie needed to be removed from Dr. Grinsby's care and transferred to University and Dr. Blackwell.

Larry had written testimony from Dr. Blackwell that he got Sunday evening. She had called him immediately after getting all of our combined messages. In her testimony, she explained the facts of Ernie's illness and mitochondrial disease in general over the phone. She then followed up with an email that contained a more detailed explanation to be used in court.

The courtroom filled up quickly and by the time the first case was called, the place was packed with criminal cases including speeding ticket challenges, DUI arrests, child support, and a variety of other somewhat minor offenses. As I listened, I learned that most of these were plea arraignments and follow-up court date assignments that could be disposed of quickly.

The judge heard a half-dozen of these before he finally called our case. I was in the back of the courtroom, smack dab in the midst of accused offenders and their families or friends. I had a hard time hearing what was being said up front between the judge, the prosecutor, and Larry.

But what I did see and hear was the prosecutor handing the bailiff a document and the judge saying something about sending the case to family court. The bailiff handed the document to Larry; his body language told me just about everything else. Larry regarded the document, closed his briefcase, and headed out of the courtroom.

Larry met me in the hallway just outside the courtroom and ushered me down the corridor a bit where we could speak privately.

"I'm afraid that this isn't going to be a simple solution, Tim." Larry began while he continued to read the document he had been handed. "Apparently, someone called CPS to look into Ernie and Elsie and their alleged mistreatment. Based on Ernie being the focus of most of this–and what I was able to skim–it was likely Ruth's reporting that did this. She must have begun this a while ago because CPS has already issued a report."

"Oh for Christ's sake Larry. Ruth! June was right about her." Tim said with disgust.

"Yeah, well, it looks as though they compiled all Ernie's records of hospital visits and...ugh, yeah, some interviews with Dr. Grinsby, a couple of neighbors–unnamed–and the principal and a few teachers...and it seems like they looked into Elsie as well."

"Oh crap, Larry," I couldn't believe what I heard. "Should I get Elsie out of school? Are they going to try and take her?"

"No, no you can't do that anyway, Tim. No, they didn't find any cause for removing Elsie from the home..." Larry was still looking over the document. "They recommend family interviews with CPS... yeah okay and the crux of this is, 'based on our findings and on the recommendations of the attending physician, Dr. Grinsby of Brinker Hospital, we have determined it is in the child's best interest that he remain in the temporary custody of Brinker Hospital and staff until such time as CPS, with the cooperation of the family and in consideration of Family Court proceedings, if initiated, can determine the right course of action to secure the child's welfare. We further recommend that Brinker Hospital staff be the sole determiners of when the child may be released to CPS or if determined by CPS or court proceedings, to the custody of the child's parents or other guardian."

"You have got to be f–ing kidding!" I said loud enough to draw the attention of several people in the corridor. "Jesus, Larry. This basically says that Dr. Grinsby has complete control of our son, and then CPS takes control, and we are last on the list."

"Sorry, Tim but yeah it's..."

"And none of these imbeciles has any clue what is really going on with Ernie!" It was hard to keep my voice down.

"I know, Tim. It looks bad; but what this means is that we can go to Family Court and file an emergency appeal, make our case to them, and get this fixed. You have to try and stay calm until then."

"Calm? Oh Larry, this *is* calm. I have to go tell June now. You want to see out of control? You come with me and explain this to her." Tim stated with an exacerbated voice.

"I'm sorry Tim. Do you want me to explain it to June?" Larry sheepishly asked.

I felt a bit guilty for taking my wrath out on the one person who was doing everything he could to help.

"Oh Christ, Larry." I finally said. "No. No, I'll tell her. You go do whatever it is you have to do to get Ernie back to us. I didn't mean to take it out on you...it's just...it's just my kid is in a coma and they can't help him and now we have to go to court to prove we aren't monsters and that Ernie has a real disease that only *one* person around here can treat. It's a living nightmare, Larry."

"Understood, Tim—and I don't take any offense." Larry offered as he rested his left hand on my right shoulder. "I'm in this with you and June...and Ernie...and I'm going to do everything I can to get your son back to you. You just have to trust me."

"Yeah. Yeah I know. And I do trust you, Larry, and so does June. We just don't trust Ruth, Dr. Grinsby, and this whole damn system. I appreciate your help, Larry—I better get to the hospital. And I need to spend a few hours in the office today before I lose all my clients."

We shook hands before he headed one way down the corridor, and I went the other.

***

While Tim was at the courthouse dealing with that event, I was anxiously awaiting his phone call and the start of visiting hours.

As much as I wanted to be with Ernie, I decided that it was best to wait for Tim to join me. Otherwise, because of the strict rules that were imposed on us, Tim would miss visiting hour and would have to wait until the afternoon opening. When I hadn't heard from him by 10 am, I called him. It went to voice mail. When he hadn't called back by 10:30, I tried again. Voice mail again.

I decided I had waited long enough and headed for Ruth's desk to arrange for my escort to Ernie's room. Just as I took a step, my phone rang. It was Tim.

I stopped and turned my back to Ruth. "Where are you?" I asked.

"Ughh, just leaving the courthouse now. There were a lot of people and cases besides ours that I had to wait through."

"So, what happened? Did they say we can move Ernie?" I asked anxiously.

"Well, uh, no. It wasn't really a court case hearing; it was all pre-liminary stuff. We have to go to family court to sort things out." Tim said. I could hear the weariness in his voice.

"So, you mean nothing happened? They still can keep us from Ernie and from making decisions for him? What do you mean family court? When? Today?" I asked while growing more agitated.

"It's...it's complicated, June. I'm getting into the car now and heading your way. I'll explain when I see you." Tim said trying to dodge having the conversation, he knew would set me off further, just then.

"Tim, what aren't you telling me?"

"Twenty minutes. I'll be there in 20 minutes. Did you see Ernie?" Tim changed the subject.

"No. I was waiting for you and was just about to go up when you called. Tim..."

"Okay. Good. Wait for me. We'll go up together."

"Tim...Tim..."

He hung up. Now I was furious at him for not telling me the whole story–AND at Larry for not getting anything done.

I walked back into the waiting area and plopped myself into one of plastic chairs to pout like a disgruntled teenager who missed a rendezvous with her boyfriend because her mother dragged her to the grocery store.

By now it was 10:45 a.m. and I had still not seen Ernie, nor gotten an update on his condition. He was up there all alone and would need me there when he woke up. And truthfully, *I* needed to be there. I needed to be his reassurance that he was okay and with his Mommy looking over him.

While I thought about Ernie in that Intensive Care room, his pale face, the tubes and machines monitoring him and keeping him alive, that horrible feeling of foreboding returned. I had managed to keep the feeling at bay all morning until now. But something triggered its return. Maybe, it was the phone call from Tim or just having too much time with nothing else to occupy my brain that caused it. Whatever the reason, there it was.

I looked around the waiting area for someone to express my angst to. I hoped to see a friendly face, maybe a priest or Rabbi; anyone who might be open to listening to the problems of others. I needed to release my frustration and fear. But, as I looked around, I saw only faces etched with their own worry and I realized that they were all living with their own stories of dread and weren't likely looking to embrace mine. We were all short stories, with our own characters and plots, sharing space in an anthology of distress. I would have to attempt to employ my least favorable attribute...patience.

I watched my cell phone clock pass every minute of my agitated calm. After 17 minutes crept by, Tim arrived. I nearly leapt out of my chair and hastily ran to him.

"Finally!" I exhaled as I reached Tim. "Come on, let's go see Ernie," I ordered as I raced toward Ruth.

Tim followed in silence, stumbling a little trying to keep up with me. When we reached Ruth, we didn't have to say a word. She knew why we were at her station and immediately said, "I'll call up and have a nurse meet you at the elevator."

Ruth seemed surprisingly emotionless and I couldn't read her face. Tim, who would normally smile at Ruth no matter how he felt toward her, was stoic too. I wondered if his lack of facial condescend was related to the conversation he wouldn't have on the phone with me and the courtroom proceedings. But, I had neither the time nor desire right then to ask. My malaise over what had transpired at the courthouse had been replaced, at least temporarily, by my need to see Ernie. Tim and I rushed to the elevators.

We rode the elevator without speaking. When the doors parted, the promised nurse was waiting to take us to Ernie's room.

"How is he?" I asked, keeping pace with her.

"I don't have any news that I can give you," she said apologetically.

"Dr. Grinsby will speak to you soon."

She guided us to Ernie's room, stood for a moment at the doorway, and then left. Ernie looked much the same as he had the night before, with the exception of an added dialysis machine to the consortium of apparatus that was managing his life. That wasn't a positive change.

Tim and I, each in our turn, repeated our tradition of kissing Ernie's forehead then sitting on the edge of his bed and speaking to him. We expressed our love, told short stories of all the special things we were going to do together when he got out, that had now grown to include a promised trip to Disneyworld, and encouraged him to wake up.

The only response was the humming and swirling sounds of machines while they filtered Ernie's blood and filled his lungs with air. With each pump of the ventilator, the room was refreshed with a new wave of melancholy that eventually sucked the enthusiasm from our story-telling and left us to bow in silence to its majesty.

About 15 minutes later, Dr. Grinsby entered Ernie's room briefly interrupting the solemnness.

"Mr. and Mrs. Gallagher, how are you today?" He spoke as if he were greeting acquaintances in the lunch room.

"We're...we're okay." Tim offered at first. "Actually doctor, we're not good at all." He approached Dr. Grinsby. "We don't see any improvement in Ernie from yesterday, and now he's on a kidney machine *and* still on the ventilator. What's going on with our son?" Tim was nearly pleading with his questions.

"Mr. Gallagher. Your son's condition is pretty much the same as yesterday. We did say that we were concerned that his kidneys were shutting down and it turns out we were right; we've taken necessary steps to counter that with the dialysis machine. He remains in a coma but that is to be expected. We continue to monitor his situation and make assessments as we go."

I stood from my spot on the edge of Ernie's bed to address Dr. Grinsby.

"Dr. Grinsby, what new assessments are you talking about? Ernie is worse than yesterday. All you have done is hook him up to machines and wait and watch. You still have no clue why he needs the machines or what is causing his problems. Do You?"

"Well we don't have an exact answer..."

"Great!" I said sarcastically. "So, have you reached out to Dr. Blackwell for her input?"

"Mrs. Gallagher, as I explained before, Ernie is receiving expert care here and has the best doctors and medicine that can be provided."

"And as I explained before, you have no clue what is wrong with him. You admit as much, even now. And yet, you absolutely refuse to reach out to an expert who *does* know, and to get my son the help he needs. What possible sense does that make?"

"Mrs. Gallagher, we don't believe it is in your son's best interest to chase after conceptual diseases and controversial therapies. We rely on facts and proven medical modalities."

"Yeah, well here's a fact for you," I'd run out of patience. "You are clueless. You have no diagnosis and therefore you have no course of treatment. You just have more machines. The only thing you're proving is that your 'modalities' are inadequate!"

My temperate reactions were growing in volume and intensity; Tim could see where this was leading. I was headed for a mess of angry, fearful emotions. Tim was hardly feeling better about Ernie's situation, but removed himself from his own emotions enough to de-escalate the situation.

"June, let's say goodbye to Ernie and go back downstairs. I just got a text from Larry." As he said that he stepped in front of me, effectively blocking my view of Dr. Grinsby. I looked at Tim and then to Ernie but didn't move. Dr. Grinsby took this moment of silence to make his exit.

"June, I don't like this, and I certainly don't like that doctor much any more than you do. But right now, we have to be as calm as we can and hope and trust that Larry can fix this."

"I know. I know Tim. I get it. I sound like a shrew most of the time. But when it comes to Ernie or Elsie, I don't care how people perceive me or about being liked or even being understood. I only see my baby hurting and people getting in the way of helping him and nothing else matters but getting Ernie what he needs. Sometimes I don't think you get that." Tears were starting to form now as I tried to explain to Tim.

Tim hugged me close then gently took my face in his hands.

"Oh June. You're wrong. I do get it. I even admire it in a way. Your passion. Your unrelenting fight for your child. Our child. It's just... well...it's just that one of us has to keep things in perspective and in some sort of control. Ya know? And, well, that's my role. I'm good cop and you're, umm...well you're the *other* cop." He hugged me again.

He couldn't see my half-smile at his humor. Tim was offering understanding while also attempting to lighten my mood. After a moment, we broke our embrace to gaze at Ernie. He was lying there, seemingly lifeless, yet living in perpetual sleep.

I sat on his bed, leaned over, and kissed his forehead then gently took hold of his hand. "I love you so much my beautiful Ernie." I cried softly. The feeling of dread returned. Tim moved behind me and held my shoulders. I placed my free hand on top of his right hand.

"What are we going to do, Tim? Will we ever get our son back?" I asked, staring hopelessly at my son.

"We're going to do whatever it takes, June. We're going to do whatever it takes." Tim gave my hand a light squeeze then kissed my cheek. "Come on. Let's go downstairs and talk." Tim helped me up. He took my spot next to Ernie's bed, leaned over, and kissed Ernie's forehead. "I love you buddy. I'm going to fix this."

Tim took my hand. We left his room and headed downstairs to the waiting area. We still had the courthouse events to discuss.

***

When we got downstairs, Tim explained what had happened at the courthouse, including the report from CPS that officially took Ernie from us–as well as the fight that was about to ensue with Larry leading the way. I calmly listened to his explanation and retelling of events while becoming apoplectic internally. My stomach convulsed with pain, my face reddened with anger, and my body started to shake with constrained rage while I tried to keep things in Tim's "perspective."

"When–Are–We–Getting–Ernie–Back?" Was all I managed to stutter in response to Tim before I collapsed on the floor. Tim cried out, "Shit!" before he rushed to my side and held my head while repeatedly calling my name. People gathered around us, and Ruth rushed over to see what had happened before running back to her station to call for help.

A doctor ran out of the emergency exam area and was quickly by my side, taking my pulse while asking Tim what had happened. The doctor was shining his pocket flashlight in my eye when I came back to awareness.

"June! June, are you okay, babe?" Tim asked with concern while holding my hand.

"What happened?" I asked in a whispery voice.

"Ma'am did you hit your head when you fell?" The doctor asked while he held my head up and felt the back of my skull for any signs of a lump or bleeding.

I was still too woozy to respond.

"No," Tim said. "No. She just sort of collapsed, straight down to the floor and then more to the side, and then rolled onto her back. We were talking, and she just...I think fainted."

The doctor helped me sit up. "How do you feel?" The doctor asked.

"Okay. I just, all of a sudden I just blacked out." June explained, still in a subdued voice.

"And are you dizzy now, or do you have any pain anywhere?"

"No," I answered, squinting my eyes against the dots in my vision from his penlight. "I–I feel okay. Tim, help me up."

Tim and the doctor helped me to my feet. I stood there a little wobbly but otherwise intact. The small crowd dispersed.

"Have you had fainting spells like this in the past?" The doctor was trying to make certain this was a simple case of fainting.

"Huh? Oh. No. No, I…this never happened before…except when I was a lot younger once I think."

"Are you under a lot of stress right now?"

I looked at the doctor for a long while before answering. I didn't know how to answer that question. I knew the answer–it was yes, I am under a ton of stress! But what I didn't know was whether I should give the long version, the are-you-kidding-me facts, or just let it go. I figured he was just looking for an affirmative or negative response and not trying to be my instant therapist, so I simply answered, "Yes."

"Well. That can do it. A build-up of stress which can also mean not eating or sleeping well–can have consequences. Fainting would not be unheard of. Of course, that is just one aspect. You don't appear to have any injuries from your fall, but I recommend you see your doctor and get a physical exam just to be safe."

"Thanks, doctor. "I'll make sure that happens."

"Okay folks. Have a good day." The doctor said and then he went back to the emergency area.

Tim guided me to a nearby chair to sit while I recovered a bit more before we would leave.

"Are you okay?" Tim asked, hovering over me before he sat down.

"Yeah. Yeah I'm fine, Tim. I think it was just what the doctor said–no sleep, not eating well and all the stress. It just caught up with me."

"Yeah," Tim said and sat down, not taking his eyes off of me. "Well. Truth is, you looked like you were about to blow a gasket when I told you about the courthouse. I think your blood pressure just got out of control or something. You are definitely going to the doctor this week and have that check-up."

"Ughh okay. Tim. But I just fainted."

"I'm serious!" he said, leaning forward, elbows placed on his knees. "You were red-faced and shaking before you went down. And you know it. This wasn't you just getting light-headed from getting up too fast. I can't have you ending up sick and in the hospital along with everything else. Ernie needs you healthy, and Elsie needs you, and I need you. So, no fooling around with this."

Tim was not arguing with me. He was telling me in no uncertain terms what I had to do. And he was right. Underneath my pretense, I was shaken by what I felt and what had happened.

"Okay. I'll make an appointment with my doctor today for this week."

"I mean it."

"I know, Tim. I promise I'll make the appointment."

"Okay. Good." Tim declared. He drew me in and gave me a hug. "And maybe look into some yoga classes or meditation thing...couldn't hurt." He added wryly before we broke our embrace.

I should have been mad at him for that addition, but I knew he was genuinely upset by what had happened and that this was his way of meditating things back to calm.

"Don't you have to go to work or something?" I asked.

"Oh crap, yeah. I do actually. Just for a few hours and then I'll come back. You'll have to drop me off though and I'll hitch a ride back from someone at the office. I need to get back to Larry too. See what's going on. What are you going to do?"

"I'll drop you off, then maybe get something to eat and come back here to wait. I'll see if Ernie wakes up and maybe I can just sneak in another visit with him. Then I'll go get Elsie from school and bring her back here with me."

"Yeah. Okay. Are you sure you're okay to drive?"

"Yep. I feel fine, really. Let's go so I can get back." I said and stood.

Tim stood and we headed for the door. We didn't think to leave the building via Tim's secret side door. We assumed the reporters had abandoned us. We were certain our story was already old news, so we headed straight out the front entrance of the hospital.

We were wrong.

The courthouse appearance produced a record of the proceedings that morning which kindled new interest in "our story." The moment we went through the doors, a handful of reporters with camera crews cozied up to us and began hurling questions.

"June, is it true that Child Services has taken custody of your children?"

"Is there any truth to the rumor your son was poisoned?"

"Mr. Gallagher, is your son's coma the result of abuse or neglect?"

We were blinded by the lights and eager to escape the unwanted attention. But that last question drew me back toward the light and to the rage from which I had just recovered. Tim, sensing what was building in me once again, took me by the arm and pulled me forward, away from the inquisition.

But I was not going to let this challenge go unanswered. I freed my arm from Tim's grip to confront the reporter. Tim called after me. I knew he was concerned that I would react too harshly and suffer another spell. I took a deep breath, relaxed my muscles as best I could, and then, facing every camera aimed in my direction, spoke.

"Our child has a very rare disease which this hospital does not recognize or have any experience with treating. They refuse to send him to his specialist at University Hospital where he can get proper care. Our son Ernie is the victim of a doctor's arrogance, unwarranted interference from a would-be social worker, and a system that favors making parents criminals over understanding a child's needs."

"Mrs. Gallagher," called one woman reporter, shoving a microphone closer to my face, "an anonymous source has said there is a CPS report that references your son's many hospital visits, doctor visits, and related emergencies. Are you saying this report is false?"

I took another deep breath before I answered. Tim was now at my side and had hold of my arm again.

"We have never seen any such report, and I will repeat what I just said. Our son has a rare disease that this hospital staff is incapable of treating. Our lawyer will soon be getting our son out of here and to University where he can be treated by his own specialist."

"That's it." Tim added in a stern voice. He led me away by the arm and this time I didn't resist. I walked along beside him to our car. Thankfully, the reporters kept their distance, maybe they got what they wanted. We buckled ourselves in, Tim turned on the car and drove off calmly.

"Freaking reporters," he said as we cleared the hospital parking lot. "I don't think we should have talked to them June. Larry said..."

"You didn't talk to them, Tim. I did. And Larry isn't here. There was no way in hell I was going to let those questions of abuse go unchallenged and then have them write some made-up follow-up story or show us ducking away, tails between our legs, as if their suggestive questioning had merit."

"Yeah. Yeah, I guess not. Tell you the truth...you were really strong but calm with your answers. I was kinda impressed."

"Meaning relieved?"

"Well, yeah, that too. Seriously though, you just basically challenged the hospital on record. So they probably aren't going to be warming to us visiting and might start an attack of their own."

"They challenged us first by taking Ernie against our will and then giving false information for a CPS report. And, frankly Tim, I don't give a rat's...butthole...what they think. And what more can they do?

They have our son, they control our visitation rights, and the CPS supports their control. What are we supposed to do?"

"Yeah, I know. We really have to trust Larry can challenge the CPS report and show the court what is really going on." Tim said and then we paused our conversation for a bit before Tim continued. "One odd thing though, I am fairly certain that the CPS report is completely confidential. I wonder who leaked it to the press?"

"Really? Well my guess is some court worker or…or maybe Ruth. I wouldn't put it past her."

"Ehhh, well I hate to say it, but yeah, she would be on the top of my list too. Or someone else at the hospital."

The rest of the ride to Tim's office went by mostly in silence. We occasionally speculated about what Larry's next steps might be or tried to guess who might have leaked the report. I dropped Tim off at his office and then headed for a nearby sandwich shop. My appetite was not screaming for food, but I was still concerned that maybe my fainting spell had something to do with not eating well, so I gave in to that logic and bought a tuna fish sandwich, Diet Coke, and barbecue chips. Not exactly the definition of "eating well" but it was food, which meant energy, which in turn meant maybe not being so run down and prone to fainting.

When I returned to the hospital, the news crews were just packing up, preparing to go to their next assignment or perhaps back to their stations. I wondered why they were delayed in leaving after our interlude, but I felt relieved that I could enter the hospital without being hassled, so I quickly shrugged it off.

When Ruth saw me enter the hospital, she immediately picked up her desk phone, turned to face away from me and began a conversation. I got to her desk just as she was hanging up—it was a very brief call, but I was fairly certain I was the subject of the exchange.

I inhaled deeply, put on my best face and then approached Ruth's desk. I wanted to see Ernie again, but didn't want this to count as one of my three visits per day.

"Hi, Ruth," I said nonchalantly. "Can I sneak up to see Ernie?" Her hesitation and confused expression told me I should add something more to my approach. "Actually, I need to talk to Dr. Grinsby about Ernie's condition."

Ruth took a moment before answering.

"Yes, okay," she finally said. "I'll call up to the nurses' station to let them know you're coming."

"Okay. Thank you."

I stared at her for a few seconds then made my way to the elevators. Something about her demeanor told me that something was not right. She acquiesced to my request, which was odd in itself, but she did so with an undertone of uncertainty–I felt she wanted to say "no" but couldn't.

By the time I had reached Ernie's floor and the elevator doors opened, I dismissed the odd feeling as just my bias toward Ruth. I was getting to see Ernie and that's all that mattered.

A nurse didn't meet me at the elevator bank, which I thought was odd, so I let myself into Ernie's room. All of the life-giving machines were still humming and swooshing while Ernie continued his long sleep. I kissed my little boy's forehead then set down my purse and sat on the edge of his bed, held his hand, and talked to him.

"Hi, honey. It's Mommy again. How's my big boy? Daddy had to go to work, but Elsie is going to come by a little later and Daddy will be back soon, too. We all miss you and love you. All your animals are missing you too–especially the kangaroo–and your nice comfy bed. Your friends at school miss you. Oh, and Charlotte called to make certain we said "hello" from her. She misses her favorite student."

I brought Ernie's hand close to my face and rubbed it against my cheek, planting little kisses on his hand in between caresses. His hand was so cold.

"Please Ernie. Please come back to us. I need my little boy so much...I love you to pieces. Please wake up, honey." I wept into his cold hand briefly warming the skin with my tears. I knew I should be brave for my little love and say only good things and not cry. But I was lost. Hopelessly lost. Powerless to help him or to even get him somewhere that offered hope. I thought my love would be enough to wake him, to bring him back, but it wasn't. Even our special bond couldn't reach him and that realization had made me sink into depression and fear.

I struggled to swallow my tears and stop the tremors that had taken command of my midsection. It took me several minutes before I could win the fight for control over my body and regain some semblance of sway over my emotional outburst. The river of emotions that flowed from my eyes dwindled to a trickle.

A moment later, Dr. Grinsby entered the room and cleared his throat loudly. I was grateful for his announcement, clearly performed for my benefit, because it gave me a few seconds to gather my senses. I wiped my tears on the back of my hand, stood, and smoothed the material that had gathered my slacks into folds. I turned to face Dr. Grinsby.

"Just checking in on your son," he said. There was something strange in the way he looked at me. "Just seeing if there are any changes or significant events to be aware of."

I said nothing.

"You know, Mrs. Gallagher, your appearance in front of the reporters this morning is not going to help your cause." Grinsby added in an awkward change of subjects. "The hospital will not react well to being, well, attacked and misrepresented, and may even revoke your visitation privileges. We wouldn't want you to be kept from seeing your son, now would we?"

I looked at Grinsby in silence for a short while longer. An unexpected calm washed over me, substituting the ire that wanted to rule my emotions.

"You know, Dr. Grinsby," I calmly said, "I have no control over what you or this hospital does. I don't know your motivation or your logic or whatever is driving this desire you have to force your ignorance into my child's care. I know *my* motivation—and my husband's—and it is a very singular one: to get our child the best care he can have that will bring him back to us. And I know that he will never get that here. So, whatever we have to do, we will do. Whatever the hospital has to do in their own interests, I am certain they will continue to do. We have no intention of backing down, and we will use whatever resource it takes to help my son. *Whatever* resource it takes."

When I finished, I picked up my purse that I had placed on the floor near Ernie's bed and walked determinedly past Grinsby who was struck with silence. When I got to the door, I turned back to take a last look at my sleeping son and then looked toward Grinsby.

"Ernie." I said to a dumbfounded Grinsby. "My son's name is Ernie. You've only ever called him my son. I just thought you should know who you are treating."

***

It was just after 1 pm when I left the hospital. The reporters were all gone. I drove to Elsie's school and found her sitting on the curb outside the entrance. She wasn't wearing the heavier fall jacket she had on when she left home. She wore a deep blue, long-sleeve cotton blouse and jeans and sneakers. She didn't have her school books or her backpack either. Elsie seemed down when she got in the car with me.

"Hi honey. Everything okay? Where's your jacket and backpack?" I asked as we drove away.

"I'm sorry Mom..." Was all she got out before she began to cry.

I drove just a bit more, turned into the first side street I came across, and pulled over.

"Elsie. Honey what's wrong." I asked while stroking her hair. "They made me talk to them."

"Who honey? Who made you talk to them?"

"The lady from the child's place and the principal. They said they could take me away from you if I didn't talk now." Elsie tried to explain while trying to catch her breath through the tears she choked off.

I undid my seatbelt and slid over closer to Elsie. I took her face in my hands and kissed her forehead.

"Oh Elsie. It's okay, just breathe, honey. It's okay. You didn't do anything wrong." I assured her as I held back the anger that wanted release. I hugged her into me the best I could, given the confines dictated by her seatbelt. "What did they ask you?"

"They wanted to know about my migraines and missing school, and any arguments at home and about Ernie, and was I happy, and I don't know...a bunch of stupid stuff!" She was agitated, living it again for me and pulled away from me.

"You said I didn't have to talk to them, but they said I did or I would have to later and they could take me...and stuff like that."

"Honey. Honey. They were wrong. They had no right to make you say anything and they knew it. It's *their* fault not yours. You didn't do anything wrong. It's okay." I held her face in my hands again as I spoke. "Elsie, did they say anything else before you left?"

"No. They made notes on some paper, the lady from the child place did. Then she said she wanted me to wait while they called someone. But I just got up and walked out and then ran out here to wait for you." I used my thumbs to wipe the wetness from the corners of her eyes then took hold of her hands.

"Okay, good. Don't worry about it, honey. Your father and I will deal with them, and Larry our attorney. Nothing's going to happen. So just forget about them. So, I guess that your jacket and backpack are still at school?"

"Yeah. I didn't have time to go to my locker. I just wanted to get out of there." Elsie said as she sniffled and used her sleeve to wipe a few more tears from her eyes and face.

"Yeah I know, no biggie." I made a decision. I steered the car away from the curb and did a U-turn. "I'm going to go get your backpack and jacket. Is your phone in your backpack?"

"No! No, Mom! You can't! They might attack you!"

"Oh my God, Elsie. Now you're being a little dramatic. I'm not going to say anything to anyone. I going to go to your locker, get your stuff and leave."

"Okay, but Mom, what if they try to make you talk to them, or what if they come out to the car to get me?"

"I know how to handle them, Elsie. I'll just ignore them. And you lock the car doors and just ignore anyone who comes to the car. I'll be five minutes tops. What's your locker number and combination?"

Elsie gave me her locker and combination which I entered into my cell phone notes app before exiting the car. I had parked at the farthest end of the school driveway, away from any potential onlookers. When I entered the school, the corridors were empty; the kids and teachers must have been in classes. I quickly found Elsie's locker, entered her combination into the lock and retrieved her backpack and jacket. No one saw me and I saw no one. I was almost disappointed. I would have loved to have given the principal and whoever that other woman was a very large piece of my mind.

Instead, I was literally back with Elsie in the promised five minutes. "Here ya go," I said while I got into the car and handed Elsie her things. She immediately tossed everything onto the back seat. "Did you get any lunch, honey?"

"No."

"Okay, well, let's go get you some lunch and then we'll head to the hospital and see Ernie or...maybe wait to see if your dad can get there early and we can all go up together. Do you have homework to do?"

"Can we go for sushi? Just a little homework."

"Umm, yeah, okay. I guess we have time. Then you can do your homework at the hospital while we wait."

***

After lunch, Elsie and I returned to the hospital. Elsie took a seat while I approached Ruth to ask if there was any change in Ernie's condition. We didn't exchange any forced pleasantries. I asked for an update on Ernie and she called up to the nurse's station on his floor. They said Ernie's condition had not changed but that Dr. Grinsby would be around later to check on him again. We decided to wait and see if Tim could join us soon before we used up one of our visitation coupons.

After my conversation with Dr. Grinsby, I was afraid hospital officials might be tightening their reins on us, and I didn't want to draw attention to myself by pushing for an extra visitation.

We went to the cafeteria so Elsie would have a reasonable work area with a table and chair. I nursed a very old cup of coffee and read a dated issue of *Time* magazine that I had taken from the waiting area. At 4 pm, Tim texted me to say he had hitched a ride and was on his way to the hospital. He also told me to meet him in the cafeteria (fortuitous), and not to try and see Ernie without him. I texted "okay". I assumed he wanted me to wait because he didn't want to be left out of the visit or risk not being let up later on.

I was wrong.

Thirty minutes after Tim's phone call, he joined Elsie and me at our table. He looked harried; his hair was tousled, his tie hung loose around his neck and showed that two top buttons of his shirt were unfastened. His rumpled shirt was half out on one side.

"Hey," Tim said as he kissed my cheek. "Hi, Elsie." Elsie barely looked up from her cell phone when he kissed her on her head. "Did you see Ernie?" He asked as he pulled a plastic chair closer to me.

"No, we didn't see Ernie. You said not to." I answered as Tim finished his chair move. "What happened to you?" I looked him up and down. Even seated he looked a mess.

"Huh?" Tim asked as his eyes took the same tour of his body mine had just completed. "Oh. I went to the gym before I left, to get in 30 minutes of cardio, and I had to rush out of there or I would have missed my ride."

"So, what's the news from Larry?"

Tim looked at Elsie who put down her phone ready to engage with us. "Well, the noontime news reports ran your, um interview from this morning. He didn't like it."

"Why? He didn't like me telling the truth?"

"Wait," Elsie interrupted. "Mom, you were on TV again?" Elsie was really interested now.

"It was nothing Elsie," I said. "The reporters were waiting for your dad and me outside the hospital when we left."

"And you didn't tell me at lunch?" Elsie was incredulous. "Wow, Mom, that would have been a good thing to know."

"Ughh, I mostly forgot about it. And you had your own things you were going through."

"Wait, what thing was Elsie going through?" Tim was now left out of the loop.

"They tried to intimidate her at school to get her to say things about home life," I said, turning my direction to him. "But nothing happened."

"At school? Who asked what?" Tim pushed further.

"The principal and some woman from CPS I think,"

"Oh yeah, yeah, yeah. Okay. That's what Larry said would happen. He knew it. That's why he didn't like the TV thing. He told us–you–not to talk to the press. Now we're in it." Tim locked his fingers behind his head as he scolded me with an "I told you so" tone.

"Woah, Tim, slow down," I said. "What are you talking about?"

Tim continued his scolding. "Larry said that the hospital would react badly to your blaming them for Ernie's condition, and for not getting the right treatment and for taking him away from us. And not just the hospital, the whole system will 'circle the wagons,' as he put it, and make us the Enemy with a capital E. Now they probably won't let us visit Ernie."

"What are you talking about?" I asked, irritation rising. "Are you saying that my interview got CPS to go after Elsie? And what do you mean we can't see Ernie? I saw him around noon and no one said anything to me...except Dr. Grinsby."

"Yeah, that's what I'm saying," Tim said, looking at me. "What did Dr. Grinsby say?"

"Just that he didn't think that saying things about him and the hospital would go over well." I admitted reluctantly.

"Well guess what? He was right. The minute I walked into the hospital, old Ruth was standing guard at her desk and picked up the phone in a hurry when she saw me walk past her and toward the elevator. She called after me, but I just ignored her. I bet she was alerting security. And I bet if we go up there right now, they will tell us we can't see Ernie."

"Oh my God," my heart was in my throat and my stomach clenched. "Tim, that's not right. They can't do that. We didn't *do* anything."

"Yeah they can," he said, giving his head two exaggerated nods. "We called them out in public and they are the ones in control."

I stood up and headed toward the elevators.

"Mom! Where you going?" Elsie asked as she rose and started after me.

"Geezus, June! Where are you going?" Tim echoed as he followed Elsie.

"We're going to see Ernie," I tossed over my shoulder before reaching the elevators. Tim and Elsie caught up with me before the elevator arrived. "We're going straight up to his room. No stopping in to check with Ruth."

"Do you think that is wise, June?" Tim got out just as the elevator door opened and I stepped in, followed closely by Elsie.

"I don't care if it is wise, Tim. I want to see Ernie and they either let me or we find out they won't. You coming?" I stuck my arm out to stop the doors from closing.

"Yeah, yeah okay." Tim reluctantly agreed and jumped into the elevator narrowly escaping the closing door as I let my arm drop. Elsie giggled. "But I'll do the talking. Don't say *anything*, and if they refuse to let us in, you keep quiet and...and we'll go downstairs, and I will call Larry. No scenes or...or..."

"Getting arrested?" Elsie finished Tim's sentence which drew a sharp look of reproach from me. "I'm just sayin' Mom, geez don't get all mad at me."

The elevator reached the second floor and the door opened before I could respond to Tim or Elsie. We made our way to Ernie's room. Sure enough, we were greeted by a security guard standing in the doorway. We stopped in front of him.

"I'm sorry ma'am, sir. But your visitation rights have been revoked by the hospital and I'm to escort you out of the hospital." The security guard said standing taller to emphasize the intent behind is words.

"What do you mean our..."

"June!" Tim snapped before I could finish my sentence. Then he spoke to the guard.

"Why are our visitations rights being taken away? Tim asked reasonably as if he didn't know. "And why do we have to leave the hospital? That's our son in there and we have a right to visit him."

Before the guard could respond, Ruth squeezed out from behind him and stood in the corridor next to Tim.

"The hospital was named as the temporary guardian of your son and we have determined it is in your son's best interest if you did not have access to him at this time." Ruth said firmly, with little emotion and without making direct eye contact with Tim.

"What the *hell* do you mean it is in Ernie's best interest if we don't see him? We're his damn parents you *idiot!*" I practically screamed in her face.

Tim grabbed my arm and forcibly pulled me back toward the elevator. "June, that's it." he said between clenched teeth, jabbing his finger on the DOWN button. "Get in the elevator. I mean it."

I was red-faced. I could feel the same rage building in me that led to my earlier collapse. I looked at Tim. He loomed over me with his six-foot frame and glaring eyes. "I'm not looking for a debate," he said.

I turned and got into the elevator which had arrived. "Elsie, you too." Tim directed to Elsie as he held open the elevator door. Elsie stepped forward but turned toward Ruth.

"Is Ernie okay? She asked, her eyes a bit watery, as she tried to peak a look past the security guard and into Ernie's room.

"Yes. Yes, he is about the same." Was all Ruth offered still offended by my outburst but perhaps softened a bit by Elsie's concern.

Elsie joined us in the elevator, as did the guard. We made our way to the first floor and were escorted out of the hospital, without speaking another word.

***

The drive home was silent; we were each in our own funk. Elsie, who would normally have her face stuck in her phone, spent the trip with her cheek pressed against the window, staring out. Tim had opted to drive my car. He busied himself in an exaggerated navigation of the road. I sat motionless with my arms across my chest, peering straight ahead thinking.

I was angry at the hospital officials, at Dr. Grinsby, at Ruth–especially Ruth–and frightened for Ernie and all of us. He was about to enter a third day of being in a coma. He had never been this sick for so long. I wondered if it really would make any difference if he were at University Hospital with Dr. Blackwell; maybe there was nothing anyone could do. Maybe everything was in God's hands and I just needed someone to hold accountable. I didn't have any answers. I just had anger and fear to hang on to–and hang on I did.

When we finally reached home, we each sought out our own comfort place, that one niche where we could refuel and pretend everything would get better.

Elsie went to her room to close off the world and enter her realm of music. Tim grabbed a scotch and plopped himself on the couch, He picked up the remote and channel surfed until he found a sports event to watch—golf.

I scrunched into my corner of the couch, comforter wrapped around my legs and waist, grabbed my crossword off the coffee table and stared at the black scratches, pretending I could discern a word or phrase.

Tim and I still had not said one word to each other. While we were active with visiting Ernie or waiting to see him, going to court, being at the hospital near Ernie, we had purpose. We were doing something to move forward to help Ernie. Or, at least we had the pretense that what we were doing mattered.

But sitting here on the couch now, we had nothing. We had lost our last connection to Ernie—our visitation rights. We had been labeled "bad parents" by hospital and CPS officials, and likely by now, the public. And I couldn't help but believe it was all because of *my* failings.

If only I had gotten Ernie out of the hospital faster. If only I could have held my tongue in front of the reporters. If only I could be the hero for my son that others said I had been for a stranger. Why did I not have the strength to command my own passions when my Ernie needed me to? Would it be so bad to just be wrong for his sake?

I turned away from Tim and my crossword and looked toward the opposite living room wall. I was searching, longing for the numbness that had driven me to slump into my corner moments ago, bereft of thought. But it was gone. My reflections on my shortcomings, that had led to Ernie's fate, had driven that sweet nothingness away; in its place crept a feeling of dread and the silent tears that accompanied it.

Tim reached into his pocket for his phone. It was on vibrate so I didn't hear it ring. "It's Larry." He said aloud before answering. It was enough to bring me back from my despair. Maybe Larry had the answers I couldn't find. Maybe he could relieve me from my guilt. He wasn't God, but he was the closest thing we had to a reason for hope. I reached across the coffee table to pluck a tissue from the flowery box of Kleenex that rested on the far end. I quickly dried me eyes and the snivel that had made a slow run from my nose.

Tim put Larry on speaker phone.

"Hi June and Tim," Larry said. "So, where we are…We are in family court first thing tomorrow morning to challenge the CPS findings and the hospital. I guess you know that the hospital management has dug in now. We're going to challenge their knowledge about Ernie's condition and their ability to treat him. I am also challenging the hospital management's assessment that their hospital and staff can better serve Ernie than University Hospital and Dr. Blackwell. We will also attack CPS' assertion that you are negligent parents.

"Dr. Blackwell has agreed to testify as an expert in mitochondrial research. I arranged for your family doctor to testify that he has seen no evidence of abuse over the years that he has treated Ernie and Elsie. I need both of you in court to testify as well.

"The first goal is to get visitation reinstated. Then I'll push for getting Ernie transferred to University Hospital and Dr. Blackwell's care. So that's the strategy going forward. Any questions?"

"Just need to know what time we should be there, Larry," Tim said.

"What about reporters? And does Elsie need to testify?" I asked.

"We might want Elsie there…yes, bring Elsie. As for the reporters…normally I would say stay away from them. But…you made a statement already and the hospital retaliated and defended their stance, so now there is a story about the hospital versus parents.

"And," Larry continued, "you have been accused of being bad parents. The courts don't listen to news stories. Theoretically. But hospitals, who need public support, do. Maybe, if we don't get visitation back tomorrow, bad publicity will put pressure on hospital heads to reinstate it on their own. But this will have to be a bigger effort than the few reporters who showed interest so far. I don't know if it will help. Maybe it's best to say nothing. I will draft a statement we can present tomorrow outside of court if reporters are still interested. But if we quietly just get visitation back...we're better off."

"Okay," I said. "Well, visitation is great, yeah; but we need to get Ernie out of that place. He isn't getting better and they aren't treating him, and I'm worried the longer he is in there the worse it is for him." I argued.

"Yeah. Yeah, I understand June. We're going to present that to the court tomorrow. But it isn't likely they will rule on that part right way. We'll push as hard as we can."

"Is there anything else you need from us?" Tim broke in.

"Just be prepared to defend any and all trips to the doctor or hospital that Ernie or Elsie have had. Why they went and generally how long Ernie has had his episodes and health problems along with what you have done to help him. We want to show that as parents, you have done everything possible in the face of an unknown disease, to get your son help. There will be challenges and accusations from CPS witnesses so, just keep your answers as muted and factual as possible. But I'll go over this tomorrow before court with you."

"Okay," Tim said. "So what time?"

"Meet me in front of the courthouse at 8 am so we can spend an hour going over things."

"Do we need to bring anything?" I asked.

"No. If things go further, we will need medical records and a calendar of times Ernie or Elsie were kept out of school with reasons for it. More detail. But for now, we're good with what we have."

"Okay," Tim answered. "Okay," I repeated.

"Great. See you both tomorrow morning at 8."

Elsie never made another appearance downstairs that night. When I went upstairs to check on her, she was sound asleep. She was lying on her side, fully dressed. Her headphones were still attached to her phone and both were partially buried under her. I didn't want to risk waking her, so I left her as she was. She had an odd indentation in her forearm when she came downstairs the next morning.

Tim and I spent the remainder of the evening making notes about Ernie's hospital visits, his days out of school, the tutoring we arranged for him, and all the ways his disease had presented itself from birth. We also made notes about Elsie's migraines and mine, and wrote up what little we knew about mitochondrial disease and family history, and how it presented itself in Ernie and Elsie…and me.

We knew Larry said we probably wouldn't need paperwork at this time, but Tim and I wanted to make certain we could tell a reliable story with clarity when we needed to. Dr. Blackwell would add the medical expertise and together, we would show that as parents, we were doing the right thing for Ernie—not abusing him. Once again, we had a purpose and a sense that what we did mattered for Ernie. That was just enough to keep my guilt and despair at bay long enough to guide us to bed and to much-needed sleep.

CHAPTER EIGHTEEN

FOLLOWING LIZZIE'S LEAD

Court the next morning was a tense affair.

Tim and I left Elsie at home rather than subject her to another round of inquisition. We arrived at 8:am and met with Larry as planned. Dr. Blackwell joined us at 8:30. She seemed confident in what she would present and in her support of us and Ernie.

She was very concerned to learn Ernie remained in a coma and on life support and dialysis, but she wouldn't commit to an opinion that if Ernie were transferred to her care, she would be able to reverse his condition. She could only offer treatment not considered by Dr. Grinsby.

That news allowed my fear to creep back into focus, but I tried hard to push those doubts far back in my mind and to concentrate on remaining positive and sticking to our goals for the day–to get visitation rights reinstated and Ernie moved to University Hospital and Dr. Blackwell's care.

I put Dr. Blackwell's warning into a mental folder labeled "cautious optimism" and filed it away for future examination. I rationalized that she was being non-committal because her profession required it. I didn't consider that she was also simply being exact.

Family court is a private affair. There are no reporters or general public allowed into the proceedings. The judge in our case, the Honorable Judge Cain Hurley, allowed for scheduled witnesses to be present during testimony in addition to lawyers and plaintiffs.

In the end, none of us were called to testify.

Judge Hurley, against Larry's protestations and insistence that Ernie's well-being needed an immediate resolution, would only rule on visitation rights. He ruled that everyone needed to come back the next morning to call witnesses and offer testimony regarding Ernie's guardianship. That meant Ernie was going to be under the care of Dr. Grinsby for yet another day. Tim and I were silently apoplectic–I was visibly shaking with self-control.

The judge was quick in his questioning and his decision-making. He asked the CPS lawyer what proof she had that Tim and I would present a risk to Ernie if we had monitored visitation. She went on about our attempt to get Ernie out of the hospital, but the judge cut her short.

"Miss Gleason, CPS had no custodial rights over Ernie Gallagher when Mr. and Mrs. Gallagher attempted to remove their son from Brinker Hospital. Is that correct?" The judge queried.

"No, your Honor," attorney Gleason said. "I mean, that is correct, we had not opened a case at that time."

"I see," the judge said. "And since that time, during any visitations at Brinker Hospital, has either Mr. or Mrs. Gallagher attempted to remove their son from the hospital?"

"No, your Honor."

"Has either Mr. or Mrs. Gallagher acted in a manner that imposed a threat to the welfare of their son during visitation?"

"Your Honor," attorney Gleason said testily, "the Gallaghers have made public statements attacking the rights of the hospital's guard-ianship as well as the Child Protective Services actions and we be-lieve..."

"Miss Gleason," Judge Hurley interrupted her, "I didn't ask if the Gallaghers took issue with what is happening with their child. These proceedings themselves have been called to challenge your position and that of the hospital. Are you suggesting that these proceedings would pose a threat to the child's well-being?"

"No, your Honor..."

"Glad to hear it. So, are you suggesting that the dispensation of free speech that the Gallaghers have as a constitutional right to express to the press or anyone else, is a threat to the welfare of the child?"

"No, your Honor."

"Do you have anything to offer this court that clearly shows that the child's welfare is in jeopardy from visitations from his parents?"

"No, your Honor."

"Very well," Judge Hurley said. The process of removing a child from the arms of a parent is not lightly entered into. We take very seriously the accusations and determinations offered by the Child Protective Services professionals and support their role in protecting our most precious and vulnerable citizens. Our priority here is for the safety and well-being of the child. However, this court is neither blind nor deaf to the needs of the parents and in the absence of a ruling on custody, or proof of threat to the child, the court must consider those parental needs as well as the benefit that parental contact may provide the child.

"This court has heard no reason to suggest that the Gallaghers pose a threat to their child that would constitute revoking visitation rights; we find the hospital acted in its own self-interest in so doing. It is the ruling of this court that monitored visitation rights, previously established by the hospital, be immediately reinstated without delay or amendment. Court will resume on the matter of custody at 9 tomorrow morning."

And that was the end of that.

We got visitation rights back, but no Ernie. Larry seemed a bit stunned by the proceedings and how quickly it was handled. He was also dismayed that we would have to wait another day for the custody preliminary hearing.

But considering how this judge worked, he determined that we had better be prepared with all of Ernie's medical records and health issues before tomorrow morning. He was pleased to learn that Tim and I had already begun putting all of that together and included as many dates as we could remember—mostly what month and year certain episodes happened.

Larry asked us to add as much detail as we could and make a chronological calendar as best we could. He admonished that we just recall the facts as that would help, while giving testimony, to control our emotions and make a clearer presentation.

He also suggested that concentrating on factual events will brace us for any emotional attack by the CPS attorney and keep us from giving any appearance of being unstable or emotionally unfit. Although he didn't look my way, I couldn't help but imagine that what he said was meant for me. He was well-aware of my past passionate reactions to anything that threatened my Ernie.

After we left the courthouse, we went to pick up Elsie, then headed for the hospital to visit Ernie. Elsie wanted to see Ernie as much as we did. Larry was to meet us there to make certain the hospital staff (mostly Ruth) were aware of the court decision and adhered to the ruling. Then he would return to his office to work on our case.

When we arrived at the hospital, we were greeted by a gaggle of reporters. Most were from local newspapers and television stations with one crew from a national news program.

We were stunned at the size of the crowd, as was Larry, who met us in the parking lot. He tried to back us off the main entrance and move us toward the side entrance Tim had pointed out to him. I froze just after we had all turned and taken a step along Tim's path. That caused the rest of our group to also pause.

"June. Come on honey or the reporters will catch up to us." Tim urged.

But I didn't move. Something familiar drew me back to the gathering at the front of the hospital. I looked intently at the group of reporters. There, standing next to a cameraman, with a microphone in her hand, was Lizzie.

She winked at me in answer to my disbelieving stare. I let a little smile chipmunk my cheeks in return. I knew what I needed to do. I took a deep breath, stood straight and tall and walked determinedly toward the media hive, not stopping until I had firmly planted my feet in front of Lizzie and her cameraman.

My little enclave followed like ducklings waddling after their mother. They didn't question me or try to stop me. They probably resigned themselves to the fact that this was going to be a "June moment" and no force on earth would deter me. Even Larry followed in silence, looking a bit like a prisoner being led to a bloodied wall.

Lizzie moved her microphone to just in front of my face to get ready for her friendly inquisition. The other media gathered around, each holding out their own microphones, cameras, and cell phones. They knew Lizzie, and her nationally recognized program; she was the big fish in this little news school and they were happy to let her take the lead.

"Mrs. Gallagher," Lizzie said, "Your son Ernie lies in a coma in this hospital. I'm very sorry to hear that. Tells us what happened."

Facts Junie,, I reminded myself. Don't be an emotional hag. It's Lizzie, just talk to her like you would at lunch.

"My son Ernie has had a long history of strange medical events in his life, ever since he was a baby. No one—until recently—has been able to tell us what is wrong with him or why he has these health issues."

"And he is being treated at this hospital?"

"No," I said emphatically. The staff here have no idea what is happening with Ernie's system. They have no diagnosis and no treatment. They are simply monitoring my son's coma. He is usually treated at University Hospital. Dr. Elizabeth Blackwell is his doctor there and has been the only person to identify what is wrong with Ernie; she has been treating him. He has mitochondrial disease.

"So, why is Ernie here and not at University?"

"Ernie collapsed at school last week and they sent him here—even though I had left strict instructions not to ever send him here, but to send him to University Hospital if he ever had issues during school hours."

"And did you try to have Ernie transferred?"

"Yes, but they wouldn't do it. They wouldn't let us take him out of here."

"And didn't you actually get arrested when you tried to remove your son?"

"Yes, that happened too, when I tried to remove him from here to get him to University and under Dr. Blackwell's care. They had no legal right to keep him, but the security guards physically tried to stop me. At that time, Ernie was walking on his own and perfectly capable of coming with me—but the hospital security thugs stopped me. The police were called and (*calm June, calm*) and while I was fighting the guards off, I accidentally hit one of the officers. And they arrested me."

"And the hospital kept Ernie?"

"Well...Ernie collapsed during the commotion. They took him to emergency and...he hasn't woken up. And they refuse to let us move him."

"So, your son lies in a coma, in this hospital, where doctors have no idea what is wrong with him. And they refuse to transfer him to University Hospital where a doctor there has identified his disease and can offer treatment. Is that accurate?"

"Yes. Exactly." I jumped on Lizzie's succinct summary. "Dr. Grinsby—the doctor on staff here who has taken over Ernie's care—has admitted that he nor anyone else here has any idea what is wrong with Ernie. And he refuses to recognize that mitochondrial disease exists or has any bearing on Ernie's condition."

I could feel myself getting emotional now. There was no stopping it. Tim sensed it and stepped forward to take my hand and offer support. I looked at Tim, and then back at Lizzie. "Our son might be dying in there; these people refuse to say they're wrong and they won't let him go..." I barely finished as the tears started running down my cheeks.

This was the first time I had openly shared my dire fear. I said out loud that Ernie was "dying in there." I couldn't go any further. Tim embraced me and Elsie joined his side to be wrapped in his other arm as she too cried. Larry stepped forward.

"I think that's enough for now, thank you." He addressed Lizzie and the rest of the reporters.

"Who are you? For the record." One reporter asked.

"Larry Greenbalt, of Greenbalt and Foster. I'm the Gallagher's attorney."

Lizzie broke in again.

"Mr. Greenbalt, what are you doing to get Ernie released? And are you planning to sue the hospital for wrongful detainment?"

"We are in court proceedings now to have the Gallagher's son moved to University Hospital. This morning visitation rights were re-instated by the court..."

"Are you saying the hospital refused visitation rights?" Lizzie asked.

"Yes," Larry said. "They took the privileges away after our last press conference where June was critical of the hospital. But the court reversed that this morning. As for any lawsuit, right now our efforts in the courts are focused on getting Ernie's parents named guardian again and getting him the best care he can receive."

"How did the Gallaghers lose guardianship of Ernie?"

Larry cleared his throat and went for it. "Child Protection Services, at the urging of one of the hospital employees, determined, without proper procedures I might add, that the Gallaghers are mistreating Ernie because of his several hospital visits and medical issues. That is of course ridiculous. The Gallaghers are exemplary parents and have only acted in Ernie's best interest at all times. We're confident that the courts will recognize that Ernie has a rare childhood disease that has affected his entire life and resulted in many doctor and hospital visits and health issues. We intend to prove that at tomorrow's hearing and to get Ernie back under the guardianship of his parents. That's all we have to say at this point."

Larry turned from Lizzie and the camera and shepherded us toward the front doors of the hospital. Lizzie was not done, however. She turned to her cameraman to put a long period on the interview. I slowed my steps so I could hear her.

"Not long ago, June Gallagher, a loving mother of two and a devoted wife, forced her way into a mangled car to battle intense flames and torn metal in a desperate effort to pull a stranger's child from certain death.

Now—this hero to all mothers—is in a fight for her own child's life. Her reputation and that of her husband, Tim, has been trampled on by Child Protective Services and this hospital staff. She has been arrested while trying to fight off hostile security guards who were holding her son against his parent's will, and now she must challenge the court system *and* CPS, in order to get her son back while there is still time to get him the care that can save his life from the grips of a devastating disease. This is Elizabeth Cochran for *Eye on America*."

***

Tim, Elsie, and I waited behind Larry at Ruth's perch while he shared the court's ruling with Ruth. I kept a watchful eye on the hospital front door. I hoped that Lizzie would come bursting through at any minute. I wanted to see her. I *needed* to see her. But she didn't appear. I assumed she had to keep a certain level of separation, or that maybe she had to go on to another story.

I was surprised that Lizzie's big Chicago morning show sent her to cover this story which is well outside their area.

Later I learned that the Chicago show had an *Eye on America* segment that brought local stories from anywhere to national light through network affiliates. I don't know how Lizzie got them to promote my story, she had only been at the new job for a couple of months. But then, that's part of the magic of Lizzie.

Anyway, Larry turned to let us know everything was set with a somewhat reluctant Ruth. We could have our visitations under the same conditions–three times a day, one hour each visit, accompanied by hospital staff.

That was all I needed to hear. I set off for the elevator without even thinking about "checking in" with Ruth. Elsie was on my heels while Tim remained behind to get any last-minute instructions from Larry.

When the elevator deposited us on the second floor, our companion nurse was waiting for us. "Gallaghers?" was all she said. We nodded in unison; she led us to Ernie's room. The nurse didn't stay with us. I got the impression she was above political intrigue and was only concerned with her patients' health. I also believe that she didn't see us as a threat and may have even sympathized with us.

When Elsie and I entered Ernie's room, and got our first glimpse of him, we stood a moment in equal disbelief and shock, before approaching his bed.

Ernie was paler and thinner than I had ever seen him and well beyond how I had imagined he would appear. His frail little body lay overwhelmed by tubes and wires and machines that surrounded him. They were inanimate guardians of the still-life that lay in front of them; giving him life from their mechanical hums. I was scared. In my head I echoed the fear that had been given words during my interview –"Our son is dying..."

I shook my head, tossing the words from my brain. I moved to sit on the edge of the bed and took Ernie's hand. Elsie edged her way closer to Ernie and began to cry softly.

"I love you Ernie. I love you my sweet, sweet little boy." I cooed as I brought his hand to my face and tenderly kissed it.

Elsie stood next to me watching. "I love you Ernie..." Was all she managed to speak before her quiet tears turned to storms from her eyes and, in concert with her wails, drowned the din of the machines. She began to shake as she repeated several more times, "I love you Ernie", in a distorted voice.

I laid Ernie's hand down, then grabbed Elsie and hugged her close while she sobbed on my shoulder, her arms hanging limp by her side. I rubbed her back and assured her, "It's okay honey. It's okay." I pulled myself from the embrace and held her firmly by one arm while I rubbed her tears with my blouse sleeve.

"Elsie," I said gently. "Look at me. Look at me honey." Elsie, still sobbing, brought her attention to my face.

"Ernie is going to be okay. You know he always comes through these things, right? He's just a little thin right now because he can't eat real food. But you know…you know when he wakes up the first thing he is going to say is 'I'm hungry,' right?"

She nodded. I tried to make things a little lighter. For Elsie. For me. Part of me wanted desperately to join her in her emotional release but I knew that I had to stay positive, to stay strong. For Elsie. For me. For Ernie.

"And you know he is going to beg us to take him out of here and get IHOP pancakes," I said with a grin, managing to evoke a little smile from Elsie's puffy face.

"Why don't you go downstairs and get me a coffee, and maybe get one for Daddy too?" I suggested. "And get a napkin or something to blow your nose. You have snot running down your face. Ewww."

I went for cheap humor hoping that it might help Elsie leave her gloomy place. It worked. She rolled her eyes with an, "Okay Mom."

"Do you need money?"

"No. I still have my lunch money." She headed out of the room and met Tim at the doorway.

"Hey, where you going?" I heard Tim ask.

"Getting coffee for Mom." Elsie answered without looking up.

"Oh, get me one too. Black." Tim barely managed to get out before Elsie ran toward the elevators.

When Tim walked into Ernie's room I was on my knees, slumped over with my head resting on Ernie's bed, his hand tucked under my chin. I had made it just long enough to get Elsie out of the room before I collapsed in an emotional heap.

I heard Tim enter, and figured he was standing there stunned by Ernie's appearance as Elsie and I had been. I think he thought I was praying, seeing me kneeling at Ernie's bed. He got on his knees next to me and wrapped one arm around my shoulder. I stirred and practically threw myself head first into his chest and wept.

For several minutes, we stayed like that. I cried into Tim's chest and he rubbed my back while he told me everything would be okay.

"Ernie just needs to eat some real food," Tim said gently. "He'll probably wake up and first thing, he'll say 'I'm hungry'." Tim assured me. I wept harder. Then I broke from Tim's embrace and stared into his warm eyes. *Who will be strong for you Tim?* I thought while I softly wiped the single tear that was caressing his cheek. *Who will lie to you?*

I managed to gather myself in time before Elsie's return. She too seemed to have recovered somewhat as she handed us our coffees and sipped on her soda. I wanted to question her choice of morning drink but thought, *"Why? In the grand scale of our lives, what was one soda?"*

We spent the remaining part of the hour visit talking to Ernie and each other. Repeating favorite Ernie stories or just talking about people who were asking about him and recounting all the things we would all do when he woke up.

We never left the hospital until night-time visiting hours were over. We were either in Ernie's room during our allotted times or in the cafeteria eating, drinking coffee, scanning our individual phones, and making small talk. The head nurse on Ernie's floor wouldn't allow me to sleep in Ernie's room with him although I begged profusely; I so wanted to be there when he woke up. I was desperate to believe that he would.

No one mentioned the underlying fear; we didn't speak about the invisible thread of dread that we knew connected us. We all needed the hope that came from the denial of its existence.

We left the hospital sometime around 9 pm. We were emotionally exhausted. The long day of waiting—of sitting and agonizing over Ernie—and the energy we each expended in our effort to be upbeat for Ernie and one another, had taken its toll.

When we walked through the hospital doors into the crisp night air, we were grateful that the reporters had abandoned their stations. No one was lying in wait for us.

But, our gratitude was short-lived. When we arrived home, the ever-vigilant hoard was camped on our front lawn. We gave a collective sigh when we first saw them. We had to enter through the front door which meant steeling ourselves against the gauntlet of reporters. Oh, how I wished we went through with the planned garage sale last summer. My side of the garage was full of years of collected 'treasure'. My garage opener battery died months ago, and Tim's was clipped to his car's visor which was safely locked inside his side of the two-car garage.

We exited our car and huddled close together as we made our way to the front door. The usual barrage of questions came at us, seemingly from every direction, but we kept our heads down until we made it to the front door. A hand grabbed my arm as we waited for Tim to unlock the door. I was about to swipe at the person when I saw it was Lizzie.

"Lizzie." I said startled to see her.

"Mrs. Gallagher, I would like to ask you a few questions in private. It could be beneficial to your case." Elizabeth needed to keep this professional to those in ear-shot of what was said.

"Well. Okay." I agreed. "But only for a few minutes. We are all very tired and want to get to bed early." I was tired, but I was awake enough to get what was going on. When Tim opened the door, Lizzie entered with us. Once safely locked inside, Lizzie and I hugged.

Tim stood in the hallway observing us while Elsie made her way to the living room couch and plopped into it on her side.

"Junie," Lizzie said. "I'm so sorry about Ernie. How is he doing?"

Lizzie immediately asked upon breaking our embrace.

"He's...he's doing okay...the same." I looked to Tim for support. Tim nodded. I continued, "But what are you doing here? I mean yah here, but I mean back home? And how did your program hear about us and what is going on here? Better yet, why do they even care?" I sounded like the reporters at my door as I harangued Lizzie with questions.

Lizzie followed me into the living room as she listened to all of my questions. She stopped long enough to introduce herself to Tim. I hadn't realized that she and Tim had never met.

Elsie shyly said "hi," then sat up and hugged one corner of the couch. I sat in my usual corner. Lizzie sat between Elsie and me. Tim offered up drinks; we politely declined so he took a seat in the big chair that sat diagonally across from the couch.

"So, to answer your questions Junie, my friend," Lizzie began, "I'm here because...well because you need me here even though you might not know it. And you need the press here."

"I *am* glad you are here, but how did you manage it and...why–no offense–do we need the press?" I asked.

"Yeah, our lawyer, Larry said we really should avoid the press and well...that judges don't react to the whims of the press...umm yeah no offense there either." Tim added.

"Okay, soooo, first off your lawyer is wrong, no offense," Lizzie quipped back to Tim with a wry smile. "Judges here are appointed by politicians. Politicians are elected by people. People vote with their emotions, and nothing is more emotional than a sick child being ripped from their mother's arms. And when that mother is the hero who risked her own life to save another child...well...it doesn't get more emotional than that. And honestly, all that makes it more of a story that our producers want to pursue. And that's why I am here, to answer the second big question."

"Well, okay but tomorrow morning we're going to court to get Ernie released back to our custody, so the story will be over." Tim argued back.

"Really? You have a government agency, favored by the establishment, arguing against you. You have heads of a hospital and doctors with established ties to that same local government and community backing up the agency, and you have a judge, who, while maybe trying to be objective, is obligated to side with established thinking.

"You have one doctor who will be made out to be a quack, citing a 'made-up disease' and two parents whose judgment and fitness to be parents has been called into question. You want to go to court against that?" Lizzie was direct in her challenge.

Tim and I sat in silence. Lizzie looked at each of us. "Don't worry, that was a rhetorical question." Lizzie said softening her tone. "You need opinion on your side. But more than that, you need outrage on your side. You need *national* attention which will bring out other people who have your shared experience and *other experts* to come forward. And, you need them *now*! Trust me on this."

"I don't know what to say," I finally responded. "This sounds like we won't get Ernie back tomorrow or...or maybe for a week."

"Well, I don't know about that," Lizzie said. "My producer has been out here all day contacting women's support groups, knitting circles, professional organizations...anyone she can find that might come to the courthouse tomorrow morning to rally for your cause. We even have a couple of national organizations that are sending people here. There should be a good crowd at the courthouse tomorrow and it will build from there. We get that kind of response, and our show will give us more coverage and...more of the regionals and national stations will send their reporters swooping in, afraid of missing a great human-interest story."

"But why Lizzie?" I asked, puzzled. "I mean yeah, I know you're my friend, but why would anyone I don't know–say in California–care enough about our story?"

"Because, Junie my dear, people everywhere have children," Lilzze said, patting my knee. "And no one wants to see a nice upstanding couple have their ill child ripped from them and put at more risk and...forgive me for saying this, but maybe even die from the mishandling by government and hospital officials. It's you against the government. It's Ernie's life versus the arrogance of the hospital doctors. It's one doctor's challenge against the established thinking about a rare disease they fail to see. It's everyman's fight against whatever holds them down–real or perceived–a fight against the odds and a chance to share in a victory that might just mean saving a child's life."

Lizzie was passionate in her response. And she made sense. As disheartening as it was to hear that we would likely not get Ernie back after tomorrow's proceedings, or maybe for another few days if at all, it was encouraging to know that Lizzie was providing a whole lot of ammunition to arm our fight for our child.

I had trust in Larry to represent us, but he was no match for the firestorm that was Lizzie. I felt strangely more confident that she would add more to our argument in court than Larry and any witnesses he could bring forward.

Lizzie didn't stay long enough to make small talk. She had important efforts to coordinate before covering the court proceedings in the morning, so she made a quick exit. After she left, Elsie gave Tim and me bear hugs then went straight to bed.

Tim and I followed shortly thereafter. We took a few minutes to clear our heads and steady ourselves for the morning. I wanted to speak with Tim before he got into bed. I knew once he assumed his horizontal position, he would be off to slumber in a minute. And, truthfully, I hoped I would experience the same welcomed respite once I placed my head onto the down of my pillow. We sat on the steps leading upstairs.

"Tim. We aren't going to get Ernie back tomorrow are we?" I quietly asked with a despondent voice.

"Ehhhboy. I don't know June. I...I guess not. Not from the picture Elizabeth painted."

"Do you think she is right?" I asked. "And do you think we are doing the right thing with all this press she is planning?"

Tim let out a long sigh before responding.

"I think Elizabeth has...she has a more cynical way of looking at things. But...I think she's right. The way she laid everything out... cynical maybe, but it made sense. When you look at the case through her eyes...I mean how she presented it, Larry doesn't stand a chance. We need something on our side that...that umm...at least says 'Hey, people are watching you.' It isn't just them ruling on our case. It's them being watched and...and being judged by a lot of people. I think Elizabeth was...well, spot on with that."

"Okay," I agreed. "I think so too. One thing I don't question about Lizzie—well two things—her friendship and her amazing energy. I don't think she has an off-button and I don't think she backs away from any challenge. She's a full-steam-ahead kind of gal."

Tim and I chuckled.

"Yeah...she reminds me of someone...I mean her passion anyway." Tim looked at me with a wide grin which I returned.

"Okay. I'm off to bed. I'm sending Elsie to school tomorrow. She's had enough time off and she doesn't need to be part of tomorrow's circus...especially if nothing definitive is going to happen."

"Okay," Tim said and stretched his arms toward the ceiling. "Let's go up. I'm exhausted."

And up we went; Tim to his instant slumber and me to my restless attempt at sleep. I was constantly interrupted by my always-on mind, that was full of worry and doubt...and fear.

***

The next morning, I was up before Tim and greeted him in the kitchen at 7 am. I had made a pot of coffee and was preparing a hearty breakfast of eggs, bacon, toast, and orange juice to sustain us through what was certain to be a long morning in court.

Tim looked surprised to see me and the breakfast. He gave me a peck on my cheek followed by a "looks good," before he poured a cup of coffee for himself and offered one to me. I accepted, and we carried our coffee and a plate of bacon and eggs each to the table to eat.

Despite the tantalizing aromas and rumbling stomachs, neither of us dug into the meal. Tim ate some of his eggs and chewed on a piece of crispy bacon before setting his plate aside to concentrate on coffee and juice.

I pushed my eggs around the plate but managed to bring only one forkful to my mouth before I too pushed my plate away. When Elsie came down five minutes later, she looked as badly as I felt from lack of sleep. She dropped into the chair next to me and began to nibble on my left-over bacon.

"Do you want some eggs?" I asked.

"No. Is there any more bacon? And juice?" She responded sleepily.

"You're going to have just bacon for breakfast Elsie? No Eggs?"

"That's what *you* had, Mom," she snapped at me. I could tell it was her lack of sleep that was driving her curtness and, given how exhausted we all were, I decided to let it go. Tim, who was quietly observing the two of us, said nothing. I assumed he was looking for a cue from me that someone should redress Elsie. When I didn't react, he let it go too. I guessed he was too emotionally spent to weigh in.

"Okay. I'll get you some juice and yes, there is more bacon." I got her the juice and bacon and returned to the table.

"School today Elsie."

"Screw that Mom. I'm going to the courthouse with you."

Tim quickly rose from his chair, with his plate in hand and glared at Elsie.

"You're going to school. And don't *ever* talk to your mother like that again." Tim commanded Elsie with a scary edge to his voice. Then, he brought his dish to the sink before returning to the table to finish his coffee. Tim rarely got upset, but when he did, Elsie knew not to challenge him.

Elsie stared at her plate of bacon.

"Elsie," I said gently, "You heard what Elizabeth said last night. Court is going to be a long, slow day, and we probably won't have any real news. And you've missed enough school. If anything important happens, I'll come get you. I promise." I reassured Elsie.

Elsie nodded her head in agreement and abruptly left the table and ran upstairs. I knew she had begun to cry. She was upset from being yelled at by Tim and from being denied the chance to participate–even if only as a spectator–in the fight for Ernie. I didn't reprimand Tim for yelling at her. He was right to be upset with her, but mostly because it dawned on me that perhaps Tim's night was not as peaceful as I had assumed.

Tim and I stayed at the table sipping our coffee without speaking until Elsie came running back down the stairs and bounded toward the front door to make her exit for the bus. I yelled after her to take her lunch money just as she slammed the door behind her.

A few seconds later, I heard the door fly open again followed by the stomp of feet running up the stairs. She left the front door flung wide open and the cold morning air rushed into the house. I could feel it making its way down the hall and adding its chill to the already cold kitchen.

A few seconds later, I heard her stomps descending the stairs and heading toward the kitchen. Elsie stood in front of me, a jacket flung across her arm and her hand held out, palm upward.

"Lunch money," She said, slightly out of breath.

I didn't have my purse with me, so I relayed the message to Tim. "Lunch money, please."

Tim looked up from his phone which had drawn his attention for the last few moments. Without a word, he reached into his back pocket, pulled out his wallet, opened it and held out a five-dollar bill in Elsie's direction.

Elsie reluctantly made the three-step journey toward Tim's end of the table and plucked the fiver out of his hand.

"Close the door and don't slam it on your way out please," Tim requested dryly after she took the money.

Elsie retraced the three steps back to me, turned to walk away, and then turned back toward me. She glanced at her dad and then back to me again.

"I'm sorry I swore at you, Mom," She said loudly, then she tore back out the front door, slamming it behind her.

Tim looked at me. I looked at Tim. Tim shook his head and stood up with his empty coffee cup in hand and walked over to place it in the sink. I smiled. I knew she slammed the door deliberately; just as I knew she apologized to me and, ignored saying anything to her father. This was her adolescent way of saying "You don't exist" to Tim.

I knew it was her spiteful, manipulative way of getting even for being yelled at. I didn't smile because I thought it was a good thing or because I thought she was right to act that way. I smirked as a sort of mock celebration that my little acorn had landed so close to me. For better or worse, Elsie is her mother's child.

***

Nothing could have prepared Tim and me for what greeted us at the courthouse.

We expected that Lizzie and her crew would create a small gathering of support for us. But we never would have imagined the crowd that had formed on the courthouse steps and beyond.

There were more than one hundred people—many with signs that read "Let Ernie Go!" or "Parents, not Government!" or some other related message. Camera crews and reporters from state-wide and local media had descended on our little town and planted themselves amongst the sign-bearers.

Larry was at the top of the courthouse steps anticipating our arrival. When he saw Tim and me standing across the street, hesitant to approach, he waved us over. That simple gesture told us we should come forward but it also, unwittingly, told the media that we were here.

Hand-in-hand, Tim and I made our way across the street and up the stairs, weaving through the crowd of supporters and reporters crammed in around us. Larry descended the stairs to meet us part way up. He turned around and stuck both arms out, attempting to cleave the crowd and make a clear path.

It was mayhem. The reporters' questions came streaming at us, often accompanied by a microphone thrust in our face. Larry was as much out of his element as we were. He looked harried and nervous as he ushered us forward insisting to the reporters that there would be no comments or answers to any questions.

When we reached the top of the stairs, two courthouse guards, whose primary concern was keeping the crowd from entering the courthouse and not our safety, held the doors open for us to proceed. Larry stood aside and gestured for us to enter first. Tim and I started forward, but I stopped just short of the threshold. I heard Lizzie's voice in my head, saying, *Because Junie my dear, people everywhere have children.*

I turned sharply and walked to the front of the cement stoop, leaving Tim and Larry to wonder momentarily, what my intentions were. I waited until all the reporters were in front and around me and the crowd's din lessened. I took a deep breath and spoke into the clump of microphones that were presented just below my face.

"We're not going to take any questions," I began; Tim stepped beside me and held my hand. Maybe he had heard Lizzie's voice in his head too. I looked at him gratefully and then back out over the crowd. I spotted Lizzie at the bottom of the stairs. She had not taken a reporter's role this morning. She had left that to another on her crew. She stood, instead, in support of us–of me. Her face, beaming bright like a beacon of hope, brought me comfort and strength as I continued.

"We are overwhelmed by the support you have shown us, and we are so, very grateful that people we don't even know would take time out from their lives to come stand by us this morning," I said, my voice shaking a little with emotion. "My husband, Tim, and I, and our daughter Elsie, just want one thing–to get our Ernie the best possible care he can get. We believe that care can only be found under the guidance of Dr. Elizabeth Blackwell at University Hospital. We are Ernie's parents. Only *we* have the love for him, experience with Ernie's disease, and the right to determine what care our son gets. Not some misguided government agency or ill-informed doctors, no matter how well-meaning they may be.

"Our fight today–and for as long as it takes–is for that right; for the rights of parents everywhere to determine what is in the best interests of their children. Our Ernie...our Ernie lies in a coma, barely alive, with no treatment options being offered. We want to give Ernie the only real chance he has and not be at the mercy of people who do not know or love our son. And for that, we have been branded bad parents. We hope, today, to show the court how far from the truth that is. And to finally get our Ernie back. Thank you."

When I spoke, there was a calm in my demeanor and in my voice, which betrayed the nerves spasming in the pit of my stomach, screaming to be released. Yet, there were also traces of passion and tears of emotion, as I spoke about Ernie's coma, that told everyone in attendance that my words were the pleas of a loving, desperate mother and not the rehearsed act of a polished orator.

CHAPTER NINETEEN

MORE JUDGE HURLEY

The courtroom was strikingly absent of any of the noise of the world just outside the courthouse doors. Tim and I were the last to arrive to the session. In attendance were the CPS lawyers, Larry, and a member of his firm we did not know, and the witnesses for each side; Ruth, Ernie's school principal, our neighbor and my former friend Ginny, Dr. Grinsby, Dr. Blackwell, Ernie's pediatrician Dr. Reynolds, and Tim and me. There were two others in attendance we did not recognize.

We all rose as Judge Hurley entered the room and then took his seat, flapping his hand for us all to sit down. He didn't waste any time with pleasantries or calling out the proceedings; he launched straight to the issue of the commotion outside.

"The matter before us is a very private matter concerning this family and the agencies assigned to protect the children of our community," Judge Hurley began. "This hearing is not for the benefit of the general public—or more specifically for the entertainment of the media. I will not have these proceedings turned into an orchestrated circus to the supposed benefit of either side in this dispute. Mr. Greenbalt, I strongly suggest you use your influence to discourage the participation of the entourage camped outside this courthouse and to suggest their departure. I suggest you elicit the Gallagher's support in those efforts as well. And that is all I will say on this matter presently."

"Your honor," Larry spoke as he rose from his chair, surprising the judge who had not directly solicited a response. "Respectfully, your Honor, neither my firm nor our client are responsible for the public interest in this case nor their interest in the welfare of Ernie Gallagher. As you stated yesterday while reinstating visitation rights, 'the Gallaghers have a constitutional right to express free speech.' As does the press and any individual or group that has an interest in making such expression. We cannot be held responsible for nor be required to be monitors or arbitrators of any such constitutional exercise."

The courtroom inhabitants, already silent with decorum, held their collective breaths at Larry's apparent challenge to Judge Hurley. Everyone except Tim and me. We looked at each other with slight grins etching the sides of our mouths. I wondered if Larry had suddenly heard Lizzie's voice as well; he no longer argued against publicity. In his way, he seemed to emphatically support it.

"Mr. Greenbalt," the judge said, "there is a difference between allowing free speech and in stoking the flames of discord for personal benefit. I warn you to heed the difference."

Larry took his seat but gave no response either in agreement or further explanation. I got the sense this was deliberate, and that Larry had no intention of agreeing to douse any flames of discord.

The CPS lawyer, Miss Gleason, called her first witness. They began with Ginny. This was going to be awkward for Ginny and for a few seconds I felt sorry for her. After she was sworn in and her relationship to Ernie and our family was established, the CPS lawyer began her more relevant questioning.

"Mrs. Morgenstern. You have, on several occasions, had the Gallagher's daughter Elsie under your care for a few hours or even overnight. Is that correct?"

"Objection your honor. This case is not about Elsie Gallagher."

"Your honor," Miss Gleason responded, "we are trying to establish parenting habits of the Gallaghers and their relevance to their son."

"Overruled, but let's not go too far from the case at hand." The judge was quick to decide.

"Mrs. Morgenstern..."

"Actually, it's Ms. Bessinger. My husband and I divorced three years ago, and I have been on my own since then." Ginny proudly corrected.

"Oh, umm, I see." Miss Gleason addressed Judge Hurley. "Your Honor, our records were not updated to this name change. We will need to re-swear in the witness?"

"No need." He said. "Let the record show the witness sworn in as Ginny Morgenstern is acknowledged to be known as Ms. Bessinger. You may continue counselor."

"Thank you, your Honor. Ms. Bessinger, during your time caring for Elsie Gallagher, did you ever see any signs of abuse or neglect?"

"Objection your honor!" Larry interrupted. "Ms. Bessinger never cared for Elsie; she was simply an occasional babysitter."

"Correction noted," the judge said. "Stick to the facts Miss Gleason."

"Ms. Bessinger, during the time you were watching Elsie Gallagher did you ever notice any signs of abuse or neglect?"

"Well...well, there were many times that I was asked to care for Elsie at a moment's notice. June, Mrs. Gallagher, was often too busy to pick her up after school or from soccer practice. And Elsie had horrible headaches much of the time she was with me and would spend a lot of her time lying down."

"I see," Miss Gleason said. "And was there a specific instance that gave you concern?"

"Oh that, yes. One time last month, Elsie was practically dumped at my doorstep..."

"Objection your honor!" Larry called out.

"Ms. Bessinger, please be as factual as you can without using unwarranted embellishments," Judge Hurley said.

"Well, I mean June told me at the last minute that she could not come get Elsie. I wasn't expecting to have her that long. Elsie was playing with my son Brian–they are close in age. Elsie kept rubbing her stomach and looked to be in pain. After about an hour of this, she pleaded with me if she could go lie down on Brian's bed. I asked her repeatedly what was wrong, but she refused to tell me and just ran upstairs to the bathroom. She was in there for quite a long time and when she came out, she went straight to Brian's bed and went to sleep until her mother finally picked her up. I was very worried for her."

"Thank you, Ms. Bessinger. No further questions." Larry rose to address Ginny.

"Ms. Bessinger, did you relate this story to Mrs. Gallagher at any time?"

"Well, no...I..."

"So, you were very concerned but never told her mother–your neighbor and friend–about her daughter's ailment? Correct? Larry didn't wait for a response. "Did you ever discuss Elsie's headaches with Mrs. Gallagher?"

"Well, yes."

"And what did Mrs. Gallagher give as a reason for the headaches?"

"She said that Elsie often had migraines. But she never said why."

"That's all I have for this witness, your Honor.

Dr. Grinsby was next. As I looked around the courtroom while Dr. Grinsby was being sworn in, I noticed that the security guards who assaulted me at the hospital were conspicuously missing from the courtroom.

"Dr. Grinsby." Miss Gleason began. "Why is Ernie Gallagher in your care? What is his medical condition and history?"

"Well," Dr. Grinsby made himself comfortable, crossing his legs at the knee and folding his hands in his lap. "Ernie Gallagher has been presented to our hospital as well as University Hospital over the past several years with myriad medical emergencies: broken bones, periodic seizures, uncontrollable vomiting, extensive weakness, learning disabilities, and other maladies."

"And what diagnosis has been offered to explain these many physical abnormalities?"

"None really. There is no definitive diagnosis anywhere in his records that indicates one medical cause or explanation for these many issues."

"I see. In your expert opinion as a physician and your many years as both an emergency room attending physician and as a family practice doctor, have you any opinion as to the cause of Ernie Gallagher's many medical issues?"

"Well, I would need more time with Ernie and we would need to question him, which is not currently possible, but based on the records and my experience, I would be inclined to consider that the patient's medical condition is the result of abuse or possibly parental neglect."

"Dr. Grinsby, is this suspected neglect the reason you are holding Ernie Gallagher at the hospital now?"

"Well no, not entirely. We are holding him because he is in a comatose condition and is in urgent need of constant care and monitoring. We are keeping him alive while we attempt to diagnose the root cause of his condition."

"I see." Miss Gleason said. "And in your expert opinion as the attending physician, is there any care that Ernie Gallagher could receive elsewhere, that he is not receiving now?"

"Absolutely not. We are doing everything possible to care for this patient. He is in expert hands."

"And, in your expert opinion, would the child's welfare be put at risk if he was released or moved to another facility?"

"Yes. He is much too fragile to move."

"Thank you, doctor. No more questions." Once again, it was Larry's turn.

"Dr. Grinsby, what is the source of your knowledge of Ernie's medical history?"

"Well, he is currently my patient; I have also read the medical records provided by his pediatric physician and from University Hospital, and his emergency admittance records."

"I see. So, other than what is happening with Ernie now, you have no personal or direct experience with any of his ailments. Is that correct?"

"Well, no, but it is often the case where medical records are consulted when personal interaction has not been an option."

"Can you tell me where Ernie's bruises are on his body?"

"I don't understand the question?"

"Well, doctor, you said you suspected abuse or neglect. I simply would like you to tell the court the signs of abuse on Ernie's body that support your hypothesis?"

"Well, he doesn't have bruises now. But his medical records show clear indications of potential abuse."

"So, the medical records you examined detail bruises from abuse that you can point out to us?"

"No, not exactly."

"Doctor, you said that you relied on medical records, absent any personal experience with Ernie over the years. So please point out the records, I have them here for your reference if you need—where abuse has been indicated?"

"There are no direct comments or indications in the records individually that suggest abuse. However, taken together in frequency of events, there is ample indication of potential abuse."

"So, doctor, if a child has undiagnosed epilepsy, for example, and ended up in the hospital on multiple occasions, with no indication of abuse on any records, you would assume the child was abused simply from the number of times they were admitted to the hospital? You would not consider an alternative reason or diagnosis such as epilepsy–in my rather simplified example. Is that correct?"

"Ernie Gallagher does not have epilepsy." Dr. Grinsby answered defensively as he uncrossed his legs.

"No, according to your diagnosis from the current records, you have no idea what Ernie is suffering from. Correct?"

"Well, yes. I mean no, we don't have any *one* specific cause of his coma."

"And neither would a doctor who is unfamiliar with epilepsy. That doctor would have to jump to the conclusion that it must be abuse, because he has no clue what is wrong. Isn't that what you are saying about Ernie, doctor?"

"No. I am not saying that at all." Dr. Grinsby rubbed his palms on his pant legs. "I never said it was definitive that Ernie Gallagher was abused. I simply stated that…that there is the potential of abuse as the result of looking at patterns of medical records."

"Not looking at patterns of medical records, doctor–you just said that there are no examples of abuse in the records. Rather your supposition of the potential for abuse is based on the sheer number of medical records. Isn't that more accurate?"

"I suppose. Yes." Dr. Grinsby shifted uncomfortably in his chair.

"Ernie Gallagher is in a coma doctor?"

"Yes. For the past several days."

"Has any treatment you have provided brought Ernie out of that coma?"

"Not currently, but a coma is not a simple matter especially when it is from an unknown cause."

"Ernie is currently being kept alive by various machines, such as a respirator. Is that correct doctor?"

"Yes, that is correct."

"Are these machines connected to the wall?"

"I'm afraid I don't understand the question."

"You stated that Ernie is too frail to be moved. You also stated that you are not currently giving any treatment that will result in a change in his condition. You ruled out moving Ernie because he is being kept alive on machines. So, I simply want to know if these machines are attached to the wall or if they are portable?"

"Well, technically, they are on wheels for the most part I suppose..."

"So, doctor, if it were absolutely essential for Ernie's well-being, he could be moved along with his life-giving machines. Correct?"

"Well, I suppose it would be possible, but it would not be recommended."

"Are you saying that if Ernie's life was in danger, and a treatment was available elsewhere, you would not move him to this new place to save his life?"

"That is supposition—no such place or treatment exists." I saw a bead of sweat from Dr. Grinsby's forehead.

"Would you move him, doctor, if treatment that could save his life existed elsewhere?"

"Yes."

"Thank you doctor. No further questions." Larry began to return to his seat and then did an abrupt about face.

"I'm sorry, your Honor. One last question before you step down doctor."

"Make it brief counselor," The judge instructed.

"Rather than move Ernie to satisfy your concern over transportation, would it not be possible to bring in someone who could administer a treatment that is not currently being offered to Ernie?"

"Well...yes if one existed, but we have some of the best experts in their field at Beamount..."

"Doctor, if an expert could be brought in, in a field that was foreign to you or the rest of the hospital staff's expertise, would that be a viable option?"

"Yes."

"And have you done that Dr. Grinsby? Have you brought in an outside expert?"

"Well, no but..."

"And given that no one at Brinker Hospital has been able to treat, let alone diagnose Ernie's condition, shouldn't you make that consideration?"

"Objection your honor!" Miss Gleason interrupted. "Counsel is not allowing the witness to answer questions."

"Yes, and that is more than one question, Greenbalt," The judge admonished Larry.

"Apologies your honor. I have no more questions."

As I listened to Larry's questioning of Dr. Grinsby, I gained new respect for him. He was methodical, concise, and very prepared. His mild manner and strict adherence to fact made him unthreatening and unable to be contradicted. He also was not afraid to push beyond polite constraints when necessary and turn a confident, adversarial witness into a befuddled companion to our argument—as he had just done with Dr. Grinsby.

The rest of the morning went about the same. Ernie's pediatrician, Dr. Reynolds, was called and again gave no indication of abuse; his testimony was about the many visits from Ernie and the unexplained illnesses.

Miss Gleason clearly relied on making the most out of Ernie as a medical mystery which indicated abuse or neglect. But, in every instance, Larry countered with logic and pointed out the lack of any direct facts.

Oddly, Ruth was not called on to testify. I suspected that her lack of authority as the initial instigator of the baseless abuse theory, made her a potential liability to the CPS case; they might call her later if needed. But I was certain Larry would call on her to expose the inappropriate and illegal actions of the Brinker Hospital staff and security guards, and by CPS itself.

Judge Hurley was aware a child's life hung in the balance and he seemed eager to push both sides along. He urged the lawyers to present their strongest witnesses in the hopes that one side or the other would have a powerful enough argument for him to rule on and not delay the case with any further proceedings.

This gave Tim and me a little hope that perhaps the process would not result in the delay we anticipated, and that something concrete—hopefully in our favor—would present itself by the end of the day.

There were over a thousand people waiting for us when we left the courthouse for lunch break. News crews from every major network were there as well. When we saw the enormity of the scene, we stood at the top of the stairs, frozen in disbelief. Even Dr. Blackwell, who joined us for the break, was dumfounded. The crowd rushed up the stairs and surrounded us in a matter of seconds. Many in the group shouted the slogans written on their individual signs. "We're with June." or "Let Ernie Go!" or "Parents not Government!" and others.

The reporters again stuck their microphones in my face, and the questions began while Tim took up his position of support at my side. The well-wishers and reporters had little interest in Dr. Blackwell or Larry. She used her anonymity to squeeze her way to the bottom of the stairs in an effort to get to her car. We had already decided Dr. Blackwell's car would be our get-away vehicle.

"June, how is the trial going?" "Are you going to get Ernie back?" "How do you feel, June?" "What would you like everyone out here to know?" "Have your children been abused?" I was peppered with questions like buckshot. Lizzie's familiar voice reached me above the spray of all the others just as she stepped out from the hovering hoard. "June, are you going to see Ernie during your break?" My rock was right there in front of me.

"Yes. Yes, Tim and I are going to the hospital now to see Ernie. We are so overwhelmed by everyone's support, really. But we have to get to the hospital and we have so little time. Please understand."

"Mr. Gallagher, how do you feel the proceedings are going?" One reporter asked while he stuck his microphone in front of Tim—he was not expecting to be questioned.

"It's going as well as can be expected," Tim's response was curt, disappointing the reporter. It was clear that Tim was not going to be the crowd pleaser or drive ratings with his simplistic answer.

"June, are you confident you will get Ernie back under your custody and to the care he needs?" Lizzie quickly diverted the crowd back to me.

"Yes. I have to believe we will. No mother would think otherwise. No parent could accept anything less."

"That's it folks," Larry said as he took charge. "Thank you for support. As Mrs. and Mr. Gallagher have said, it is greatly appreciated, but they must get to the hospital now. Please let them through and please respect their privacy at the hospital. Thank you." After his short statement, he led the way through the crowd that parted as he approached. The well-wishing continued from stranger-after-stranger as we descended the stairs and made our way to Dr. Blackwell who was waiting in her car, with the engine running.

After we all piled into Dr. Blackwell's car, she sped off in the direction of Brinker. We arrived at around 1:20 p.m. which meant that by the time we got out of the car, managed getting past reporters and reached Ernie's room, we would have 20 minutes at the most to visit with Ernie. Just enough time to give him a kiss and tell him we loved him.

We were all relieved to see that only a few supporters were gathered. It wasn't that we weren't grateful for their presence, we simply didn't have the luxury of time to speak with them. We were on a very tight schedule, much of which was not in our control. Security guards constrained them to the visitor parking lot away from the main entrance to keep them from interfering with normal hospital operations. That made it possible for us to avoid the group and enter the hospital unimpeded.

Ruth hadn't made it back from the courthouse. She had been replaced by someone we did not recognize and who seemed not to recognize us. Before Larry presented himself to this new person, I grabbed his arm.

"Larry," I whispered. "I don't think this person has any clue who we are. Rather than waste time while she calls this person or that, Tim and I are just going to go up to Ernie's room. Give us five minutes and *then* introduce yourself."

"Eghh,, well, I don't want to get on their bad side just now," he whispered back.

"What's that old saying?" Tim said with a smirk, "better to ask for forgiveness than permission." Besides, given the news coverage and the sign carriers outside, I don't think there is any side other than 'bad' when it comes to June and me."

"Well, okay," Larry agreed. "I'll cool my heels as they say while you get a head start. Dr. Blackwell and I will grab a bite and wait in the cafeteria for you and I'll make a few calls. There are two doctors who have flown in—one from Philadelphia and one from Seattle—who are experts in mitochondrial disease and they have volunteered to testify. Apparently, your case is intertwined with their interests and they want to seize this opportunity to bring awareness and recognition to the disease and their own patients. I have to coordinate getting them to the court before we head back there and brief them on what can be expected."

"That's great Larry. Then it won't be Dr. Blackwell on her own trying not to seem like she invented some illness. I had read about a few experts in the country after Dr. Blackwell told us Ernie had mitochondrial disease, but I never imagined they'd be interested in our case." I said with genuine excitement.

"Well, yeah, that's the idea," Larry said. We can use them to make Dr. Grinsby look inadequate in his experience rather than having Dr. Blackwell and you appear to be on some fringe aspect of medicine."

"Great," Tim said, impatient now. "Come on June, we should get up there. See you back down here in 20 minutes, Larry."

"Yes, but not a minute longer," Larry said. "As it is we will barely get to the courthouse on time and this judge won't welcome using the crowd as an excuse for being late."

Tim and I nodded then quickly made our way to the elevators and up to Ernie's room. Ernie was as pale as ever, still lying motionless, with his arms by his side. He looked like a posed, sleeping little angel.

I sat on the edge of his bed and pressed his hand to my face, gently caressing it with the soft warmth of my cheek. "I love you Ernie," I cooed several times before bringing his hand back down to his side. Tim sat on the other side of the bed. He gently petted Ernie's knee as he spoke to him.

"Hey big guy," Tim said quietly. "I miss you. I've been working on the trip to Disney and we're pretty set to go as soon as you're ready. Elsie sends her love. She really, really misses you. She won't even sit on the swings until you're home and she can give you some big pushes."

"Not too big kiddo. You might fall off again." I teased.

But, Ernie's expression didn't change. He didn't smile or blink his eyes. His hand did not hold mine. The steady rhythm of the ventilator breathed his only response and nothing we said roused him from his slumber and brought him back to us.

The battle that we were all waging for his life was being played out in the courtroom. But the real struggle was Ernie's own fight, somewhere deep inside himself, to find his way back to us; and there were no signs that our little love was winning.

After a few more promises of the wonderfulness that awaited him if he could just wake up, accompanied by a few more gentle kisses to his cheek and forehead, it was time for Tim and me to leave. As short as the time was, we still had managed to miss our deadline. Tim and I ran from Ernie's room to the elevators and then ran from the elevators to the exit in time to meet Larry at Dr. Blackwell's car. We made it only three minutes late.

The crowd in front of the courthouse had swelled again, now blocking traffic on the main street to the front of the courthouse. We were on the morning and afternoon news casts all across the nation. Larry was fielding invitations to have us on morning talk shows on all the major networks. Saving Ernie had become a sort of national pastime.

Dr. Blackwell let us off on the same side street where we had met her after the morning session. The crowd was quick to notice us and chanted louder than before, "Mothers not Government!" "We're with June!" They made our way over and began to surround us. As they bellowed their chants over and over again, I was thankful they were on our side.

Larry pushed through the throng and cleared a small path toward the top of the courthouse stairs for us to follow. All along the way, people, mostly women, shouted "We're with you, June!" "We love Ernie too!" "We're praying for Ernie and for your family!"

It was heartwarming to hear so much support, and yet, disheartening to accept that the desperation in their voices echoed the melancholy in my heart. None of this mattered if Ernie did not come back to us.

We stopped at the top of the stairs to acknowledge the crowd and the reporters again before we ducked into the courthouse. This time, it was Tim who found his voice. He draped his arm around my shoulder and together we stepped in front of the microphones. Tim didn't wait for the reporters to introduce their questions.

"Our family is very grateful for all of your support and for your prayers for our son, Ernie," he said calmly. "Very grateful. And for the many news organizations who have brought our story to life. We never intended to garner this kind of reaction, nor did we realize how many people our story would touch. It's really remarkable. We just came from visiting Ernie at the hospital. He is still in a coma and very frail. We have heard about your unwavering support. We want to ask for your continued prayers for his recovery and to ask you to continue your phone calls and emails to the Governor, our state representatives, Senators…everyone in government whose support you can influence. We hope to win this court battle, but if not, we must find another way to reverse this terrible course that has put our son's life in such danger. Thank you."

That was it. Tim had gone all-in to bring public opinion and outrage to influence these proceedings or to promote the next wave of attack. I was certain this would anger the judge when he found out later, but I was also fairly certain that Lizzie was right–all of this pressure on elected officials would have to trickle down to this courthouse in some way. If not to force a result, at least to encourage the judge to question the strength of arguments from CPS and Brinker Hospital officials.

Larry quickly ushered us into the courthouse noting that we were more than five minutes late. But we weren't the only ones. Luckily for us, something urgent had kept Judge Hurley from his usual promptness and we were able to take our seats a full five minutes before he made his entrance.

"All rise for the Honorable Judge Hurley," the baliff called.

We rose and sat when the judge indicated. Something was off.

Although he never gave the appearance of an overtly pleasant man, Judge Hurley now looked particularly distracted and distraught when he entered the courtroom. That didn't seem to be a good omen, since it was Larry's turn to present our side.

"All right. Let's move these proceedings along. And I warn you, counselor Greenbalt." The judge said, "no theatrics, no stalls, and no grandstanding. There is no jury and you won't win me over. Let's get some actual actionable facts into this case. You may proceed."

"Thank you, your Honor." Larry replied. "I would like to call Dr. Sarah Blackwell, of University Hospital."

After Dr. Blackwell was sworn in and Larry established her medical credentials, he began a methodical presentation of our case.

"Dr. Blackwell, you have been treating Ernie Gallagher for several weeks now, is that correct?"

"Yes. The Gallagher's case was referred to me by another physician at the hospital, Dr. Chawla."

"And why was that doctor?"

"Ernie was admitted to University Hospital, presenting with multiple symptoms that Dr. Chawla could not identify as collectively belonging to any single disease or cause. Upon examining Ernie's records, Dr. Chawla also noticed he had many examples of varying health issues over the last several years, that she could not explain. She was familiar with my work with mitochondrial disease and thought, given Ernie's history, it would be worthwhile if I examined Ernie."

"So, Dr. Chawla recognized your expertise in mitochondrial disease."

"Objection your honor!" Miss Gleason said while quickly rising. "Counsel has not established that mitochondrial disease exists, therefore, we cannot recognize Dr. Blackwell as being an expert in a non-existing field."

"We will withdraw the question your Honor, until we have called our other expert witnesses to testify as to the existence of this disease, as well as to Dr. Blackwell's competency in the area in question."

"Sustained." The judge ruled.

"Dr. Blackwell. Is mitochondrial disease a real thing?"

"Objection your Honor!" Miss Gleason jumped up again. "Once again, counsel is asking the witness to establish her own so-called disease."

"Your honor," Larry said, "With your indulgence, I would like to call two expert witnesses who can attest to the existence and reality of mitochondrial disease. Then I would like to immediately recall Dr.

Blackwell."

"You Honor! We have not been notified of these two witnesses."

"Well, you are aware now," Judge Hurley said. "This isn't criminal court, so I'll be a bit lenient here for now, Miss Gleason. Counselor Greenbalt, you may call your witnesses but confine your questioning to their expertise in...what is eghhh, yes mitochondrial disease." Judge Hurley said reading the from his notes..

And that's what Larry did. Dr Blackwell stepped down, and one at a time, Larry called up Dr. Marvin Hesh from Philadelphia Children's Hospital, and Dr. Bruce Deshaun of Seattle Children's hospital.

Each of the doctors established their credentials as well as the existence of mitochondrial disease They provided written case studies and patient diagnosis and treatments, as well as independent research studies concerning the mapping of MtDNA in patients with mitochondrial related abnormalities.

Miss Gleason and her team of CPS attorneys were unable to challenge the presented research and offered no rebuttal.

Larry pushed each doctor a bit further and asked if they could establish Dr. Blackwell's expertise in mitochondrial disease.

"Objection!" Miss Gleason fairly screeched each time.

"Over-ruled," Judge Hurley answered each time.

Doctors Hesh and Deshaun firmly established that Dr. Blackwell was a recognized expert in the field of mitochondrial disease research and treatment, and that she had been a major contributor to several studies as well as a key presenter on mitochondrial disease before Congress.

With that established, Larry re-called Dr. Blackwell.

"Dr. Blackwell, as an established expert in mitochondrial disease, and as Ernie Gallagher's physician, is it your expert opinion that Ernie suffers from mitochondrial disease?"

"Mitochondrial disease is very difficult to diagnose," Dr. Blackwell said. "We have to consider the patient's overall health and symptoms in order to properly diagnose the disease. And the patient can have myriad illnesses under the umbrella of what we call mitochondrial disease. Testing for the disease beyond that can be a lengthy and difficult process.

"We performed a muscle biopsy on Ernie, one of the most common, though costly and invasive diagnostics used, which came back inconclusive. We also sent out blood samples to a firm that has developed a new DNA test that can look at both the DNA and the MtDNA for mutations. Those results came back conclusive. Ernie indeed does suffer from mitochondrial disease."

Tim and I looked at each other. This was news to us. Of course, we "knew" that was what our Ernie suffered from but didn't realize it had been confirmed conclusively.

"Dr. Blackwell, can a child with mitochondrial disease have multiple disorders or health episodes?"

"Yes," she answered. "It is not only possible, but quite common. A person with mitochondrial disease may have multiple health issues, including seizures, long periods of vomiting, learning difficulties, digestive issues and more serious aspects including complete organ failure, sight impairment and others. Or they may suffer for years with severe migraines and show no other health abnormalities."

"I see. And did Ernie Gallagher present with any of these symptoms?"

"Yes. He presented with a history of many: seizures, vomiting, extreme low energy, organ failure, learning challenges...over a period of several years."

"So, a child with mitochondrial disease could have a long, varied record of health issues resulting in multiple doctor visits, emergency room admittances and related issues even at school requiring the intervention of the school nurse. Would that be fair to say?"

"Yes, that would be typical. And unless the doctor or hospital has knowledge of mitochondrial disease, the child would likely go undiagnosed and untreated."

"And, Dr. Blackwell, in your expert opinion, would you say Ernie Gallagher's many hospital emergencies and doctor's visits records are directly related to his mitochondrial disease?"

"Yes."

The other side sat rather dumbfounded during this whole series of questions. They had nothing now to combat Dr. Blackwell's testimony. And, I was more convinced, from their lack-luster attempts in trying to challenge Dr. Blackwell's testimony–as well as the obvious absence of Ruth and Beth Myers, the original CPS case worker, that these attorneys knew they had a very weak case.

Larry dismissed Dr. Blackwell and called me to the stand. Before I could make my way to the witness stand, the judge waved me off and called both councils to a meeting in chambers.

I took my seat again and waited nervously in anticipation of what that meeting might mean. Tim and I were suddenly hopeful that maybe the judge was going to do something radically in our favor. We also surmised that he could do the opposite.

Ten minutes passed. Then 15. After 20 minutes both councils returned to the courtroom. Tim and I stared intently at Larry trying to see some sign on his face of how the meeting went. He glanced our way but remained stone-faced. Tim grabbed my hand. I think we were both convinced that the meeting outcome was not in our favor. After 45 minutes, the judge entered the courtroom and read from a written statement.

"This case has had an immediacy to it that has led me to make some procedural moves that might be considered unorthodox. However, a child's well-being and possibly life hangs in the balance at this moment, and that has taken precedence over following a stricter adherence to procedure.

"There are several questions and issues that have been troublesome concerning the Child Protective Service's actions and adherence to their own policy and procedures, as well as the actions of Brinker Hospital Staff. These need to be considered.

"For their part, CPS officials did *not* complete all of their preliminary or following reports in this case as required. Nor did they inform the parents of the child of their proceedings or even make proper attempts to conduct an interview with the parents as is required.

"As for Brinker Hospital, I can see no clear reason or right for their actions in calling in security officers to impede the Gallaghers removal of their son from the hospital prior to their child's collapse. From the reports provided me, it seems their actions were improper to say the least, and potentially represents an illegal detainment of an individual.

"However, this case made its way to this courtroom *after* those facts; in consideration of the child's current state, as well as records provided of past health issues that may be associated with abuse or neglect. It is in that light, that I have considered the evidence presented here or provided on written reports.

"The Gallagher's son, by all accounts, has endured a great many health issues resulting in multiple emergency visits to local hospitals, as well as repeated care by his physician and many incidents at school. These multiple health-related issues, while concerning and certainly detrimental to the child's development, do not however, follow any typical signs of neglect or abuse. We see no reports of bruising, broken limbs, starvation, lack of care, or any noticeable indication of abuse. We are left, therefore, with investigating the cause of the multiple health issues and any potential relationship to abuse or neglect absent of any typical or expected signs.

"Dr. Grinsby, the attending physician at Brinker Hospital, offered no testimony or knowledge of the child's current condition nor any explanation of past, potentially related causes. He admittedly has no plausible diagnosis and could not conclude that the child has suffered from abuse or neglect. Nor did Dr. Grinsby support or have any direct knowledge of or experience with the one potential diagnosis offered by another physician who has cared for the child—mitochondrial disease.

"Through the testimony of highly-credentialed medical witnesses, doctors Hesh and Deshaun, we learned that the child's many health deficiencies are within the spectrum of mitochondrial disease. We further learned that the child was, until Dr. Grinsby and Brinker Hospital intervened, under the care of Dr. Blackwell, a recognized expert in the field of mitochondrial disease.

"Dr. Blackwell clearly testified that the realm of health issues suffered by the child are likely routed in mitochondrial disease. Dr. Blackwell further testified that recently acquired DNA testing, has proven that the child does indeed suffer from mitochondrial disease.

"In the absence of any proof of child abuse or neglect, and with the acknowledgment of expert testimony as to the actual cause of the child's current and past health emergencies, this court rules that the child has not been a victim of abuse or neglect."

I didn't realize I'd been holding my breath until that moment, when it whooshed out of my lungs. Tim squeezed my hand even harder.

Judge Hurley continued, "It is further recognized that the child may not be currently cared for at a facility or under the direction of qualified staff that have the necessary expertise in the related health field from which the child suffers.

"The court rules that Timothy and June Gallagher retain unimpeded legal guardianship of the child to include any and all decisions related to the care of the child, health facilities, and physicians. This ruling is to be implemented immediately and without challenge.

"This court now stands adjourned." He banged his gavel and left through the door behind his seat.

Tim and I leapt to our feet and hugged each other. Tears of overwhelming joy streamed down my cheeks. Larry shoved some papers in his briefcase then turned to Tim and me with a big smile on his face. I wanted to run over and give him the biggest hug and kiss he had ever experienced but, given where we were, I decided to contain myself and offer a mouthed, "thank you" his way.

We were going to our Ernie back.

I said it to myself and to Tim several more times before we left the courtroom. "We're going to get Ernie back!" I loved the sound those words made as they caressed my lips and made their way to Tim's ears and anyone else's who cared to hear. "We're going to get Ernie back."

Tim and I stopped in the foyer of the courthouse waiting for Larry before we exited left through the front doors. We wanted nothing more than to run to Ernie, but we knew we needed Larry's help one more time, to get through the throng that awaited our victory.

Dr. Blackwell took turns congratulated first me and then Tim. We both thanked her profusely for her time and caring to testify for us and brought her into a bit of an awkward embrace. I didn't care if it was messy. I didn't care about anything other than what our victory meant.

I meant to ask Dr. Blackwell about the DNA test that she testified had come back positive, but I was too distracted and overcome by emotion follow through. That could wait.

When Larry finally appeared in the hall, I let go of Tim's hand, which I had squeezed white. I ran over to Larry and threw my arms around him. Larry was unprepared for my emotional onslaught. I nearly knocked him over and I continued squeezing him until Tim made his way to our side. "Thank you, Larry. Thank you for giving us our son back. You're my hero...forever." I said as tears once again streamed down my cheeks. And I meant it.

When I finished gushing all over Larry, he extended his hand to Tim expecting Tim to reciprocate. But Tim was overcome with emotion. He brushed Larry's hand aside and gave him a big bear hug. Larry chuckled a little nervously, but, when they broke, I detected the signs of emotion glistening in Larry's eyes. As calm and removed as he might have wanted to be, I could see that Larry was touched by the role he played in saving our son.

"Hey, it's my job," he said, disentangling himself from Tim and patting him on the back. "I'm glad it went our way. You're good people and that made it...well that made it...makes it a good feeling."

That was all the very humble Larry said before he led us toward the courthouse door. "Ready? They're going to need a few words from you both. When you step out that door they will have already heard the ruling and they will likely react as though they have *all* won. So, get ready."

The guards opened the courthouse doors and Larry led us outside.

We were greeted by a large crowd that had come out despite the rapidly dropping temperature and black, lowering sky. They erupted as we appeared. The cheers and applause were deafening. Tim and I and even Larry, were taken aback by the emotional outburst.

Reporters, more than from the morning, were two rows deep. Their satellite trucks lined both sides of the street. Cameras, with their blinding lights were pointed at us, microphones were horseshoed around us, and even reporters with nothing but cell phones or pencils and pads, were clamoring to get a good spot to record our reaction. All simultaneously cackled their nearly indistinguishable questions at us.

Larry moved his hands up and down to get the crowd to quiet down. With all the microphones in place on shared stands, Tim and I stepped forward. The crowd quieted. Tim spoke first.

"I just want to say thank you to everyone here and to those who aren't here but have supported us. We can never adequately describe what you have meant to us and to getting our son back. We are thrilled at the outcome and we are anxious to go see our son and work on getting him the care he needs. Thank you."

"June, this must have been a very difficult experience for you and your family. Can you tell us how you feel." It was Lizzie, beaming and near tears of her own, who was asking the question. But it was the question most likely on everyone's lips.

"I feel…joy. Overpowering joy. And relief." I said with a huge smile that helped propel the tears quickly down my cheeks. "I cannot find any words worthy enough to express how grateful our family is to Larry, our lawyer and hero, and his firm. He is amazing. And all of you. How do I say thank you adequately enough to all of you for coming out here as you have to support us? I can only tell you, that you matter. That what you have done, matters." I went on as I tried to wipe the tears that continued to flow down my cheeks. Someone shouted from the back of the crowd and held out a handkerchief.

"Here June," the man said. "It's clean. You take it. I've got plenty more at home."

The crowd chuckled. The handkerchief was passed from person-to-person until it reached the row of reporters in the front. I leaned over the microphones and caused them to squeal as I took the handkerchief. I made a goofy face. The gathering laughed again. I held up the handkerchief and shouted 'thank you' then wiped my eyes. Everyone cheered.

Larry was right. They were sharing this moment, this victory, as if it was their own and I felt I needed to acknowledge that. I quieted the crowd before I spoke.

"I know many of you have come here driven by your own stories of desperation and love and your own hopes of being heard. And I know, that for many of you, our victory is not our own, but one you shared in. Thank you for bringing your hopes and fears to us and for sharing such a personal part of yourselves with us. We hear you. And we hope that what you have helped to accomplish here today, in some small way, brings you some of the joy we feel. Take what you need. We gladly and gratefully share it with you."

The crowd erupted in applause and cheers once again. It was such an emotional high and a connection that I had never before felt. Tim wrapped his arm around me while he wiped his own tears from his eyes. He was feeling it too. A moment when humanity was in concert, absent of any political divide or personal gain. We were one giant gob of "feel good."

Someone in the crowd yelled, "June for President!" which caused a ripple of laughter. Larry took that as his cue and stepped to the bundle of microphones.

"Folks," he began, "the Gallaghers appreciate your support. But, as you can appreciate, they are anxious to get to Ernie and take whatever steps needed to get him moved to where his doctor can provide the best care. So, thank you and please, let's clear a way for them to leave."

Larry ushered Tim and me down the courthouse stairs with Dr. Blackwell following. The well-wishers and the press parted as Larry asked. Everyone still felt the "group hug" and wanted to be supportive and respectful of our need to get to our son.

Many offered personal messages and congratulations while others patted our backs as we made our way down the stairs and to Dr. Blackwell's car.

Finally, we piled in and sped off toward Brinker Hospital–and our Ernie!

My phone had been turned off the entire day and it wasn't until I turned it back on while riding to the hospital, that I saw the 110 text messages waiting for a response. Many of them were from strangers, who somehow got my cell number, wishing me well. Many were from Elsie wanting to know what was going on and when we were going to come get her. It was late in the day, so she'd already taken the bus home.

Tim's phone had a similar number of messages, so we both sat quietly reading and deleting. There was no time to respond to most of them. In the middle of reading through the onslaught of messages, Tim turned to me and said that some of the texts he'd received were from his parents. They had seen a television report of our story and cut their Italy trip short to come support us.

Tim had only told them that Ernie was very sick and that the hospital was fighting with us about his treatment. He never mentioned our attempt to sneak Ernie out or my arrest or the courtroom fight. But, because our story had been picked up by so many media outlets, it became noteworthy ex-pat fodder for European television as well.

His parents had arrived in town just this afternoon and wanted to know where to meet us or what to do to help. I wasn't close with them nor was Tim. But they were good to us in their way and we certainly had room for more support. I was surprised and touched that they made so much effort to come be with us.

I suggested that Tim text and ask them to pick up Elsie, who by now was at home, and meet us at Brinker Hospital. I called Elsie to give her the good news and to let her know her grandparents were in town and would pick her up and bring her to the hospital. When I told her the news about Ernie, she cried. That made me cry. Tim stopped his texting to observe me crying into the phone with Elsie. He smiled knowingly, then went back to his task.

When Elsie was finally calm enough to talk again, she started to pepper me with all sorts of questions: what happened in court, were we moving Ernie to University today, who called her grandparents, and so on. We were nearing the hospital and I didn't have time to answer any of them completely. Besides, her questions didn't follow a logical progression. They were just her stream of consciousness flowing freely at me. I told her that her grandparents would be there in five minutes and to be ready. We would all go see Ernie together and after that I would answer her questions. Then I hung up before she could think of another question to ask.

We arrived at Brinker Hospital at about the same time I had finished reading or deleting all of my texts. Tim was still working his way through his list but put his phone away the minute we entered the hospital parking lot.

Another group of reporters—or perhaps the same group in very fast vehicles—were just outside of the front entrance to the hospital, being kept at bay by several hospital security guards. There were also about a hundred well-wishers gathered, waiting our arrival. A few police vehicles were being used to keep supporters from blocking entry to the hospital and from interfering with emergency vehicles and entryways. Unformed officers were also manning barricades they had erected to keep the crowd at bay.

We wanted to acknowledge the supporters' presence but at the same time, we wanted to get inside and to Ernie as quickly as possible. Larry suggested it would be best if Tim and I gave a very quick thank you to the crowd and he volunteered to take on the reporters and give a statement on our behalf.

Larry, Tim, and I made our way to the crowd while Dr. Blackwell entered the hospital. She wanted to take a look at Ernie and his charts before we got upstairs to determine if she should have him moved or petition the hospital to allow her to treat Ernie there.

As with the courthouse supporters, there were cheers and applause offered us while we prepared to speak. It was a smaller crowd, but they were just as emotionally charged as the courthouse group. We could feel their good will with each chant of, "We love you Ernie!" It was odd to hear a hundred strangers offer their love to our son, but it was welcoming, nonetheless.

Tim took my arm as we faced the microphones. "You go ahead, June," He said lovingly.

"Thank you for being here," I said and smiled. "Tim and I, and Ernie and our daughter Elsie, all appreciate your prayers and your support. Without all of you, I don't know if we would have made it this far. We are grateful. So very grateful. Thank you to all of you here and to the many at home—I looked in the direction of the three cameras pointed my way—who have offered their prayers as well. We still have a long way to go to get Ernie better and back home with us, so please, when you go home, still think of us and pray for us. Thank you."

Larry stepped forward while Tim and I retreated. Larry thanked the crowd and took questions from reporters.

Tim and I made our way toward the entrance of the hospital and eventually through the front doors and into the lobby. Ours felt like a grand entrance. It wasn't colorful or full of pomp. But, it was beautiful if seen through the prism of parental love. We would never have to skulk or act as on tenterhooks, heads bowed and hiding, afraid to step out of line.

We held our heads high and walked with bold determination, almost strutting forward to Ruth, who was waiting at her perch. We were conquerors come to claim our bounty—our son's life. Nothing and no one could stop us now.

When we reached Ruth's desk I announced, "We're the Gallaghers. We're here to see our son, Ernie."

Ruth barely looked at us. She bowed her head and said, "I'm so sorry," and then shriveled into her chair. She offered no other comment. We stayed for just a moment, regarding the weight of her defeat. She said she was sorry–an apology that seemed out of place to me yet somehow sincere. I tossed it off as the nervous reply of guilt.

Tim took my arm and we strode toward the elevator. No, I take that back–we nearly skipped. I knew that Ernie was still in a coma and that there were still many challenges ahead, but I couldn't stop my euphoria that increased the closer I got to his room.

When the elevator doors opened on the second floor, I ran the few steps to Ernie's room. I nearly collided with two technicians who were wheeling Ernie's heart monitor and ventilator from his room.

My heart beat so fast I thought it would pound through my chest when I realized what this meant–Ernie was awake!

Dr. Blackwell was behind the technicians and tried to intercept me but I thrust myself forward and propelled myself toward Ernie's bed. She had better luck with Tim and managed to pull him out of the entrance to the room and into the hallway.

I stumbled onto the side of Ernie's bed and yelled out for all to hear, "Ernie! Oh Ernie you're awake!"

I threw my body as gingerly as my overwhelming love would allow, right next to his still body, my tears streaming a river of joy. I kissed his soft, precious cheek. It was so cold. *Why do they keep these damn hospital rooms so cold?* I thought. *He needs a blanket.*

I looked at his face. His eyes were closed. "Ernie," I said much softer. "Ernie, honey, it's Mommy. Open your eyes baby."

He didn't. I took his little hand in mine. It was as icy cold as his cheek. "Ernie? Oh God, no. Ernie no, no, no, no, no." I sobbed uncontrollably over his, lifeless body.

I sat up and shook his shoulders. "Ernie you wake up! You have to wake up!" I was no longer sobbing. A deep blackness had engulfed me.

Tim stormed into the room, tears burning his cheeks. He grabbed me and tried to stop me from shaking Ernie alive.

"June. June stop it. Please, please stop it." Tim tearfully pleaded with me. "You're hurting him."

I broke from his grip and stood. I didn't offer any warmth to Tim. I couldn't. My tears had dried, and my emotions were as still as the little body in front of me. I went numb. Completely numb.

Tim slumped over Ernie, crying. He moved his face closer and closer to Ernie's and touched noses. Nothing. Sobbing, Tim tried tickling Ernie's rib cage. "Come on, little man. Wake up."

I backed out of the room. As I turned to leave, a face said something to me. Dr. Blackwell's I think. I didn't completely recognize sounds or people or even the hospital corridors. I saw everything through a haze, as though I wore a cheesecloth mask. And, in my head, I heard this awful humming sound. Not the low-key hum of a fan or other machinery. It was a repetitious juxtaposition of a high note with a low note, that beat in time with my broken heart; over and over again it pounded.

I fumbled my way to the elevator and down to the lobby. I had no reason. There was no plan or forethought that moved me. I was in motion for motions sake—a zombie-like shell unable to relate to anything around me.

I looked through my haze toward what I did recognized as the front door. A vague memory of people gathered out front, slipped through my grogginess, and warned me away from there.

I shuffled toward another set of doors somewhere to the side. I stepped out onto the sidewalk and then stumbled across the road, into the cold, gray dusk. A light snow and unseasonably chilled air were foretelling winter's arrival.

I felt neither.

I turned to face the building I had just left and stood staring blankly at it. A vehicle whizzed toward me then swerved to avoid hitting me. I didn't move. Someone screamed at me from inside the vehicle.

"Lady, what the…this is an emergency entrance, get out of the damn road!"

I didn't respond.

"I sat on the curb behind me. I held my knees close up under my chin and waited. For what I didn't know. Maybe I was waiting for this nightmare to end.

A figure approached me. A voice spoke in my direction which I didn't acknowledge. As the figure got closer, the voice got louder; it was a man's voice I turned my head slightly to peek at the figure through my gauze mask He spoke again as I sat there collecting tiny snowflakes on my head.

"June?"

Something about his voice was telling my head, deep, deep inside that I should know him. He got closer.

"June. Is that you?" The voice spoke again.

My haze cleared a bit. I lifted my head and looked up at the man now standing in front of me. I recognized the blue uniform and then I saw a familiar EMS emblem sewn onto his blue shirt.

"June. Are you all right?" The man asked as he took a seat on the curb next to me and wrapped the jacket he had removed around my shoulders. I looked more closely at him now. I looked into his warm brown eyes. My vision came back clearer to me, bringing with it, the ugliness of my reality.

I looked beyond the man, to an ambulance parked at the emergency entrance. *He must have brought someone to the hospital I thought.* I looked back into the man's caring face. He stared intently at me while he held me close in his arms and rubbed my shoulders to keep me warm.

I recognized him. He was the EMS man who comforted me when I rescued Kalea from the burning car. He had found me at my most vulnerable moment and protected me. I suddenly felt safe I didn't have to hide my pain inside my numbness. I could let it out. Share it.

"June. Is everything okay?" My friend asked again. I sobbed.

"I couldn't save him," I said. The first few tears ran down my face and dripped from my chin.

"Who June?" he asked. "Who couldn't you save?"

"Ernie." I let out a guttural sob. "My...son...Ernie. "I...couldn't... save...him." I collapsed into his arms, dug my head into his broad chest and wept.

EPILOGUE

"How are you feeling, June?" That's the question I got most often. It's an innocuous question when asked of anyone else. Three years ago, I would have taken it as such myself. "How are you feeling, June?" Do they want to know if my cold has gone away? Did I get over my migraine last night?

No.

They are asking if I might finally be over the death of my son. Not over the loss. But can I function normally again? Can I just pretend for them and myself that everything is back to normal with me now? Like that cold or migraine—is the sickness behind me? Maybe we can have brunch?

I don't blame them. My friends, the few whom I have reconnected with from college, didn't sign up to wallow in sadness with me. They want to have normal conversations. To smile on occasion and to not feel like they have to be on guard for any word they might say or idea they suggest. Don't bring June into that gloomy place and ruin the day.

They want these things for themselves. But they want them for me as well, I know. They see my pain. They just struggle against being dragged down into that abyss with me. It's difficult for them. It's impossible for me.

I'm not alone in that black hole. Tim is in there with me. Or he was. He has work to occupy his brain. And he's Tim. He's found a compartment to put the loss in and lock it up. He had to go on and pretend for Elsie and me. But I still see the sadness lingering in his eyes. On a Sunday while he rakes leaves I see him stop and stare at a newly raked pile. He's waiting for Frankenstein to emerge, I imagine. He's waiting for his son's giggles.

We don't make love anymore.

There are no special nights. We tried. More than once. My body just won't feel pleasure while my heart has stopped feeling joy. We have had moments of tenderness and caressing. Our therapist says that's a good sign, a sign that we're healing. Three years is a lot of therapy with so little wellness I think.

We began seeing a therapist after Christmas the year Ernie left us. We had to. The holidays were impossible to get through. We realized we couldn't do it on our own. I think therapy is another compartment for Tim. We go once a week to deal with the loss of our son and that's where he places the hurt. That lets him function normally the rest of the week. I envy him that peace.

Tim and I went into a deep depression. Tim couldn't go into work until mid-January. I stopped eating. Hell, I stopped all functioning. I was hospitalized for six months and at one point, under suicide watch.

Elsie had no one to talk to about losing her brother. Tim and I were too far gone ourselves to be much use. She withdrew inside herself. Her school work suffered and she stopped relating to friends. Child Services visited our home to check on Elsie just after I got out of the hospital. I was grateful it took them that long to come around because they surely would have taken Elsie from Tim and me if they'd come any sooner. Tim and I were able to muster enough spirit to satisfy them that Elsie was being taken care of and she was fine.

She wasn't.

One day, about eight months after Ernie passed away, Elsie came bursting into the living room while Tim and I were arguing over something trivial. We argued a lot.

"Shut up! Shut up! Shut up!" She screamed as her entire body shook. "I lost my fucking brother! I hurt too. I hurt too." She began to sob and fell to her knees. "I love Ernie. I miss him so much. Why doesn't that matter to you?"

Tim and I stood, stunned for a moment then dropped to our knees next to Elsie and swooped her into an embrace. The three of us shook and sobbed together. The next week Elsie began therapy sessions. By the end of that year, her grades had improved, and she spent time with friends. She even went to Junior Prom–with a date. I fussed over her dress and makeup and did everything I could to make the event special for her. To be her mother again. It helped bring me a few moments of happiness that I thought were lost forever.

The episode with Elsie and watching her blossom again drew me out of my shell enough to function. Tim had work and I had being-a-good-mom to Elsie–being her pod partner. My child needed me and my love still. And I needed hers. Her brightness helped me through my dark times. She had found a way to bounce back better than either Tim or me.

I would still catch her lying on Ernie's bed playing with his plush kangaroo. I tried not to let her see me; I didn't want to embarrass her. It was her private moment. One time, about a year after Tim and I had begun therapy, I wandered into Ernie's room. It had taken me that long to even think about going in there again. We kept his door shut. I stood in front of that door for over an hour before I opened it and stepped inside. I was shaking. I didn't cry. Other than the episode with Elsie, I hadn't cried in a very long time. I was too numb for emotion.

I walked over to Ernie's bed and sat on the edge. I took his pillow out from under the comforter and held it to my face. I wanted so much to feel his warmth, to breathe in his special scent. Neither were there.

I looked over at the plush kangaroo. Elsie had given that one to Ernie during one of his hospital stays. I squished the stuffed animal's head hard to my face and thought I smelled Ernie. I gathered the entire toy into an embrace and squeezed. Something hard poked me in the cheek. I turned the animal around and found his secret pouch. I reached inside and pulled out a Snickers bar. *Oh Elsie. My darling, loving Elsie* I thought. I wanted to cry for her. But I couldn't find any tears.

I put the kangaroo back in its spot and left the room. I kept the door open. My therapist said that was a positive sign. I might have believed him had I not insisted we move, right after that, to a small ranch house the next town over. I couldn't bear the constant reminders that Ernie was here once, watching TV in that living room, eating tuna fish sandwiches at that kitchen table, and tucked into his warm bed in that bedroom. I was close to a relapse.

Lizzie never gave up on me. She calls often. When she comes to town she doesn't ask how I am or if I want company. She's Lizzie. She just pops over and invites herself in. She is a ray of sunshine in my dark world. There are moments spent with her that I think, maybe… maybe I will get better. We talk about her work and she tells me funny stories about the people she interviews. On occasion, she forces me to go out to lunch and be "gal pals" as she calls us. Sometimes she takes me shopping. Often, I really don't want to go do anything. But she's Lizzie. I can never say "no" to Lizzie.

The real amazing thing about her…she lets me go to my dark place if I need to. She holds me, cries with me, and never asks if I feel all right. She knows intuitively that I will never be "all right." I hope to be something else, someone else; someone who can cope better. That's the best I can do and Lizzie accepts that. And in her way, she helps to gently push me toward being someone who can cope.

I do think I am making some progress. That's what my therapist says. But he's been wrong before. If I am getting to a better place, I don't believe it is because of him. It's because of Tim and Elsie and Lizzie. They are my rocks and my reasons for trying.

In July, following Ernie's passing, Kalea and her Aunt Lashay came to see us. It was more than I was prepared to handle emotionally. They came at dinner time hoping that the three of us would be home. I greeted them a bit robotically; I was only six months out of the hospital and still barely functioning. Tim and Elsie were sitting in the living room watching TV. We hadn't made any commitment to dinner yet. Lashay was carrying a large, brightly colored bag and Kalea had a plate covered with tinfoil. Kalea looked as beautiful and sweet as the first time we met.

"I know you couldn't have had any kind of holiday with things the way they were." Lashay nervously explained once we were all seated in the living room. "So, Kalea and I thought we would bring you Christmas in July. It's nothing fancy. We just wanted to let you know we're thinking about you and we share your loss. We wanted to do something." Lashay said as she grabbed the big bag from the floor.

"And I made these for you." Kalea said handing me the tinfoil-covered plate. "They're my mom's chocolate chip cookies. I mean, well they're from her recipe."

Then Lashay handed a gift from her bag to each of us and we opened them in turn. Tim went first. He received a handsome blue dress shirt with white stripes. Elsie opened her present. Lashay bought her a pretty silver bracelet with a silver teddy bear charm hanging from it. It was the kind that she could add charms to.

"I picked this one out for you." Kalea said when it was my turn.

I opened it slowly, afraid my emotions might be released from what lay within. Inside was a glass Christmas ornament with an angel painted on it. The angel held a scroll in her hands. On the scroll was written, "Ernie".

I handed the ornament to Tim then threw my arms around Kalea and held her close to me. "Thank you Kalea." I said softly. "Thank you. I love it and Ernie would love it too."

When I let go of her, she was a mess of tears. Tim, Elsie, and Lashay were crying as well. Only my eyes remained dry. I felt the moment deeply, but I was not able to show my feelings the way the others were.

Elsie broke the sadness in her inimitable way. She grabbed the plate of cookies I had placed on the table and declared, "So, I guess it's cookies for dinner then." She stuffed a cookie in her mouth. Everyone laughed. I smiled.

I ordered take out for everyone and we had dinner together. Their visit and the gifts, the thoughtfulness of what Kalea and Lashay did, was special beyond words.

***

We visit Ernie's gravesite as often as we feel we can get through it. Sometimes it is just Tim and me, sometimes Elsie and me, and sometimes all three of us. Lizzie has gone with me too. Sometimes, I go by myself. I don't tell anyone because I just want to be alone with my son. And, I don't want to answer the therapist's questions about why I went and what did I feel.

So many years ago, I saw gravestones of babies and young children and got teary-eyed. They were often adorned with a little lamb, or engraved with the face of the child, or have an angel on top, or maybe a baseball bat. They always made me feel sad.

For Ernie, we didn't do anything like that. We just had a simple white stone, with words engraved on it along with his name and the date he passed.

Yesterday was Ernie's 13th birthday. I wanted to be with him. It was a work day, so Tim was at his office in the afternoon. Elsie was home. I picked some flowers from the little garden I had started in the back yard. It was suggested as part of my therapy. I grabbed my purse and opened the front door to leave just as Elsie came out of the living room.

"Mom. Where you going?" She asked.

I didn't want to draw attention to what I was doing or remind her that it was Ernie's birthday.

"Just out. For a walk."

"You have a new boyfriend?" Elsie teased, nodding toward the flowers in my hand.

I stuttered something inaudible.

Elsie walked up to me where I stood, hand on the doorknob. "Mom," she said gently. "It's Ernie's birthday." She took my hand from the doorknob and held it. "I would like to be with him today, and you too. It's not something you should hide from anyone. Especially not me or Dad. We all love him still. How about I go with you?"

I felt something. Something familiar. Something that pitted in my stomach. And behind my eyes, that place where tears are formed, another sensation. *My little girl is becoming an amazing woman*, I thought. And it touched me.

"Sure," I said. "I would love your company. And Ernie will too."

Like two peas in a pod, we walked hand-in-hand down the long driveway to my car that I parked on the street. We drove to Ernie's cemetery, stopping first for two Diet Cokes, a tuna fish sandwich, and two Snickers bars to bring with us. We ate lunch with Ernie. We talked about Elsie's school and my garden and Lizzie and Tim. I actually told a couple of funny stories about Tim from college. It wasn't a morbid time.

When we stood to say our goodbye to Ernie, I asked, "Elsie, how do you do it?"

"Do what Mom?" She asked. We were both still gazing at Ernie's tombstone.

"Cope. Go on. How do you seem to mange to still embrace life the way you do? Is it just youth?" I asked. I was hopeful my wise child might know something I didn't.

"I get sad sometimes Mom. Really sad. And I cry. I even left a Snickers bar inside Ernie's kangaroo one time." She laughed. I didn't let on that I knew.

"But how do you let go of your sadness? How do you even feel enough to cry?"

"The way you taught me, Mom."

I tipped my head to the side and looked at her inquisitively.

"Movies Mom. I play one of my little Ernie movies in my head. Like today, when I woke up and realized it was Ernie's birthday. I got depressed and cried a bit. Then I played one of my movies. The one where Ernie calls everyone a panty head and then we do the pantomime for you and Dad. It makes me laugh."

And she did, standing there at Ernie's gravesite. She smiled and then laughed.

"I'll wait for you at the car Mom," she said. She gave my cheek a kiss then grabbed our bag of lunch trash and walked off toward the car.

I stood looking at Ernie's gravestone. I searched my head for a movie. At first, none would come. Then, I read the words on Ernie's gravestone again. *Beautiful, Beautiful, Beautiful, Beautiful Ernie.* And I remembered.

The reels in my head started to move and images flashed in front of me as though they were happening right there where I could touch them. Ernie was sitting at the kitchen table and I was making him breakfast. I was humming and then I sang to him, *Beautiful, Beautiful, Beautiful, Beautiful Ernie.* He laughed and giggled each time I sang it. He was alive in my movie. And in my heart. I smiled as I played it over and over again.

Then a tear crawled out of my right eye and made its journey down my dry cheek. Another followed. Then one from my left eye. Another joined the first two and then both eyes were flowing. Not with sadness. But with pure joy. I was crying. And laughing-or as near to a laugh as I could remember how.

It only lasted a few moments. But it was there. I was feeling and coping. Maybe I could go forward as whatever person I had to be— could be—to honor life and Ernie. I don't know. It was a lot to take in.

As I turned to join Elsie at my car, I suddenly thought, *I should take Lizzie up on her offer to see Chicago. I'll call her when I get home and see when she can have me come visit.*

I told my therapist about what happened. He said it was a real breakthrough and a positive sign. Then he and Tim talked back and forth about his day and what did Tim think about my experience.

While he spoke to Tim, I just sat there and wondered if Lizzie knew a good place for "beast" Bloody Marys. I think *that* was a real breakthrough.

ACKNOWLEDGMENTS

My sister Janice –there would be no Incorgnito Publishing Press without your continued support and enthusiasm for making this venture a success. Love you!

My brother-in-law Dean –for getting dragged into another "investment opportunity" and saying yes!

My Niece and Nephew –Alexandra and Andrew are the reason for our name. Their appreciation for Welsh Corgis, resulted in - Incorgnito. Gotta love those Corgis!

The authors we represent –I have such admiration for your talents and the risks you take putting them out there for all to judge. And, I appreciate the trust you have placed in Incorgnito to represent your gifts. You collectively and individually have inspired me to attempt to join your ranks as an author.

Our contractors –Star Foos, Daria Lacy, Mauro Sorghienti, Taylor Basilio, Jennifer Collins, Julianne Winter, Matthew Bucemi, Liga Clavina, and many others, the skills you bring to our books as designers, artists, and editors makes our books better. It's a treat to be exposed to talented people, here and abroad, who choose to work with Incorgnito.

Midpoint Trade Books –As Incorgnito's distributor, you have opened new paths to bring our titles to many more people. Your continued advice and experience have helped us to grow.

Lieutenant Jason Clawson - And his fellow officers at the Pasadena, California Police Department, for the extensive tour and explanation of being arrested and processed. And for letting me go afterward.

The Mito Families –Mother's Child is the completion of a commitment I made several years ago as President of Cure Mito. What I learned in that role, about the suffering of children with mitochondrial disease, and the lack of recognition and resources to fight it, inspired me to write this book. I hope it isn't too late to be a positive influence.

Heidi Wallenborn, my editor –your extensive experience and skills as an editor, helped tremendously to bring this story to life. And, you made me a better writer. Most importantly, you made me believe I could actually do it. You gave me the gift of encouragement, without which, I would never have attempted this book.

About The Author

Michael Conant is the publisher and founder of Incorgnito Publishing Press.

Before entering the world of book publishing, Michael spent over twenty years in b2b publishing. He served as a circulation, sales, and marketing executive, managing products across several industries, with a concentration in financial publications.

Prior to his foray into publishing, Michael pursued his love of theater as an actor, singer, director, and producer at regional theaters, dinner theaters, and at several Off-Off Broadway theaters. Michael introduced New York audiences to the American premier of Hal Shaper's musical adaptation of Jane Eyre, which featured Michael as Rochester along with a very young Alyssa Milano as his ward, Adelle.

Shortly after moving to Pasadena, CA, Mr. Conant was introduced to Cure Mito, an organization of "Mito Moms" dedicated to funding Mitochondrial Disease research in support of Dr. Richard Boles at Los Angeles Children's Hospital. Michael helped the group secure non-profit status and was elected as the organization's first president.

In between his publishing duties and new writing efforts, Michael plays a lot of tennis with his South Pasadena, Arroyo Secco teammates. He also spends free time visiting with family and getting "puppy" kisses from his niece's lovable, crazy Bernedoodle, Bentley. (b3ntley_zefluff on Instagram)

Mr. Conant is also the co-author of *David Margrave: The plumber who outwitted the IRS*. He may be contacted at mconant@incorgnito-books.com https://www.incorgnitobooks.com

This book is a work of art produced by Incorgnito Publishing Press.

Heidi Wallenborn
Editor

Star Foos
Artist/Designer

Daria Lacy
Graphic Production

Janice Bini
Chief Reader

Michael Conant
Publisher

December 2018 Incorgnito Publishing Press

Direct inquiries to mconant@incorgnitobooks.com

CPSIA information can be obtained
at www.ICGtesting.com
Printed in the USA
LVHW020007060219
606521LV00002B/3/P

9 781944 589660